"A strong debut launching an Ancient Rome–inspired romantic fantasy series. . . . The main characters have excellent chemistry, meshing right from the start. In addition to the richly imagined world and a delightfully entertaining tale of magic and intrigue, Raby also delivers an understated yet versatile magic system and a convincing, sensitive portrayal of Vitalia's efforts to reclaim her life from post-traumatic stress." — *Publishers Weekly*

"Raby's debut heralds the arrival of a terrific new fantasy romance voice joining the genre. *Assassin's Gambit* is a multifaceted tale of the sacrifices demanded in the battle over an empire. The hero and heroine of this story are on opposite ends of the spectrum, but are smart enough to see the benefit in collaboration. Raby ably demonstrates that she has a gift for storytelling and readers will absolutely look forward to the next installment of the Hearts and Thrones Series!" — *Romantic Times* (4 stars)

"Impressive . . . the best debut book/author this year . . . a wonderful epic fantasy romance." — The Book Pushers

"Shades of *From Russia with Love* . . . damn good. Yes, it is a romance. A very good one. The characters are memorable and I found myself lost in the world. You can't ask for more than that." — Hoover's Corner

"A thrilling story." — A Little Bookish

"A great read. It was wonderful to see two intelligent individuals continue to value and treat each other with respect. . . . I am looking forward to the next in the series." — Dear Author . . .

"A great setting and protagonists worth rooting for. I will definitely be waiting for Hearts and Thrones #2." — All About Romance

"Unlike any romance I've read. The hero and the heroine are completely original and utterly fascinating. Those who love *Game of Thrones* will enjoy this new series. . . . Savvy, smart, and imaginative. This book has action, intrigue, and two lovers who desperately need each other. Simply amazing!" — Bookaholics Romance Book Club

SPY'S HONOR

THE HEARTS AND THRONES SERIES

AMY RABY

A SIGNET ECLIPSE BOOK

SIGNET ECLIPSE
Published by the Penguin Group
Penguin Group (USA) LLC, 375 Hudson Street,
New York, New York 10014

USA | Canada | UK | Ireland | Australia | New Zealand | India | South Africa | China
penguin.com
A Penguin Random House Company

First published by Signet Eclipse, an imprint of New American Library,
a division of Penguin Group (USA) LLC

First Printing, October 2013

SIGNET ECLIPSE and logo are trademarks of Penguin Group (USA) LLC.

ISBN 978-0-451-41783-1

Printed in the United States of America
10 9 8 7 6 5 4 3 2 1

*To Mom and Dad, who sent rockets into space
and also launched a daughter*

ACKNOWLEDGMENTS

First, thank you to my editor, Claire Zion, and my agent, Alexandra Machinist, for believing in these books and for making them so much better.

Working nearly three thousand miles away, on the opposite coast, I don't have the privilege of personally meeting everyone, so thank you to all the wonderful people at Penguin and at Janklow & Nesbit. Collectively, they transformed a gangly collection of bits from my computer into a finished, polished novel.

To my family: sorry for always making you turn off your videos so I can write without distraction. You don't need to watch those videos anyway!

To Angie Christensen: thank you for the myriad ways you've been helpful. You made it possible for me to keep up with the kids' activities and still meet my deadlines. And to JoAnn Ten Brinke, thank you for being my walking buddy and motivating me to get out of the house every morning.

This book has been through multiple incarnations, each time critiqued by a different set of beta readers. Thank you to my first readers, Jessi Gage and Julie Brannagh of the Cupcake Crew, for your insightful critique, lovely conversation, and valued friendship.

Thank you also to my second readers, from Writer's Cramp: Barbara Stoner, Mark Hennon, Kim Runciman, Stephen Merlino, Steven Gurr, Tim McDaniel, Amy Stewart, Thom Marrion, Janka Hobbs, Marta Murvosh, Michael Croteau, Kirsten Underwood, and Courtland Shafer. Each person in this group brings a different strength, whether it's structural editing, line editing, or detailed knowledge about some specific subject. Nothing gets past Cramp!

And to my online critiquers: Marlene Dotterer, Bonnie Freeman, Kelly Jones, Olivia Fowler, Lisa Smeaton, John Beety, Tara Maya, Heidi Kneale, and Jarucia Jaycox Narula—thank you all for making this a better book.

1

The guards dragged open the double doors, and Rhianne swept into her cousin's sitting room. "Is the council over? I need your fifteen tetrals."

Lucien whirled on his wooden leg, jumpy as a winter partridge. He wore his imperial garments, the silk syrtos and thin jeweled loros that marked him as the son and heir of the Kjallan emperor. His dress suggested he'd only just returned from the council or was about to head out again, since he never wore the loros in his private chambers except to receive important visitors. Rhianne could not blame him. As the emperor's niece, she possessed a similar garment and found its weight onerous. Lucien, whose left leg had been amputated below the knee and who walked with the aid of a crutch, probably liked it even less.

He glanced at the door. "This is a bad time."

She could see that it was. Lucien had neither retreated to his Caturanga board for a war game nor settled on one of the many chairs and couches in his finely appointed sitting room to read one of Cinna's treatises on battle tactics. He was standing in the middle of the room and seemed to be waiting to receive someone, and she was not that someone. She glanced back at the door, but aside from the guards, she and Lucien were alone. "I only need the tetrals. Hand them over and I'll go. We can talk later."

Lucien frowned. "This business with the money—it has to stop."

Rhianne straightened her shoulders. He'd never balked over this before. "We agreed to it. Fifteen tetrals from each of us. And besides—"

"There are more important things going on right now." Lucien's eyes went anxiously to the door. "And I can't afford to upset him any more than I already have."

"Who? His Royal Unreasonableness?"

Lucien grimaced. "We should stop calling him that."

Rhianne smiled sadly. Lucien was trying so hard to grow up, and he seemed to forget sometimes that she, three years senior to his tender seventeen, already had. And she wasn't leaving without her tetrals. "How am I supposed to come up with the full amount if you don't pay your share? When you've got an obligation to somebody, you don't walk out on that obligation because something else comes up—"

"It's not just me," snapped Lucien. "Your name came up at the council meeting."

She couldn't imagine why. It was a war council, and why should anyone, in the context of talking about the war with Mosar, bring up the emperor's niece? She was royal, but from a side branch of the family with a somewhat questionable pedigree. She wasn't important the way Lucien was.

"Well," thundered a voice from the doorway. "If it isn't our yapping dog from the War Council."

Rhianne, recognizing the deep tones of her uncle the emperor, sank into a welcome-curtsy. She glanced at

Lucien long enough to see him steel his expression and bow to his father.

"Emperor," said Lucien coolly.

Now she understood why Lucien was off-color. He and Florian were about to have a fight, and in these frequent and unavoidable conflicts, the son always fared worse than the father. She ought to have left when Lucien told her to. "I'm sorry to intrude," she said. "I'll leave you to your privacy."

"No, no," said Florian, his eyes on Lucien. Though the emperor and his heir were cut from the same cloth, the resemblance one noted on first glance was superficial. They shared the same black hair, black eyes, and aquiline profile, but Florian was broader, and taller by several inches. Florian reminded Rhianne of an eagle, with his sharp eyes, craggy nose, and severe face. His two elder sons might have been stamped woodcut copies, their resemblance to Florian was so strong, but Lucien and his sister, the two youngest, with their slighter builds and finer features, took after their late mother. Lucien was handsomer and smarter than his father, but Florian had never forgiven him for losing his leg to a trio of Riorcan assassins or for becoming his only choice of heir when the assassins had also murdered Lucien's elder brothers.

"Stay," Florian now said to Rhianne. "I should like to hear your opinion of a son and heir who openly criticizes his father in a council of war."

Rhianne winced. "Well, without knowing the particulars—"

"Father," Lucien broke in, "it is a *private* council, and its purpose is the discussion of strategy. If the council members cannot speak their minds—"

Emperor Florian backhanded him, hard, across the

face. Lucien cried out, and his crutch clattered to the ground. Bodyguards, both Florian's and Lucien's, stiffened, ready for action, but nobody touched the pair.

"The *legati* are there to speak their minds," hissed Florian. "*You* are there as a courtesy. *Your* purpose on the council is to agree enthusiastically with everything I say. Is that clear?"

Lucien nodded. Limping on his wooden leg, he recovered his crutch and straightened his syrtos. His hand moved instinctively to his face, a protective gesture, but then dropped back to his side. Florian tolerated nothing he could interpret as a sign of weakness.

"Rhianne understands—don't you, my dear?" said Florian. "We have enemies, and to protect ourselves, we must present a united front. Family solidarity. Isn't that right?"

"Absolutely," said Rhianne. "But when Lucien led White Eagle battalion in Riorca, he was regarded as a brilliant military tactician. If the War Council isn't the right place for his ideas to be heard, perhaps there is another place?"

Florian laughed. "You were right the first time, when you said you needed to know the particulars. This idea of your cousin's was practically treason. He wants us to call off the war with Mosar."

Rhianne turned to Lucien, who grimaced without meeting her eyes.

"I don't call that brilliance. I call it cowardice," said Florian, turning to Lucien. "And I will not hear it from you again. Is that clear?"

Lucien nodded.

"Speaking of family, it's time to expand it," said Florian. "Rhianne, you shall marry."

A shiver crept up her spine. Marry? Most of the men were away at war. She hadn't met anyone she desired to marry. And there were practical considerations. Marrying would almost certainly take her away from the Imperial Palace, and then who would deliver the tetrals? Certainly not Lucien, the way he'd been talking. "Did you have someone in mind?"

Emperor Florian nodded. "Augustan Ceres, commander of our forces at Mosar. When he finishes the military operation, I plan to offer him the governorship of the island, and you shall be his bride."

"I'm to be a war prize?" She glanced sidelong at Lucien, whose eyes were downcast. He'd already known.

"Not a war prize, a governor's wife!" said Florian. "You've always wanted to travel to foreign lands. Now you shall, to Mosar."

"I've never met Augustan."

"Easily remedied," said Florian. "I shall summon him back to Kjall long enough for a brief engagement before he returns to the front."

"And if I don't like him?"

"You will," said Florian.

And if she didn't, he'd smack her like he had Lucien until she changed her mind.

"Now, if you'll run along, I have a few more things to discuss with your cousin," said Florian.

Rhianne walked numbly toward the door.

"One moment," called Lucien, swinging rapidly toward her on his crutch and wooden leg. When he reached her, he whispered, "We'll talk later," and slipped something into the inside pocket of her syrtos. She could tell by the clinking sound that it was the fifteen tetrals.

*   *   *

What perplexed Jan-Torres, Crown Prince of Mosar, about the slaves of Kjall was that they had so much freedom of movement. He'd been watching them, concealed beneath his invisibility shroud, from outside the slave house on the grounds near the palace for much of the evening, and as far as he could tell, they were unfettered.

Where are the chains? He posed the question to Sashi, his animal familiar, through their telepathic link. *Why do they not run away?*

Perhaps they will starve if they run away. The ferret, perched on his shoulder, turned his head to watch a yellow-haired Riorcan exit the slave house and head off into the trees. Janto had discovered a well there earlier, and a latrine. The men had trodden a well-worn path to each.

Now Janto frowned. Hunger alone would not enslave a man. There had to be another answer, and he needed to learn it if he was going to pass successfully as a palace slave. He couldn't hide under his invisibility shroud forever, not if he was going to track down his missing spy. And finding the spy was imperative. That was why he'd left the battlefield in Mosar to come here. He needed the information the spy possessed.

You will find him, said Sashi.

He is probably imprisoned or dead, said Janto. *But I appreciate your faith.* Even in peacetime, Janto hadn't been a popular prince. His people preferred warriors, not scholars, as their leaders, and the shame of the tragedy at Silverside Cavern still hung over his head. But none of that mattered now. The threat of losing Mosar to the Kjallans overshadowed all. He had a spy to find and a secret to uncover. *I'm going to look inside,* he told Sashi. *Stay close, and stay hidden.*

With a chirp of acknowledgment, Sashi scampered down Janto's sleeve, leapt to the ground, and disappeared into the darkness alongside the slave house. Janto waited for a group of slaves to return to the house, then, still invisible, slipped through the door with them.

The muffled conversation he'd heard from outside became a roar. Light spilled over him, along with the smell of food—something foreign and not very appetizing. Six long tables just inside the door were crowded with people eating supper, all of them men. Beyond the tables, a partially enclosed sleeping area was crammed so tightly with canvas pallets that there was barely room to walk between them. Warmth poured off the heat-glows mounted on the wall.

Looking back at the tables, Janto saw that the men were divided into three groups. About a third were Mosari like himself. Another third were Riorcans, and another third unidentifiable—Kjallans, he supposed, from conquered provinces. Though no barrier separated them, the groups did not mingle.

He walked past one of the Mosari tables, looking closely at each man's face, careful not to touch anybody or otherwise reveal his presence. It had been years since he'd last seen Ral-Vaddis, his missing spy, but surely the man hadn't changed much. Janto would recognize him.

No sign of him at the first table, so Janto moved on to the second. No Ral-Vaddis, but another face caught his eye. Hadn't that fellow once been a signaler in the palace? Poor man; how had he been captured? He moved on to the third table, and the fourth. His spy wasn't here. And he couldn't see any hint, from inside the slave house, of how the slaves were kept under the control of their Kjallan masters.

He glanced back at the second table. Might the signaler be of some use to him?

On a table in the corner of the room sat several logbooks, an ink pot, and a quill. Probably the overseer did his bookkeeping there, but he wasn't in sight now. Janto picked his way to the table and extended his shroud just enough to cover the writing utensils. He tore a piece of paper out of a logbook and wrote the word *Outside* on it, followed by his royal signature, the letter *J* atop a *T.*

Returning to the table, he slipped the folded paper into the signaler's hand. The man turned, startled at the unexpected contact, but there was no one for him to look at. Janto headed for the door and slipped outside behind someone heading to the latrines.

Sashi, he called, lowering a hand to the ground. The ferret came running from out of the shadows, up his arm, and onto his shoulder. *We might have company.*

You found Ral-Vaddis?

Someone else.

The signaler burst out of the slave house and looked around frantically in the moonlight.

With an arc of his hand, Janto extended his magical shroud to include the signaler, an act that rendered both of them invisible to everyone else, but visible to each other.

The signaler jumped as Janto materialized. "Three gods! Is it really you? Your Highness . . ." He started to get down on his knees but thought better of it, glancing about him.

"We're invisible. You're in my shroud. Follow me." Janto's shroud concealed their visibility and sound, but it didn't prevent them from disturbing ground cover or being stumbled into by other people. He led the signaler into the cover of the forest.

When he halted beneath the branches of a great oak, the signaler dropped to his knees and bowed his head. "Your Highness."

See? Your people love you, said Sashi.

Silverside, Janto reminded him. *He'd prefer my father or my brother, but he'll take what he can get.* "Don't do that; it could get me in trouble," he said. "And don't say Jan-Torres either. Call me Janto."

"Your family name?"

"It's a common name, shouldn't give me away," said Janto. "Didn't you used to be a signaler in the palace? What's your name, and how did you end up here?"

"My name is Iolo." He stood. "After the palace, I did some work on merchant ships. I was a signaler on the *Canary* when the Kjallans took it off Bartleshore. But why are *you* here? I hope we haven't lost the war."

"Not yet."

"Is it not going well?"

"My father's doing the best he can, given that the Kjallan army is ten times the size of ours," said Janto. "I'm looking for a man named Ral-Vaddis—"

"Ral-Vaddis is here?"

"You know him?"

"The shroud mage. I know *of* him."

"He said he had valuable intelligence for us, that the Kjallan emperor was about to make a critical strategic error, one that could cost him the war. He was going to get back to us with details. But he never did."

"And you came to find him? Why you? I can see why someone who could turn invisible was necessary, but surely there was another besides the Crown Prince—"

"Casualties have been high. I run Mosari Intelligence, and shroud mages are as rare as albino brindlecats. There *was* nobody else."

Iolo's face fell in dismay. "I wish I could help, but I haven't seen Ral-Vaddis."

"But you can help me, nonetheless," said Janto.

"How?"

"By answering some questions. Why do the slaves in Kjall not run?"

"What do you mean?"

"You have no chains on you. Why do you not run away?"

"Because of the death spell," said Iolo.

Janto opened his palms in confusion.

"When I was brought here as a slave, a death spell was cast on me, but it has a delayed effect. It doesn't work right away. Each day, if I do my work and follow the rules, they cast an abeyance spell that delays the death spell by another day. If I run off, I won't get my abeyance spell. But you could fix that. Couldn't you?" His eyes lit upon the ferret that was the source of Janto's shroud magic. "You're a mage. You could remove my death spell."

"A shroud mage has no power to remove a death spell."

Iolo looked at the ground. "Oh."

"If I could, I'd free all of you," said Janto. "You work in the Imperial Palace, do you not?"

Iolo nodded. "The Imperial Garden."

"If you want to help me, teach me to pass for a slave myself, and get me into the palace," said Janto. "It may not be enough for me just to sneak around and overhear things. I need to be able to talk to people, interact with people — other slaves and maybe even Kjallans. There are things I must learn quickly if I'm to have any chance of finding Ral-Vaddis and discovering what it is he knows."

"I can do that, Your Highness," Iolo answered with a smile.

2

As Rhianne crawled on hands and knees through the hypocaust, the palace's underground heating system, she simultaneously cursed and blessed its existence. It was hot and cramped and ridiculously uncomfortable, yet without it she'd never be able to sneak out of the palace without her escort tagging along after her and reporting her every move to the emperor. Her poor, naïve guards believed her to be taking a nap in her bedroom right now, just as they had every other time she'd sneaked out. They must think her a prodigious sleeper.

Brushing a cobweb from her hair, she counted the massive heat-glows spaced at intervals along the floor. Forty-five, forty-six, forty-seven . . . This was where she turned left into the narrow passage. Good thing she wasn't frightened of small spaces. The hypocaust was sweltering even with only one of every five glows activated, but tempted as she was to deactivate them, she interfered with nothing down here. She would leave no evidence of her passing.

At the end of the narrow tunnel, the crawl space opened vertically into a passageway, allowing her to stand and walk normally for a few steps until it ended at a door, the hypocaust's lone service entrance. It was guarded, but as long as the guards possessed no magic, Rhianne had nothing to worry about. She opened the door and stepped through it, throwing first a confusion spell and then a forgetting spell over the guards who turned in her direction. She continued on her way.

She proceeded from there to the palace stables and then, on horseback, down the switchbacks to the Imperial City of Riat. When her journey was complete, she led her white mare into a tiny stable adjoining a modest home in the merchants' district.

"Who's there?" called a gruff voice as she dismounted and pulled the reins over the mare's head. The huge figure of an old palace bodyguard appeared in the doorway that connected house and stable, casting a shadow over the straw-filled stall. The voice softened. "Oh, it's you. The boy will take your horse."

A Riorcan slave slipped into the stable and took the mare's reins. Rhianne climbed the stairs and trailed the big man into the house. "How are you, Morgan?" she asked.

"Getting by."

"I brought your pension." Rhianne pulled the thirty tetrals from her pocket.

Morgan turned and rocked on his feet, frowning at the coins. Finally he extended a hand, and she poured them into his palm.

"You don't have to do this," he said.

"Someone has to," said Rhianne. "Are you doing those exercises the Healer recommended?"

Morgan nodded. He puttered around his kitchen, searching for a pair of clean mugs. "I don't know where that boy puts anything," he groused, reaching for a high shelf but grunting when his arm wouldn't straighten.

"He puts things *away*," said Rhianne. "If you'd just

look where they're supposed to be—I'll get those." She pulled two mugs off the high shelf. "You're not doing the exercises."

Morgan didn't answer. He took the mugs and poured a reddish drink from a pitcher into each.

"Do I want to know what that is?"

Morgan grinned. "Try it. You'll like it." He gestured at the sitting room. "Have a seat. Catch me up on the palace gossip."

Rhianne perched on a settee and sipped her mystery drink. It was sweet and fruity and strongly alcoholic. She coughed discreetly. "It has a kick."

"Fig juice, honey, and gin." He settled onto a couch across from her.

"Disgusting." She took another sip.

"So, what trouble has your cousin gotten into lately?"

Rhianne rolled her eyes. "He spoke out against the war in Mosar during a council session. Now Florian's ready to mount him on the wall."

Morgan laughed. "Wish I'd been there."

"It's not funny," said Rhianne. "Florian struck him, and it's not the first time."

"I mean I wish I'd been at the council meeting. Florian's not used to having anyone call him on his horseshit, and Lucien's just enough of a pissant to do it. The problem with those two is that they have only two things in common—stubbornness and pride—and everything else about them is different. Florian's such a hothead. You know—act first, think later. But Lucien's so controlled, he can stare at that Caturanga board of his for an hour just contemplating the moves. The two of them don't value the same principles or see eye to eye on anything. I've never seen a father and son who are such opposites."

"Lucien suffers," said Rhianne. "He puts a brave face on it, but Florian's hatred torments him."

"Of course it does," said Morgan. "But wait and see. If Lucien survives these years under Florian's thumb—and I know they are not easy—he will make a fine emperor someday. One of the best."

Rhianne leaned back in her chair. "You say this, having served his elder brother?"

A shadow crossed Morgan's face. "I'd have saved him if I could. You know I would have. But Sestius would have made, at best, a mediocre emperor, and the same goes for Mathian. I know it was Riorcan assassins who did it, but . . . sometimes I wonder if the Vagabond may have meddled with us, just a bit."

"Calling on the gods now? You'd better keep those treasonous thoughts to yourself," said Rhianne.

"Well," said Morgan with a twisted smile, "I don't work in the palace anymore. To treasonous thoughts!" He raised his mug, apparently with no expectation that Rhianne should raise hers, and drank deeply.

Sometimes Morgan frightened Rhianne with his bitterness and plain speaking, but at least he came by his faults honestly. He was former Legaciatti, once the personal bodyguard of Sestius, Lucien's eldest brother, who had been heir to the Imperial Throne. Assassins had attacked the pair of them, killing Sestius and leaving Morgan for dead. Morgan survived, but his injuries were crippling; he could not continue in his duty as a Legaciattus. He was entitled to a lifetime pension, but Emperor Florian had been so furious at his failure to save Sestius that he'd dismissed Morgan from the service empty-handed.

Morgan, during his service, had always been kind to

Rhianne. He'd tipped her off a couple of times when Sestius was in a rage so that she could stay out of his way, and he'd always seemed to be conveniently blind when she and Lucien had played their childhood pranks. She and Morgan hadn't been close back then, since in his service he'd been attached to Sestius. Nonetheless, she'd perceived him as family, as a sort of distant uncle. He had no real family, of course; none of the Legaciatti did, and after his disability, he would have been destitute had she and Lucien not come up with the scheme to support him with their personal spending money.

"You tell your cousin to keep his head down," said Morgan. "Florian is not a man to be crossed. He bears grudges."

"You would know, I suppose," said Rhianne.

"Lucien's goal right now should be to sit back, quietly learn as much as he can about governance, and *survive*. He'll have his turn to run the empire, in time—if his father doesn't kill him first."

"Lucien's afraid there won't be an empire left for him if Florian governs so recklessly."

"Such dramatics," said Morgan. "He's, what, seventeen? A difficult age."

"I have news too," said Rhianne. "Apparently I'm to be married."

"Are you?" Morgan sat up straighter. "Who's the lucky fellow?"

"Augustan Ceres."

Morgan's eyebrows went up.

"I didn't choose him," Rhianne added quickly. "Florian simply informed me I was marrying him. He'll have the governorship of Mosar when it's conquered."

"Mosar? You're leaving, then."

"Yes, but don't worry," she said. "I'll find another solution for your pension. Maybe Lucien can deliver it. Or I can send it from overseas."

"You're a good woman," said Morgan. "But don't involve Lucien. The poor boy's got enough to deal with."

Rhianne swallowed. "Do you know anything about Augustan?"

Morgan shook his head. "Seen him around the palace a few times, but he wasn't there much—always out on assignment. A great legatus, I've heard. Handsome fellow." He smiled tentatively.

Rhianne waved a hand. "I don't care if he's handsome."

"Sure you do," said Morgan. "You wouldn't want an ugly old man like me."

"You're not ugly, and thirty-six is far from old," said Rhianne. "It's nice if a man is handsome, but that's not the most important thing. The most important thing is what sort of person he is. Is he kind? Is he generous? Is he loyal?"

"Those are the second most important things," said Morgan. "The first most important thing is how big his cock is."

"Oh, be quiet," said Rhianne. "So, what's the news from your corner of Riat?"

"Nothing of import," said Morgan, but he filled the next hour with tales of the crazy widow next door and the fortune-tellers across the street, plus a story about a donkey that sat down in the middle of the road and refused to budge until someone scared it off with a squealing pig. For that hour Rhianne managed, at least for a little while, to forget her own worries.

3

Infiltrating the Imperial Palace as a garden slave turned out to be easier than Janto had expected. There were a couple dozen such slaves, and when Janto joined the horde at the back gates of the palace in the morning, dressed in a single-belted gray slave tunic so that he blended in with the group, no one remarked on his presence. The head gardener, a creaky Kjallan fossil, didn't know the slaves by name or even seem to regard them as individuals, so the biggest problem Janto faced was having no gardening skills, nor any experience with manual labor. That and having to hide Sashi, whom he concealed with his invisibility shroud and instructed to stay close while disturbing as little ground in the garden as possible. He could see Sashi himself, since the shroud was his own creation, but the ferret looked faded, almost ghostly, behind the veil of his magic.

He took instruction from Iolo as he went. The garden itself was stunning. Janto had never seen such a variety of trees and plants in one place. Most of them were leafless, which he found creepy and strange. Mosari trees never lost their leaves while they lived, and walking through a forest of bare trunks made him feel as if he were walking through an arboreal graveyard. But he understood they were only dormant, waiting for the spring, and as he spread mulch around the tree trunks, he tried to imagine what each tree would look like when it came to life again.

This is a terrible forest, complained Sashi, scampering invisibly at his heels and keeping to the dirt paths, where his passage would not bend grasses or stir leaves.

How so?

No rats, no voles.

Are you certain? asked Janto. It seemed plausible that rodents might find places to nest in the thicker ground foliage.

Can't you smell? Sashi drawled with a look of condescension.

Janto smiled. His ferret loved to lord his superior senses over Janto when he could. *I'll take you hunting later. In a real forest.*

As he wrestled a wheelbarrow of mulch from one section of the garden to another, with Iolo trailing after him, he discovered the garden was divided by country—here were Inyan plants, there were Sardossian ones—and he was astonished when he arrived at a Mosari section. It was warm, wonderfully so, with heat-glows strategically placed to simulate Mosar's tropical climate. He recognized many trees and plants. There was an avocado tree, fruitless and pruned rather strangely, but he recognized its distinctive leaves. He spied a Poinciana and a lemon tree, along with other familiar plants whose names he did not know. Most of them looked a bit odd, and some were unhealthy. He felt as if he were looking at a copy of a copy of a Mosari garden, recognizable but not quite right in its essentials.

This forest is sick, fussed Sashi.

You're quite right. I wish we were at home.

Sitting on a bench beneath the Poinciana tree was a woman—a Kjallan noblewoman, no doubt, since a uniformed bodyguard, female but substantial-looking, stood watchfully at her side. The noblewoman was perhaps twentyish, of average height, pretty, with walnut-colored hair that hung in ringlets. She wore the feminine version of the syrtos, which flattered her figure, and over it was draped a loros, a thin band of jewel-encrusted brocade. At the sight of the loros, Janto adjusted his estimation of her rank upward by several degrees. In all likelihood, she was a member of the imperial family.

"Who is she?" he whispered to Iolo.

"Don't know," he whispered back. "Very high rank. Stay away."

Janto pushed his wheelbarrow closer to the woman. He'd come here to spy on the imperials, and here was an imperial, although he doubted a sheltered Kjallan princess knew much about the war.

The scent of orange blossoms wafted toward him as he neared her. The princess's voice was soft and liquid as honey, and she was speaking Mosari! Reading it from a book, it appeared. She was misprouncing most of the words, and she had the most atrocious accent he'd ever heard. Poor woman—nice to look at, but it seemed she had dandelion fluff for brains. He listened anyway, mesmerized.

Rhianne could see that the Mosari travelogue she'd found in the library wasn't going to be much use. It had a single page of helpful phrases for travelers, but if she was going to spend the rest of her life in Mosar, she needed to learn the whole language, not just a few helpful phrases. Still, it was all she had, and until she found better, she'd make the most of it.

"*Cona oleska,*" said Rhianne to Tamienne, her bodyguard. "Means *good morning.*" She repeated the phrase under her breath, trying to commit it to memory. "*Cona oleska, cona oleska.*"

"*Cona oleska,*" echoed Tamienne.

She sighed and looked up from her book. She noticed the slaves were now working near her in the garden. She wanted to learn the Mosari language, and here she was, surrounded by Mosari men, every one of whom spoke it fluently. The problem was that none of these slaves spoke more than a few basic words of Kjallan. Still, perhaps she could practice a "helpful phrase" or two on them.

One slave was quite close, shoveling mulch. "*Cona oleska,*" she called to him.

The slave raised his head and, to her astonishment, spoke in fluent submissive Kjallan. "With respect, great lady, you just wished me a 'good mountain.'"

Tamienne was instantly in motion, cuffing the slave across the face. "*Your Imperial Highness,*" she growled.

"Leave him be, Tami!" cried Rhianne.

"I beg your pardon, Your Imperial Highness," said the slave.

Tamienne retreated, glaring balefully at the slave.

"Come closer," Rhianne ordered him.

Wordlessly, he did so.

Rhianne could not help thinking that there was something distinctly unslavelike about this man. Though not especially tall or imposing, he stood before her with the carriage of a warrior, and his comfort in addressing her suggested his rank in Mosar had once been high. He couldn't have been in Kjall long because his coloration was still sun touched, his golden hair a shade lighter than his skin but cut short, unlike the Inyans, who braided theirs down their backs. His sea-blue eyes regarded her with more amusement than fear, and she found herself wanting to know his story and maybe touch that lovely bronze skin—not that she was the type to consort with a slave. "What's your name?"

"Janto."

"I wished you a 'good mountain'?"

"You put the stress on the wrong syllable. You said *oh-LES-ka*. It's *OH-les-ka*."

"OH-les-ka," she mimicked. *"Cona OH-les-ka.* Is that right?"

"Yes. But your accent is atrocious." He smiled, and she was taken aback by how beautifully his features lit up.

She smiled back. It was so funny to hear him speak words in the submissive grammar that weren't submissive in their nature at all. Perhaps since he was a foreigner, he was not aware of the irony. "I would fault your Kjallan accent if I could, but I'd be lying. It's perfect."

"Thank you," said Janto. "I had an exacting tutor."

"I have a feeling you weren't a gardener back on Mosar."

"No, Your Imperial Highness," said Janto. "I was a scribe in the Mosari palace."

"You're literate, then?"

"Yes."

And he spoke with such confidence. If he'd truly been only a scribe, he'd been a valued one. "How did you come here?"

His eyebrows rose. "To the Imperial Palace?"

"Yes. To Kjall." She realized as soon as she'd said it that it was a stupid question. Obviously he'd been enslaved, and whatever had happened to him, it had been recent, so the pain would still be raw. And he was young—around twenty-five, she guessed, which made his situation sadder still. She was curious, but she should not satisfy her curiosity by poking at fresh wounds.

With a wry smile, he looked around the garden. "Imperial Highness. This is a beautiful place, and you are a beautiful woman. I don't think you wish to hear my tale of woe."

Rhianne did, in fact, want to hear his tale of woe, but she accepted this as Janto's polite way of saying he preferred not to talk about it. Still, if she got to know him a little better . . . but he was a slave. He could be transferred anywhere at any time, at the whim of the overseers. "Your talents are wasted hauling dirt. I would like to give you a new job."

"Yes, Your Imperial Highness?"

"I'd like you to tutor me in the Mosari language."

He raised his eyebrows in surprise but didn't say anything. She supposed she had shocked him, but she couldn't resist. It had been a long time since she'd met someone who intrigued her as much as this man. A slave, yes, but educated and diplomatic. Obviously well bred. And gods, that smile.

"I'll be here every morning at around this time, and you can teach me," she said. "I'll speak to the head gardener about your absence from your other duties."

"May I ask why you wish to learn my language?"

Rhianne hesitated. She could hardly tell him it was because she was supposed to help govern his country after it had been conquered. That was just cruel. "I'm . . . supposed to travel there later. I thought it would be good if I knew the language."

Janto folded his arms. "During the war?"

Rhianne shook her head. If he was going to push for an answer, he was going to get one he didn't like. "No. After we conquer it."

"Perhaps your efforts will be wasted," said Janto, his chin up. "You might lose."

She looked down at her book, embarrassed now that she had tried to hurt him. "I can't imagine it would ever be a waste to learn another language. I'll see you tomorrow morning. Be prompt."

"Prompt as the sunrise, Your Imperial Highness." The slave returned to his wheelbarrow.

Janto left the Imperial Palace grounds under cover of his shroud with Sashi on his shoulder. He watched Iolo and the others pick up their signed chits that indicated they'd done a full day's work. As he understood it, the chits entitled them to their abeyance spells and allowed them to live another day. The brutal, dehumanizing system seemed typical of the Kjallans.

Invisible, Janto stayed close to Iolo, who, as agreed, slowed his pace and fell behind the others. When they were alone, Janto extended his shroud to cover the both of them. "I think that went all right."

Iolo shook his head. "You were crazy to talk to the Imperial Princess. I about had a stroke when her bodyguard went after you."

He touched the tender spot on his cheek, only just now remembering the assault by the bodyguard. Once he'd started talking to the princess, all other thoughts had fled from his mind. Gods, he'd never anticipated meeting someone like her. "The bruise is a small price to pay. I need access to the man at the top—or at least to his half-witted military strategies—and this woman gets me close."

"I don't question your courage," said Iolo. "But there are other ways to get what you're after."

Janto sighed. Iolo had spent the last couple of days teaching him everything he needed to know about pretending to be a palace slave. His initial fear that Iolo would be overawed by his rank had turned out to be unjustified. Iolo eagerly challenged Janto on decisions he didn't agree with. That was good; his advice seemed insightful, and his outspokenness meant Iolo would be useful as a long-term ally and adviser, not just a temporary tutor in the ways of Kjallan slaves. But it was also annoying. "You don't question my courage," said Janto, "but you question my judgment."

"If you want me to advise you, Your Highness—"

"By all means be honest with me," said Janto. "I've no use for a sycophant. But don't dodge the issue; come out with it. You believe my decisions are suspect because of Silverside."

Iolo winced. "That's not what I said."

"It's what you're thinking," said Janto. "Everybody thinks it. I made a bad decision, and we lost a dozen mages. It was a mistake, one with a tragic outcome. But I've made good decisions too. No one can be right all the time."

Iolo nodded, but Janto didn't feel he looked convinced.

"I need access to the imperials," said Janto. "And they're not gods. They're ordinary people with human failings. Kjallans sequester their noblewomen. That princess has probably never so much as set foot outside the palace walls, and I'll bet you anything she's dumber than a clump of seaweed." As he walked in silence, he decided it was a good thing Iolo wasn't leaping to take that bet. The princess had been curious, and curiosity often meant intelligence. He'd have to be careful around her. He'd never meant to talk to her so much in the first place, but she was so fascinating. The words had poured almost unbidden from his throat.

"Well, I've found something for you," said Iolo. "I've discovered someone who knows Ral-Vaddis."

"What?" Janto looked up, jolted from his thoughts of the princess. "Why didn't you tell me right away? This is wonderful news!"

"There's a woman named Sirali who works in the palace kitchens. She knows him."

Janto eyed him sternly. "But can we trust her?"

"Don't worry, I was discreet. And I know the slaves here. We can trust Sirali."

"Then I need to speak to her right away."

"I've made arrangements," said Iolo. "She'll meet with us tomorrow night."

4

Rhianne dove into the pool with barely a splash, then rolled over and let the warm water carry her to the mist-covered surface. She felt as if she were floating in a cloud of orange-scented vapor. She closed her eyes to deepen the illusion, blocking out the sight of the white marble roof and walls. As she lay there, her friend Marcella splashed by, oblivious to the pool's comforts and obsessed, as usual, with exercise.

After a moment, the splashing stopped, and a smattering of droplets fell onto Rhianne's face.

"Are you asleep?" asked Marcella.

Rhianne straightened in the water, treading. "Not anymore."

"I heard the good news." She grinned.

"What news?"

Marcella splashed her playfully. "Your betrothal!"

"Oh, that." Rhianne pushed a stray lock of wet hair out of her face, disappointed there wasn't actually any good news. "Honestly, I'm not thrilled about it. I've never met Augustan."

"Cerinthus has nothing but fine things to say about him," said Marcella. "I understand your nerves—I was worried about my marriage too. But it's all worked out beautifully, and I've never been happier."

"I'm glad things have worked out so well for you and Cerinthus." Rhianne took a deep breath and dove beneath the surface, swimming down and down until her ears hurt, all the way to the pool's marble bottom. Cerinthus was a bootlicker. That he praised Augustan, a higher-ranking officer, didn't mean a thing; he praised anyone who outranked him. While Rhianne hoped his excellent treatment of Marcella stemmed from a deep-seated love for her, her cynical side knew it was at least partly motivated by the fact that Marcella's father was an influential legatus upon whom Cerinthus's military career was entirely dependent. She hovered at the bottom of the pool for as long as she could stand it, bubbles streaming from her mouth. When her lungs cried out for air, she swam to the surface.

Marcella took her hands and squeezed them. "I pray Augustan will be as wonderful for you as Cerinthus has been for me. And think of the things we could do, the four of us, when the war is over! We could go hunting together, hawking together. And our children, Rhianne! Our children will grow up as friends—"

Rhianne ducked her head, suddenly sad. "It won't be that way. Augustan is to have the governorship of Mosar, and I'm to accompany him."

Marcella's face fell. "You're leaving Kjall?"

Rhianne nodded.

"But you'll be all alone on Mosar!"

"Well," said Rhianne, trying not to sound bitter, "I'll have Augustan."

Later that afternoon, dried off and dressed, she found her cousin Lucien on her fifth visit to his rooms. He was reclining on a couch in his sitting room, his nose deep in one of Cinna's lengthy tomes. An elderly hound sprawled atop him.

"You're impossible to find these days." She gathered up the silk train of her syrtos and settled into a chair across from him.

"Well, here I am." He scanned a few more lines of Cinna and set the tome aside. "Florian's always got me busy with something. War councils, meetings with his financial advisers, lunch with the governor of Worich. It never ends. And I'm not allowed to talk, by the way, unless I'm 'enthusiastically agreeing' with him."

Rhianne shook her head. "Sounds like a wonderful time."

"Asbolos is better company," said Lucien, rubbing the hound's ears. "It's good training, at least. I'm learning a lot, and I *will* have to run this empire someday."

Looking at Lucien, Rhianne couldn't help thinking how much he'd changed from the boy he had been, long ago, before the assassins had changed everything. As a child, he'd been superfluous like her, a spare family member to be married off someday. Ignored by Florian, the two of them had learned the ways of the hypocaust and sneaked out of the palace on a regular basis, exploring and getting into mischief and riding off into the woods to talk for hours on end. But no longer. Lucien was crippled and couldn't go crawling around the hypocaust anymore, and now he was heir to the Imperial Throne. He barely had time for Rhianne in between all his responsibilities. He still cared for her; she didn't doubt that. But it wasn't the same, and even in his presence she felt the deep ache of loneliness. She was losing him, and she would lose Marcella, and she would lose Morgan too.

Silence stretched uncomfortably between them. "Three gods, you spoil that dog," she said, just to have something to say.

"No more than you spoil Morgan."

Rhianne shook her head. "Morgan's earned what he gets." It was a similar situation for the dog, however, an ancient animal the houndmaster had intended to drown for being too old to work anymore. Lucien, who'd hunted with Asbolos when the animal had been in his prime, had stepped in and adopted him, much to his father's annoyance. "Does Florian still give you a hard time about Asbolos?"

"I just shut him in a back room when I'm expecting His Royal Unreasonableness. Not that he doesn't drop in unexpectedly now and then and chew me out for being too weak and softhearted to run an empire."

"It's not weakness," said Rhianne.

"No," agreed Lucien. "It's loyalty. Florian doesn't realize it, but when he threw Morgan out on his ear, he weakened his position with the Legaciatti. I'm not saying they'd go so far as to depose or assassinate him, but they know now that he doesn't have their back. And if push comes to shove, they won't have his. That's what I learned when I was stationed with White Eagle—your people need to know you'll stand behind them."

"Of course they do." Rhianne eyed the Cinna tome. Lucien was the military strategist, not she. But loyalty to one's friends seemed such a basic concept. One didn't need to study thousand-page books to know it was important. "So what do you know about Augustan Ceres?"

"He's coming here," said Lucien. "Florian had already summoned him, even before he spoke to you."

"He's coming *soon*?"

"A matter of days."

Days. She didn't feel ready. But maybe she never would. "What sort of person is he?"

Lucien frowned. "I don't know. He's always been on assignment in the south, and I was in the north. He's got a reputation. . . ."

"What sort of reputation?"

"He's strict. Stern."

Rhianne bit her lip. She'd been hoping for a kind, jovial husband. Someone who made jokes, like Morgan. Someone thoughtful, like Lucien.

"It's not necessarily bad," offered Lucien. "Most good officers are on the strict side. They're clear about their expectations, and the men like that."

"I'm not a soldier," said Rhianne.

"Of course you're not. I'm not implying he'd be strict with *you*." Lucien gave a nervous laugh. "You'd be his *wife*, not his, uh . . ." Whatever word he was searching for, he didn't find it.

Rhianne tried to calm the anxious flutter in her stomach. It was no use getting worked up about a man she had never met and was hearing about thirdhand from a soldier's point of view. Augustan might turn out to be wonderful. She couldn't help wondering about him, but she would not pass judgment until she could evaluate him in person. "So after I go to Mosar, what are we going to do about Morgan?"

Lucien sighed. "I don't mind contributing the fifteen tetrals, but if you're expecting me to go crawling through the hypocaust in your place, well . . ." He held up his crutch. "Come up with another plan."

Rhianne dropped her chin into her hands. "Morgan said not to involve you. Is there anyone else we can bring into this little conspiracy? Celeste?" As soon as she said it, she knew it was ridiculous.

Lucien shook his head. "Out of the question."

Celeste, Lucien's younger sister, was only eight years old and in the constant company of her nurse and tutor. She had not yet soulcasted. Rhianne could safely evade guards and travel through the city of Riat with the aid of her mind magic, but until Celeste acquired her own magic at around the age of twelve, it was ludicrous to consider sending her on such a mission.

"When I become emperor, I'll reinstate his pension, but that won't happen any time soon. Florian is likely to outlive Morgan. What about sending the money from Mosar?" said Lucien. "Once you're married, you should have the authority to do that. And the island is wealthy—you'll have money to spare."

"I think that would depend on my husband. Will he allow it, considering that it violates Florian's wishes?"

"Augustan doesn't have to know what the money's for," said Lucien. "Not exactly. Just say you're sending money to support Kjallan war veterans."

"What if he doesn't allow me to have money of my own?" said Rhianne.

"He'd better," said Lucien.

Rhianne's heart leapt when she saw the slave Janto waiting under the Poinciana tree at the appointed time. She'd been looking forward to this meeting all morning. When he spotted her and turned with a smile of recognition, her stomach practically melted. Which was ridiculous. A princess should never be nervous or excited about meeting a slave. She stood up straight and made herself enunciate clearly, "There you are." She took a seat on the bench. "I thought we'd start with this." She held up a book of Mosari fairy tales.

"A children's book?"

It still stunned her to hear such perfect Kjallan words come out of his mouth. Most foreigners stumbled over the different grammatical forms. Janto, speaking in the submissive since he was her social inferior, hadn't made an error yet. But perhaps he knew only the submissive. "Something easy, since I'm just getting started. Do you know all three grammatical forms of the Kjallan language?"

"Of course," said Janto. "Now I'm speaking to you in the diplomatic form," and he rattled off a few lines of Plinius, a well-known Kjallan writer. "Now I'm speaking to you in command." More Plinius.

He switched as fluently as a native speaker. And while he shouldn't have been speaking in command, he didn't stiffen up or take on an apologetic air, the common mistakes that gave away those who weren't comfortable in the form. Rather, he spoke command with a charisma that almost had her wanting to obey *his* orders. Which was disconcerting. "You astonish me."

"Why?" He grinned. "Did you think my people spent all our time frolicking about on the beach?"

A flush crept up her cheeks. "No. I just mean it's unusual for a nonnative to master all three grammatical forms so thoroughly."

He shrugged. "I have a talent for languages."

She slid over on the bench, making room. "Will you sit down?"

He glanced at Tamienne. "Your attack dog is eyeing me."

"If you mind your manners, you've nothing to worry about from my attack dog." Though part of her wished her bodyguard wasn't there. Yes, Tami protected her, but she was also a chaperone. Rhianne would never be able to touch this man, not even in the most innocent of ways, with Tami present.

He sat, leaving a frustrating hand's width of space between them, and handed the book back to her. "Show me what you know."

Rhianne opened the book to the first story, about a prince, an old woman, and a magical goat. She read aloud haltingly, translating to Kjallan where she could and asking for help when she didn't know a word. Janto turned out to be a patient and nonjudgmental teacher. The sweet citrus scent of a nearby lemon tree wafted over them as they worked, and the Mosari tale was adorable. She would have thoroughly enjoyed herself except that Janto was being excruciatingly careful not to touch her, always pulling his hand away from the book before their fingers met. No doubt he was worried about Tamienne, but it was aggravating. She could feel the heat of his body, the strength of his presence, but at this rate that was all she would ever feel.

"So here's something that's driving me crazy," she said. *And it's not the only thing driving me crazy.* "Earlier, the prince was referring to the old woman with the pronoun *xhe*, and now the pronoun is *nhe*. Why do Mosari pronouns change all the time? It makes no sense."

"It makes perfect sense. He says *xhe* at first because she's a stranger. Later he says *nhe* because she has become, to him, *na-kali*. That's a word with no translation in your language, but it can be thought of as 'future friend.' It suggests friendly intent and common ground. Now, if they were truly friends, he'd call her *alhe*, or *kali* if he were addressing her directly, and if they were intimates or family members, *sei* or *su-kali*. *Su-kali* is also how our mages address their familiars, and vice versa, since that's a close relationship."

"How do you keep track of it all? Aren't there seven forms for each variant?"

Janto shrugged. "Yes, but it's no harder than learning three separate grammatical forms for an entire language. Rather easier, in fact."

"Which one of those pronouns would you use for me?" asked Rhianne.

"None of them," said Janto. "You'd be *jhe*. Uncertain friend."

She wished she could be more. "Do I want to know what the sixth and seventh forms are?"

"The sixth is *dre*—enemy. And the seventh form is reserved for the gods. *Otte*."

"You have a special pronoun for the gods?"

"Of course we do," said Janto. "Think about it. Our pronouns communicate the relationship between two beings, and none of the relationships I just described—stranger, friend, enemy—describe the relationship between a mere mortal and a god. Thus we give that relationship its own pronoun. *Otte* from man to god, *otu* from god to man."

"What about between the gods themselves? Say, between the Soldier and the Vagabond?"

Janto shrugged. "Depends on the context. Probably *sei* because in most of our stories about the gods, they treat one another as brothers."

"I have a different sort of question for you." Rhianne marked her place and closed the book. "How long have you been a slave?"

Janto hesitated before answering. "Why do you ask?"

"I want to know if you were captured before or during the war. Don't worry, I won't ask for details."

"During," he said.

"You fought, then, on Mosar?"

He eyed her warily. "Yes."

"Then you have some familiarity with Augustan Ceres."

"The commander in charge of the invasion?" said Janto. "I have the sort of familiarity that comes from fighting against him. I've never sat down to dinner with him."

"What's he like?"

"He's a monster," said Janto.

Rhianne shivered. Surely he was exaggerating. "I understand he's in charge of the forces that invaded your country, and you would naturally harbor ill feelings toward him—"

"I don't personally despise every enemy commander who targets my country, Princess. I understand they're under orders and they're doing their jobs. But Augustan Ceres really is a monster."

"How do you mean?"

"Early in the attack, when my people saw how outnumbered we were, the royal house sent your Commander Augustan a party of envoys under Sage flag to offer terms of surrender. They were generous. Preferential trade agreements, annual tribute."

"You can't blame him for not accepting," said Rhianne. "Our military men are instructed not to accept conditional surrender."

"It's not that. He refused to return our envoys, even though they'd come under Sage flag. He led them out on the beach and staked them, in the full view of those watching from the cliffs. In war, he is ruthless and cruel. When we took Kjallan soldiers as prisoners of war, they were more frightened of him than they were of us. They desperately did *not* want to be traded back. I never learned why."

A cold knot of fear gathered in her belly. This was the man she was supposed to marry, a man who would murder a group of envoys who'd come to negotiate under Sage flag? But then, Janto would naturally be biased, and maybe she was naïve about the realities of war. "You don't know his reasons for doing what he did. He commands the entire Kjallan invading force, and you cannot know his mind. It's not Augustan who's ruthless and cruel. *War* is ruthless and cruel."

Janto gave her a pitying look. "I cannot agree, Princess. War is harsh, but there is no call for Augustan to be cruel to his own men. For him to murder men under a Sage flag is not only dishonorable; it offends the gods. I would rather be a slave, with my honor intact, than to be wearing that man's sandals."

Rhianne bit her lip so hard she tasted blood. He had to be wrong. He *had* to. Of course he was. He was Mosari, and the Mosari hated all Kjallans, especially the ones involved in the invasion. One could hardly blame him—his country and his people were at stake. She clutched the book of fairy tales to her chest and stood. "I think I've had enough language work for today."

5

J anto waited for Iolo beside the well, rubbing his arms and shivering beneath the oaks. Since his arrival on Kjall, he had yet to feel truly warm. Over his head, the full Vagabond moon, ghostly blue, shone through a tangle of bare branches. The Sage was also up, just a sliver, but the Soldier was not, which made for a dark night.

Leaves crunched along the path, and Janto turned. It was Iolo. He gestured and brought the man into his invisibility shroud.

Iolo stopped short. "That always takes me by surprise."

"I suppose it must, my appearing out of nowhere." Crouching, he lowered his hand to the ground and called through the telepathic link. Sashi came running from where he'd been hunting nearby in the forest and ran up onto his shoulder with a chirp of greeting. "Where's this woman we're supposed to meet? Sirali, right?"

"She's jumpy," said Iolo. "She wouldn't meet near the slave house, so we've got a walk ahead of us."

"Dark night for it."

"Vagabond moon, though." Iolo smiled up at the sky. "An omen for mischief." He headed into the woods, and Janto followed.

The forest was not a natural one. The trees, evenly spaced, were all the same variety of white oak. Some smaller plants and trees had sprung up in the gaps—weeds, Janto supposed—but the cultivated forest was remarkably open, allowing easy travel.

"How does it work, your shroud?" asked Iolo.

"You're familiar with the spirit world?"

"Yes . . . well." Iolo looked confused. "It's the source of all magic?"

"It's an entirely separate world. No one understands it fully, but it exists parallel to our own. Your physical body resides in our world, and your soul resides in the spirit world."

Iolo blinked. "Even if I'm not magical?"

"We're all magical because we all have souls," said Janto. "You can call magelight—anyone can—because magelight is your soul's reflection in the spirit world. But other forms of magic are more complicated. Magic is simply a transference from the spirit world into the real world through a Rift, but opening a Rift is extraordinarily difficult. To simplify the task of magic, one creates a sort of permanent Rift that can be used at will, and one does that by soulcasting. By entrapping a part of one's soul in another creature, or sometimes an inanimate object, one creates a fracture in the barrier between worlds."

"Your ferret," said Iolo. "You cast part of your soul into him. But how do you use him to create a shroud?"

"I find the fracture between worlds," said Janto, "the one I created by soulcasting. I open it and pull it over myself like a veil, placing myself in the between-space, neither in the real world nor the spirit world. The only hint that I'm in a shroud is my vision's a little fuzzy, and sometimes I get that rainbow effect around the edges of the veil—see there?" He pointed.

"I see it," said Iolo. They walked in silence. Then Iolo slowed, looking about. He seemed to find what he sought—a particular tree, which he examined. He altered course. Janto squinted at the tree as he passed it. There was a score mark on it in the shape of a circle.

"Did you hear my conversation with the princess today?" Janto asked.

"Gods, no, I stayed well away. That bodyguard of hers." Iolo shuddered.

"She asked me something strange. She asked what I thought of Augustan Ceres."

"Who's he?"

"The commander of the invasion—I guess you wouldn't know if you were enslaved before the war."

"Why would she ask what you thought of the enemy commander?"

"That's what I'm trying to figure out. She got mad when I told her he was a nasty piece of work. I'm beginning to think he's her lover or something." And Augustan didn't deserve her, the bastard. But maybe he was misinterpreting Rhianne's interest. She'd been asking as if she'd never met the man. Maybe he was a relative—a distant one. They were nothing alike, after all.

"You said she had seaweed for brains."

"I take that back," said Janto. "I never have to repeat a thing when I'm teaching her, and Mosari is not an easy language for foreigners. So she's not stupid. Perhaps a little naïve."

"I don't know why you talk to her at all. Isn't it dangerous?"

Janto shrugged. "Everything I do here is dangerous.

Talking to Rhianne may be the least dangerous thing I do, because while I'm not a trained spy, I *am* a trained diplomat. I know how to talk to people like her, so at least I'm playing to my strengths."

"But what do you hope to accomplish? She's not going to leak war intelligence to you. She probably doesn't know any."

"I'm not sure yet what I hope to accomplish with the princess," said Janto. "I just know that having a link to the imperial family is better than not having one." Also he just plain liked being around her. He knew Iolo would neither approve nor understand, and that it couldn't go anywhere. But some things couldn't be denied, and his desire to be near Rhianne was one of them.

They continued through the forest. The ground rose beneath Janto's feet, and the soft dirt became solid stone. Surf roared as a breaker rolled in somewhere below him. They'd reached the sea. There were no more trees ahead of them, and the empty sky glittered with stars and the crescent Sage.

"Careful," said Iolo, gripping his arm firmly. "There's a drop-off in front of us."

Janto could see it, or at least imagine it, the total blackness of the empty air below them and then the ocean, which stretched toward the western horizon, dotted with glow beacons. The glow beacons would be navigational aids, identifying hazardous places for ships, or perhaps marking a channel.

"Are we in the right place?" asked Janto. "Where's Sirali?"

They turned simultaneously, looking for her, and Janto spotted her, pressed against a tree and scanning the forest.

Janto dropped his shroud and approached with Iolo at his heels. "Sirali?" he called.

Her head whipped toward them.

"This is the shroud mage I told you about," said Iolo gently. "The one who's looking for Ral-Vaddis."

"Right, and what do you know of Ral-Vaddis?" she asked.

"I'm the man who sent him here," said Janto. "And since he hasn't reported in for a while, I've come to look for him."

"Prove it," said the woman. "Show me you're a shroud mage."

Janto approached her slowly. At first he thought her an older woman, but the more he scrutinized her, the less certain he was of her age. It was more that she looked worldly, that any naïveté or innocence she might have possessed had somehow been scrubbed away. Her accent suggested she'd grown up in a Mosari fishing village. He plucked Sashi off his shoulder and cradled him in the crook of his elbow. "Do you see me? Do you see my familiar?"

Sirali nodded.

"Watch closely." He went invisible and watched with satisfaction as Sirali's eyes went wide. He became visible again. "Proof enough?"

"Right, and Ral-Vaddis is gone. I don't know what happened to him."

Sashi leapt out of Janto's arms. *I'm hungry,* he said. *Mouse scent here.*

Good hunting, said Janto as the creature scampered into the trees. Then to Sirali, "Start at the beginning. How did you know Ral-Vaddis?"

"I work in the palace kitchens," said Sirali. "Sometimes

I serve people in their rooms, or at meetings or parties. Not the big parties, and not the imperials—slaves don't have access to them people. But I hear things sometimes."

"I don't doubt it," said Janto.

"Right, and Ral-Vaddis approached me one day. He said Mosar wanted to know the things the jack-scalders said. He wanted to meet with me once a sagespan—"

"Jack-scalders?" That was a term he hadn't heard in a while. Near-universal warding spells had rendered pox lesions virtually extinct.

"Kjallans." She wrinkled her nose. "This is the place we met, right here. I told whatever I heard. And then he stopped coming."

"Do you have any idea why?" asked Janto.

Sirali shrugged. "Got caught, maybe."

"And yet he didn't give *you* away. Did he?"

"Right, and he didn't."

"Don't you think if they'd caught him, they'd have interrogated him? And if they'd interrogated him, they'd have gotten your name out of him?"

Sirali was silent.

"They would have," said Janto. "If there's anything the Kjallans are good at, it's torture and interrogation."

"Ral-Vaddis was an important spy," said Sirali. "I'm a kitchen slave who heard things."

Janto gave a bitter laugh. "You think you weren't important enough for them to come after you? If he'd given you up, they would have. Something else happened. Either he didn't get caught, or he died before he could be interrogated. Did you know anybody else who knew Ral-Vaddis? Perhaps someone who worked for him the way you did, hearing things in the palace and passing them along to him?"

Sirali shook her head. "I met with him alone. I figured he met with other people too, but he didn't want us to know about each other."

Janto nodded. That made sense, though it was aggravating now. There could be a dozen or more slaves like Sirali scattered throughout the palace, people who'd worked with Ral-Vaddis, and one or two of them might know something about what had happened to him. But how was he ever to track them all down? "Tell me about the wards in the palace. What types do they lay, where do they lay them, and how often?"

"Across doorways," said Sirali. "Don't know what kinds or how often."

"You're sure they're always across doorways? You've never seen one laid across a hallway?"

"Right, and I've not. Might make it hard for slaves to get around if they had wards over hallways."

"Sirali, I've a task for you. Do you still hear things, in the kitchens and such?"

"Sometimes."

"I'd like you to continue to report on what you hear, once per week, but to me instead of to Ral-Vaddis."

"Right, and I'll do that," she said. "Whatever stops the jack-scalders from taking Mosar."

Rhianne hurried to the Imperial Garden, anxious to get to the appointed meeting spot. She wasn't late—in fact, she was early. But she wouldn't risk missing even a moment of her time with Janto. She was beginning to strategize about what she might do after the wedding and the move to Mosar. Could she not convince her uncle to let her bring Janto along? Janto *was* Mosari, after all, and he *was* teaching her the language. He could continue in that role, and act as her cultural adviser or something. Janto wouldn't mind, would he? Mosar was his home. And this was all perfectly innocent.

All right, in her mind and fantasy life, none of this was innocent. But in the real world, with Tamienne keeping a watchful eye over the two of them, they hadn't so much as touched fingers.

Janto was waiting for her beneath the Poinciana tree. He was early too.

"Cona oleska, na-kali," she called to him.

Janto's face broke into his beautiful grin.

Rhianne sighed. "Please tell me I didn't wish you a good mountain again."

"No. You said, 'Good morning, my alligator.'"

"Three gods. I thought I had it right this time!"

"When you add the *na-* modifier, it changes the vowel sound in *kali*. It's confusing, I know. Say it like this. *Na-kow-li.*"

She repeated the altered pronunciation until she got it right. Then she glanced at him shyly. "It's not as if you *look* like an alligator."

"Perhaps if I were toothier." He gestured to the bench.

She sat, clutching the book of Mosari mythological tales she'd brought. It would be harder going than the fairy tales, but she was ready for a challenge. In more ways than one. Gods above, she wanted to touch this man. She eyed the necklace of glass beads he wore around his neck. That seemed a reasonable excuse. "Where did you get this? Can I see?" She reached for it.

He drew away, placing a protective hand over the necklace. "Mosar."

She withdrew her hand. Rebuffed again. "Why wasn't it taken from you when you were enslaved?"

"Because it's worthless."

"Yet you care about it."

"If you had but a handful of possessions," said Janto, "you would care about them too."

"Fair enough." If only she could figure him out. She was almost certain he liked her, but he wouldn't touch her. Maybe it was just Tamienne. "Look, I won't be here for the next few days."

"Oh?"

"Augustan Ceres is coming. . . ."

Janto's jaw dropped.

Rhianne blinked and considered how that must sound to him. "It has nothing to do with the war," she amended. "That's still ongoing. But Augustan has been recalled for a few days. For his betrothal."

Janto's eyes narrowed. "To whom?"

"Me," Rhianne said in a small voice.

Janto was silent for several seconds. "Did you have any choice about this?"

"Of course not. Do you think a Kjallan imperial princess gets to choose her marriage partner?" It was the one enormous downside of being what she was. That she would have to marry one man for political reasons while secretly craving another, wholly unsuitable man.

"She might, perhaps, choose among several eligible suitors."

"Well, that is not what happened," said Rhianne. "And as for his being a *monster*, I would like to point out that you are Mosari and have an extraordinarily biased opinion."

"You are quite correct," said Janto.

Rhianne eyed him. His response was proper and polite, yet it chafed. For the past few days, he had not hesitated to push back when he'd disagreed with her, and she'd rather enjoyed arguing with him. He reminded her of Lucien, the sort of man she could enjoy an easy back-and-forth with and not worry that, like Florian, he was going to lose his temper, or, like so many of the lower-ranking men around the palace, he would be intimidated by her rank and refuse to challenge her. But now he was simply agreeing with her even when she knew perfectly well he didn't, and she feared it was because he felt sorry for her.

She felt sick to her stomach. "So I won't be here tomorrow or the day after. We can meet again in three days."

Janto nodded, and they began their language work.

They weren't far into it before Rhianne began to regret her choice of book. The first mythological tale was an adventure story in which the three gods, portrayed as brothers, overcame a series of trials by relying on their separate strengths. First, the Soldier defeated a giant serpent by stabbing it with his pike. Then the Sage negotiated with an evil rhinoceros and helped it by solving a problem with a polluted water supply; afterward, it allowed them to pass. The Vagabond got them past a troll by challenging it to a boasting game. The story was clever, but . . . "This is offensive," she told Janto.

"Offensive?" said Janto. "How?"

"It portrays the gods as equals," said Rhianne. "The Sage, in this story, is just as effective as the Soldier, and so is the Vagabond, while in reality—"

"That's the whole point," said Janto. "The story demonstrates that peaceful negotiation or trickery can accomplish as much as brute strength."

"Yes, yes, well done, but in so doing it portrays the

Sage and Vagabond as the equals of the Soldier, when in fact the Soldier is the primary god and the Sage and Vagabond are his subordinates—"

"Only Kjallans believe that," said Janto. "Surely you know that belief is not universal. It's not shared by Riorcans or Sardossians or Inyans, and it's certainly not shared by my own people. We consider the gods to be equals. Brothers, in fact."

She wrinkled her nose. "That's sacrilegious."

"To us, it's offensive for you to elevate the Soldier above the other two gods."

"Well." She glanced at him. "Perhaps your country—and Riorca—are losing to our forces because your sacrilege offends the gods."

Janto went very still, and a flush of anger crept up his cheek. "We are losing, and Riorca has already lost, because your forces outnumber ours ten to one."

Rhianne bit her lip. It pained her to torment him, but he sat there pitying her, as if he were *superior*. How could he be so calm, so proud, so secure in himself, when he was a slave and his country was about to be conquered? Shouldn't she be the one pitying him and explaining to him the error of his ways? "Kjall was not always a large country, you know. Long ago, my ancestors occupied only the southwestern corner of the continent—*this* corner, where Riat sits now. We conquered our neighbors. We grew and became prosperous because the gods willed that we should. I forgive you for your anger, because you've been taken from your homeland, and I can only imagine how painful that must be. But like it or not, the Soldier demands that strong nations should rule weak ones, as the Soldier himself rules over the Sage and the Vagabond."

"And your emperor," said Janto. "Did he attack Mosar because the Soldier told him to or because he coveted our sugar crop?"

"It's not my place to question the emperor."

"I wonder, do you support this philosophy yourself? Larger nations should rule smaller ones?"

"I said stronger nations should rule, not larger nations."

"But it is Kjall's size that gives it the advantage over Mosar."

Rhianne shook her head. "Not only size. Our military tactics and training are superior."

"How can you know, when you know so little of Mosar?"

She gave him a sour look.

"You are a woman," continued Janto. "Do you believe women should be ruled by men because men are physically larger?"

"That's . . . not the same thing."

"I fail to see the difference. I think the Soldier as envisioned by your people is something of a bully."

"Stop it!" He hadn't even raised his voice, yet his words were like knives. Her family had ruled Kjall for generations. He was wrong. Biased. Of course he was; he was Mosari. "You're twisting my words around! At least on Kjall we don't engage in unnatural practices like casting our souls into animals."

"I assure you, on Mosar we find it equally strange that you cast your souls into inanimate objects."

"Gemstones," corrected Rhianne.

"Last I heard, gemstones were inanimate objects," said Janto. "Our scholars have researched the origins of magic, and we have reason to believe that the first mages used animal familiars, that the type of magic we practice on Mosar is the oldest and most time-honored and is what the gods intended us mortals to use. Your riftstones are, we believe, an aberration—a means of gaining the magic through an unintended and inappropriate pathway, and one that lacks some of the benefits of soulcasting. After all, you can have no telepathic bond with a gemstone."

"Telepathic bond?"

"Do you not know?" said Janto. "A Mosari mage shares a telepathic bond with his animal familiar and can speak to him through the bond."

She blinked. "But what would you have to say to an animal?"

"After soulcasting, it's not an ordinary animal. It carries part of one's soul, and it's sentient. It will be one's companion for the rest of one's life. How can a lifeless riftstone compare to that?"

Rhianne looked at him sharply. He spoke with such conviction that she could swear he had once been a mage himself. "You know an awful lot about it for a palace scribe."

"The Mosari palace is full of mages," said Janto. "Just like the Imperial Palace."

Rhianne reached for the gold chain that hung around her neck and withdrew, from beneath her syrtos, a glowing purple amethyst. "Our riftstones aren't exactly lifeless."

Janto stared. "Is that your riftstone? What sort of mage are you?"

"A mind mage," she said.

"Confusion and forgetting spells? That sort of thing?"

"Also truth spells and suggestions. It's boring, I admit,"

said Rhianne. "All the women in my line are mind mages, and all the men are war mages. You'd think we might be more creative. But it's tradition. And mind magic is protective. It allows me a little more freedom than I would otherwise have." She slipped the amethyst back beneath her clothes. "Janto, what you said before about the Soldier. That's not what we believe. The war is not about one nation *bullying* another. The Soldier desires to bring order to the Five Nations, bring them under one banner, put an end to war and strife. For now, there may be some pain, some suffering, but in the long run it's for the good of all. It is the Soldier's will, as inevitable and unstoppable as his long march through the skies."

"Imperial Highness," said Janto, "do you know what your Kjallan army does when it captures a Mosari village?"

"No." Her heart sank. She knew it couldn't be good. Why did he have to tell her these things when she liked him so much, *wanted* to like him, and he obviously hated her people? He probably hated her too. No wonder he wouldn't touch her.

"They kill the children."

Her eyes met his.

"For the slave ships, your people want young, able-bodied men and women," said Janto. "The old and the very young they have no use for. They line them up on the beach and slaughter them."

She looked down at her book. This was how he saw her, as the offspring of mass murderers.

"Is this how your people put an end to war and strife? By slaughtering children? Princess, this is a horrific corruption of the Soldier's purpose. The Soldier stands for courage and strength, not brutality and aggression."

6

Rhianne sighed as her attendants fussed over her, making every fold of her gown lie flat and even and every curl in her hair fall in just the right place. It was ridiculous. She was going riding, so in no time at all it would be a mess.

Augustan's ship had arrived during the night. He'd been escorted up to the palace and ensconced in a stateroom, so she had been told. She was due at the audience chamber, midday, for their formal introduction.

The gown was one of her favorites, green and ivory with gold accents, attractive but reasonably practical; she could wear it in the sidesaddle. Florian had tried to convince her to wear the imperial orange, but with her coloring she simply could not wear orange and come off looking like anything but a butternut squash.

A knock came at the door.

"Tami?" called Rhianne.

The door cracked open. "It's time."

Rhianne hopped off her chair and headed for the door, trailed by her entourage, eager to get this frightening business over with. She straightened her shoulders as she walked down the hallway. Perhaps if she could muster the outward appearance of confidence, it would stop her hands from trembling.

When she entered the audience chamber, her eyes went everywhere, searching for the man who must be Augustan, but there was no one in the room she did not already know. Florian stood on a raised platform. The marble throne—one of several he used, in multiple chambers—loomed just behind him, but he was not sitting in it today. The jewel-encrusted loros glittered on his chest. Lucien, immediately to his right, stood balanced on his wooden leg, hands tightly interlaced behind his back as if he wished he could sit on them. The other people in the room were Florian's usual set of advisers and Legaciatti.

"You look spectacular, my dear," said Florian, gesturing to the empty spot on his left.

Rhianne took her place beside her uncle, straightened her gown, and waited.

"Bring him in," called Florian.

A door opened at the far end of the room and three men appeared, one in front and two just behind him—Augustan and his entourage, Rhianne guessed. All were in military dress. If the man in front was Augustan, he was handsome, at least. The three walked smartly up to Florian and knelt before him, bowing as one.

"Rise," said Florian. The men obeyed. "Augustan Ceres." Florian stepped forward and clasped wrists with the foremost man.

"Your Imperial Majesty," answered Augustan.

As they completed their formal greeting and Augustan introduced his two underlings, Rhianne scrutinized him. She couldn't fault him in the looks department. He was typical Kjallan in many respects: big and muscular, dark in coloration, though his hair was closer to brown than black. He had a pleasing face, although its lines suggested he didn't smile much, and a scar cut a small jagged line across his chin. She supposed one could hardly wage war as long as Augustan had without collecting an occasional such memento of battle.

"I would like to introduce you," Florian was saying, "to my niece and adopted daughter, Rhianne Florian Nigellus, Imperial Princess of Kjall."

"Legatus," said Rhianne, stepping forward and clasping his wrist.

His face broke into what looked like an unaccustomed smile.

She sat through the usual litany of platitudes and welcome speeches from her uncle, which seemed to bore Augustan as much as they bored her, and finally the two of them were dismissed to the stables for their planned ride, escorted by a dozen servants and Legaciatti. The horses were waiting for them, tacked and ready to go, although Rhianne's mare, Dice, was wearing the hunt saddle instead of the requested sidesaddle. The groom, when he spotted Rhianne's gown and realized his mistake, went as white as the mare and led the animal back inside for a tack change.

Augustan swung up on Flash, the dapple gray gelding with a curious tail that was ivory on one side of his body and black on the other. Dice came back wearing the sidesaddle, and the apologetic groom boosted her up and handed her the riding crop. Rhianne hooked her right leg over the saddle horn and smoothed her gown. She preferred riding astride, but Florian had insisted on a formal gown, and he was the emperor, so that was that. The irony was that riding sidesaddle was more precarious and thus more dangerous than riding astride, so, far from being chivalrous, asking a woman to ride sidesaddle demanded more skill from her and asked her to take greater risks than a man. But Rhianne had long given up trying to make sense of it.

She was at no great risk riding Dice. The mare was gentle, with smooth gaits, and her name came from her coloration, not from any tendency toward risky behavior. Dice's natural color was what horsemen called flea-bitten gray—white flecked with black spots—but the stable staff bleached out the spots, having decided pure white was a color more appropriate for the mount of a princess.

Augustan steered Flash alongside her. "You ought to have that groom whipped."

"Because of the saddle?" She shook her head. "It was a natural mistake. I usually ride this mare with the hunt saddle."

"Don't permit your staff to be lax and lazy around you. It speaks to a lack of discipline. You are a princess, and they should fear to displease you."

Rhianne stiffened her shoulders. She liked Dice's groom, who had a close personal connection with the mare and spent hours every day grooming and massaging and exercising the animal, keeping her happy and in top condition. She would not jeopardize that over a tack error. Was Augustan always so rigid and punitive? So far he was fitting bullet-to-bore with his reputation as a stern disciplinarian.

They set off, trotting and cantering down well-worn bridle paths, trailed not so discreetly by their entourage, now also mounted. Rhianne led the way since she knew the lay of the land. South of the Imperial Palace was the city of Riat, but on the other three sides were lands belonging to the imperial family, pastures and plains dotted with lakes, and forests of all types, most of them cultivated, but there were two ancient, old-growth forests that the continent's many wars had miraculously left untouched. Rhianne led her fiancé-to-be on a tour through some of the finest of these lands, and when the horses began to tire, she and Augustan dismounted at the side of a lake and picnicked, their entourage setting out blankets and food.

"You are not quite what I expected," said Augustan, biting into a pigeon tart.

"Oh?" Rhianne looked at him sidelong. "And what did you expect?"

"A more delicate, retiring sort of woman. Don't get me wrong. I'm quite pleased with you."

Rhianne wasn't sure how to answer this. She was glad he didn't dislike her. On the other hand, he was *pleased* with her? He spoke like a parent praising a child.

"Are you pleased with me?" asked Augustan.

"Legatus, we've barely met."

"That's fair," said Augustan. "It was good of the emperor to bring me here so we could get to know each other a little before the marriage."

Rhianne nodded. "How is the war going?"

"Very well," said Augustan. "We've nearly wiped out the last pockets of resistance. I expect we'll have it wrapped up soon."

It was good news, but Rhianne couldn't help but feel a pang for poor Janto. His country was about to fall, and once it did, his people would be enslaved forever. She touched her chin. "How did you get this?"

Augustan mirrored the gesture. "Musket fire. That was years ago."

"You were shot?"

"Grazed." He smiled crookedly. "Bullet left its mark, though."

"You have been many years at war," said Rhianne.

"Indeed. This governorship of Mosar will be a new adventure for me, commanding people in peacetime. Although leadership is nothing new. I consider your uncle a great example."

"Do you?" Rhianne raised an eyebrow.

"Absolutely. He's decisive; he's bold. And he can be charitable too, as you must know."

Florian did have his positive traits, but Rhianne could not, for the life of her, think of a time he had been charitable. "What do you mean?"

"Well, for example, when he adopted you and shielded you from the shame of your birth."

Rhianne stared, shock rippling through her body as if he'd slapped her in the face. Surely he could not have actually said that. "The *shame* of my *birth*?"

"Don't be coy," said Augustan. "You know what I mean."

Her cheeks prickled with warmth. "Legatus, my parents were *married*. I am a legitimate child."

"Yes, but they eloped, did they not? Emperor Nigellus did not approve the match."

"He didn't approve, but according to Kjallan marriage law, he didn't have to. The contract was legal."

"Still," said Augustan, "when Florian adopted you, he gave you his name so that you carried the imperial name, not your father's."

"He did," said Rhianne. "But on the other hand, it was a bit of an insult to my real father, who didn't give me up by choice. I wonder sometimes what my life would have been like if I'd been raised by my parents instead of by Florian."

"Well, I always considered the adoption a grand gesture on Florian's part." Augustan wrinkled his brow, as if he found her a puzzle. "You know I would never hold it against you, your father's low birth. You may not appreciate it, but your uncle was right to get you out of that situation. Just because the parents have done wrong doesn't mean the child will."

"Of course. I never imagined you would hold it against me," said Rhianne, still stunned. Did he think her damaged goods? If so, why did he want to marry her? For her name, of course—Florian's name—and the governorship of Mosar. Unless she was much mistaken, he had no respect for her as a person. "The horses are looking refreshed. Perhaps we should head back to the palace."

"If Her Imperial Highness wishes it," said Augustan, rising to his feet in one fluid motion. "I have some betrothal gifts for you—one-of-a-kind items from Mosar I think you'll find very special."

"I can't wait," said Rhianne dully. She didn't mind being challenged by a man. Janto challenged her. Lucien challenged her. Somehow when those two forced her to question her assumptions, she felt herself growing and stretching, becoming wiser and more knowledgeable. Janto disagreed with her often, even grew angry at times, but on some fundamental level he believed in her. Augustan's criticism—and for that matter, even his praise!—made Rhianne feel small. No betrothal gift, no matter how one-of-a-kind or special, was going to make up for that.

7

With Augustan and his entourage in residence, and a betrothal ceremony in the works, the palace was stirred up in the manner of a trodden-on anthill. Janto would not waste this opportunity. With the staff preoccupied, it was time to invade the palace and brave the magical wards that were the bane of a spy's existence. Sirali had said that the Kjallans didn't place them in the hallways, only across doorways and probably only in sensitive areas. He prayed she was right.

Just inside the slave entrance was an enormous, bustling hall. Janto twisted sideways to avoid a wheeled cart piled high with laundry, then dodged a pair of burly slaves carrying sacks of flour, his shoes slipping on the polished floor. Though this was only the service wing of the palace, it was striking in its beauty. Vaulted ceilings rose to lofty heights. From them, semicircular light glows hung in alternating colors of orange, blue, and white. Each glow was as large as a man. Silk hangings, bright with color, cascaded down the marble walls.

Fine place, he commented to Sashi, who clung to his shoulder.

Ugly, said the ferret.

I know you've no appreciation for stone, but do you not at least like the artwork?

Sashi studied one of the hangings as they walked by, a depiction of the mighty Soldier with his pike. *It resembles a man, but he is flat and unmoving. He smells of dust and lye.*

Janto smiled to himself. *Never mind.*

He passed from the first hallway into a larger one flanked by black marble columns. The bas-relief ceiling depicted scenes from Kjallan mythology. He began to sweat beneath the woolen overcloak he'd pilfered from a supply shed. The hallway was warm, but he had yet to see a heat-glow. Where were the Kjallans hiding them?

He counted six hallways on his left, following the mental map Sirali had roughed out for him, and turned into the seventh. Here, alcoves set into the walls displayed artwork: paintings of warships and landscapes and battle scenes. War leaders sculpted in marble or bronze sat proudly atop their prancing steeds with swords upraised. Janto paused before the first nonmilitaristic sculpture he came to, that of a woman holding an infant.

In the alcove next to it, a stone statue of a mythical sea dragon sat on an obsidian table. The lines and style of the work were familiar, and he could swear he recognized the artist: a Mosari woman named Fioni. How had her work turned up here? Was it stolen? There was virtually no trade between Kjall and Mosar.

The gallery wasn't as crowded as the service wing. Most of the people he maneuvered around weren't slaves or servants, but Kjallans in syrtoses or military uniforms. He located the final hallway, which was narrow and devoid of decoration. At the end of it, a stairway descended a few steps toward a heavy iron door guarded by two Legaciatti. There would be no going through that without someone opening it for him.

Janto settled invisibly on the stairs. *Looks like we wait.*

We do a lot of that, said Sashi, untroubled.

The door to the prison might be warded, but he doubted it, since prisoners had to come in and out through that door. There were two types of wards he had to concern himself with: enemy wards and invisibility wards. Enemy wards were the most commonly used, because once placed, they lasted several days. They had to be attuned to a particular person, however, and that person had to be physically present when the ward was laid.

Invisibility wards were used sparingly if at all because shroud mages like Janto were rare and invisibility wards barely lasted an hour before having to be laid again. Such wards kept Warders so busy that they were typically only placed if there was reason to suspect a shroud mage was in operation, and then only in the immediate areas where the shroud mage was expected to be.

For the next hour, Janto amused himself daydreaming about Rhianne. What if their countries had never gone to war and they'd met in a routine diplomatic visit? Not that Mosar and Kjall had engaged in much diplomacy before the war. But if they had, he might have met her at a state dinner. Danced with her, maybe. What would they have thought of each other if they'd met in such a way?

A knocking noise roused him. One of the guards opened a tiny window in the door, looked through it, and nodded. The other unbarred the door. Janto was on his feet, and the moment they had it open to let the other man come out—another guard, as it happened—he slipped inside, turning sideways to avoid him.

As the door slammed shut behind him and the bar crashed home, he felt a jolt of reflexive terror—would he ever get back out? But of course he would. That door had to open several times a day, if for no other reason than to bring in food and water and swap out the guards.

The lighting was dim inside the prison, just some faint light-glows mounted sparingly, but he could see well enough. To his relief, the cell doors, though solid iron at the bottom, were barred at the top, allowing him to see in. To his left was a sort of guard room with cots and tables, where two guards sat, chatting quietly. To his right was the first cell, which was empty. He walked on.

The next cell housed a yellow-haired Riorcan. Beyond it, the prison hallway took a sharp turn to the left.

Janto soon discovered that the prison was a square that looped back on itself, with the prison cells on the outside of the square. On the inside were interrogation rooms. The complex was smaller than he'd expected and sparsely occupied. There were only four prisoners in residence, and none of them were Mosari. His trip had been a waste of time.

Ral-Vaddis was not here.

Rhianne shielded her eyes from the lights. They made the pain stab like the Soldier's own pike inside her head.

". . . Wouldn't you say so?" said Marcella beside her.

"What?" Rhianne tried to recall the beginning of Marcella's question. Thank the gods this was the last social event of the day. She'd had all she could stand of constricting gowns, small talk, insincere smiles, and Augustan Ceres.

"Wouldn't you say the pyrotechnics outdid themselves tonight?" repeated Marcella.

"Oh yes. Absolutely." A hideous display. With their magical light show, set to music from the imperial orchestra, they'd reenacted Augustan's capture of some Mosari stronghold right there in the ballroom. How strange to see brutality and bloodshed in the midst of silk hangings, polished floors, and chandeliers. The scene was ugly enough in its own right, but worse was looking around at the delighted faces of her fellows. Could they really see slaughter and destruction as something to be proud of? She could not help thinking of how the spectacle would make Janto feel, and she was ashamed.

Marcella's smile dimmed. "Are you all right?"

"I'm feeling wretched," said Rhianne, braving the bright lights to meet Marcella's eyes. Cerinthus, Marcella's husband, sat beside her, but he rarely said a word in Rhianne's presence; he seemed intimidated by her rank. "It's been too long a day for me."

"Ought you not to go up to your rooms and rest? Surely your uncle will understand."

"He told me I was attending or else." Rhianne smiled grimly and sipped the wine, her fourth glass. At dinner, closely watched by her uncle, she'd abstained, but now Florian was making a tour of the ballroom, introducing her fiancé-to-be to her second and third cousins and the visiting officers from the northern front. Rhianne was making up for lost time.

"Won't the wine make your headache worse?" asked Marcella.

"No," said Rhianne, blinking in irritation at the lights. "It won't make it better either, but it'll make me not mind so much having one."

"In that case . . ." With a wink, Marcella poured the contents of her own glass into Rhianne's.

Rhianne grinned. "I knew there was a reason we were friends."

She turned to see how far Florian had progressed in his tour and how much time she had left before she'd have to perform the odious chore of dancing with Augustan. There was Florian—seated and engaged in a heated argument with a first-rank tribune. She smiled wryly; her uncle did so love a good verbal sparring. Not that he played fair. Winning an argument with the emperor could prove fatal to one's career, so his opponents always made sure they lost.

Nearby, Augustan yelled at someone, a Riorcan slave woman who fled from him, cradling a tray of wineglasses. The scene gave Rhianne pause. She couldn't tell what had caused the incident. Augustan turned, caught her eye, and smiled. She could not bring herself to smile back at him. Instead, she looked away and hoped it would discourage him from approaching.

No such luck. He showed up at her table minutes later with a steaming tea mug in his hand. "Rhianne. You look stunning as always."

Marcella and Cerinthus rose from their seats, as did Rhianne, wincing at the pain in her head. "Legatus Ceres," she said formally. "These are my friends Tribune Cerinthus Antius and his wife, Marcella."

Augustan took in the insignia on Cerinthus's uniform that marked him as third rank and gave him a dismissive nod.

As they sat, he turned to Rhianne and pushed the mug toward her. "I brought you a drink. Spicebush tea. It's fine stuff—we brought it back from Mosar."

Rhianne indicated her wineglass. "Thank you, but I already have a drink."

He smiled indulgently. "My dear, it is your fourth glass. I know you do not wish to appear unseemly."

She stared at him, incredulous. Had he been watching her this entire time, keeping track of how much wine she drank? "Thank you, but I don't care for tea."

"Try it. Perhaps you will develop a taste for it." He pushed the mug closer to her and edged her wineglass away.

Rhianne considered how much trouble she would be in with Florian if she threw a mug of spicebush tea into Augustan's face.

"Well, if you are not thirsty," said Augustan, a line of irritation appearing in his brow, "I believe the crowd is eager for us to begin the dancing. Shall we?"

"With respect, Legatus, I'm not feeling well enough this evening to dance."

He stiffened with affront. "Indeed? I beg your pardon. I thought you the very picture of health." He got up from the table and walked away.

Rhianne slumped in her seat, infuriated, yet relieved he was gone. Who was he to tell her what to drink and act like she was faking when she said she wasn't feeling well? She shoved the tea away and gulped her wine. Marcella's hand fell upon hers in sympathy. Cerinthus stared at her in horror.

Moments later, Emperor Florian slid into the seat next to Rhianne. "Leave us," he barked to Marcella and Cerinthus, who scrambled to their feet and departed. "Rhianne, you are being unacceptably uncooperative."

"I'm not feeling well."

He glared at her.

"He's rude, Uncle. He tried to force me to drink tea because he thought I'd had too much wine—"

"You *have* had too much," said Florian. "I see the flush in your cheeks."

"And now he wants me to dance, when I have a headache that would send the Soldier himself packing off to bed."

"Don't be ridiculous. Do you think when Augustan is feeling poorly, he cancels the war for the day?"

Rhianne raised her eyebrows. "What a strange argument you make, Uncle. Do you imply that waging war and dancing are equally important?"

"Augustan will only be here for a couple of days, and the empire needs this match."

"He's not going to walk away because I refused his disgusting tea or didn't feel like dancing one evening. I'm your niece. He'd marry me if I had two heads and tentacles."

"It's not heads or tentacles I'm concerned about, but your tongue, which is excessively sharp."

"Augustan, by the way, hasn't expressed the slightest bit of concern for my condition."

"Neither have I."

"From you I have given up expecting it."

"No more excuses," said Florian. "Go and dance with him, or your head won't be the only part of your body that hurts."

"I'm going." With a sigh, she stood. The throbbing in her head accelerated to match her pulse. Draining the dregs of her wineglass, she searched the room for Augustan. There he was, speaking to Taia Livia and two young women Rhianne did not know. All three women were simpering in his presence. *Great,* she thought, shooting a look of exasperation at Florian. *Now Augustan will think I changed my mind out of jealousy.*

The conversation ceased at her approach. Taia and the two younger ladies dipped into curtsies, murmuring, "Your Imperial Highness."

"Taia," she answered. Best to get the moment of humiliation over with as quickly as possible. She turned to Augustan. "Legatus, would you do me the honor of dancing with me?"

A corner of his mouth quirked. "Feeling better, are you?" He offered her his hand.

"No. But I'll dance anyway." Deep in her gut, she knew that handing him even this small victory was a mistake. It would only encourage him. But what choice did she have? She had another day of this to endure, and when the war in Mosar was over, a lifetime. Gritting her teeth, she slipped her hand into his.

8

Rhianne cradled the cat in her arms as she walked, trying to make it comfortable, but it squirmed, and one of its needlelike claws poked through her syrtos. She winced and removed it.

"Your Imperial Highness," said Tamienne from behind her. "Perhaps we should leave the animal in your rooms?"

"No, I want Janto to see it." She couldn't wait to see him again. She'd survived two horrid days of Augustan, including the world's most tedious betrothal ceremony, which had lasted a mind-numbing three hours. She'd finally seen him back to his ship, waving prettily as he set sail and praying that the war lasted another fifty years. If he lost the war entirely, might the marriage be called off? Gods, she was thinking the most horrid thoughts lately. Janto and Morgan and Lucien, with their treasonous ideas, must be wearing off on her.

She sat on her usual bench beneath the Poinciana.

Janto arrived soon after and spotted the cat in her arms. His eyes went wide.

"Please tell me you're not afraid of cats." Rhianne patted the space next to her.

"House cats, no," said Janto. "But, three gods, that is a brindlecat."

She laughed. "How can it be a brindlecat? They're ten times this size. And do you see any brindling?" She held up the cat to display its plain brown coloration. It had no stripes at all.

Janto sat beside her. "Brindlecats are born without stripes, and what you have is a kitten. Watch the ears over the next few days—that's where they'll appear first. Do you see the claws?" He picked up one of the cat's paws. "They don't retract. This is not a house cat. Where did you get this animal?"

"Augustan gave it to me." She studied the cat— kitten—with chagrin. Maybe it really was a brindlecat. Augustan had said it came from Mosar, and brindlecats were native to that island. He'd probably had no idea what it really was.

Janto recoiled. "Is he trying to kill you?"

"Well, honestly, it doesn't look dangerous. Can you tell if it's a boy or a girl?"

Janto inspected the cat. "It's a girl. Princess, you have to cage this animal. She may not be dangerous now, but if you feed her properly—and it would be cruel not to— she's going to grow quickly. Within a month, she will be deadly."

"I can't imagine." However, Rhianne could see a little of what he was talking about. The kitten's claws and teeth were larger than she'd seen before, and the animal wasn't exactly sweet-natured. "Don't you think I could make a friend out of her? If I handle her every day?"

Janto looked horrified. "Absolutely not. Brindlecats are wild animals. If you're the one who feeds her, she'll probably refrain from clawing you to pieces. But she'll make a mess of your floors, she'll shred your furniture, and she'll play so rough she leaves gashes in your arms. This is not a pet."

"Three gods," said Rhianne. "I don't think Augustan had any idea."

"I should hope he didn't."

Rhianne stroked her brindlecat kitten. Janto was probably right that the animal would grow dangerous quickly, but she would enjoy her while she could.

"Didn't you bring a book today?" asked Janto.

"No," said Rhianne. "I thought we could just talk. I want to learn more about Mosar—your customs, your way of life. Is it true your people live in caves?"

Janto's eyes narrowed. Perhaps he thought she was insulting him. "It depends what you mean by caves. In the Mosari language, we have two words meaning *cave*. The first is *lerot*, a beast cave, naturally occurring, usually rough and inhospitable. The second is *usont*, a man-made cave carved into the mountain by one of our stone-shapers. We live in *usonts*."

"And what's an *usont* like?"

"Like any indoor space, except carved of stone. Our stoneshapers' magic can make the walls, ceilings, and floors flat and the corners right-angled, like your Kjallan houses built of wood. But stoneshapers can also make graceful curves, undulations, strange textures, rooms that are perfectly round. Parts of the Mosari palace would astonish you."

"It sounds interesting. But why do you live in caves rather than houses?"

"Because of the storm season. During the late summer and fall, Mosar is battered by storms so severe that they would rip apart the sorts of houses you build here on Kjall. During the storm season, we send our ships to safer waters and retreat into our *usonts* for safety. The rest of the year is our growing and building season, and we erect some temporary structures then. But there's not much wood on Mosar. What we have, we wouldn't waste on houses. We use it for ships."

"Does it not drive you crazy, sitting in a cave all through the storm season?"

Janto raised his eyebrows. "Does it not drive *you* crazy, sitting in the Imperial Palace all year long?"

Rhianne bit her lip. She sneaked out on a regular basis. But he didn't know that.

"In answer to your question," said Janto, "no. Our *usonts* make up entire cities. There is much work to be done indoors, whether it's more building, or artwork, or scholarship, or magical training."

"Tell me something else," said Rhianne. "What's something Mosari people do when it's not the storm season? Something fun."

Janto shrugged. "Lots of things. We hunt lorim eggs."

"What's a lorim?"

"A seabird. They nest by the millions along our cliffs in spring and early summer, just before the storm season. You can hardly hear for their squalling, and when they fly, their wings darken the sky. Mosari youngsters—boys and young men, mostly, but some of the girls get in on the fun—like to climb up the cliff face and harvest the eggs. We've a law that you must leave two eggs in each nest, so by late season, the easy eggs have been harvested, and you've got to climb way up to find an eligible nest."

"You've done this personally?"

"Oh yes," said Janto. "You're a coward if you don't.

The cliff claims a few lives each year, but it wouldn't be exciting if it weren't a bit dangerous. It's not easy clinging to the rocks with your fingertips while the birds' wings beat in your face."

Their conversation was interrupted by the arrival of Rhianne's lunch, a crystal tray piled with cold venison, soft cheese, biscuits, oranges, and sliced apples.

"You want some of this?" she asked.

"I wouldn't say no to it."

She set the tray down between them, and they shared.

"Have you ever been to Sardos?" asked Rhianne.

"No."

"Their language is a lot easier than yours. The pronouns aren't so ridiculous."

Janto's eyebrows rose. "You speak Sardossian?"

"Yes. *Bellam khi oberym.*" *Good morning, my alligator.*

He laughed and answered, "*Qua oberym, bellam khi iquay.*" *I understand, my alligator. Good afternoon to you.*

"How many languages do you know?"

"Five."

Her jaw fell. "*Five?*"

"Mosari, Kjallan, Inyan, Sardossian, and Riorcan. Except my Riorcan is awful. Maybe we should say four and a half."

"And you're a palace scribe? Seems to me your talent is wasted."

"Languages are more of a personal interest for me, but I've done translation work and foreign correspondence."

Translation work and foreign correspondence? She didn't doubt he'd done plenty of that, but as a palace scribe? That seemed less and less likely. She'd been suspecting for a while, and now she was convinced: this man was Mosari nobility.

Lucien was at his Caturanga board when Rhianne found him, playing a game with some minor official she knew vaguely by sight but not by name. Lucien gave her a cursory glance. "Give us a few minutes. The game's almost over."

She nodded and retreated to a couch to thumb through his books.

Behind her, she heard the sounds of the game finishing and the two men discussing it, their voices raised in passion—it appeared Lucien had won. Then the official left, and Lucien limped over on his crutch and wooden leg. "No one around here can give me a challenge anymore. You should play more."

"Caturanga?" Rhianne rolled her eyes. "That's a man's game. I couldn't be less interested."

"Nonsense," said Lucien. "There's a woman tearing up the tournament circuit in eastern Kjall as we speak. What are you here for? Is it time for the tetrals?"

"Not yet. I came to ask you about something else."

"Make it quick. I've got a meeting in half an hour."

"I sort of got in an argument with someone about the war in Mosar, and I think I came off looking like a fool."

"With Augustan?" Lucien shook his head. "He's the commander of the invasion. If you argue with him about that war, you *are* a fool."

Rhianne considered correcting him, but she decided against it. Lucien might not approve of her discussing the war with a Mosari slave. "I realized I don't know that much about Mosar. Or even much about Kjall, politically and economically. I think the histories I've read were . . . shall we say, self-serving. Florian doesn't involve me in meetings the way he does you, and—well, you know a great deal. You've got your own ideas. You're opposed to the war, for example."

"You don't want to hear *my* ideas. They're unpopular. *Treasonous.*"

"But they're right. Aren't they?"

He shrugged. "Yes."

"I want to hear them."

"All right, but it's on you." He pointed an accusing finger at her. "Don't complain to me if you repeat this stuff to Florian and he goes up like a pyrotechnics display. In fact, you'd better not repeat anything to him at all."

"Of course I won't," said Rhianne. "So why is the war in Mosar a bad idea?"

"Because we can't afford it."

"You've already lost me. We have an enormous army, and we're a wealthy nation."

"Right on the first count, wrong on the second," said Lucien. "We're a poor nation, and the size of our army is part of the reason for it. Our economy is based on plunder, tribute, and slave labor. We invade a neighboring nation, plunder their wealth, take slaves, and extract tribute from them henceforth. But the tribute payments don't grow—in fact, they diminish over the years because the captured provinces do not flourish under the harsh conditions we impose on them. We solve the problem of our dwindling treasury by invading someone else, but after we conquered Riorca, there wasn't anyone else left. We have the entire continent."

"So we invaded the island of Mosar," said Rhianne.

"Yes, and now you see how uncreative Florian's thinking is. Invading Mosar is a stopgap solution, and we've reached the point where our constant wars are making our problems worse, not better," said Lucien. "We have to face the real problem, which is that our empire is too far-flung and too backward—"

"Backward?"

"You've never been to Sardos or Inya. If you had, you'd know they're ahead of us. The Inyans can build bridges the likes of which we can only dream of, and the Sardossians—well, Sardos is a bit of a mess, but I assure you they don't leave so many of their natural resources unexploited."

"What do you mean we don't exploit our resources?"

"Just one example," said Lucien. "There are mines in Riorca, rich mines where we could be extracting iron and copper and gold, but they've been shut down for decades because of the unrest in that part of the country. If we could stabilize the north, calm the unrest—but no, Florian sends our troops overseas to conquer Mosar." He shook his head. "And speaking of Mosar, they're ahead of us too. They've got musket technology far superior to ours. Their weapons are breech loaded, not muzzle loaded."

"But if we take Mosar, it will be good for us. Won't it? We can copy their muskets."

"It won't be good for us," said Lucien. "In the short term, yes, there'll be plunder, and we can copy the musket design. But Riorca has been a nightmare to manage. We conquered it decades ago, and there are still pockets of rebellion. And they've got the Obsidian Circle assassinating our people. You think it will be any easier with Mosar? It will be worse. The farther away the conquered nation, the harder it is to manage from Riat. You'll be in the middle of that mess, you and Augustan. We would do better to pull out now, establish some favorable trade agreements with Mosar, and focus on stabilizing the north."

"This is a lot more complicated than I imagined." Would she and Augustan really be stuck in the middle of an unstable, violent mess when they tried to govern Mosar? She'd thought the worst of her problems would be a husband she didn't get along with. She hadn't considered that she might also be dodging assassins and rebels.

"I've barely scratched the surface." Lucien gave her a weak smile. "And I've got to go to my meeting. Would you like to come along? If you sit in on these meetings, you'll pick up a lot. And if you'll be trying to help govern a conquered Mosar, you'll need it."

"I suppose I should." Janto had coaxed her to look beyond the simplistic explanations she'd heard from her tutors, the ones that glorified Kjall and skirted around all the tough questions that had nagged at her even as a child. On a gut level, she'd always known those explanations did not make sense. She was ready to discover a more complex reality.

9

"He's not in the prison," said Janto.

He sat with Iolo and Sirali in a forest clearing beneath the meager light of the orange Soldier moon, pooling his information with theirs and finding it depressingly scanty.

"Maybe there's another prison," said Sirali.

"Could be," said Janto. "But he's not in the one beneath the palace."

"Right, and the war's going well from a Kjallan perspective," said Sirali. "Augustan's men were crowing about the progress they'd made."

Everyone was silent. That was not good news.

"I think Ral-Vaddis is dead," said Janto.

"You can't give up yet," said Iolo.

"We give our spies a poison pill. They're to use it if they're captured, so they don't give up their informants when they're tortured. I think he must have used it. Otherwise he'd have given up Sirali."

Sirali hugged her knees to her chest.

"And this mystery bit of information he said he had, what he thought might win the war," said Janto. "I can't imagine what that could have been. I don't think it exists."

"It *does* exist," said Iolo. "If Ral-Vaddis is dead, you have to find that intelligence."

"I *don't know how*," said Janto. "Ral-Vaddis was a trained spy. I'm a prince and a diplomat. I know many things, but not how to do what he did. I'm trying, but Ral-Vaddis did his best, and I think it got him killed."

"You have shroud magic, same as Ral-Vaddis had," pointed out Iolo. "In Mosar's hour of need, we all do our best, even if it isn't what we were trained to do."

Away in the woods, a woman screamed.

Janto turned in the direction of the sound. He called telepathically to Sashi, who came running and scrambled onto his shoulder. "What was that?"

"There's nothing you can do," said Iolo.

"Why?" said Janto. "What's going on?"

"It's Micah," said Sirali. "The slave overseer."

"What do you mean? Who's screaming?"

The woman's voice cried out in the Mosari language, "Stop! Let go!"

Janto leapt to his feet. That was one of his people being threatened. What harm could there be in at least seeing what was going on? Here was a situation where maybe he could do some good—not like this endless stream of failures in searching for Ral-Vaddis and phantoms of war intelligence that didn't exist, or if they did, that he would never find. "I'm going." He flung a shroud over himself and ran in the direction of the voice.

Ahead, a distant light shone through the trees. He followed it, panting from exertion. The trees ended abruptly at a clearing where he found a building identical to the men's slave house with warm, yellow light shining through the windows. In front of the building, two figures struggled. The larger figure was a man—Micah, the slave overseer?—and the smaller figure was a woman, trying to escape his grip. Any sapskull could see what was afoot.

Micah was a huge Mosari man, well-muscled and intimidating. Janto wished he could fight him invisibly, since he had no weapon and the man outweighed him. But that wasn't an option. He didn't intend murder, only intervention, and if Micah reported an invisible attacker to his Kjallan masters, invisibility wards would go up all around the vicinity.

Sashi, on his shoulder, bared wicked teeth. *He may be big, su-kali. But he will be slow.*

Let's hope so, su-kali.

Together we will kill him, said the ferret.

No killing, insisted Janto. *We will hurt him a little.*

He released his shroud, leaving Sashi invisible, and stepped into the moonlight. "Let her go."

"Vagabond's breath," Micah swore, gripping the woman's arm as she tried to pry his fingers off it. "Who are you?"

Janto didn't answer.

Micah peered at him. "You're not one of mine, are you? But you can't be anyone else's. Get out of here."

"Let her go," repeated Janto. He was committed, but he realized now how big a risk he was taking. This was the overseer, who knew all the slaves by sight.

Micah leered at him. "The only reason I can think of that you haven't left yet is that you want to watch."

The woman he held prisoner stomped on his foot, hard. Micah yowled. She twisted out of his grip and took off running into the woods.

"Horse fucker!" roared Micah. He flung himself at Janto and flung him to the ground.

In his youth, Janto had been trained in unarmed combat, against his adolescent will. He'd been uncoordinated, gawky, his younger brother pinning him two bouts out of three. Now, for the first time in his life, he was glad of that training, because despite what Sashi had believed, Micah was not slow.

Janto aimed a knee at Micah's groin. Micah shifted to block it, and Janto, taking advantage of his distraction, twisted out of his grip and punched him hard in the face. Then he felt a crushing pain as Micah's fist connected with his jaw.

Kill! came Sashi's battle cry, and through the telepathic link, Janto knew the ferret had sunk his teeth into Micah's leg.

Micah yelled and grabbed at the animal, and Janto scrambled into the darkness beneath a tree. Sashi must have withdrawn too, because Micah was on his feet, cursing and looking around. Janto circled into the moonlight and charged him from behind. He managed to bowl over Micah and get in several good blows before Micah's fist found him again, and pain exploded in the side of his head. He rolled into the shadows and called on his shroud. Hopefully he'd given the woman enough time to get away.

Sashi? he called.

The ferret scrambled up his shoulder from out of the darkness. *Good fight, but we should have killed him.*

While Micah lunged around, searching for him in the darkness, Janto hurried through the trees, back to Iolo and Sirali. When he spotted them, he extended his shroud to include them. "He does this regularly? Rapes the slave women?"

They stared at him, horrified, and he realized he presented a less-than-pretty picture: dirty and mussed, he probably had some blood on him and bruises forming.

"You attacked him," Iolo accused.

Sirali looked awed.

"Just long enough for her to get away," said Janto. "He's half again my size, and I don't carry a weapon."

"Did he *see* you?" said Iolo.

"It's better he should see me than not," said Janto. "If the Kjallans become aware there's a shroud mage in their midst, they'll start placing invisibility wards."

"You should not have done it, Your Highness," said Iolo. "I said before, I don't question your courage, but—"

"My judgment," said Janto. "I know."

"Right, and . . . of course it was the right thing," stammered Sirali. "Micah does this to lots of women."

Iolo turned on her. "But he's got to find Ral-Vaddis! He's got to find intelligence to help the war effort! He's made an enemy of Micah, he's aroused the man's suspicions, and he might get caught. We don't have any other shroud mages. Only him!"

"I came here to help my people in any way I could," said Janto. "That woman is one of my people."

"You have to put the most important things first," said Iolo. "It's awful what Micah does to those women, but if we lose you, and Mosar loses the war, how many more of them are going to be raped or killed by Kjallan soldiers?"

Sirali folded her arms. "I think if a prince would let his people get hurt right in front of him, he deserves to lose his kingdom."

"What about everyone else in that kingdom?" snarled Iolo. "What do they deserve?"

"Right, and if it were *men* being hurt instead of *women*—," began Sirali.

"Quiet, both of you," said Janto. "What's done is

done." He only hoped it didn't turn out as disastrously as Silverside. "Sirali, you say he does this frequently?"

She nodded. "He picks out a slave. Does what he likes with her."

Janto bit his lip. "What can we do to stop him from doing it?"

"Kill him," she said cheerfully.

Yes, kill. Sashi bared his teeth.

"Oh, no," said Iolo. "You couldn't possibly. There'd be an investigation."

"Iolo's right," said Janto. "But start thinking. I helped one woman tonight, but that won't help the one Micah chooses next time. Come up with an answer."

10

When Rhianne arrived at the bench under the Poinciana for her language lesson the next morning, Janto wasn't there. Annoyed, since it was beyond ridiculous for a slave not to show up for an appointment with an imperial princess, she sat down to wait for him. Ten minutes dragged by, and he did not come.

"Do you suppose he might be sick?" she asked her bodyguard.

"We could ask the head gardener," replied Tamienne.

"What about that man?" Rhianne angled her head toward an anxious-looking slave who kept glancing over at her as he pulled weeds. "Maybe he knows something." She raised her voice. "You there."

The man stood, trembling but confused.

"Pox it," said Rhianne. "Probably doesn't speak Kjallan." She switched to Mosari, hoping she wouldn't need any difficult words. "Where is Janto?"

A flood of frantic Mosari erupted from the man.

"Wait, wait," she called. "I don't understand. Come closer."

He approached.

"Speak slowly and use easy words. Please. Where is Janto?"

"Guards came," said the man. "Took him."

"What?" she cried. "Why?"

The man looked frightened. He shook his head and shrugged.

He knows something, but he doesn't want to tell me, thought Rhianne. "What guards? Where did they take him?"

"Legaciatti," said the slave. He pointed toward one of the garden exits.

Rhianne nodded. "Come on, Tami. We have to find him."

"He said *Legaciatti.* If they took him—," began her bodyguard.

"I don't care." If Janto's crime had been something minor, like insubordination or being late to work, ordinary guards or the slave overseer would have dealt with it. Since the Legaciatti were involved, Janto was accused of something serious—theft or the assault of a Kjallan, perhaps. Or they might suspect him of being a spy. From what she'd seen of Janto, it didn't surprise her terribly that he'd wound up on the wrong side of Kjallan law, but it did frighten her. She realized just how much she didn't want to see Janto come to harm.

Janto was trapped. He'd been refilling his wheelbarrow in the company of three other slaves when a bruised and angry-looking Micah had stalked through the gate not twenty paces away, flanked by two orange-garbed Legaciatti. Janto could not throw a shroud over himself with an audience so near. He'd tried to discreetly slip away, but it hadn't worked. Micah had spotted him.

Micah grabbed him by the tunic and hauled him before the Legaciatti. "This is the one. This is the slave who attacked me last night."

Sashi, invisible, came running. *I'll bite him, su-kali!*

Do not, cautioned Janto. *Stay hidden and stay close.* His ferret, who lived in the moment and lacked the capacity to regret past errors, would not chide him for failing to kill Micah the night before. But Janto had regrets enough for both of them.

"He's not on the books?" asked a Legaciattus with a scar on his lip.

"No. I don't even know his name."

Lip Scar jerked his chin at his uniformed partner. "We'll take it from here."

The Legaciatti led Janto out of the garden and down a long pathway through the courtyard. They entered a small, simply furnished outbuilding with a table and four chairs. Sashi, still invisible, slipped in the door before they closed it and pressed himself into a corner, out of the way.

Kill them now? asked Sashi.

I don't have a plan yet, said Janto. *Sit tight.* Killing, unfortunately, was beyond his means. They were armed, and he wasn't, and one or both of them might be war mages.

Lip Scar pushed Janto into one of the chairs, cuffed his wrists, and sat down across from him. "Get a mind mage," he ordered his partner, who nodded and left.

A mind mage. Janto felt sick with despair. They would use a truth spell on him, and then he would have two choices, either of which would reveal him. He could use his magic to repel the truth spell, but the mind mage would know if he did that, and he would give himself away as a mage. If he didn't repel it, the mind mage would know when he lied. One way or another, he faced torture and death. Iolo had been right. Unless he could talk his way out of this, the best he could hope for was to take his poison pill.

"Tell me," said Lip Scar, speaking Mosari. "How is it that we have an Imperial Garden slave with no paperwork, who is unknown to the overseer?"

"Sir, I believe you need a better overseer."

Lip Scar snorted. "Oh?"

"The overseer spends his time ravishing the slave women. He has no interest in learning the names of the male slaves, or in keeping his paperwork up-to-date."

"He says you attacked him."

"He assaulted a woman," said Janto. "It was an unfair fight, so I evened the odds."

"You are not to assault your overseer under any circumstances," said Lip Scar. "But disciplinary matters among slaves are not my concern. We'll see how your story holds up when the mind mage gets here." He shuffled through some papers, initialing a couple of them.

Your tame Kjallan is at the door, said Sashi.

Janto blinked. *Tame Kjallan?*

The door opened. "I heard you needed a mind mage."

Janto turned and stared. It was Rhianne. The second Legaciattus followed her into the room.

Lip Scar leapt to his feet. "Your Imperial Highness! I requested a mind mage, but I would never have presumed to trouble *you*."

Rhianne flashed him a dazzling smile. "It's no trouble at all, Bruccian. I ran into your partner outside, and he said you were looking for one, and it happens I've no other obligations this morning. What sort of spell do you need?"

"A truth spell," said Lip Scar. "We've reason to believe this man may be a spy. He's been posing as a slave in the Imperial Garden, but the slave overseer doesn't know him and says he's not on the books. He also says this man attacked him last night."

Rhianne scrutinized Janto's face as if she'd never seen him before. "He's clearly been in a fight."

"Yes," said Lip Scar. "That's not important. I want to know whether he's a spy."

"I'll find out." She turned and stared at Janto imperiously. "Slave," she said, "give me your hand, and do not be afraid. This won't hurt."

Janto's palms were sweating. He wiped his hand on his slave tunic and offered it to her. She took it with an expression of distaste, which he hoped was feigned.

An electric sensation crept up his hand—her mind magic, invading him. He stared at her hand on his, the point of entry, but it was all happening invisibly, in the spirit world: a breach of his soul. As the tendrils of her magic seeped through and enveloped him like a fog, he felt his own magic screaming rebellion, gathering to repel the foreign magic. But he held it in check and allowed her truth spell its nauseating hold. He could see no way out of this except to put his faith in Rhianne. She had a quick mind and a kind heart. He had a feeling she would not let him down.

"We're ready," said Rhianne.

Lip Scar leaned forward and spoke to Janto. "Who and what are you?"

Apparently this man wasn't the type to ask a few

warm-up questions first. "My name is Janto. I'm a slave assigned to the Imperial Garden." His voice sounded strange inside his own head. There was an echo within, some sort of rumbling overtone.

Lip Scar glanced at Rhianne.

A moment's infinitesimal hesitation. Her eyes met his. "Truth," she reported.

"Are you controlled by a death spell and under the oversight of Micah?" asked Lip Scar.

"Yes," said Janto.

Lip Scar's eyes went to Rhianne.

"Truth."

Gods, she was lying for him. He owed her a debt, and he would never be able to repay it.

"Are you a spy?" asked Lip Scar.

"No," said Janto.

"Truth," reported Rhianne.

"Is Micah remiss in his responsibilities regarding paperwork and keeping track of slaves?" he asked.

"Yes."

"Truth," said Rhianne.

"Did you assault Micah because he attacked a slave woman?"

"Yes."

"Truth," said Rhianne.

Lip Scar sat back heavily. "Your Imperial Highness, please release him from the spell. I've no further need for this man."

Janto closed his eyes in relief. The fog of the truth spell dissipated within him like the smoke of a discharged pistol, and Rhianne dropped his hand.

"I'm pleased to help," said Rhianne. "Slave, I'll write

you a chit to explain your absence from work." Rhianne took a blank sheet of paper from the table, scribbled a few words on it, folded it, and handed it to Janto.

Puzzled, he took the paper. Later, walking back to the garden, he opened the note. It read *Bow Oak Bridge, midnight.*

11

Janto thought hard about whether to meet with Rhianne as requested. In the end, he decided his honor demanded it. She had rescued him. She knew exactly what he was and had covered for him, an act her people would consider treason. If she'd stuck her neck out for him to that extent, he owed her some sort of explanation.

The Bow Oak Bridge spanned a gravel-strewn creek just northwest of the Imperial Palace's service entrance. Every morning and every evening, hundreds of slaves trod its ancient oaken planks smooth on their way to and from work. Farther north was the larger bridge, the one wide enough for carts and carriages. The Bow Oak Bridge served foot and horse traffic only, and, for the purposes of his "tame Kjallan," was more private.

In the darkness, Janto heard the water chattering to itself and smelled its dampness, but he could not see it. He crossed the bridge shrouded from the slave side to the palace side, not wanting his footsteps to echo hollowly on the wood, but as he stepped off the bridge onto the dirt footpath, he dropped the shroud, leaving only Sashi invisible. He slowed his steps, looking for Rhianne on the path ahead and among the trees on either side.

"Stop there," called Rhianne's voice. "Are you alone?"

He turned in the direction of the voice and found her just off the path, dressed in dark colors to blend with the night and half hidden behind a great oak. "Of course." Was she alone? He supposed she might have that bodyguard with her. *Is anyone with her?* he asked Sashi.

I smell another, answered his familiar.

He kept his expression carefully bland. *Find the other person and tell me who it is.* The creature chittered acknowledgment and scampered invisibly away.

"Come here," she called. "Into the trees."

Wary but still inclined to trust her, Janto headed toward her. He'd never seen Rhianne in the dark. Darkness did interesting things to a woman—reduced her to essentials, as it were. If she wore her fine imperial trappings, they did not show in the dim moonlight. Only her outline, her face, and her hair, rendered in shades of silver.

Her beauty was undiminished. Indeed, he might say it was enhanced. She was but a woman, pure and simple and enchanting. The curve of her throat, lit by a patch of lustrous sagelight, was so lovely it was all he could do not to reach out and touch it.

There is a man back here, said Sashi. *He points a gun at you.*

So much for the magic of a beautiful woman in the dark. *Legaciattus?* asked Janto.

Not in uniform.

Warn me if he looks like he's about to shoot, said Janto.

Rhianne took his hand and spoke in a voice that was barely more than a whisper. "I committed treason to save your life. For that, I want some assurances from you."

"What assurances?"

"I want the truth."

The electric feeling crawled up his arm again—her truth spell. As it seeped through and enveloped him, once more his magic rebelled against it, but again he held it in check, permitting the invasion. A gun on him, three gods. He swallowed. "You shall have it."

"You are a Mosari spy," she prompted.

"Yes," said Janto.

"What do you seek in Kjall?"

"Information to help us win the war," he said. "And another spy we lost touch with."

Rhianne nodded. "Anything else?"

"No."

She sighed, and tension melted from her face and shoulders. "Are you armed?"

"No."

"Are you magical?"

Janto winced. He'd hoped she wouldn't ask that. "Yes."

Her eyebrows rose. "What sort of mage are you?"

"I'm a shroud mage."

Understanding dawned in her eyes. "Are you an assassin? Do you intend harm to me or anyone in the palace?"

"No and no." *The gunman?* he inquired of Sashi.

Just standing here.

Rhianne released his hand, and the truth spell dissipated. "I want you to understand why I did what I did. I saved you not because I'm a traitor to my country but because I know you are no villain. You only wish to help Mosar, and nobody with a modicum of sense would blame you for that. If I hadn't lied to the Legaciatti, they would have tortured you to death. You don't deserve that. But I won't betray my people any more than I already have. I can't let you remain here."

"Princess—," Janto began.

She held up a hand. "You *must* leave. You have three days in which to do so. After that, I will raise the alarm that a shroud mage is active in the Imperial Palace. The place will be salted with invisibility wards, and you *will* be caught. The other spy you're looking for. What's his name?"

Janto regarded her warily.

"I'm trying to help. If we caught your spy, I can find out for you. I don't see any harm in giving his family peace."

"It wouldn't be right for me to give you his name," said Janto. "But we lost track of him a month ago, if that helps."

"I'll find out what I can and leave a message for you under this bridge within the next twenty-four hours."

"Princess, there's one more thing."

"I can't help you win your war," said Rhianne. "I'm sorry about it. I think the war is a terrible mistake, but that decision isn't mine to make."

"It's something else," said Janto. "The reason I got caught was I stumbled on the slave overseer assaulting a woman. I fought him off, and he turned me in to the Legaciatti the next day. But he assaults the slave women regularly. I had been planning to find a way to stop him. If you force me to leave, I cannot do it."

Rhianne's brow wrinkled with concern. "You're certain? If I spoke to the slave women, would they corroborate that story?"

"I believe they would," said Janto. "If they trusted you

enough to talk to you. Or if you used your magic on them."

"I'll see what I can do," said Rhianne. "Who's the overseer?"

"A Mosari man named Micah."

"All right. You don't need to worry about this problem anymore. I'll take care of it."

Silence stretched between them. Janto didn't want to leave, knowing he might never see her again, but he could think of no more excuses to extend the conversation. She'd told him to leave the country, and she had every right to do so. It also saddened him that she'd brought a gunman to this meeting and kept the man hidden. He was a threat to her country, so he understood why she'd banished him, but he would sooner die than do harm to Rhianne. He wished she knew that. He didn't want to reveal Sashi, but maybe she would confess to the gunman's presence if he prompted her. "No bodyguard with you tonight?"

"Don't need one," she said cheerfully. "You've got a gun pointed at you right now, just in case."

"Really?" That was his princess, all honesty. "Who's holding the gun?"

"Somebody else. Don't do anything stupid, because he never misses."

"Please believe me when I say that I would never hurt you. Not in any circumstance. I'll miss you, Rhianne."

"It's Rhianne now, is it?" She smiled. "Thank you for the language lessons, even if you were just spying on me the whole time."

"At least one good thing has come of this war," said Janto. "I didn't believe there were any kind and decent

Kjallans in the world, but in meeting you, I've discovered otherwise. You're as lovely on the inside as you are on the outside, and I hope your fiancé appreciates what a prize he has."

She looked away.

Janto winced. Normally he got a better response when he complimented a woman. "Did I say something wrong?"

"No," she whispered, staring at a spot near his foot.

He pondered her for a moment, perplexed. "I'm sorry if—"

"Don't say anything," she said. "Just don't." She reached for him.

Gunman? Janto asked Sashi in alarm.

Swearing to himself in Kjallan, answered Sashi. *But he hasn't cocked the gun.*

Janto took Rhianne into his arms, something he'd longed to do almost since the day he'd met her. Her hair slipped through his hands like silk as the scent of orange blossoms washed over him. There was a hitch in Rhianne's breathing. She was upset, and who could blame her? She was to marry the horrid Augustan. She'd spent two days with him, and he gathered the man had made a poor impression. Rhianne, despite being a Kjallan imperial, was no villain in this drama, but another victim, like himself and all the other Mosari. He rubbed her back, wishing he could do more for her than offer this scant comfort. But if he couldn't save his own people, how could he save her?

Her body felt electric against his, charged, like the pregnant air during the Mosari storm season. And his inevitable physical response reminded him of how long it had been since he'd touched a woman. He tilted her chin upward and wiped away the wetness beneath her eyes. "Someday, when no one's pointing a gun at me, I'm going to kiss you."

She looked up, her eyes bright. "Kiss an imperial princess of Kjall?"

"Princess or not," he said, "you are a woman in need of kissing."

Rhianne licked her lower lip. "But you're leaving. We won't see each other again."

Janto smiled. "I wouldn't be so sure of that."

He let her go, stepped back, and disappeared under his invisibility shroud.

"Are you crazy?" Lucien fell in beside Rhianne on the footpath, slipping the pistol into a pocket of his syrtos. "If Florian finds out about this—"

"You're not going to tell him, and I'm not," said Rhianne. "Besides, it's over. I told him I won't be seeing him anymore." *Someday, when no one's pointing a gun at me, I'm going to kiss you.* What did he mean by that? Was he really going to pop out of nowhere at some point and kiss her? He was a shroud mage. He said he was leaving, but he could be following her right now.

She rather hoped he did pop out of nowhere and kiss her, sometime when Lucien wasn't around. It was exciting to think about.

"Who is that man?" said Lucien. "*What* is he? I couldn't hear half of what you were saying."

"That's for the best. Trust me. No harm is being done here." She hoped not. She hadn't meant to commit treason—not exactly. But Lucien had shown her that what her country was doing was *wrong*. It was wrong for them to attack Mosar, and it would be wrong for them to torture and kill Janto simply for trying to stop them. If her people would simply imprison him, perhaps disable his magic and send him home at the end of the war, then she could have exposed him as a spy with her conscience intact. Not that she would have taken any pleasure in seeing him jailed, given how much she liked him. But send him to his death? How could she do such a thing and not despise herself for the rest of her life?

"Oh, sure, nothing to worry about." Lucien rolled his eyes. "That's why you needed me to hold a gun on this fellow for half an hour."

"It was just a precaution. You don't have to worry about it anymore. It's over." Except for a few details she needed to take care of. And maybe a kiss.

12

It took Rhianne less than an hour to track down Janto's missing spy. The prison archivist had on record a Mosari shroud mage whom they'd caught with an invisibility ward and taken into custody thirty-five days earlier. They had hoped to interrogate him, but he had died suddenly, foaming at the mouth. After his death, a dark gray ferret had appeared and darted for the exit. They had cornered and killed it. They had never learned the man's name.

With a heavy heart, Rhianne copied the relevant page and hid the copy in an interior pocket of her syrtos to deliver to the bridge later in the day.

Now she was left with the harder task, dealing with the abuse of the slave women. She wished she could take this problem to Lucien, but he didn't have the authority to act without Florian's approval. And if Florian and Lucien disagreed—well, she'd just be creating more friction between father and son. Better to go directly to Florian and take the heat herself, if there was heat to be taken. She was in the right on this one, and her uncle was no proponent of the mistreatment of women, but it was hard to say how much he would care about the plight of slaves.

She found him in the Sardossian section of the Imperial Garden, sitting ramrod straight on a stone bench, his syrtos and loros impeccable to the last folds. Wiry trees with butter yellow blossoms formed a rough semicircle around his bench. He spotted her, and his craggy face broke into a smile. He beckoned, and she went to him. Brushing away the fallen blossoms, she sat on the bench.

"I'm glad you came," said Florian. "I meant to send for you. I've heard an interesting story from your bodyguard. Apparently you've befriended a Mosari slave in the gardens—these very gardens!" He indicated them with a sweep of his hand. "And later he was arrested on suspicion of being a spy."

The little hairs prickled on the back on her neck. Tamienne had *snitched* on her? *That duplicitous, ungrateful* . . . But she had to stay calm. It would not do to appear flustered in front of the emperor. "I can't believe Tamienne spoke to you about such a trivial matter."

"You saw fit to intervene in his interrogation and serve as the mind mage administering his truth spell? That's irregular."

"You want to know what really happened? That slave, whom I'd recruited to teach me the Mosari language, was being harassed by an overseer who was raping slave women he's supposed to be in charge of. The Mosari you speak of tried to stop him. I *did* administer the truth spell. I *know*."

Florian frowned at her.

"This is why I came to speak to you today," Rhianne continued, still trembling a little from the shock of Tamienne's betrayal. "The overseer, Micah, rapes a slave woman every night. This—this cannot be good for productivity, and we need to put a stop to it."

"Melodrama between slaves doesn't concern me," said Florian. "This Micah—he's Mosari?"

"Yes."

Florian shook his head. "That's just what those Mosari animals do."

"Not all of them!" cried Rhianne. "Not the slave who intervened. And, Uncle, it's *wrong*. Whether this happens on Mosar or anywhere else, we shouldn't be allowing it to happen here. No woman, Kjallan or Mosari, slave or free, should have to suffer that."

"The slave who intervened probably wanted the woman for himself," said Florian. "These are people who live in caves and soulcast into animals, Rhianne. They're not like us."

"That's entirely untrue, Uncle."

"I forbid you to meet with this slave again. He's a bad influence."

"I've no interest in seeing the slave again." She was sending him away anyhow. What if Florian's suspicions led him to investigate further and learn that Janto's name really wasn't on the slave books? "But about Micah—"

"Leave the slaves to their petty excitements, Rhianne. It's none of our affair. And you're not to participate in interrogations at all. It's beneath you. Dirty work, meant for the lesser families."

Rhianne wilted. She'd told Janto she would solve this problem because she'd thought it would be easy. Now it didn't look so easy.

Florian squeezed her hand. "I've been pleased to see you in some of our state meetings lately. It's refreshing to see a pretty face among my grizzled old officers and counselors. I shall miss you terribly when you go to Mosar. It broke my heart when your mother left."

Rhianne swallowed. She had few memories of her

mother, only fragments and scattered images, and hated being reminded of what she'd lost.

He cocked his head at her. "Are you happy, Rhianne?"

She looked away. "Sometimes."

"Your mother," said Florian, "she was not happy. Even as a youngster, I saw it. She was restless." He gave her a probing look. "You remind me of her."

Rhianne avoided his eyes, not knowing what to say. What she really wanted—freedom to explore, to learn, to make her own choices in life—he would not grant her. And the more she asked for it, the more he would resist. "I'm happy, Uncle. I'm not going to run off like my mother did."

"You'll enjoy Mosar," he said. "You've always wanted to see another country. And marriage has a settling effect. It did for me."

"Uncle, I don't like Augustan."

"You barely know him," said Florian. "He's a brilliant man. A wonderful strategist, not a speck of cowardice in him."

"That doesn't mean he'll make a good husband."

"Give him time, my dear. You spent all of two days with him. Get to know him better before you make such strong judgments."

Rhianne sighed.

"You'll give Augustan time?" prodded Florian.

"I suppose." What choice did she have?

In the late afternoon, Rhianne sneaked out through the hypocaust and made her way to the Bow Oak Bridge. She wished she had a solution for the slave women, but she'd promised Janto information about his missing spy, and at least she could give him that before he left Kjall. Morning clouds had matured into a light drizzle, and she pulled her cloak's hood over her head as she approached the bridge.

No one was out walking. She had the place to herself, which was good.

Under the bridge, a shallow creek rattled over a bed of pebbles. She wanted her note out of sight and out of the rain, so she followed a rough trail down to the water, looking for a hiding spot beneath the bridge. Possibly she could tuck the note up in the bridge's supporting beams, but that might be hard for Janto to find.

Something splashed in the creek. She turned, but there was no one there. She stood still, watching. Perhaps a fish had jumped?

A pebble rose of its own accord. Then it fell into the water with another splash. Her heart thrummed against her ribs. Janto? She remembered his promise from the other night, and a warm tingle of anticipation ran through her.

A rock on the other side of the creek dislodged itself from the ground and rolled down the bank. Farther up the bank, grass bent, as if by a stiff wind.

Rhianne ran up the trail and crossed the bridge to the other side. She found the patch of bent grass, which was slowly straightening. In the woods, a pile of dead leaves flew into the air. She hurried to it. Nothing there, but a little farther on, a branch bent on a bush. She ran to the bush. "Janto?" she whispered.

Someone tapped her on the arm.

She whirled, and Janto grinned at her. A weasel-like animal sat on his shoulder.

She pressed a hand to her fluttering heart. "You could have just said something."

His grin widened. "That wouldn't have been as much fun." He lowered his hand so the animal could run down it and jump off, and swept her into his arms.

She'd been thinking about this kiss since the night before, imagining it, even wondering if she should protest, though she knew deep down she wouldn't. She'd never kissed a man before, yet some rebellious side of her had been wanting to kiss Janto almost since the day she'd met him. It was unseemly for a princess to get involved with a slave. But Janto wasn't a slave—not really. And gods, did she want her first kiss to come from Augustan? Janto's lips were warm and soft, and his mouth fit hers perfectly. She wondered about that—were mouths supposed to fit? Did that always happen?

Nervous and bewildered, she tried to figure out what was expected of her. What was she supposed to do with her lips, her tongue? But when Janto tilted her head just so, as if to savor her, she grasped that all she had to do was give herself up and surrender to his kiss. He held her, one arm around her waist and the other stroking her hair, her throat, coaxing her to yield. Something fluttered deep inside her. Her legs trembled, and she relaxed into his grip. He led, and she followed, and her mouth knew exactly what to do.

"Gods, Rhianne," he whispered against her lips.

"How long did you wait for me?"

"All my life." He grinned. "Oh, you mean just now. A while, but you were worth it."

She twisted out of his arms in sudden fear. "We could be seen. You're visible now."

"No, I'm not," said Janto, taking her by the hand and drawing her gently back. "And neither are you. When I become visible to you, one of two things just happened.

Either I dropped my shroud, or I extended it to include you. If I extended it, and that's what I did, we're both invisible to the outside world but visible to each other."

"Oh." She looked around, taking in the bridge and the forest. "We're both invisible?"

"Yes. No one saw you kissing a filthy, animal-loving Mosari."

She pressed herself against him, shivering with pleasure as his arms snaked around her. "And no one saw you with a cruel, thieving Kjallan. Was that your familiar I saw?"

"My ferret, Sashi," said Janto. "He's gone hunting. He doesn't like to be around for this sort of thing."

Rhianne laughed softly and enjoyed the sight of his warm smile. But then her expression grew dark again. "You have to leave the country, you know."

"You're making it difficult."

"I mean it." Sobering, she pulled away and unfolded the paper from the prison archivist. "I found your spy."

He snatched the paper from her hand, and his eyes moved rapidly over its contents. When he came to the key passages, his expression changed. He swallowed, blinked, and sat heavily on a nearby rock. "The prison archives. Of course. Your people record *everything*."

"Is that the man you were looking for?"

He scrubbed his face with his hands. "I believe so. I should have found this myself. I was in that prison."

"You wouldn't have found it in there," said Rhianne. "It was older and in storage."

He shook his head and stared at a spot off in the trees, looking pale and sick. "You'd know where to look. His name was Ral-Vaddis. Doesn't matter if you know now."

Rhianne bit her lip. He looked desolate, parched of

his usual spirit. Surely he must have known the spy would be dead. But if he'd come here to search for the man, he must have harbored some hope that the man lived, and she'd smothered that hope. He'd greeted her with a kiss, and all she had to offer him was crushing disappointment. She wished she could kiss him again, but clearly his mind was on other things. "I'm afraid the rest of what I have to say isn't much cheerier. I couldn't get anywhere on stopping Micah. I tried, but . . . well, it didn't work."

"What did you try?" asked Janto.

"I asked the emperor to intervene, and he refused."

"Surely that's not the only way to solve this problem."

Rhianne hesitated. She hadn't planned to pursue this further once Florian had turned her down. But Janto was so upset about the dead spy, and he was going to lose his entire country soon. She hated to disappoint him again, and he was right. There had to be another way. "I know someone who's a great tactical thinker. He might have an idea."

Janto turned to her, his face lighting with a shred of hope.

"We can talk to him together, maybe come up with a plan. If it's not something I can carry out, it might be something you could, with your shroud, or . . . who knows. If I arrange to have the door opened for you, can you sneak into my rooms?"

"How are your rooms warded?" asked Janto.

"There's an enemy ward across my door, attuned to me. You should be able to pass that. I would hope you could."

"I can pass it. What about wards in the halls? And how do I find your rooms?"

She drew him a quick map in the dirt. "There are no wards in the halls. Only across doorways." She eyed him significantly. "But there *will be* invisibility wards in the hallways if anyone suspects there's a shroud mage operating in the palace. That's how your Ral-Vaddis got caught, and you'll get caught too if you don't leave. I'm giving you two more days before I raise the alarm."

He gave her a wry smile. "Then we'll work quickly. You'd better get back so you can open the door for me."

13

Janto believed he had found the entrance to Rhianne's rooms. Before the arched doorway stood her bodyguard, Tamienne, and another orange-garbed Legaciattus. Two huge, black ironwood doors stood sentinel as well, barred shut through heavy silver rings as thick as Janto's wrist. One might think Rhianne was a prisoner in her own chambers.

Janto waited in silence until a tapping of footsteps down the hall indicated the arrival of a uniformed servant, who bore a jug of wine on a tray. The guards removed the bar and, grasping the silver rings, dragged the doors open to let the servant through. Janto trailed after him.

Inside was a receiving room, lavishly furnished with couches, chairs, and carved tables. Rhianne lounged on one of the chairs, reading a novel. With a flick of her wrist, she indicated an end table, and the servant placed the wine upon it.

Janto, unable to reveal himself until the servant left, wandered in farther and placed Sashi on the floor to give the place a sniff. An arched entryway led from the receiving room to a sitting room with a well-stocked bookcase and seating for ten people or more.

I smell brindlecat, said Sashi.

Janto remembered the brindlecat Rhianne's fiancé had given her. Now he scanned the room with alert eyes, searching for the predator. A ferret was no match for a brindlecat kitten. He saw no signs of it, but such creatures loved to hide and spring on their prey unawares. *Ride on my shoulder, just in case.* Janto lowered his arm, and Sashi scampered back up.

The door shut behind the departing servant. Rhianne rose to her feet, looking around eagerly, and Janto released his shroud. "Alligator," he said.

She turned, and a smile lit her face. He started to speak, but she pressed a finger to her lips, beckoned, and moved through the archway into the sitting room.

Janto followed her as she passed under a second archway into an enormous bedroom. He swallowed and stared at the bed, a cream and gold monstrosity piled high with goose down pillows.

"Don't get any ideas," said Rhianne. "This is the farthest room from the door guards and the place we're least likely to be overheard."

Janto hoped his embarrassment didn't show. "I would not dream of debauching an imperial princess of Kjall. Unless, of course, she wanted me to."

A flush crept up Rhianne's cheeks, and she looked away, muttering something about needing wine.

Janto had been half joking. Of course he'd like to sleep with her, but she was a Kjallan princess and he was a Mosari spy. That he was also a crown prince didn't signify, given that their nations were at war and he couldn't reveal his identity. Their lives were on different trajectories. He had no wish to put her in a situation that might cause her grief. A kiss was one thing, bedsport another.

He waited while she retrieved her jug of wine and poured herself a glass. Her blushing intrigued him—she seemed as embarrassed as he was.

Was she a virgin? He didn't know what the rules were for Kjallan princesses, but when he'd kissed her, she'd been so tentative, and her pulse had fluttered under his hand like the heartbeat of a bird. Most Mosari women went to the marriage bed sexually experienced, and he'd heard it was the same in Kjall, but perhaps the imperial family was different. If she was a virgin, and Augustan was to be her first lover . . . well, one could only hope Augustan was a gentler man in the bedroom than his reputation on the battlefield suggested.

"Wine?" Rhianne's hand trembled as she offered him a glass. "Let's stick to business. We're here to help the slave women. Nothing else."

"Of course."

"Wait here," said Rhianne, setting down her glass. "I'm going to send word to someone who may be able to help us. You'd better hide your animal." She indicated Sashi. "My friend doesn't know what you are."

"Right." He shrouded Sashi.

Rhianne left, and Janto sipped his wine, looking about, trying to settle his mind on something, *anything* except the bed in the middle of the room. His eyes lit on the ruins of a bedroom chair. Its damask upholstery was shredded, the wood deeply scored. Horsehair littered the ground beneath it. He blinked. What in the Soldier's name?

Rhianne padded softly back into the room.

Janto indicated the chair. "What happened there?"

She followed his gesture. "Oh. Whiskers got carried away."

"Whiskers?" Comprehension dawned. "Is that what you call the *brindlecat*?"

"I figured she ought to have a name."

"Yes, but *Whiskers*? I told you to cage that animal."

Rhianne wrung her hands. "I know, but she's so little. And there's something wrong with her. She's not eating."

Janto looked around the room, searching for the cat. "What are you feeding her?"

Rhianne surprised him by extracting the scowling kitten from underneath a settee and thrusting the animal at him. Even he had to take sympathy on it. The poor thing was skin and bones.

Gods, keep her away from me! squealed Sashi, who leapt from Janto's shoulder and fled to the far end of the room.

She can't see you, Janto assured him.

She can smell me.

Janto held the kitten firmly, just in case.

"I tried a lot of things," said Rhianne. "Every kind of meat I could think of, raw and cooked. Fish. Milk. Cream. She won't have any of it."

He ran his hands along the kitten's protruding ribs. The creature sniffed thoroughly along his shoulder, where Sashi had been, and hissed. "And *how* are you feeding her?"

"I put the food on a plate or in a bowl and leave it for her."

"Ah. You have to feed her by hand."

"Three gods, why?"

He set the kitten on the floor. "Because she's a brindlecat. Whiskers here was surely raised in the zo crèche on Mosar as a future familiar for a war mage.

When brindlecats are very young, still in the nest box, their keepers surround them with meat laced with bohr leaf. Bohr leaf has no detectable scent, but it induces vomiting. Meanwhile, they're fed clean meat by hand. Soon they learn never to touch anything unless it comes from a keeper's hand. At sexual maturity, their habits are refined even more, and they're fed only by their intended zo partners. We can't have enemies soul-sundering our war mages by tossing their familiars tainted meat."

"I didn't realize she'd be so complicated to care for," said Rhianne.

"I told you, she's not a house cat."

Just then, from back in the receiving room they heard the heavy scrape of the bar being drawn and the door opening. A man's voice called, "Rhianne?"

"That's my cousin," Rhianne said softly. "Let me do the explaining." In a louder voice, she called, "In the bedroom, Lucien!"

Janto nearly spilled his wine. Lucien? Her cousin? Was Rhianne bringing the Imperial Heir into his presence? He craned his neck for a look as her cousin entered the bedroom.

Lucien was a black-haired, fresh-faced teenager with a wooden leg who walked with the aid of a crutch. He wore imperial dress and a loros wider than Rhianne's, though not so wide as the emperor's. Yes, this was the heir.

On Mosar, the rumors flew about this man, and they were so contradictory that an accurate picture of him could hardly be constructed. He was brave. He was cowardly. He had strong opinions. He never said a word. He was rebellious. He supported the emperor.

Lucien spied Janto and stopped short. "Three gods, Rhianne."

"It's not what it looks like," she said.

"How did you get him past the door guards?" said Lucien.

Rhianne shrugged. "We found a way."

His eyes narrowed. "You *did* bring him in through the front door . . . didn't you?"

"Of course. This is innocent. I just want to help Janto find a way to stop the overseer from assaulting the slave women."

"Talk to Florian," said Lucien. "I don't have that kind of authority, but he does."

"I tried talking to Florian. He doesn't care about the slave women."

"Rhianne!" cried Lucien. "You can't solve everybody else's problems! Not Morgan's, and not the slave women's."

"Why not?"

"Because Florian—"

"Florian should be solving these problems, because he's the emperor, and he has the power to do it," said Rhianne. "If he won't do the job, I'll find a way to do it for him."

"Just because there's an injustice in the world doesn't mean *you* have to fix it. You take too much on yourself. You didn't create the problem—"

"Lucien, if everybody thought that way, what kind of world would we live in?"

"Think of the danger! If Florian saw us here with this man—"

"What's he going to do?" snapped Rhianne. "Marry

me off to Augustan and send me to a conquered province full of rebels who hate me? That would be a fine punishment."

Lucien, defeated, sank into a chair. "We'll discuss this later. What do you want from me?"

Rhianne gestured to Janto.

"We need a way to discourage the slave overseer from attacking the women," said Janto. "I fought him off once, but my assumption is he was back at it the next night. We need a way to discourage him permanently. The overseer himself must report to someone. If that person were to order him to stop—"

"Could *you* go to Florian?" Rhianne asked Lucien. "Or someone else in the chain of command? Nobody listens to me."

Lucien rested his forehead on his palm and shook his head. "No. I'm in more trouble with him right now than you are, and if I . . . no."

"Rhianne, what about your magic?" said Janto. "Could you plant a suggestion or something? Make him decide not to attack the women anymore?"

Lucien's eyes glinted with anger. "*Her Imperial Highness* is not getting personally involved in this, Mosari. She has too much of a tendency to let her heart override her good sense."

"It wouldn't work," said Rhianne. "My suggestions are short in duration and limited in their power. They can't change how a man thinks or alter his behavior over the long term."

"Killing him or crippling him is out of the question," said Janto. "Other considerations aside, there'd be an investigation. What we really want is to frighten him somehow. Humiliate him."

Suddenly, Lucien looked up. "Perhaps the sackcloth treatment."

"What's that?" asked Janto.

"If an officer bullies his men too much, they gang up on him one night, stuff him in a sackcloth bag, and beat on him with hollow training staves. The staves leave bruises but don't break bones. It isn't exactly legal, but it's an old tradition, and most people look the other way when it happens. It reminds bad officers that their purpose is to lead, not to be tyrants."

"That might work," said Rhianne.

"Can we get staves and sackcloth?" asked Janto.

"I can," said Rhianne. "Do you think the slave women will agree to take part?"

"I don't know," said Janto. "I'll ask a friend."

"If women are going to carry this out, you might want something heavier than hollow staves," said Lucien.

"They'll hit harder than you think, Cousin," said Rhianne. "And we can't risk killing him; that would lead to an inquiry. Do you suppose visible bruises will be a problem? It will be better for all of us if Micah keeps the attack a secret, but he won't be able to if the evidence is on his face."

"Just don't hit him in the head," said Lucien. "After you put him in the bag, protect his head with something. A helmet would work, but in the army they prefer an empty chamber pot. And stop saying *we*—you're not to be personally involved, Rhianne." He leveled an icy stare at Janto. "Mosari, if you want to carry this out, fine. But if anything happens to Her Imperial Highness, I'm holding you responsible."

"I would never let anything happen to Her Imperial Highness," said Janto.

Rhianne picked up Lucien's hand and squeezed it. "You won't say anything to Florian, will you?"

"Of course not," said Lucien. "Cousin, it's time for this Mosari to go back to wherever he comes from. And you come back with me. I want to talk to you."

14

As Rhianne headed to Lucien's rooms, trailed by her perfidious tattletale of a bodyguard, she debated just how much she could and couldn't tell her cousin about Janto, since it was clear he intended to ask. She had never in her life kept secrets from Lucien, and it killed her to start now, but she couldn't tell him Janto was a spy. That was too big a burden for Lucien to carry.

The guards opened the doors to her cousin's chambers. She took a deep breath as she entered.

Lucien paced the floor. Leaning on his crutch, he waved at Tamienne. "Out. This is a private discussion." He gestured at his own guards, and everybody departed, closing the doors behind them.

Rhianne strode across the room and flung herself onto one of Lucien's couches. "Why can't I make her do that?"

"The privileges of rank." Lucien sat across from her. "Look, you can't keep getting involved in these things. First there was the seamstress with the blackmail problem—"

"I got her out of that mess fine, and I just used forgetting spells all around, so where's the harm?"

"Then the stableboy who was being abused—"

"Got him out too, and no harm done there either." Rhianne smiled. "Who'd have known our little trip to the Consualian Games would have led to all this?"

"You'd better not have told that Mosari fellow about the Consualian Games. Or the hypocaust."

"Of course not."

Lucien relaxed a little. "Then there was Morgan, and now this Mosari fellow." He ticked them off on his fingers. "Cousin, you've got a good head on your shoulders, but sometimes when you get a bug in your ear about something, you lose all sense of reason."

"I know it's something you don't understand," said Rhianne. "But you're not me. Florian did a terrible thing to my mother, and I've grown up without her, and I don't know where in the world she is." Her voice broke, and she squeezed her eyes shut. "I'll never find her. But somehow I feel that when I help these other people Florian has harmed, then maybe, just maybe, I'm making her proud."

"Rhianne," he said softly, "I *know* she's proud of you. *I'm* proud of you. And I will always keep your secrets. I just worry. It's one thing to help out the less fortunate of our own people, but that Mosari—he's an enemy. You told me you weren't going to have any more to do with him."

"After we get this problem solved, I'll never see him again."

Lucien sighed. "Who is he really, and why does he call you *Rhianne*?"

"He used to be a scribe in the Mosari palace. He's educated. Very knowledgeable, very intelligent. I enlisted him to teach me his language."

"If he's a palace scribe, I'm a ditch digger. That man is

Mosari nobility, or at least he used to be. There's no doubt in my mind."

"I suspect that as well," said Rhianne. "But it doesn't matter. His country will be conquered, and when that happens, it won't matter what family he came from."

"On the contrary," said Lucien. "When we conquered Riorca, we purged their aristocracy down to the last man, woman, and child. Augustan will do the same in Mosar. If your Mosari is part of that aristocracy, he needs to conceal his ancestry. He's not doing a very good job of that now."

"We're *purging* the aristocracy?" said Rhianne. "Is that the word we use? Three gods." And she was sending Janto out of the country, presumably to go home to Mosar. Where, all too soon, he'd be rounded up and staked along with his family, courtesy of her lovely fiancé. Worse, maybe the purge wouldn't take place until she and Augustan were married. Then she'd have a front-row seat for the whole affair.

"You're in love with him, aren't you?"

Rhianne blinked, astonished the conversation had taken this turn. "With Janto? In love?" She was honestly surprised by the question. But not just because Lucien had asked it. She was surprised to discover her own feelings in reaction. Still, this was not something she could tell her cousin. "No . . . not in love."

"You have feelings for him."

She was more comfortable with that phrasing. It still surprised her that Lucien had picked up on it. But then, the changes that had happened in Lucien during the past few years ran deeper than the physical. It was unfortunate that Florian saw Lucien's sensitivity as a weakness, when in fact it was his greatest strength. Lucien picked up nuances Florian not only failed to perceive, but lacked the capacity to understand.

"It was Janto you had the arguments with, wasn't it? About the war." Lucien gave a snort of laughter. "And here I thought it was Augustan."

Rhianne leaned back in her chair. "He's opened my eyes about a few things. And so have you."

"You're flirting with treason," said Lucien.

Already there, Cousin. "You said yourself the war is bad for Kjall."

"There's a big difference between saying that in a Kjallan Council of War and saying it to a Mosari nobleman who, for all you know, may be funneling information to the mother country. They have spies."

"I don't tell him anything like that," said Rhianne. "We're just trying to stop the slave overseer from raping the women."

"Cousin." Lucien hesitated, biting his lip. "You don't like Augustan. It was obvious when he was here, and I don't blame you. I didn't like him either."

Rhianne lowered her eyes.

"Do you think this thing with Janto . . . Are you perhaps looking for an affair before your marriage?"

"Why would I do that?" Rhianne said carefully.

Lucien shifted in his seat. "Because you'd be crazy not to? If I had to marry a woman I didn't like, and I probably will someday, I'd be running around trying to sleep with as many women as possible beforehand."

"Ugh." Rhianne made a face. "I didn't want to know that."

"I'm saying have an affair. Get it out of your system. No one would begrudge you that, not even Florian," said Lucien. "But not with a Mosari man! Not with that Janto.

That would be a scandal the likes of which the Imperial Palace hasn't seen since your mother ran away."

You have no idea. "Affairs don't work for me the way they work for you. You see a pretty woman, and you want to sleep with her. I need to get to know a man before I want to sleep with him. And a lot of the time, what I find out about him makes me *not* want to sleep with him."

"So get to know some Kjallan men. Maybe you'll find one you like. But please," said Lucien. "I say this for your own sake. Don't get involved with the Mosari beyond this slave overseer business. It can only end badly, for you *and* for him."

As Rhianne headed back to her rooms, she decided Lucien was half right. Having an affair, "getting it out of her system" before she married Augustan, wasn't a bad idea. But there was no way it was going to be with a Kjallan.

After Janto had worked out the details of the plan with Rhianne, he took it to Iolo and Sirali and explained how the sackcloth treatment worked. "We'll use magic to make it fail-safe," he said. "Next time Micah assaults a woman, Rhianne and I will approach him under cover of my shroud, and Rhianne will hit him with a confusion spell. That's how we'll get him into the sack. You see? No risk to anybody."

"No such thing as no risk," said Iolo.

Janto turned to Sirali. "We've got everything taken care of except the support of the slave women. Will they participate? Can you recruit them for us?"

"Janto—," began Iolo.

"I'm asking Sirali," he said.

Sirali thought for a moment. "Dangerous for them."

"Yes, but consider the potential benefits," said Janto. "And with a mind mage on our side, the danger is mitigated. From Micah's perspective, he's going to wake up in a sackcloth bag, having no idea how he got there, and then he'll get beaten up. If things should go horribly wrong for some reason, Rhianne can make him forget the whole episode."

"Three gods, Janto, I can't believe you're doing this!" said Iolo. "What about finding that intelligence for Mosar?"

"Ral-Vaddis is dead, and I fear the intelligence he meant to pass along died with him." There was also the fact that Rhianne was forcing him to leave the country within two days, or she'd inform on him to the authorities. He hadn't told Iolo or Sirali about that yet. The odds of his finding the intelligence within that time window were vanishingly small.

"You can't give up! You don't know for sure that the dead spy was Ral-Vaddis—"

"Yes, I do," said Janto. "There were no other Mosari spies stationed here."

"And even if it was," continued Iolo, "you are the only hope Mosar has. You can't risk everything we have on punishing this slave overseer."

"I understand your concern, but these women are Mosari. I'm their prince, and it's my duty to protect them," said Janto. "I'm going ahead with this—that is, if Sirali agrees to her part. The risks are low, and it's worth doing. Iolo, I won't ask you to participate."

"You think it will work?" said Iolo.

Sirali snorted. "Right, and I want to do it even if it *doesn't* work."

"It will work," said Janto. "When Micah climbs out of the bag, he'll see all the slave women there. He'll know they're united in their opposition to him, that further abuse will land him in the sackcloth again. And Lucien says the authorities don't intervene in these cases—this sackcloth treatment is a Kjallan tradition of sorts. Part of their military culture." He turned to Sirali. "Can you recruit the slave women?"

"Yes." Her eyes gleamed. "When's the soonest we can do this? Tomorrow night?"

"Tomorrow night." And then he would leave the country.

Maybe.

15

Janto, invisible, waited for Rhianne by the well, his stomach churning with a familiar mixture of excitement and nerves. The sackcloth treatment. While the plan was a little frightening to carry out, at least he was *doing* something. The end result might be good or it might be bad, but at least he'd make a difference. This wouldn't be like his fruitless search for Ral-Vaddis.

Branches rustled as someone approached through the trees. Janto moved toward the sound and released his shroud. "Alligator?" he called.

Blue magelight flared in the distance. The odd-shaped figure it illuminated looked unfamiliar at first, but he soon sorted out that it was Rhianne with a bulky sackcloth bag thrown over her shoulder. He ran forward to take the bag from her.

Rhianne grunted her thanks. The chamber pot at the bottom rattled as it bumped against the wooden staves. "I forget how handy the Legaciatti are when it comes to hauling heavy things," she said. "I hope I'm not late."

Janto shook his head. "See that light through the trees?"

Rhianne nodded.

"That's the men's slave house. The door has opened a few times, but Micah hasn't come through it yet."

"So we wait?"

Janto nodded, shrouding both of them.

"Where's your ferret?"

"Hunting."

"What does he hunt?" said Rhianne. "I saw him when you had him in my rooms, but only for a short while."

"I'll bring him back so you can see him." He called to Sashi through the link. The ferret dashed back through the leaves and scurried up Janto's arm. *Rhianne wants to see you. Be nice, will you?*

Sashi chittered his irritation. He didn't like socializing.

No biting, Janto reminded him, and placed the ferret in Rhianne's arms.

She stroked Sashi like she would a cat. "He's lovely. His fur's stiff along his back, but soft everywhere else."

I want to bite her, said Sashi.

Janto took the ferret back. "His coloration is atypical, the strawberry and white. Most ferrets are brown or gray. His color might have made it harder for him to hunt if not for our shared magic. He hunts invisibly."

It is all skill, said Sashi. *I could do it without the magic.*

"I never realized that," said Rhianne. "That your magic was shared. Wait. Janto!" Her hand fell upon his arm: he felt it as a rare, electric touch. "The door's opening."

Janto delayed a moment, wanting her hand to stay where it was. But he watched the door and said, "That's Micah."

Two routes led from the men's slave house to the women's. The first and more direct was a forest path that snaked through the trees. The second route was somewhat more circuitous but wider and brighter in the moonlight, taking a short trail to the paved road, following it for a while, and then taking another trail to the women's slave house. Micah was heading for the paved road. Janto grabbed the bag of gear and hurried after him. He had to rush. Micah, huge and athletic, moved without hesitation or uncertainty, covering the distance with long, swinging strides.

"He must make this trip a lot," Janto whispered to Rhianne as they turned from the road onto the second trail.

At the women's slave house, Micah went straight up the steps and through the door.

They waited several anxious minutes. "He'll come out, right?" asked Rhianne. "He's not going to just attack someone inside?"

"He should come out," said Janto, though he was wondering the same thing.

Micah emerged, dragging a woman by the arm. She wasn't fighting, but she didn't look happy. The pair descended the steps.

"All right," said Janto. "Spell him."

Rhianne jogged toward Micah. Janto could not help but tense as his princess approached a man twice her size, but she moved without fear. Either her mind magic gave her confidence, or she trusted Janto's invisibility shroud. His fists clenched helplessly as she reached out and touched Micah's arm. Micah brushed at the spot, as if a leaf had fallen on him. And he *changed*. The fire drained from his eyes, leaving behind a dull, glassy stare. His shoulders drooped into an apathetic slump. The woman he'd been dragging yanked her arm from his loosened grip and pelted back into the slave house, slamming the door behind her. Rhianne grinned at Janto. She led Micah by the hand, and he followed, tripping over roots and branches.

Janto said, "That is the most disturbing thing I've seen in a long time."

"Let's get him into the sack," said Rhianne.

Janto wrestled the sackcloth over Micah's head. "How long does the spell last?"

"As long as I want it to."

When Micah was covered head to toe in sackcloth, Janto pulled him to the ground and tied his feet so he couldn't escape. Rhianne probed the other end of the sackcloth to locate his head and placed the empty chamber pot over it. They stepped back to observe their handiwork.

"Think that'll hold him?" asked Janto.

Rhianne's forehead wrinkled. "Maybe you should tie a few more knots."

Janto tied a few more. No wonder she was concerned. The sackcloth looked scanty and weak for a man of Micah's size. Still, they were as ready as they'd ever be. He released the shroud over himself but left Rhianne and Sashi invisible. "Make sure he stays spelled for now," he told Rhianne, and headed for the slave house door.

Before he could knock, the door opened and Sirali emerged, followed by a dozen women. "Right, and we were watching from the windows how Micah got stuffed in a sack by an invisible man."

"Happy to entertain," said Janto. He stepped back as more women filed out, four or five dozen at least. He picked up the wooden staves and handed them out. Most of the women carried them gingerly and upright, like flag standards; only Sirali gripped hers as if she meant to use it. "He's got a confusion spell on him right now. That's why he's quiet. When we're ready, I'll have the spell removed so he understands what's going on." He directed the women to surround Micah. They did so, but stood well back from the sackcloth-covered form, and for the first time, he worried the plan would not work. "Ready?"

The women murmured something that might have been assent.

"Ready," said Sirali.

He nodded to an invisible Rhianne, who gestured with her hand.

Micah exploded into life. *"What in the gods' names—,"* he cried. His fists punched at the confines of his sackcloth prison, and his legs, though tied together, kicked frantically. The chamber pot over his head went flying. He was furious as a badger in a trap, and the trap was no match for the badger. *"What's going on? Who's out there?"* he roared.

The women backed away, some of them dropping their staves. Even imprisoned in sackcloth, Micah was frightening. He seemed to have discovered the rope that held his feet and was tearing at it, ineffectually since the rope was on the outside of the bag and his hands were on the inside. But he would free himself soon enough if the women just stood around. They had to begin with the staves, or it would be too late.

Janto grabbed a staff from the forest floor and ran forward. Sirali was closer than he was, and her staff slammed into Micah first.

Micah cried out, *"You fucker!"* But before he could renew his struggles, Janto's staff struck him, then Sirali's again. Another woman landed a blow, a soft one. Then she wound up and hit him with a resounding thwack. Micah's efforts to escape grew more frenzied and disorganized. Instead of working out a way to get at the knots, he reacted to the blows and punched back at the sackcloth.

The rest of the women stepped forward, bolder. Janto got in a few more blows and handed off his staff to the woman nearest him.

Sirali handed off her staff. She carefully replaced the chamber pot on Micah's head, then supervised the women, passing the hollow weapons from one to another and intervening when one woman used the staff too viciously and when another aimed too close to the chamber pot. Micah continued to curse, but not as loudly. His attempts at escape slowed and then ceased as he curled up to protect his vulnerable parts.

Janto retreated to where Rhianne waited, below a tree, so he could observe without being in the way. It was less his battle now than the women's. He rested his back against the tree. Rhianne slipped her hand into his and leaned into him, shivering. Her presence gave him comfort. Instinctively, he put an arm around her.

"It's disturbing," she said, after watching for a while in silence.

"An unpleasant business," agreed Janto.

The women had lost their fear. Some of them looked scary now, their faces contorted with rage as they rained blows upon the sackcloth bag. Micah stopped cursing and began to plead for relief.

"You think we should let him out?" asked Rhianne.

"No," said Janto. Micah was tough. Halfway measures wouldn't work. He had to be thoroughly frightened and humiliated.

The beating continued until the women's fury had abated and the only sound that came from the bag was Micah's hoarse, sobbing breath. Janto caught Sirali's eye and nodded. He hid himself under the invisibility shroud.

Sirali collected the staves from the women and

dropped them on the ground. She tossed away the chamber pot and untied the rope that bound Micah's feet, then retreated into the circle of women who stood around the bag.

At first there was no movement from within the bag. Janto worried they'd overdone it and killed him.

Then the sackcloth moved. Micah backed slowly out of the bag, taking several minutes to extract himself. After freeing his legs and torso, he pushed the lip of the bag over his head with shaking hands. He was wild-eyed, his hair and clothes mussed. He looked up, saw the women surrounding him, and froze, so still it seemed he'd stopped breathing. His head turned slowly as he took them all in.

As if on cue, they filed back into the slave house. They walked differently than before. Straighter. Prouder.

Soon nobody was left in the clearing except Micah. Janto and Rhianne watched him from the safety of the shroud. After a while, Micah stood, shaky and bent with pain. He turned and trudged back to the men's slave house.

When he was well away, Rhianne let out a sigh. "Gods," she said. "I don't know how I feel about that. What an ugly business! But I think it succeeded."

"Did you see the look on his face when he came out of the bag and all the women stood around him?" said Janto.

"That part was an inspiration," admitted Rhianne. "And I think it will help, as far as deterring future attacks on the women. He clearly didn't understand how he ended up in the bag. That had to frighten him."

Janto nodded. "If he doesn't know how he was captured, he can't strategize to find a way to avoid being captured again. The only way is to avoid angering the women."

"Janto, look." Her hand on his arm again. "Is that the woman we saw before?"

"Where?" He followed her gaze. The door to the women's slave house had opened, and the woman Micah had dragged out, the one he'd meant to assault in the first place, was heading into the woods. "What's she up to?"

"I don't know," said Janto. "I think we should find out."

He trotted after her invisibly, with Rhianne at his side. The woman ran down the snaky forest path that led to the men's slave house. Toward Micah? Did she intend to hurt him even more? Or was something else going on? Then she headed into the trees, slowing to a walk and looking all around. She put her hands to her mouth and made a sound like a bird calling.

Through the trees came an answering call. She turned and jogged toward it, slowing to a walk when she reached a small clearing.

A man stepped out from behind a tree trunk.

Janto clutched Rhianne's hand, instinctively stepping in front of her, though they were both invisible. But the woman they were following seemed to expect this stranger. She ran to him, and they embraced. Then the woman began to talk. Janto was too far away to hear, but from the gestures, it was clear she was describing the events that had taken place at the women's slave house.

"Is he her lover?" Rhianne whispered beside him.

The couple embraced again, their two forms merging to one in the moonlight. Janto knew he'd passed beyond legitimate investigation into voyeurism, and he ought to turn away from watching this private moment, but the sight reminded him of own private yearnings: a homeland and a family he wanted desperately to see again, a Kjallan princess he desired but who was intended for someone else. Something ached deep in his chest. "I believe he is."

The distant figures separated just enough to share a kiss.

"Let's leave them alone," said Rhianne.

Janto nodded, swallowing the lump in his throat. He turned, still holding Rhianne's hand, and began walking back the way they'd come.

"I never think about that, you know," said Rhianne. "That the palace slaves have lives outside of fetching my supper trays. Or if they don't, they want to."

"They're my people—some of them—so I think about it a lot."

"I suppose you must. I feel we've done something right for these people tonight. Something good."

"I believe we have," agreed Janto.

Rhianne nestled against his shoulder as they walked, her warmth delicious in the cool evening air. "Janto, I have something to ask you."

"Ask."

"Not here. Let's—let's get the equipment first."

In silence, they returned to the clearing by the women's slave house. They packed the staves and ropes and chamber pot into the sackcloth bag, and Janto hoisted it onto his shoulder. "Where to?"

Rhianne looked about helplessly and pointed in what seemed a random direction. Janto shrugged and followed her.

16

Rhianne didn't know the area and didn't have anywhere specific in mind. She just wanted a private, secluded spot with enough room to spread out a blanket. She found a quiet glade that seemed adequate for the purpose and halted. Janto lowered the bag to the ground and gazed at her expectantly.

Now for the proposal. "Janto, I . . ." Her breath caught, and she trailed off and looked away.

"What is it?" he asked gently.

Her legs felt weak. She looked around for a place to sit, but there wasn't a stump or log anywhere. She swallowed. *Courage.* "I was wondering if you would make love to me."

Janto drew back, his eyes wary. "Are you certain? Is there—will there be trouble?"

She blushed furiously. "No one will know. We're alone out here, and shrouded, and . . . Look. I don't love Augustan, and I don't want him to be the first or only man I ever sleep with. I want that man to be you."

Janto's expression softened. He held out a hand. "Come here, Princess."

She went to him, her shoulders dropping in relief. He enfolded her in the circle of his arms and kissed her, teasing her mouth open as if testing her, ascertaining for himself whether she truly wanted this. She yielded to the invasion, softening her body against him, surprising even herself as a sound of longing purred from her throat. *This* was the man she wanted, the gentle scholar who'd bantered with her in the gardens and gently prodded her to a deeper understanding of both of their countries, the spy who'd played games with her at the bridge. Not Augustan, and not some random Kjallan either.

Heat pooled deep inside her body, a paradoxical mix of pleasure and warmth and dissatisfaction, an unscratched itch that had her pressing closer to Janto, kissing him and wrapping her arms around him, trying to satisfy that unsatisfied place.

"Hold a moment," he said, restraining her. "You've not been with a man before?"

"I have not. You don't mind?"

"No. Will Augustan expect a virgin on his wedding night?"

"Kjallan women seldom go virginal to the wedding bed." She'd never intended to wait this long; she was just *choosy*. And with so many men away at war, there had never been a lot of options.

"Are you nervous?" he murmured in her ear.

"No." She wanted this, and she'd chosen the right man. However, losing one's virginity was supposed to hurt—sometimes there was even blood—and that worried her. Perhaps she ought not to bend the truth. "A little."

"We'll go at your pace," said Janto. "If you don't like anything or you change your mind, you tell me to stop, and I will." He looked around. "I don't think the forest floor is going to be very comfortable."

"I brought a blanket." She went to the bag and fished out a blue coverlet, which she spread on the ground.

"You *planned* this."

Her cheeks warmed. Indeed she had. "You're leaving the country soon, so it's my last chance."

Janto knelt and fingered the blanket, gauging its thickness. "This won't be as nice as a bed. Especially the sort of bed an imperial princess is accustomed to."

"I don't care." She sat beside him. "Better you and a blanket on the hard ground than Augustan and all the feather pillows in the world."

He flashed her an affectionate smile. "Are you warded? I've been away from my people for a while. My own wards might have faded by now."

She'd considered that already. "My wards were applied a few days ago. I won't get pregnant."

He held out his arms again. She went to him, and he bore her gently to the ground. He examined her syrtos and fingered its double belts. When the knots stymied him, he gave up on them, straddled her, and removed his slave tunic instead.

Janto didn't look Kjallan—not remotely. His chest wasn't pale but golden, bronzed by the tropical sun of his homeland and dusted with a smattering of light brown hair. He was watching her, she realized, drinking in her admiring gaze. He leaned down and kissed her gently. She felt nervous about touching him, but she sensed he wanted her to, so she raised her hands uncertainly and stroked the sides of his body. As her confidence grew, she let her fingers explore, outlining the muscles on his back and shoulders. He leaned into her touch, yet he looked tense.

"Are you all right?" whispered Rhianne.

"Quite all right. Being with a virgin presents certain challenges. I want you very badly, but I don't want to hurt you." He reached again for the dual belts of her syrtos.

Much as it tickled her to see him struggle with the oddities of Kjallan fashion, she helped him unknot the belts. Then she sat up so he could pull off her syrtos and unlace her corset. At last they were skin to skin, and the wonderful but strangely urgent sensation returned, the unscratched itch that made her want to get closer to him, always closer.

Janto gathered her into his arms. He was big and warm and . . . big. Janto was not the tallest or burliest of men, yet compared to her, his size was substantial, and until he'd taken her into this intimate embrace, she had never been so aware of it. His erect cock rested against her thigh, and that too was intimidating. It was astonishing to think she would be taking that into her body. He stroked his tongue into her mouth, and her thoughts fell away. She wrapped her arms around his neck, deepening the kiss. Her breasts brushed his chest, sending a delightful tingle through her body, but mostly she wanted to get closer. She looped a leg over his, capturing it. Her breathing quickened.

He wrestled with her, chuckling as he broke her hold on his mouth. "Easy. I know what you want, but I can't give it to you if you hold me so tight."

"I need—," she murmured, and, uncertain exactly what she needed except *him*, she captured his mouth again.

He broke the hold again. "Lie back."

Reluctantly, she did so. She wanted so much to hold

him, to be close to him, but to her disappointment he wasn't moving in for a kiss at all. Well, at least she was initially disappointed. Instead, he was doing something with his tongue on her breast. That produced a wonderful shivery feeling that went all the way through her and made that unscratched-itch feeling more delightful and more unbearable at the same time. She arched her back, both from the torture of it and to shove her breasts closer to him.

"Rhianne." He laughed. "You are an absolutely delightful lover."

"I am?" She was surprised to hear it. "Well, you're torturing me."

"I'm not; you're just very sensitive." He licked her nipple and grinned at her convulsive shudder. "See?"

She stared back, nonplussed. How was she supposed to respond?

"Stay there," said Janto. He moved farther away, down toward her hips, and parted her legs. She trembled a little. That part of her was so private, so intimate. He leaned down and licked.

Oh gods. That was what she needed. She was about to tell him to do that again, but there was no need. He was at it already, and she was awash in sensations she hardly knew how to process. She felt restless and uncertain, like there was something she ought to be doing except she didn't know what it was. But Janto gripped her legs, stilling her. She let herself relax and just enjoy what he was doing with his tongue. The compulsion to press herself into him was gone, and she understood that he had been right; this was what her body had been craving.

His strokes, gentle at first, became stronger. Something was building inside her. It felt lovely, so she let it spiral upward, until the sensations became so overwhelming that her body was no longer her own. Her hips moved of their own accord, and Janto shifted to accommodate them. For a moment, she feared he would stop what he was doing, which was unthinkable, but he didn't. He drove her on.

Then everything changed. Sweetness flooded her, so joyous, so luscious that she threw back her head with a cry. Her body shuddered in Janto's grasp. Time slowed, and a languorous feeling seeped through her.

Janto returned to her arms, covering her body with his own.

"Am I ready now for the other part?" she said.

"You should be."

She was afraid of the hymen-breaking, but it needed doing, and better Janto should do it than Augustan. She shifted beneath him, tilting her hips to meet his. He began to enter her, slowly and gently.

She shut her eyes. Pain. Searing pain.

His movement stopped. "Does it hurt?"

"A little," she said in a tight voice.

He remained still and kissed her on the forehead. "I'm sorry."

"Just go in. I'll be fine."

"No. Let's talk for a moment while your body adjusts." He took one of her breasts in his hand, circling her nipple with his thumb.

She arched her back at the electric sensation. There was that unscratched-itch feeling again, just a hint of it. But she was sensitive, almost *too* sensitive.

Janto noticed and stroked her in less erotic places—

her sides, her back. "You smell like orange blossoms," he said. "It's one of the first things I noticed about you. It reminds me of home. Do you use a scent?"

"It's the baths," said Rhianne. "Scented water. I always choose orange blossoms."

"Tell me about the baths. Is it true you all bathe naked in a giant pool together?"

"Not at all," said Rhianne. "The pools are divided by sex. Men in one, women in another. Most people have to share, but since I'm from the imperial family, I get a bath all to myself if I want it." The pain was receding, and she felt herself beginning to relax.

Janto moved.

There was the pain again, sharp and piercing, but after reaching a crescendo, it began to recede. She felt Janto inside her. It was a strange feeling—a sense of fullness, and his body so close to hers.

He leaned over her, quite still, not yet thrusting. He cradled her face within his hands and kissed her. "I'm sorry to take you by surprise, but you were tense, and I needed you to relax. You're not afraid any more, are you?"

"Should I be?"

"I don't think so," said Janto. "I'll be gentle. If it hurts, say something and I'll stop."

She nodded and wrapped her arms around him, pulling him possessively close. He began to move, slowly, his eyes on her face as he sought evidence of pleasure or pain. There were a few twinges of pain—it was not gone entirely—but they were bearable, and she tried not to let the evidence of their existence show. The pain was not Janto's fault; it was the natural result of her inexperience, and she feared that if he stopped now, he would go unsatisfied. Besides, as he built up a rhythm, pleasure began to overshadow those twinges.

The unscratched-itch feeling was back, but with less urgency. It was more a languid enjoyment of the sensations, a *yes, that's nice, keep doing it* feeling rather than the insatiable longing she'd experienced before. She entwined one of her legs with Janto's, and he accelerated his rhythm. It was so wonderfully intimate, him inside her body, taking pleasure and giving it. Janto groaned. She worried at first that he was hurting. Then she realized it was the opposite. He stiffened and drove against her, spilling his seed.

He withdrew and dropped onto his side, looking spent as a rained-out thunderhead. A light sheen of sweat covered his body. He grabbed his tunic and draped it over them to prevent chills, then pulled her into his arms. "Are you all right?"

"More than all right," said Rhianne. "But do you think . . ." She hesitated. "Will it hurt next time?" That was a stupid question. Next time would be with Augustan. Why even bring this up?

Janto didn't answer right away. "Every woman is different," he said finally. "It probably won't."

She'd given Janto her virginity, and she would never regret that choice. She could not have asked for a kinder, more considerate lover. But did it really have to end here? If next time wasn't going to hurt, why not spend that next time with Janto instead of Augustan? She couldn't send him home to Mosar anyway, not if Florian intended to "purge" the Mosari ruling class. "Will you meet me again tomorrow?"

"No," said Janto. "I have to leave the country, or somebody will turn me in to the authorities."

"Stay one more day, and I won't turn you in."

Janto turned to her. "Why? Because you want to sleep with me?"

"No." Gods, was she that transparent? "Well, maybe. Look, this is important. When you leave the country, where are you going to go?"

"I'm not sure I should tell you," said Janto.

"*Must* you be like this?" She toyed with the hairs on his chest. "I ask because you can't go back to Mosar. You'll be killed. Augustan plans to murder the entire Mosari aristocracy."

Janto stiffened beneath her fingers. Clearly the news was a shock. But he said nothing. At least he wasn't denying he was part of the aristocracy.

Rhianne nudged him. "Are you listening? You can't go back to Mosar."

"Where would you have me go?"

"Sardos or Inya. As a refugee."

Janto sniffed. "You insult me. I would never abandon my people."

"Janto!" she hissed. "If you go back, you'll be killed!"

"Better that than to live as a coward and a traitor."

She hugged him, pulling his sun-bronzed body close. How could he be so careless with his own life? "Don't say such things! And please, let's not fight. I just made love for the first time. This is not what I want to remember, you and I fighting afterward."

He kissed her, stroking her cheek. "I don't want to fight either. But you're asking something of me that I can't do."

"Stay one more day," she pleaded, "and I won't turn you in. Will you meet me by the bridge tomorrow at noon?"

Janto hesitated a moment, then said, "Yes."

He helped her lace up the corset. She put on her syrtos, rolled up the blanket, and gave him a good-night kiss. Then she headed back to the palace through the moonlit forest. His scent lingered on her body for a moment and then faded.

17

Janto waited impatiently for Rhianne at the bridge. She'd given him a critical piece of intelligence during their liaison last night, though not a welcome one. The Kjallans intended to murder the entire Mosari aristocracy.

Since then, he'd debated what to do with the information. Should the aristocracy evacuate Mosar? The aristocrats were, for the most part, also Mosar's mages, and for them to leave in the middle of the war would spoil any chance Mosar had at winning. But there wasn't much chance of that anyway.

After much thought, he'd decided the intelligence had to be passed along at his first opportunity. His father and mother, back on Mosar, would decide what to do with it.

Around noon, Rhianne trotted up on horseback, riding a white mare and leading a dapple gray gelding. She rode astride, not sidesaddle, and wore a shorter-than-usual syrtos, no loros at all, and braccae—Kjallan riding pants. He'd seen mounted soldiers wearing such pants, but never a woman.

"Can you ride?" she asked.

"Yes." He glanced around to make sure no one was watching, then shrouded all of them, including the horses. "We're invisible now. Did you not attract attention, bringing a second horse?"

She shrugged. "I used a lot of forgetting spells." She offered him the reins to the dapple gray. "This is Flash. He's big and—well, flashy. He picks up his feet when he trots, which means he's kind of bouncy to ride. But he's quiet and sensible, and if we don't go too fast—"

"I'll be fine. I've done a lot of riding." Janto took the reins, put his foot in the stirrup, and swung up onto Flash. "Where are we going?"

"I want to show you something. It's a surprise." She turned the mare and sent her into a canter.

Janto gathered Flash's reins and sent him after her, noting with pleasure how the animal arched his neck and moved up to the bit without being asked. They cantered in single file along a soft-dirt avenue. Passing through a pair of marble gates, they left the Imperial Palace grounds.

The road sloped downward as they traveled inland, away from the city and the harbor. Smoke rose from the chimneys of distant cottages. Farmland in the distant hills, dotted with pockets of trees, checkered the landscape in green and yellow.

Janto clucked to Flash, who responded with an instant burst of speed and surged alongside Rhianne's mare. "How far?"

"Just ahead." She pointed to a forest that lay cradled in the next valley. "Bow oaks. They're in season."

He'd heard of bow oaks, valuable trees for shipbuilding, much coveted on Mosar, where they did not grow. Bow oaks provided "compass timber"—wood with a natural curve used to form the rounded frame of a ship. Such trees were of great economic and military importance, but he wasn't sure why Rhianne would want to show him a forest.

They veered onto a side road, downhill into the valley. One moment there were fields on either side of them, and the next moment there were trees. Big, fine trees, obviously cultivated. Each tree leaned over to one side or the other, its trunk forming a shallow arc.

The path dwindled away to nothing, and as the trees pressed closer around them, they slowed their horses to a walk. One of the trees had a symbol marked on it in red paint: a half circle crossed with a slash.

Janto pointed to the mark. "What does that mean?"

"That tree has been selected for harvest," said Rhianne. "It'll be chopped down and hauled to the shipyards at the end of the season."

Spring seemed to have come late to the bow oaks; they were mostly just bare trunks and branches. Up in the canopy were large, ungainly white flowers and some curious growths—enormous fruits or seed pods, perhaps.

A gunshot went off behind him.

Janto drove his horse toward Rhianne to shield her from the unknown attacker. He looked around frantically but couldn't see anyone. At least they were invisible. Rhianne seemed oddly unflustered.

Another gunshot went off.

"Where are they?" he cried. "Who are they firing at?"

"Nobody's firing anything. It's the trees," said Rhianne.

"What do you mean it's the trees?"

"Officially they're called bow oaks, but sometimes we call them poppers. That sound is the trees popping." Rhianne's white mare stood calmly, as did Flash. Apparently the horses knew what was going on.

He looked up. "The trees are *popping*?"

"You see the lumps on the branches, way up there? They explode."

"How?" Janto scanned the trees. He heard another gunshot sound behind him. He whipped his head around and caught the end of whatever had happened. A cloud of yellow powder rained down over several of the trees.

"Some sort of alchemical reaction. It's how they reproduce. Why don't we walk a bit and give the horses a rest?" Rhianne dismounted, pulled the reins over the white mare's head, and set the ends on the ground. "You can leave Flash there; he ground ties."

Janto pulled the reins over Flash's head and tugged them downward to remind him to stay put. Flash flicked an ear back, insulted.

Rhianne unfastened a bundle from her mare's saddle and carried it with her. Janto suspected it was another blanket. He walked at Rhianne's side through the deep carpet of old, decaying leaves, staring at the branches overhead. He was rewarded when a popper finally exploded before his eyes. The strange lump broke open with a bang. It propelled a large yellow bullet shape into the trees, which broke into a stream of powder and rained down. "What do you mean it's how they reproduce?"

"You know how with fruit trees, you need a hive of bees in the orchard to pollinate them? These trees don't need bees. The explosion sends the pollen onto the flowers of other trees."

"So it's like . . . It's like . . ." He chuckled. "It's a bit vulgar, isn't it?"

Her cheeks colored. "Janto, these are *trees*."

"I know. But I don't want any of that stuff to fall on me."

"So what if it falls on you? It's *pollen*. You get pollen on you all the time."

"It's just—I don't know. Something about the way it's delivered." He grinned.

"Come on, don't you think it's interesting?"

"It's very interesting," said Janto.

"You told me about all the fascinating things you've seen on Mosar. I wanted to show you something on Kjall—something you hadn't seen before. You've seen so many wonders, and I've seen so few."

The anxious look on her face told him this was a bad time to tease her. She craved his approval, and if he didn't grant it, he'd hurt her feelings. "It's marvelous. I've never seen anything like it."

"Really?" She smiled tentatively.

"Really."

They walked a little farther through the forest. Most of the trees were tall and mature, but there were a few saplings about. One had a red *x* marked on its trunk.

"What does the *x* mean?" Janto asked.

"It means the tree will be culled," said Rhianne. "See how its trunk is nearly straight? The shipbuilders don't want that. They want a curve. They'll chop it down so a new tree can grow."

Rhianne found a bare stump and settled on it. Janto sat beside her and wrapped an arm around her shoulder. A popper went off nearby, startling him. Rhianne did not react at all. Bits of yellow fluff drifted through the tree canopy and landed on their heads.

"I hate to bring this up, but I've been wondering," said Janto. "You've met Augustan now, and you never told me how that went. I take it from what you said last night he didn't meet your approval?"

Rhianne looked away and was silent.

"That bad?" said Janto.

"I don't feel that he respects me. Or values me, except as a link to the throne," said Rhianne.

Janto wrestled with his conscience. In his jealous heart, he was glad Rhianne hadn't liked Augustan. And yet Rhianne could never be his. The obstacles that lay between them were insurmountable. She would marry Augustan, and he could not change that. Given that the marriage was inevitable, shouldn't he wish that she might be happy in it? Even guide her, perhaps, in that direction? "Is it possible you're asking too much of him too soon?" he said gently. "You'd only just met. He barely knows you."

"His feelings will not change. He views me as . . ." She made a face. "As damaged goods."

"Why would he think that? Unless . . . well, because of me and you. But that was later."

"He has a reason. It's a stupid reason, but in his mind it makes sense. Do you know my history?"

Janto shrugged. "You're Florian's niece. You were raised in the palace. I'm missing a lot of details."

"A great many," said Rhianne. "My mother was Florian's younger sister. I guess they were close when they were children—so Florian tells me. Many years ago, before I was born, she was engaged to, I don't know, some nobleman. But she must not have liked him, because she ran off and eloped with an upholsterer."

"An *upholsterer*?"

Rhianne stiffened. "Yes, an upholsterer. Does it bother you to find out my father works in trade?"

Janto threw up his hands. "Not at all."

"They fled east to the city of Rodgany, and then I was

born. Florian wasn't emperor yet. His father, Emperor Nigellus, was. When Nigellus died, Florian succeeded him, and I don't know how he did it, but he tracked my mother down. He came to Rodgany. I was three years old, and Florian took me from my parents. It's the earliest memory I have, Florian carrying me to the imperial barouche while I screamed and kicked, and my parents looking on, crying, but saying nothing. In the carriage, Florian held me and told me everything would be all right. I fell asleep in his lap."

"They knew they couldn't oppose him," said Janto. "What did he do to them? Anything?"

"Aside from taking me, I believe he left them alone. He won't talk to me about them."

"They might have had more children. Do you suppose you might have brothers or sisters?"

"I often wonder that," said Rhianne. "I heard they went deeper into hiding after Florian took me, so if there are more children, there's no telling where they are now."

"What a thought. Your parents are alive, and you might have brothers and sisters!" Janto shook his head in wonder. "I'd assumed they were dead."

"From my perspective, they might as well be. And Florian's greatest fear is that I'll run away like my mother did. Either I'll run off to find her, or I'll run away with some . . . some . . ."

Mosari spy? Janto wondered.

"Upholsterer," she finished lamely. "You have to understand. Florian's not a cruel man—"

Janto snorted. Emperor Florian had authorized the wholesale slaughter of his people.

"But he likes to own things. Possess things. I'm his possession, and he is determined to keep me under his control. Or Augustan's control, which amounts to the same thing."

"I have no sympathy for him. He wants to possess my entire country," said Janto.

"He does," agreed Rhianne. "I'm sorry."

Janto looked at her with a terrible sadness. If only Kjall had not gone to war with Mosar, if only Kjall were not so terribly insular in its patterns of marriage, he might be the one engaged to Rhianne right now instead of Augustan. As the heir to the Mosari throne, he should have been eligible to court her, and he would never have considered her *damaged goods*. Had he courted her in the ordinary way, as a visiting prince, he would have fallen in love with her as surely as he was doing now.

The thought did not surprise him. He did not doubt that he was falling in love. He loved Rhianne's liveliness of mind, her compassion, her bravery. Before Kjall had invaded Mosar, he'd been in a situation similar to hers, though less extreme. He'd known he would have to marry for the good of his country, almost certainly to a stranger and probably not someone greatly to his liking. He was luckier than she in that he was the man, the more powerful party in the marriage. While a hateful wife could make his life unpleasant, there were certain things he didn't have to worry overmuch about, whereas Rhianne could not ignore these concerns. Would Augustan beat her? It was his deepest fear for Rhianne, that Augustan, who did not value the unique and precious creature Janto had made love to last night, would use his fists on her, brutally trying to shape her into something she was not.

Augustan could destroy her.

Rhianne nudged him. "You're thinking about something."

"I was thinking," said Janto, "that if Augustan cannot love a woman as kind and honest and courageous as you, it is his own failing. If he does not love you, then love lies beyond his capabilities."

Rhianne squeezed her eyes shut, as if his words caused her physical pain. "Why did you have to be born Mosari?"

"Why did your country have to invade mine?"

She sighed. "Let's not waste the little time we have arguing about things we can't control." She dropped a bundle of fabric into his lap. "I brought a blanket."

"I'm developing a fondness for blankets."

"The thing is"—she winced—"I'm sore today."

"I feared you might be," said Janto.

"Is it normal?"

"Yes. It shouldn't last long."

She let her breath out in a rush. "Gods, that's a relief. I was afraid something might be wrong with me." She unfolded the blanket. "Aren't there other things we can do? Things that won't hurt when I'm sore, that will satisfy you as well as me?"

"There certainly are." He took an end of the blanket, helping her to spread it on the ground.

"And will you show me?"

"I certainly will," said Janto.

18

Rhianne wriggled out of her clothes and slipped into her lover's embrace, marveling at his easy strength as he lowered her to the ground. As Janto sought her mouth, she twined her legs round his. She felt herself melting into him, as if the nooks and crannies of their bodies were interlocking pieces, designed to fit just so. A popper exploded above them, dusting them lightly with pollen. Janto seemed not to notice or care.

He stroked the side of her face, touching her forehead, her cheek, her ear. She reached up and did the same to him, closing her eyes so her fingers could learn what her eyes already knew. Given time, she would memorize every inch of him in the most intimate detail—though perhaps they did not have that kind of time. She would learn what she could and treasure the memories.

With a groan of impatience, Janto captured her wrists and pushed them down to the blanket. She struggled experimentally, but he held her fast. A little jolt of excitement ran through her. It was a little like fear, and yet it wasn't, because with Janto she always felt safe.

"Do you trust me?" he whispered.

Rhianne swallowed. "Yes."

He took her breast in his mouth. Unable to move her

arms, she arched her back and moaned. So good, so *painfully* good. He circled her nipple with his tongue, teased her, kissed her on her neck and chin until she craved his mouth on her nipple again. Then he tortured her again.

"Tell me you are mine," he said.

"I'm yours," gasped Rhianne, wishing it could be true forever.

Janto grinned. He released her wrists and moved downward.

"Wait." She craved that wicked tongue of his, but she had a different plan in mind. "You first tonight—you said you would show me what to do."

He paused, then settled beside her. "All right."

As he pulled her into his arms, resting his cock against her thigh, she asked, "What do I do? Can I touch it?"

Her took her hand and guided it. Though his cock was hard underneath, the skin on the outside was silky as down. She stroked it gently.

Janto placed his hand over hers and pressed harder, demonstrating. "It wants a firm touch," he explained. "And gods, that feels good."

"It's better if I do it with my mouth, though. Isn't it?"

He made an involuntary noise of longing. "Yes, I like that better. If you want to try it."

It took some time to find a comfortable position, and a bit longer to figure out exactly what to do with her mouth and tongue. Janto gave her some suggestions— the most important seemed to be not to use her teeth— but she found she learned best by experimenting. Running her tongue over one particular spot around the head seemed to be Janto's favorite; it reduced him to panting and incoherent moaning. She was no expert, but it didn't seem to matter. By the look on his face and the sounds he made, she could tell he was enjoying what she was doing.

Now she understood why Janto took such pleasure in pinning her arms and torturing her with his mouth. She felt *powerful*. He was bigger than she and far stronger, yet when she put her mouth on him, she was the one in control.

"Gods," he said. "Rhianne, I'm—I'm . . ." He gasped and pulled away. With a great cry, he shuddered through his climax.

Rhianne kissed him, rubbing his back as he caught his breath and came down from the high. "I could have stayed with you through that."

"Your first time," he panted. "Didn't want to startle you. But next time . . ."

"I want to," said Rhianne.

Janto pulled her into his arms. He rested a short while, idly kissing and stroking her, and when he was ready, he took her to paradise.

Later that afternoon, Rhianne led Dice into Morgan's tiny stable. The slave boy hurried forward to take the reins.

"You're late," said Morgan from the doorway. "Was starting to worry about you."

"I'm sorry. I hope you didn't run short of money." Rhianne climbed the short stairway from the stable to the house and handed him the tetrals. "I've been busy. Augustan came for a visit, and . . . well, other things have happened."

"Augustan!" Morgan's eyebrows rose. "Are you engaged? Was there a big to-do?" He headed into the kitchen.

"Yes and yes."

"We'll open a bottle of wine." He went to a chest and pulled out a bottle. He worked at the cork a bit and winced.

Rhianne took it from him and uncorked the bottle.

Morgan grunted an apology about his feeble fingers, grabbed two mismatched cups, and poured. Rhianne trailed after him into the sitting room, where he took a seat and sipped his wine. He gestured at the chair across from him. "So, tell me about your fiancé."

"I hate him," said Rhianne.

Morgan choked on his wine and smacked his chest, coughing. "Not what I expected you to say."

"Wouldn't you think that a man who came to the palace to court his future wife would be on his best behavior?" said Rhianne. "Even if he were by nature mean and nasty, he should be perfect for those two days, because anyone can fake it at least that long, right?"

"I would think so," said Morgan. "Depends how aware he is of his behavior and how it's perceived."

"Augustan yelled at the servants and wanted them beaten for trivial mistakes, he was nasty to me when I wasn't feeling well, and he insulted me to my face. If that was his best behavior, what's he going to be like when the emperor isn't looking over his shoulder?"

"He *insulted* you?"

"Right to my face!"

"What did he say?" Morgan's forehead wrinkled. "What fault could he find in you?"

Rhianne laughed. "You're sweet. I have many faults. Ask my cousin, and he'll provide you with a list. But in this case, Augustan referred to the *shame of my birth*."

Morgan rolled his eyes. "Because of your mother."

"Yes, and my father being a tradesman."

"Clearly this fiancé of yours is a vile human being." Morgan pointed to her wineglass. "Drink."

Rhianne drank. "He *is* vile, and I have no choice but to marry him."

Morgan peered into his empty cup, swirling the dregs as if they had a story to tell. "You always have a choice, Rhianne."

She shook her head. "If I run away, Florian will catch me. He's got the whole army at his disposal. My mother didn't outwit Nigellus. He *let* her go."

"Perhaps you underestimate yourself."

Rhianne sipped her wine. She didn't think Morgan truly understood Florian, even after everything the emperor had done to him. Her uncle was tenacious as a badger; if she fled from him, he'd never stop hunting for her. Besides, she had to be realistic. For all that she might dream of running away with Janto, her Mosari lover remained fanatically loyal to his people and to his mission, whatever that was. And Florian needed her to help govern Mosar. Part of her hoped that Augustan wouldn't be so awful, that over time she'd win him over, and while their marriage might not ever be wonderful, it might at least be tolerable.

"Consider this," said Morgan. "Running away and marrying Augustan aren't necessarily your only two choices. Also, what Augustan said wasn't a slip of the tongue. One doesn't become a high-ranking legatus by being a fool. He said it deliberately."

"What do you mean?"

Morgan set his wineglass on the table. "I've known men like this before. Augustan feels threatened because *you outrank him*. You are an emperor's niece and adopted daughter; he is merely a legatus and soon-to-be provincial governor. Most men would be proud to make such a distinguished marriage, but Augustan is clearly frightened by a wife who is more powerful than he is. He wants to diminish your power by shaming you, so that you feel that you're a fraud, that you're not a true member of the emperor's family."

"I never thought of it that way," said Rhianne.

"You can't marry this man, because insults are only the beginning," said Morgan. "Men of this sort can't tolerate anyone else having power, especially their wives, and also their children. He'll mistreat the children you'll have someday, Rhianne. Have you thought of that? If you won't stop this marriage for your own sake, do it for theirs."

At a seaside cliff several hours' walk from the Imperial Palace, Janto summoned a ball of flickering blue magelight, sent it through a series of orchestrated movements, and dismissed it. He sat and waited, shivering in the darkness. Beneath him the breakers rolled in, each one crashing against unseen rocks and retreating with a disappointed hiss. The ocean was a wall of blackness broken only by a field of stars that demarcated where water ended and sky began.

In the blackness, a blue light appeared. Janto froze, watching its movements carefully. Up, to the right, a circle. Left. Another circle. It was the answering signal of his spy ship.

Once he transmitted his message to the ship, it would need four to six days to relay its coded message to the next signal station and return. That was four to six days he would be stranded on Kjall. Also four to six days during which time, if he found a better piece of intelligence, he would have no way to transmit it. But given the number of lives he might save with the information Rhianne had given him, and its urgency—his people on Mosar might not hold out much longer—he'd decided he had no real choice but to send it and hope for the best.

He'd coded his message earlier in the day and had only to put his magelight ball through its paces: up and down, side to side, around in circles, winking in and out. *Ral-Vaddis killed in action. Kjallans to purge Mosari ruling class as they did in Riorca. Relay immediately and return.*

He dismissed his magelight and waited for the answering signal. It came, and, to his surprise, it was not a simple acknowledgment. The spy ship had intelligence to relay to him as well. He'd brought paper and a quill in anticipation of this possibility, and as the signals came, he transcribed them. Professional signalers could decode as they watched, but he wasn't experienced enough for that. When the signal ended, he decoded it with quill and paper. *Kal-Torres's fleet sighted off Bartleshore.*

Now that was interesting. Kal-Torres, his younger brother, was First Admiral of the Mosari Navy. It was tradition on Mosar that the king should command the island's army while one of his close relatives commanded its navy. Janto, since he was a shroud mage, was in charge of Mosari Intelligence, a small command his father had hoped would prepare him for the larger command he would inherit later—if, after the war, there was anything left to inherit.

Kal-Torres, similarly, had been captain of a single ship in the Mosari Navy. But when the Mosari and Kjallan fleets had clashed at the beginning of the war, most of the Mosari ships had been sunk or captured, and the First Admiral, Janto's uncle, had been killed in action. Kal-Torres had broken away and escaped with a small fleet of wounded ships. It was believed they were repairing and refitting at an unknown location. Kal-Torres was promoted to First Admiral in absentia. Apparently now his little fleet was back in action, although what good it might do at this late date, Janto could not say.

He signaled acknowledgment and dismissal to his spy ship, glad to have dispatched his intelligence but anxious about being stranded for a minimum of four days, and began the long walk back to the palace.

Rhianne's attendants were just leaving when the morning breakfast tray arrived. She wasn't usually hungry in the morning, but having gone for an early swim in the baths before getting dressed, she had worked up a bit of an appetite. She grabbed one of her Mosari books so she could study while she ate, watching as the last of the servants trailed through the door and left her blessedly alone. Then she sat.

A bit of movement caught her eye. Whiskers? Surely the brindlecat had not escaped her cage.

A strawberry and white ferret leapt onto her blue damask settee at the side of the room, chittered briefly, and curled up to sleep.

Rhianne stared at the ferret, her heart throbbing, all her muscles tensed for action. That was Janto's familiar. Was Janto here? Perhaps he had sneaked into the room invisibly when the servants were moving in and out, but he hadn't revealed himself. She looked slowly about the room, searching for signs of his presence.

"Janto?" she called softly.

No answer.

With shaky hands, she reached for one of the covers on her breakfast tray and picked it up. Then she shrieked as the cover was pulled from her hand and replaced on the tray.

The heavy door to her sitting room opened a crack, and Tamienne poked her head in. "Everything all right, Your Imperial Highness?"

"Fine," called Rhianne. "Whiskers growled from her cage and . . . startled me."

The door closed again.

She couldn't see him, but there was no doubt about it. Janto was here. "What are you up to?" she whispered.

Still no answer. Then she felt a whisper-soft touch on the sides of her neck—Janto, still invisible. Her ghostly lover was behind her. She relaxed into the warm, invisible hands, letting them stroke her. Her hair rose, lifted by the ghost. She let him run his hands through it and feather it back to her shoulders.

"Gods, Janto," she said. "This had better be you and not someone else."

The hands left her, and she regretted having spoken. A quill and piece of paper lifted themselves from her desk in the corner and moved, seemingly of their own accord, through the air toward her. The paper landed on the table, and the quill wrote *Alligator*.

"I knew it had to be—" She couldn't finish because his lips covered hers, and hands cradled her face. She moaned in pleasure and reached for her ghost, hoping to capture his invisible form in her arms, but the moment she made contact, he departed, leaving her lips tingling and her body craving more. She looked around the room, trying to guess where he had gone, but he made no sign.

"All right, so I'm not allowed to grab you. Come back." She waited.

No response.

She got up from her chair, hunger entirely banished—hunger for food, anyway—and moved about the room. Where was he? She was tempted to fling her hands out and search for him as if they were playing some ridiculous children's game, but she'd only look like a fool. She wouldn't find him unless he wanted to be found.

Frustrated, she halted in the center of the room. If she couldn't chase him down, could she lure him in? She unknotted the double belts of her syrtos and removed first one belt, then the other. She parted her syrtos, and—damn it, why did she have to wear a corset? She would never get the dratted thing off without help. Improvising, she reached into her corset and lifted her breasts up and out. She stroked the nipples that peaked out and closed her eyes, pleasuring herself, all the while imagining it was Janto caressing her.

And there he was, her ghost lover, touching her breasts, licking them, kissing them. The corset was in his way. The ghost seemed to grow frustrated with it, and soon he was behind her, tugging at the straps and untying them, freeing her from the confining garment. Her loosened syrtos came off over her head, the corset fell to the ground, and her legs swept up out from under her. She bit her lip to stifle her cry of surprise—it would not do to have Tamienne poke her head into the room now and see her suspended in the air, wearing only her shift.

Janto carried her into the bedroom. She couldn't see him, but wrapping an arm around him, she could feel he was entirely substantial beneath his shroud. When they reached the bed, he tossed her onto it without ceremony.

The goose feather pillows and comforter deflated beneath her with a pouf of escaped air. Rhianne reached for her ghost lover, but her arms met only emptiness. She looked around. Where had he gone this time? Perhaps he was getting undressed.

"Close the door," she suggested.

Moments later, the bedroom door swung closed.

She sat up in bed, poised and ready to pounce on him like a cat, but she had no idea where he was. He could come from any direction. The comforter sank on one side of the bed. There he was! She swiped the air, hoping to grab him, but missed and found herself tackled, borne to the bed by her invisible lover. Heat pooled between her legs. Deprived of anything to look at or listen to since he couldn't speak through the shroud, she could focus only on sensations. His weight, pressing her into the down comforter. The strength of his arms, pinning her wrists. His skin, smooth and dry as it moved against hers. His mouth, hot and insistent as he kissed her again and again.

"I wish you would talk," she said through the kisses.

Her ghost lover released her wrists and pulled her shift off over her head. He placed his hand on her side and made a circular motion.

He was talking with his hands, but Rhianne didn't know that language. He tugged her gently into position, and she guessed that he wanted her on her side. He moved to spoon her, hugging her back to his chest. He was still invisible, but all over her, so present with his touch that it almost didn't matter that she couldn't see him. He entered her like silk. The hand beneath her reached up to cradle her breast, and the other touched that place that made her buck against him.

She couldn't hear his voice get huskier or his breathing get heavier, but she could *feel* him. Each thrust, in this odd but exquisite sideways position, was an undulation of their joined bodies, and as his excitement grew, his grip on her tightened, and the undulations came faster and harder. Her pleasure swelled within her, reaching its sweet tendrils throughout her body, until it burst, white-hot. She cried out in surprise and desperate joy as her ghost lover completed his final thrusts.

She collapsed on the bed, and when she next opened her eyes, she saw Janto's arm around her.

"*Now* you're visible. Can I finally talk to you?"

He turned her in his arms and cradled her head on his shoulder. "That's the trouble with the shroud. It's all or nothing, both sight and sound. I can't make myself audible but not visible, or the other way around."

She punched him lightly in the side. "I can't believe you came in here and made love to me like a ghost. Without saying a word!"

He laughed. "You liked it. Admit it."

"I liked it a lot. I never thought of lovemaking as a game, but that was fun."

"Why be lovers if you can't have fun with each other?" said Janto.

The thought made Rhianne a little sad. She couldn't imagine Augustan playing games in the bedroom. It would be all business for him.

"You haven't turned me in to the authorities yet," teased Janto.

"I still might."

Janto shook his head. "You're never going to turn me in."

Rhianne gave him a withering look. He had her dead

to rights. She would neither turn him in to be tortured and killed here on Kjall, nor would she send him home to Mosar to be killed there. She didn't want to be a traitor to her country. But she'd prefer that to being a murderer. "Listen. What's going on between us can't last. Your country is going to be conquered, and I'm going to marry Augustan. Neither of us likes it, but we can't change it. You have to go to Sardos or Inya. Not because I'm going to turn you in, but because there isn't an alternative. If you stay here, someone besides me will catch you."

"But if I leave, I'll miss out on another enchanting visit to the Forest of Ejaculating Trees—"

She laughed and punched him in the shoulder. "They're called bow oaks! And you haven't done much better. On our first date, you took me to a beating."

"You make a good point," said Janto. "Clearly I have no notion of how to seduce an imperial princess."

"Be serious for a moment," said Rhianne. "You have to leave the country before you're caught and killed."

"We've had this discussion already," said Janto. "It didn't turn out well."

"You want to help your people," said Rhianne. "I understand and respect that. But when Mosar is conquered, your duty to your people ends. Then you can go to Sardos or Inya with a clean conscience."

"My duty to Mosar never ends," said Janto. "Not if it is conquered, not if it is burned to the ground. Not even if it sinks into the sea."

Rhianne rolled her eyes. "Could you be any more stubborn and exasperating?"

"You are no compliant lapdog yourself," said Janto, pulling her closer. "I regret that we cannot marry and have stubborn, exasperating children."

His words brought a lump to her throat. There were nights when she lay awake staring at the ceiling, terrified of her upcoming marriage to Augustan, and fantasizing about a life with Janto, complete with children. Maybe not stubborn and exasperating ones—she imagined them intelligent and kind, like Janto—but she'd take them however they came. Janto, perhaps sensing her melancholy, rubbed her back. She closed her eyes, letting herself drift.

"Janto," she said drowsily, "do you think a husband ought to stop his wife from drinking at a party, if he thinks she is drinking too much?"

"Well, I don't know," said Janto. "Does the wife have a drinking problem?"

"No," said Rhianne. "She only drinks at parties. She might have been drinking more than usual at this particular party because she was upset."

"I'm sorry she was upset. Were other people drinking?"

"Everyone was drinking. Almost everyone."

"Was the husband drinking?"

"Not much."

"I think Augustan can go climb a lorim cliff in a thunderstorm," said Janto. "If he depresses his future wife so much that she wants to drink, he's the last person who should complain about it."

Rhianne laughed into his chest, but it was a sad laughter, one that walked a line between mirth and tears. "How did you know I was talking about Augustan?"

"You're transparent as rainwater, love," he said. "Part of your prodigious charm."

19

Janto hurried to meet Iolo and Sirali, who waited for him in the darkness beneath the trees.

"You're late," said Iolo. "We were starting to worry."

Janto shook his head. "Sometimes it's hard getting out of the palace. Closed doors and all."

"What were you doing in the palace?" asked Iolo. "Searching for intelligence or visiting your princess?"

"Both," said Janto. "Everything valuable I've learned so far has come from Rhianne. How's Micah been since the sackcloth treatment? Will we need to repeat the treatment?"

"That first evening he came to hand out abeyance spells, his face was white as a pox boil," said Sirali.

Janto nodded eagerly. "We scared him. That's good."

"Right, and a few days later, he did what we thought he'd do. He pulled a couple women aside and tried to get them to tack—"

"To what?"

"Change sides," explained Sirali. "He offered them extra rations, special favors."

"And?" This was the part of the operation that worried Janto most, that Micah might find one or two women willing to betray the others. If he could divide the women, he might regain his power over them.

"Linna was one of them he tried. He pulled her aside, asked her who set up that business the other night. She blinked at him, innocent-like, and said, 'What business?' He wouldn't explain what he meant—couldn't come out with it. He'd go at the subject sideways, and she'd sidle away."

"Did anyone, uh, *tack*?"

She shook her head. "We agreed that if anyone did, we'd spit in her oatmeal every day, and worse."

Janto feared for Sirali, since if Micah did convince someone to name the instigator, that person, not knowing much about Janto, would name her. But Sirali seemed not to fear this prospect. Janto had the impression that Sirali had already been through the worst life had to offer, so something like this didn't intimidate her much. "Was that the end of it, then?"

"No," said Sirali. "A few days later, he got cod-proud again and grabbed Mori."

"Grabbed her! You mean—"

"Right, and I'm not finished," said Sirali. "A dozen of us rushed him. We didn't plan it. Didn't even think about it. It was gods-inspired, like we all had the same thought at once. He let go of Mori's arm and ran like a field mouse from a grass fire." She grinned, exposing her crooked teeth. "He's not touched a one of us since."

Pleased, Janto held out his hand to Sirali, and they interlocked index fingers in the gesture of shared victory.

"I have figured something out," said Rhianne as Janto materialized in her sitting room the next day. "You always arrive at mealtimes. I think you're using me for food."

"I'm definitely using you," said Janto, lifting the cover off her dinner tray. "But not for food. It would help if your doors opened at other times of the day."

"If you left me a note, I might know when to expect you," said Rhianne. "Then I could arrange for the door to open at the proper time."

Janto tasted her potato-and-leek soup. "I prefer surprising you."

"If you wish to have dinner with me, there's a price to pay," said Rhianne.

He looked at her, eyebrows raised, with the spoon still in his hand.

"You will tell me something about yourself."

"Tell you what?"

"I told you about my background, how Florian stole me away from my real parents, how Lucien and I were the terrors of the palace because we were the backup children, of interest only as future marriage prospects. But I know almost nothing about you."

"I'm a shroud mage. I speak five languages. I climbed lorim cliffs as a boy—"

Rhianne shook her head. "I mean your *family*. It's obvious you're nobility. I want to know about the people close to you."

Janto drizzled oil onto a slice of bread. "How much do you know about Mosari politics and history?"

"Almost nothing."

"And the royal family?"

"There's a king and a queen. Two princes."

"Mosari nobility, what do you know of them?"

"Nothing."

"I don't want to lie to you," said Janto. "I can't tell you my zo name or the names of my family members, because if I did that, I'd be putting people in danger—"

"Your zo name?"

"You don't know what that is?" He shook his head. "You're supposed to govern my people alongside Augustan, and you know nothing about Mosar."

"My uncle doesn't believe in educating women, at least not about politics and other countries. That's why I recruited you to teach me the Mosari language myself."

"Well, when a Mosari mage soulcasts, if he does it successfully, he is given a new name. Like *Ral-Vaddis*—that's a zo name. If you have a zo name, then you're part of our zo caste. It means you're a mage."

"Is Janto a zo name?"

"No. I have one, but I don't use it here," said Janto. "Too dangerous."

"Make up names for your family members. I don't care," said Rhianne. "Just tell me about them. What are they like? Are your parents still alive?"

"They were alive when I left Mosar."

"Do you like them? Hate them? Why do I have to drag details out of you? You'd think I was performing an interrogation."

"Of course I like them," said Janto. "They're good people." When she glared at him, he added, "My younger brother and I were competitive. We'd try to seduce the same women."

"Oh?" She felt a little jealous of those unknown women. "Who usually won?"

"My brother." Janto placed a cheese slice atop a pear slice and ate them together. "He's taller. Handsomer."

"Those women were fools," said Rhianne.

"Naturally," said Janto. "Look, I'll tell you a story that might actually mean something to you. I went through my magical training with one of my same-age cousins. I'll call him Bel. Are you familiar with the root called jovo?"

"I've heard the name before, but I don't know anything about it."

"It doesn't grow here. Only on Mosar. We warn our children not to chew it, but some do anyway. It has an effect like wine but more powerful. It fogs the mind and produces euphoria. If you chew it once, you feel compelled to chew it again and again. Over time it rots your teeth, and I think it must rot your insides too, because jovo addicts die young. Bel and I went through magical training together, and we became friends. He was, at the time, chewing jovo, but he was discreet about it, and I never caught on. He soulcast into a cliff bear, which made him a stoneshaper." Janto stopped to take another bite of pear.

"We parted ways because our training diverged, but we stayed in touch. He became an accomplished stoneshaper, but his jovo chewing caught up with him. He was disciplined repeatedly for not showing up to work and for shoddy or unsafe workmanship. Finally he was brought before my father, an authority within our family.

"My father believed that the only way to induce Bel to behave more honorably was to remove him from the island of Mosar—get him away from jovo entirely. He wanted to send Bel to sea as a sailor in the Mosari Navy. After a year or two of no access to jovo, he might safely return to stoneshaping."

"That sounds like a good idea to me," Rhianne said.

"I thought so too. But Bel was horrified at the prospect of going to sea where his magic would be useless and he'd have to perform hard labor and be separated from his friends. He implored me to speak to my father and change his mind. He had learned his lesson, he said, and would never chew jovo again, if only I would spare him this fate. I liked Bel, and I believed him, and we were chronically short of stoneshapers. We needed several for a building project at Silverside Mountain. So I persuaded my father to find a spot for Bel at Silverside." Now he paused to take a sip of wine, as if bracing himself.

"Several sagespans later, there was a cave-in at Silverside, in which we lost not only Bel but a dozen other mages. In the investigations that followed, we learned that Bel had been disciplined several times at Silverside for showing up under the influence of jovo and that his inappropriate thinning of a key structural pillar had caused the collapse."

"Janto, I'm so sorry," said Rhianne. "You sound like you feel that accident was your fault. But you couldn't have known your cousin would lie about the jovo again."

"I should have known," said Janto. "In hindsight, it seems obvious. Addicts always have problems giving it up. My father's solution was the right one. At the time, I thought it was harsh, but those two years on a ship might have saved Bel's life. They would certainly have saved the lives of the other mages. The compassion I showed Bel did him no favors."

"I cannot fault you," said Rhianne. "It was the wrong decision, but you made it for the right reason. There is altogether too little compassion in this world."

"You possess it in abundance to give me that much credit," said Janto. "I have thought long and hard about Silverside and that collapsed cavern. Compassion must be tempered by judgment."

"Of course," said Rhianne. "But if good judgment were easy, we'd make the right decisions every time, wouldn't we?"

"I suppose we would," said Janto.

"Here's what I think," said Rhianne. "I think you should pull up all the jovo root on Mosar and burn it."

He shook his head. "If only it were that easy. But for now, I have another question. Have I met your requirements, Princess, and told you something of substance about my family? Have I earned the right to share your dinner?"

"I don't know why you bother to ask, since you ate half of it while we were talking even after you had the gall to say you weren't using me for food. If not food, what *are* you using me for?" Rhianne sent him a look of mock perplexity. She knew already what his answer would be.

Janto grinned, and his eyes twinkled. "Come over here and find out."

It was past dark when Janto left the palace and went searching for one of his bolt-holes to spend the night in. A stable was a good choice, sometimes a supply shed. Anywhere reasonably warm where he could throw a shroud over himself and be certain no one would trip over him. It was a harsh reality check, trading the silk sheets of an imperial princess's bed for a chilly dirt floor. He shivered just thinking about it.

As he turned the corner, he noticed to the south, away in the harbor of Riat, a soundless yellow light exploding in the air. Janto blinked as the afterimages danced before his eyelids. That was a pyrotechnic signal!

He broke into a run, heading for a nearby hill where

he might have a better view. Pyrotechnic signalers were rare and valued. They were not used lightly, and they transmitted only news of great importance.

From the higher vantage point at the top of the hill, he saw that the yellow starburst had been not a lone pyrotechnic shout but merely the highest in elevation of a flurry of pyrotechnic communications cascading across the harbor. Bright and numerous, they cast the harbor in an otherworldly light. He could see the harbor was full of ships. Some were in the process of anchoring. Others were moving in, signaling frantically, their brown canvas sails round and fat with wind. It was a scene of eerie beauty, yet it sent Janto's heart plummeting to the pit of his stomach.

Is that the Kjallan fleet, su-kali? asked Sashi from his shoulder.

It is, said Janto. There were only two possible things the fleet's return could mean. One was that his people had beaten the Kjallans off and they'd come limping home. But Janto didn't see how that could have happened. Why entertain false hope? The other possibility was the only one that made any sense.

Mosar had fallen.

20

At sunrise, a blast of trumpets summoned the people of Riat to the harbor. The horns played a brief fanfare in a six-beat rhythm. Deep, brassy cornus joined in, followed by snare drums and tympani. Color exploded overhead as the pyrotechnic mages added their visual accompaniment.

Janto, who'd spent a sleepless night observing the fleet and its communications with the Imperial Palace, dropped his shroud, emerged from the dockside warehouse where he'd taken cover, and joined the crowd of civilians watching the spectacle. With so many people around, no one would take notice of him.

The Kjallan pyrotechnics were among the most skilled he'd seen. Any pyro could pull shapes and colors out of the spirit world, but sculpting them into recognizable forms like people and animals required talent. Above the crowd, they had summoned and shaped a brace of cavalry horses. Trumpets sounded the charge, and the illusionary horses reared and galloped forward. The horses faded, and in their place appeared ocean waves. A cadence of drums beat the waves' undulating rhythm, driving to a crescendo until a ship's bowsprit crashed through them.

The airborne images began to float away from the harbor and toward the city proper. Janto hurried after them, pushing his way through the crowd toward the parade he knew lay at the center of the throng.

Breaking through the massed civilians, he saw the marching soldiers, a troop of infantry in tight formation wielding orange flags. Behind them plodded draft horses with docked tails and feathered hooves, each hauling a supply cart loaded high with who knew what, probably stolen treasures from Mosar. Tarps covered the bounty. Next marched a cadre of drummers, keeping time with a rolling beat. Along the tail of the procession, Janto saw more soldiers, horses, cannons, and supplies. The pyrotechnics and their images were ahead.

He withdrew into the cover of the crowd and pushed his way through until he spotted the pyrotechnic mages. They gesticulated with agile fingers, their brows furrowed with concentration as they called their complex creations from the Rift.

"There he is!" cried a man from the crowd. "The legatus!"

Janto whipped his head to where the man was pointing. Four men in officer's uniforms rode in a quadrille, their horses' paces nearly synchronized. Ahead of them rode four more, and leading them was a single officer, lightly armored, astride a dark bay warhorse frothing at the bit. Janto recognized the rider easily enough: Augustan Ceres. The legatus had come for Rhianne. For *Janto's* woman.

Janto stared at the man with such furious hatred, he half expected the back of Augustan's neck to burst into flames. The legatus turned and scanned the crowd, but his expression was mild, and his gaze passed over Janto without interest. Two men walked on either side of Augustan—servants, by the look of them. Each carried a wooden box. Gifts, Janto decided, for Rhianne or the emperor. More treasures stolen from Mosar, which Augustan would use to secure his theft of Janto's throne and his princess.

Kill him, suggested Sashi, *if he takes what is yours.*

Rhianne was never mine, said Janto.

You have mated with her, said Sashi matter-of-factly. *If another man steals your mate, kill him.*

He is a war mage. Impossible to kill, said Janto. *Even were it otherwise, love and marriage are not simple when it comes to my kind.*

Your kind makes things too complicated, Sashi scolded.

Janto frowned. His familiar had a point.

Rhianne awoke to the news she had been dreading. Augustan was victorious. Mosar had been conquered. The war was over, and her fiancé was at this very moment marching to the Imperial Palace from the city of Riat to celebrate his victory and claim his bride, who, unfortunately, was her.

She couldn't stop thinking about Janto. Did he know? How was he taking the news? He seemed to be all alone on Kjall. He would have no one to confide in or seek comfort from as he confronted this new reality. And he could not come to her. It was not possible. She prayed he would not attempt it, not with Augustan in the palace and so many people in and out of her rooms.

Janto was strong. She prayed he would survive this blow and see the necessity of escaping as a refugee to Sardos or Inya. With his language skills, he could start a new life there. No future remained for him on Mosar, and he would never have a future in Kjall.

Today she had her own horrors to face. Augustan had come for her, and her days of relative freedom had come to an end. Her husband-to-be would not dally at the Imperial Palace. He had a vassal state to stabilize and govern. Florian had not discussed details of the wedding, but she knew that under the circumstances, it would be rushed. She would be wedded and bedded and shipped off to Mosar in less than a week. She must say good-bye to all the people she loved: Morgan, Marcella, even Lucien. She would not be able to say good-bye to Janto.

Her lady's maid slipped into the room. "Your Imperial Highness, shall we get you dressed? Our signalers report that the legatus is at the base of the hill."

Janto, concealed within the crowd, followed the procession as it wound its way through the city of Riat. When the parade reached the city gates, a line of guards blocked the civilians and prevented them from following. The soldiers, led by Augustan, filtered through the gates and continued up the hill to the Imperial Palace. Janto, determined to learn what had happened on Mosar, donned his shroud and slipped in among the soldiers as they passed by the guards.

The soldiers marched uphill through switchback after switchback until they crested the peak and the whole of the Imperial Palace came into view. Though they still had some distance to cover, what remained was an easy march on a flat, paved road, shaded by ancient oaks. As they approached, the front gates of the palace were flung wide in welcome. Did the emperor intend to host the entire retinue?

Uniformed officials just inside the gates directed traffic, sending Augustan and the other officers in one direction, the rank and file in another. The smell of roasting meat wafted down the hallway, and Janto guessed that a banquet awaited the hungry soldiers. He hungered for information rather than food, so he followed the officers.

The officers filed into a high-ceilinged, white marble audience hall. Two rows of gray pillars flanked a central aisle. At the far end of the hall stood a raised platform, also gray, upon which three figures awaited them, one dressed in orange, one in blue, and one in white.

Such arrogance, thought Janto, *to wear the colors of the gods.*

But he did not have to look twice to recognize the figure in white as Rhianne. She stood on the left, and the young man on the right, in blue, was Lucien, the Imperial Heir. The man in the middle, wearing a broad, glittering loros over a shimmersilk orange syrtos, had to be Emperor Florian.

The emperor was tall and imposing, middle-aged and showing it, but Janto had envisioned a nastier, more vicious-looking man. Did cruelty show? Janto believed it often did, especially in the later years, when the lines of one's face began to tell the tale of one's life. Florian appeared stern and resolute, more a hard man than a cruel one. It puzzled him.

He found a quiet corner where he could watch the proceedings without being bumped into or trodden on. The officers took up places behind the pillars, leaving the aisle clear. When everyone was inside and settled, Augustan entered the end of the hall opposite Florian, escorted by two burly officers and two servants carrying the wooden boxes Janto had seen during the parade.

All fell silent, and Augustan strode down the aisle, his entourage a few steps behind him. He stopped just shy of the gray platform.

Emperor Florian spoke in a deep, commanding voice. "Report, Legatus."

Rhianne shifted subtly on her feet, relieving a muscle in her back that was beginning to cramp. She'd been too long motionless. She watched as her husband-to-be, instead of responding succinctly to Florian's order, turned to acknowledge one side of the aisle and then the other.

"My fellow officers ... Princess ... Your Imperial Highness ... my illustrious Emperor." He inclined his head at Florian and addressed the crowd. "Today is a glorious day for the empire. When first we set sail from Kjallan shores nine months ago ..."

Rhianne suppressed an eye roll. Was he going to turn this into a long speech? Of course he was; it was his moment of glory. If one could call it glory, murdering innocent people to take their land and wealth. The whole affair sickened her. Not to mention she had to stand in front of everyone looking ridiculous in a dress white as cuttlebone because Florian had this notion that the royal family should dress as the gods. As if that wasn't going to offend anybody. And he had her and Lucien backward. If anything, he should have dressed wise Lucien as the Sage and her as the rebellious Vagabond, but that was classic Florian. He'd never truly known his family.

Was Augustan building up to a point? It sounded like it.

"...And so, thanks to the courage of our fighting men and the leadership of the officers you see before you, I report triumphantly that Mosar has been brought to heel. We have accepted Mosar's unconditional surrender, and Kjall takes the former nation as its vassal state."

The audience hall erupted in cheers, and Florian stepped to the edge of the platform to clasp wrists with Augustan. From there, Florian pulled him up onto the platform. "Legatus Augustan Ceres, you are a credit to your forebears and to the Kjallan Empire. I am pleased to offer you the governorship of Mosar, beginning immediately, and I welcome you to the imperial family as my son-in-law." He gestured to Rhianne.

This was her cue to step forward and kiss Augustan. He approached with a cocky smile. She managed not to recoil when he wrapped an arm around her and pulled her close. She had to rise on her tiptoes to reach his lips, and he didn't help her by bending down, so she didn't feel guilty when she gave him only a peck. Even then, she wanted to wipe her lips afterward, but she knew better than to do that in front of her uncle.

The crowd cheered their pathetic kiss.

"I have something else to present, Your Imperial Majesty," said Augustan.

"The floor is yours, Legatus," said Florian.

He gestured to the servants carrying the wooden boxes. "Part of the task I was assigned on Mosar was to exterminate the existing royal family. That job is not complete. Some of the royals have, as one might expect of Mosari cowards, gone to ground. As the Mosari governor, I shall make it one of my first priorities to flush them from their hiding places. Nonetheless, progress has been made. Your Imperial Majesty." He swept his hands toward the servants, as each pulled from his box a severed head and held it high for all to see. "The former king and queen of Mosar."

A hush fell over the room.

Rhianne recoiled in horror. She'd had no idea those boxes contained anything so grisly. She'd expected stolen relics, perhaps artwork or jewelry. The heads were not badly decomposed, and they smelled more of brandy and camphor than of rot, but how was she supposed to react to such a sight? Never mind the grisliness of it; her stomach could handle that, as long as she didn't put anything in it for a while. But these had once been people, and they hadn't done anything to deserve this fate. Augustan was a murderer, showing off his crime as if proud of it, and her own uncle Florian was the man who'd ordered him to commit it.

"Well done, Legatus, well done," said Florian.

The officers in the room broke into polite, subdued applause.

Rhianne couldn't take any more of this farce. She turned on her heel, stepped off the platform, and left the audience hall.

The former king and queen of Mosar.

Janto had been too far away to see the heads clearly, but those words sent him reeling. He wanted to rush the platform, to slay Augustan and Florian where they stood in recompense for this unspeakable crime, but he was unarmed and surrounded by enemies. It wasn't possible. He scrambled for the exit.

Three gods, three gods, three gods. His mother and father were dead, murdered by Augustan.

Several heads turned in his direction as he raced invisibly down the center aisle. In his mad rush, he wasn't being careful. He was creating a breeze, maybe even brushing some people with the edges of his cloak. He didn't care.

Nobody followed him out into the corridor, where he fell upon his knees in a paroxysm of grief. He thought of the heads again, the heads *of his parents*. He emptied his stomach.

I'm sorry, su-kali, said Sashi, clinging to his shoulder. *We will kill them for what they've done.*

We'll do what we can.

Which, so far, had been a whole lot of nothing.

Back in the audience hall, the officers were applauding. Kjallan filth! Rhianne was the only decent human being among them. He'd watched her kiss Augustan at her uncle's bidding, her movements stiff and unyielding, every cell of her body screaming abhorrence. The Kjallans had applauded that too. Was there no horror they wouldn't celebrate?

The officers in the audience hall sounded restless, and he suspected they were about to be dismissed, probably to the feast. He hoped the sight of the heads had diminished some appetites. Clutching his stomach, he straightened and hurried along the corridor, heading for the slave entrance. While this might be a good opportunity for spying, he was in no condition for it, and given the circumstances, what was the point? Mosar was lost. As for seeing Rhianne, he had a feeling he was no longer welcome. She didn't want Augustan, but she was committed to going through with her marriage, and there was nothing he could do to help her.

He was out of the Imperial Palace and halfway to one of his bolt-holes when he realized that some days ago, when Augustan had murdered his father, Janto had unknowingly ascended the throne—for whatever that was worth. He was now king of Mosar. It was almost funny.

21

Rhianne sat quietly in her receiving room, still in her ridiculous white gown, waiting for the maelstrom that was certain to arrive as soon as Florian extricated himself from the remainder of the ceremony. She hadn't *planned* on walking out. It had just happened. Morgan had said she'd had choices. It appeared that for better or for worse, she'd just made one. Probably for worse. She'd rebelled against Florian in dozens of clandestine ways over the years, but never had she challenged him openly. She could envision no scenario in which this worked out well for her.

A thump and a grating noise outside her door told her the bar was sliding back, granting someone entrance to her chambers. She swallowed. The door opened, and, no surprise, Florian stepped through, looking angry as a harassed hornet.

She leapt to her feet, a gesture of respect that had become as reflexive as blinking, aware of the irony after she'd shown him the disrespect of walking out of the ceremony. Perhaps it would appease him a tiny bit.

He strode toward her, stepping so close she was tempted to cower. She held her ground, trembling, as he towered over her.

"I was raised not to strike a woman in anger," Florian grated through his teeth. "That's for the lower families. But *never* have I been so tempted." He pointed at a chair. *"Sit."*

Wordlessly, Rhianne sat.

Florian took the seat across from her. "This morning's ceremony was to be Augustan's moment of glory, after nine months of hard campaigning. You spoiled it with your childish behavior. You shall *immediately* make amends. You shall sit down at your writing desk and compose a brief speech of apology. This you will show to me, and after I approve it, you will go to Augustan and, in front of his servants and top-ranking officers, *humbly beg his forgiveness* for the insult you delivered him in the hall this morning."

"Uncle—"

"This is not a negotiation," said Florian. "I am giving you orders. We will follow your apology with a gift. I was thinking—"

"Uncle—"

"Stop interrupting, girl! Must I call the guards and order you beaten for your intransigence?"

"I'm not marrying Augustan."

For a moment, he was actually speechless.

Rhianne leapt into the opening of his stunned silence and spoke in a rush. "I hate him, and he doesn't care for me either. I cannot marry him. I'm sorry to disappoint you."

Florian remained silent. A muscle bulged at the back of his jaw. After a moment, he turned his back on her, pacing the room. "Let me make something clear to you. Do you see all the fine things in here?" He swept his arm to indicate the furnishings.

"Yes," she said softly.

"Take a moment to recall the other fine things you've had. Your horse and magical training, fine clothes, fine food, the imperial baths, the guards who protect you—"

"Guards who *spy* on me."

"For your protection," said Florian. "Do you think I give you those things out of the goodness of my heart? No. You are here to serve a purpose, just as I serve a purpose, as Lucien serves a purpose. Your purpose, Rhianne, is marriage. Marriage to the right man, to strengthen the family line and strengthen the empire through the governance of a new vassal state."

Rhianne drew up her knees and clutched them beneath her gown. What he said was true. She harbored no illusions about her role in the imperial family. And yet. "I never asked for these things. I never asked for this *life*. You took me. You brought me here, without my parents' consent—"

His nose wrinkled in a snarl. "You were *always* meant for it, even if my sister, your mother, shirked her responsibilities." He pointed at her. "*You* shall not shirk yours." After a moment, he blinked and sighed, rubbing his face. In a gentler voice, he continued. "Why did you walk out on the ceremony? Was it because of the heads?"

Rhianne nodded. "Uncle, it's not right. Those were innocent people Augustan murdered for no reason except that they were in his way. I cannot love a man who thinks he should be praised for such a thing."

Florian smiled sadly. "He should not have brought the heads to the ceremony—not with a lady present. I'll speak with him about it, and that will pave the way for your apology. He was impolitic, but you were rude. Both of you were at fault. You must understand he has been at war a long time, and solely among men. He forgets that women are sensitive and have no stomach for war, especially its gruesome side."

Florian didn't understand. It wasn't the gruesomeness of the heads that bothered her, but what they represented. Her country had done something horrid, and it shamed her. She couldn't write the apology he asked from her, because it would make her complicit in those crimes. Crimes against Janto and his people.

"Still," said Florian sternly, "this nonsense from you must cease. Augustan killed those people on my orders, and I gave those orders for the good of the empire. I do not expect you to understand why I make hard decisions that you find unsavory, but it is not your place to question my commands. It is your place, as it is Augustan's, to obey them. Therefore I expect your written apology, for my review, within the hour."

Rhianne blinked back tears. She couldn't do this. "I'm not writing it."

His expression darkened. "Do not try my patience. Wedding plans are under way, and I've no time to indulge your childish whims. I was raised never to strike a lady, but I will not hesitate to order you beaten if that's what it takes to convince you of my seriousness."

"Cancel the wedding," said Rhianne. Gods, he was going to destroy her for this. "Forced marriages are illegal in Kjall."

"My dear." Florian's eyes narrowed. "I'm the emperor. Do you think you can tell me what is and isn't legal?"

Rhianne shivered. "The law applies to everyone."

Florian laughed. "Your written apology. Until I have it, you are confined to your rooms. You will have no visitors, attend no events, and have nothing brought to you until you think better of your foolishness. And if you think these are the worst things that can happen to you, think again. My forbearance will last only so long."

Iolo and Sirali looked downcast when Janto met them in the usual spot beneath the trees. He supposed all the Mosari must feel as he did, though perhaps with less personal grief. Most of the others did not know the fates of their families back on the island.

"Is it true?" Iolo said softly. "The rumors about the king and queen?"

"They're dead," said Janto.

"I'm sorry," said Iolo. "That makes you king, doesn't it?"

Janto nodded.

Iolo inclined his head. "Your Majesty."

Janto waved his hand. "It's meaningless. We have no country, not that I won't do everything in my power to win it back. How are the slaves taking the news?"

"Badly," said Iolo. "There have been suicides."

Sirali nodded. "While Mosar held out, we had hope. Now we have nothing."

"I came to say good-bye," said Janto. "I'm leaving Kjall."

Their foreheads wrinkled with concern. "Where will you go?" asked Iolo.

"I've a ship that supports me," said Janto. "I sent it away a few days ago to relay some information, and when it returns, I'm going to have it pick me up and find Kal's fleet. I'll join my brother, and we'll try to retake Mosar."

Iolo's eyebrows rose. "Does Kal-Torres have the men to do that?"

"I can't imagine he does, but we'll sell our lives as dearly as we can. There's nothing else left for us. I only wish I'd accomplished more here."

"Right, and you helped the slave women," pointed out Sirali.

Janto nodded. At least there was that.

Rhianne crawled through the hypocaust on hands and knees, ignoring the stifling heat and counting heat-glows as she followed her usual pattern. She wasn't running away—not yet. That would take some planning. But she had to talk to somebody about her plight, and Morgan seemed the only option. He always talked sense, and Florian didn't keep a close eye on him the way he did Lucien. Morgan would help her figure out what to do.

She reached the access tunnel, where the ceiling became high enough to stand. She rose to her feet, approached the door, and eased it open, just a crack. There were the guards at the end of the short hallway.

Wait—why were they wearing orange? Those weren't ordinary guards. They were Legaciatti! Magical guards, immune to her spells.

She pushed the door gently shut, her heart thrumming wildly against her ribs as she prayed they wouldn't turn and see her. The hypocaust guards had always been ordinary palace guards—never Legaciatti. Why the change? Did Florian know about her secret excursions from the palace? How long had he known?

She headed back into the hypocaust, dropping onto hands and knees as the ceiling angled sharply downward. There was nothing for it but to return to the prison of her rooms. She was trapped.

*   *   *

Janto sat on the pier with his back to a post, invisible. Heavily laden boats sliced through the harbor waters, some loaded with supplies, others with troops. A battalion of soldiers massed on a nearby beach, awaiting the boats that delivered them, thirty at a time, to troop ships riding at double anchor.

A bosun's shrill voice carried on the wind. "Man the falls! Haul taut singly! Hoist away!" Janto turned to watch the shallow-draft frigate nearest him take sealed casks on board with its water-whip. Other men were up on the yards, doing something to the sails; still others clung to ropes slung over the stern. Across the water echoed the knocks of hammers and the scrape of an adze.

The fleet was preparing to sail again. He'd assumed they were going to Mosar, since Augustan was returning there with Rhianne, but it was odd they were loading so many soldiers. Why carry them all the way to Kjall just to send them back to Mosar? It didn't make sense.

Another thing that didn't make sense: he'd seen new cargo loaded—things like warm cloaks and blankets. Why would anyone need those things on tropical Mosar?

No. The troops were going elsewhere. He needed to find out where.

Rhianne lay prone on the settee in her rooms, trying not to move or even breathe too deeply. Florian had waited two days for her to change her mind, and when she hadn't, he'd made good on his threat. Her back, striped with a whip and still raw, hurt like she couldn't believe. Never again would she speak casually about someone receiving the lash as a punishment. There was nothing trivial about it.

She glanced up as the bolt slid back from her door. It couldn't be food. Florian was sending her prison rations—bread and cheese and water, three times a day—and it wasn't time for lunch yet. She wasn't permitted visitors, so it could only be Florian, whose presence she dreaded.

But it was Lucien! A pleasant surprise. She gritted her teeth and raised herself just enough to make eye contact. "I didn't think I was allowed to see you."

"Florian thought I might talk some sense into you." Lucien grinned and rolled his eyes. He looked again, perhaps noticing her awkward pose and loose clothing, and stopped short. The color drained from his face. "Did he have you *whipped*?"

"He did," she grunted. "It was much worse than I thought it'd be."

Lucien turned away, as if he couldn't bear to look, though her injuries were bandaged and covered. He limped with his crutch to the far side of the room. "I didn't think he'd go that far. How many lashes?"

"Ten."

He rounded on her, his hands balled into fists. "That leaves scars."

"Not if a Healer closes the wounds. He says he'll send a Healer when I start cooperating."

Lucien scrubbed a hand through his hair and limped back to her. He sat, leaning his crutch on the chair. "What he's doing is wrong. You know it, and I know it. But you should do as he says. If this were a Caturanga match, he'd have you in every possible way—his Traitor behind your enemy lines, his Tribune under the Soldier's influence, and all your battalions and cavalry mired in terrain while he's got a clean run across the board. He has every advantage, and you have none."

"I have my integrity," said Rhianne. "And the law's on my side."

Lucien smiled sadly. "Florian is subject to no law. But think on this, Rhianne—he won't be emperor forever." He lowered his voice. "When I ascend the throne, everything will be different. If Augustan mistreats you in any way, I'll send him packing the moment I become emperor. You have my word on it. And then you shall marry whomever you please. But until that day comes, you and I have to swallow our pride and accept our orders as they come. Florian destroys people who oppose him. I've seen him do it."

"I know you mean well," said Rhianne, "but Florian is healthy and strong. He could rule for another forty years."

Lucien took her hand and squeezed it. "You speak as if you have a choice in this matter. You don't."

"I could run like my mother did. I'd have done it already, except . . ." She sighed in exasperation. "There are Legaciatti guarding the hypocaust now. Florian must know. Or else it was a lucky guess."

Lucien lowered his head. "Florian doesn't know. I put the Legaciatti there."

"You!" hissed Rhianne. "Why would you put them there?"

His eyes glistened, liquid with guilt. "Because I knew you'd try it. And if you run, he'll find you. And that will only make things worse."

Rhianne, realizing his hand was still holding hers, flung it back at him. "Of all the people I thought might betray me, I never guessed it would be you!"

"I knew you'd be angry," said Lucien. "I only hope someday you'll understand. I did it because you'll never escape Florian's net. He has resources you can't even imagine: signal towers that offer him near-instantaneous communication with every settlement in Kjall, guards in each city who can track your progress through the food and grain you buy and the houses you sleep in—"

"I've got forgetting spells."

"Not as useful as you think. Mind magic is unsubtle. Forgetting spells leave holes in people's memories, and if Florian's agents know the right questions to ask, they'll discover them. Flight is impossible. You'll be caught and dragged back home and forced to marry anyway, and what is Augustan going to think of all this? Do you think you have any chance at all of a happy marriage when your fiancé knows you had to be beaten and dragged halfway across the country to wed him?"

As if there had ever been a chance of her enjoying a happy marriage with Augustan. "Remove the Legaciatti, Lucien."

He shook his head. "I can't watch you destroy yourself."

"Remove them!" she cried.

"No. I'm sorry."

"Get out of my room, then," she snapped. "You and I are finished."

Lucien rose wearily, turned his back on her, and limped for the door.

22

For the first time, Janto entered the north dome of the Imperial Palace, the home of Emperor Florian's personal chambers and offices. This area was certain to be salted with wards, but he was less concerned about tripping one than he had been before. With Mosar conquered and most of his family dead, part of him almost welcomed the opportunity to use his poison pill.

So far he seemed to be getting off easy. No wards yet, and with so little traffic, these hallways were easier to navigate invisibly than other areas of the palace. Legaciatti guarded most of the doors, and probably some of the rooms beyond those doors contained reams of useful intelligence, but finding a way into them would not be without challenge.

Around the corner, a pair of voices broke the silence. Janto moved toward them.

"He's not back yet," said one man.

"But I'm on his schedule," replied another.

Janto turned the corner and saw Augustan Ceres, accompanied by one of his officers, speaking to a door guard.

"He's running late," said the Legaciattus. "You can wait in the anteroom."

Augustan nodded and, along with the officer, headed toward a side room. Janto followed and was delighted to discover the anteroom had no door. He didn't enter but hovered outside, in case the arched entryway was warded.

Augustan and the officer took seats, looking irritated.

The officer spoke in a quiet voice. "You think he'll give us the ships?"

"Can't imagine he wouldn't," said Augustan. "There's still a Mosari fleet out there, and he won't want anything to happen to his precious niece."

The officer snorted a laugh. "What's the word on her? She break yet?"

Janto blinked, confused but interested. Augustan and the officer had to be referring to Rhianne, but what was this about her *breaking*?

Augustan shook his head. "He had her whipped yesterday, but she's a stubborn bitch. Not giving in yet."

Stubborn bitch? She'd been *whipped*? Surely Janto had heard wrong or misunderstood. They could not be talking about an imperial princess. They were speaking softly, and he could have missed something. Maybe they were talking about a hunting dog, or a horse.

Or maybe they weren't. What in the Sage's name had been going on here while he'd been hiding away, mourning his parents and his conquered land?

"He's going about it all wrong," said the officer.

" 'Course he is," said Augustan. "She's thoroughly spoiled. Forget the wedding—just sign the marriage papers and throw her into my cabin on the *Meritorious*. I'll make a wife of her. I'll have her on her knees on the quarterdeck before the voyage is over, sucking my cock and thanking me for the privilege."

Janto stiffened. He didn't know how he would do it,

but somehow he was going to kill that man. His fingers twitched, wanting to wrap themselves around Augustan's neck and crush it.

Yes, muttered Sashi darkly, picking up his thoughts. *Kill.*

Later, said Janto, coming to his senses. That man was a war mage, blessed with preternatural speed and strength, as well as the gift of anticipation, which allowed him to sense blows before they landed. His combat skills would be formidable, to say the least. *Right now, I need to buy Rhianne some time.*

Augustan and the other officer launched into a comparison of their sexual exploits, some of which had involved captured Mosari women. Janto listened with half an ear, not wanting to get too angry and lose his composure. Finally one of the door guards came and nodded at Augustan. "He wants to see you first."

Augustan rose. "Any word on the princess?"

"You'll have to ask him yourself." The guard led him to the door, and Janto followed.

"Come in. Don't stand on the doorstep," called Florian from inside.

Augustan stepped into Florian's office. Janto, invisible at his side, crossed the threshold with him.

Fireworks crackled and spat as fingers of red and blue lightning raced along the door frame. Shouts erupted, and Legaciatti raced into the room. Two of them backed Emperor Florian into a corner, shielding him with their bodies. Another shut the door, while others tackled Augustan and wrenched his arms behind his back. The legatus cried out in confusion and anger. He could have fought them—he was a war mage—but he seemed to have the wit not to resist.

Janto picked his way around the Legaciatti toward Florian's desk.

"It was a faulty ward!" Augustan lifted his head from the floor, but the guards shoved it back down. Two men sat on him while a third fastened manacles onto his arms and legs. "A faulty ward! I am your faithful subject, Emperor, I swear it!"

Two of the Legaciatti got up and searched the room, yanking back chairs and tables. One of them came straight at Janto. Janto backed away and out of his path. When another guard cut him off from the other direction, he scrambled invisibly onto a table. The guard yanked a chair out from beneath it. Janto slid across to the other side and jumped down.

The men completed their search. Silence fell, broken only by the sound of Augustan's harsh breathing. A Legaciattus approached the emperor and his bodyguards and saluted with a thumb to his chest. "The room is secure, sire." The bodyguards stepped away.

"What in the Soldier's hell?" growled Florian, emerging from his corner and heading toward Augustan.

Janto reached Florian's desk. Though all eyes were on Augustan, he threw his shroud over the papers lying on the table, just in case someone glanced in his direction, and gathered them into his arms. He'd hoped to slide open the desk drawers and steal their contents as well, but that seemed too risky.

"Shall we take his riftstone, sire?" asked a Legaciattus.

"Yes," said Florian. "Take it to the Epolonius Room. Send for a warder and a mind mage."

The Legaciatti rolled Augustan onto his back. One of them reached into his syrtos and retrieved the riftstone on its chain. They lifted him up and placed him in a chair, where he sat hunched forward to accommodate his manacled wrists. The Legaciattus carrying away the riftstone left the door open, granting Janto a welcome escape route. He edged toward it, hoping to get out before someone cast a new ward.

"Sire," began a pale and trembling Augustan, "I welcome your truth spell and the opportunity to prove my innocence. This is a mistake. The ward must have been incorrectly cast."

Florian frowned. "Silence. We'll have this sorted out soon enough."

Janto slipped out the open door with one last glance at Augustan. *Enjoy your interrogation.*

Janto tucked himself into an alcove, behind a statue of a Kjallan warrior, to peruse his stolen bounty. His time in the palace was limited now. Once truth spells established Augustan's innocence and Florian discovered the papers on his desk were missing, he might conclude, correctly, that an invisible spy was operating in the palace. Then the invisibility wards would go up. Janto had been reckless, but it had been worth it to see Augustan humiliated, and who knew? Maybe he would find something of value.

He looked at the first paper on the stack. *Emperor Florian Nigellus Gavros commands your presence on the Fifth Day of the Sage for the Marriage Ceremony of Imperial Princess Rhianne Florian Nigellus to Legatus Augustan Ceres. . . .*

Three gods. Had he picked up a stack of wedding invitations?

He paged through them. Invitation, invitation, invitation. Yes. A stack of completely useless wedding invitations, which had apparently been left on Florian's desk because they needed his signature at the bottom. Wonderful.

Wait—here was something else. A requisitions order from the palaestra. Training equipment. Not very interesting, but it was another document requiring the emperor's signature. He hadn't stolen a stack of wedding invitations. He'd stolen a stack of documents needing signatures.

What else? Execution orders, two of them, for prisoners currently held beneath the palace. No details in the paperwork about their crimes. Janto shivered and paged farther through the stack.

Here was something.

Captain, Skylark.

> *By imperial command, you are required to proceed through the Neruna Strait and seize control of the harbor at Sarpol. Once the harbor is secured, you will place yourself under the command of Legatus Ahala Philippus and await further instructions.*

Official orders for the *Skylark*, and juicy ones at that. What was the emperor up to? Sarpol was the westernmost port of Sardos. Was Florian really going to attack Sardos right after conquering Mosar? It boggled the mind. If Ral-Vaddis had known of this plan a while ago, this might be the intelligence he'd believed would turn the war. If Sardos, knowing a Kjallan attack was imminent, could have been persuaded to join the fight while Mosar still stood, the two nations together might have defeated the aggressors. That opportunity might be lost now, but not necessarily. Kal-Torres still had a fleet.

Janto flipped through the remaining papers and found identical orders for the captains of the *Faithful* and the *Seabird*. Just three ships for attacking Sardos? That wouldn't be enough. There was something missing, something he didn't understand yet. Perhaps the action in Sarpol was a feint. Or perhaps the orders for other ships involved had already been signed and delivered. He needed to know more—a lot more.

But first he would find out what was going on with Rhianne.

Rhianne had been dreaming, once again of being chased. She ran and ran, but there was nowhere to hide. It was inevitable: in time she must tire, and her pursuer would catch her. She wasn't sure who he was, only that she must run from him. But someone was shaking her shoulder, waking her with a gentle touch before the dream could reach its frightening conclusion. Not Florian, since he wouldn't be gentle. Perhaps her lady's maid. She slept a lot these days. There was little else to do, and unconsciousness granted her reprieve from thinking about her impossible situation. She opened her eyes.

A man crouched at her side.

She scrambled away in a reflex of terror, confusing him with the pursuer from her dream. But it was Janto. He spoke soothingly and reached for her, and as the wispy threads of her dream dissipated, the pounding of her heart eased, and she crawled into his embrace. He held her close, and she began to cry, spilling with her tears the horrors of the past several days.

He settled on the settee where she'd been sleeping

and pulled her into his lap. Inspecting her with careful fingers, he found the bandages on her back—so quickly she had a feeling he'd known to look for them. He drew in his breath sharply. "What's happened, love?"

She wanted to speak but couldn't stop crying.

He stroked her hair. "When you're ready. I don't mean to rush you."

His warm hands running through her hair began to quiet her in mind and body. What a comfort his gentle strength was! If only she could have him by her side always, not just at these unpredictable moments. She took a deep breath and let it out. Her trembling subsided. "When Augustan came, he spoke in the audience hall. At the end of his presentation, he held up . . . oh gods. You may not want to hear this."

"Go on," said Janto. "I think I already know."

"He held up two severed heads. He had executed the king and queen of Mosar. I'm so sorry. You come from a high family, and you must have known them. Here I am weeping over some stripes on my back, and things are so much worse for you—"

"The days since the return of the fleet have been the hardest of my life," said Janto. "That does not diminish what you've been through."

She sighed, her breath shaky. "I was . . . horrified by the gesture of the severed heads. So I walked out of the ceremony."

He looked down at her sharply. "You walked out? When?"

"After he held up the heads."

Janto shook his head in astonishment. "Then we both walked out. I must have gone before you. I was there, invisible, but when he held up the heads, I ran for the exit."

"You were there? I wish I'd known—I felt alone up on the platform. But my act of defiance has led to nothing but trouble. Everyone's turned against me, even Lucien. I'm imprisoned in my rooms, I'm allowed no visitors, and Florian had me whipped. He'll do it again if I don't come around. And the worst of it is that while he wants me to wed Augustan willingly, I think that if I continue to refuse, he'll just forge my signature on the marriage contract and throw me on the ship to Mosar. What can I do then? I can't fight Augustan. The man's a war mage."

Janto's arms stiffened, even as he held her. "That's not going to happen. Have you given any serious thought to running away?"

"I'd have run before now if it were possible," said Rhianne. "I used to be able to sneak out, but Lucien knows my secret route out of the palace. He anticipated me and set Legaciatti to guarding it."

"I can get you out with my shroud, but we'll have to wait for your front door to open. When will that happen next? It looks like supper's already been delivered, although that isn't your typical supper—"

"Florian's got me on prison rations. Bread and cheese. My lady's maid should be in later, but she'll be looking to help me with my clothes. It's not a great time to sneak out. Other than that, the door won't open again until breakfast. But we can go out the secret way, if you can get past Legaciatti."

"I got past the ones at your door. I came when they delivered your dinner. I was watching you sleep for a while."

"Then I don't see a problem," said Rhianne. "Wait until dark and I'll show you. In the meantime . . ." Her voice became small. "Will you lie here with me? Hold me?"

"Of course." Janto stretched out on the couch and pulled her body into the crook of his own, handling her gingerly around her bandaged areas.

She sighed deeply, feeling safe and secure with his hard, solid warmth all around her, and tried not to think about the fact that these might be her last hours of contentedness.

Hours later, after Rhianne had packed her bag and dressed in a sensible syrtos for travel, she moved a chair in her bedroom and shifted a silk rug several feet to one side. Janto watched, his eyes full of questions.

"This is the tricky part," she said, kneeling on the floor and working her fingers into a seam between two squares of the parquet floor. "Fingerholds. It's easier to feel them than see them. Ah—here." She lifted the entire wooden square out of the floor, leaving a hole that led to blackness.

Janto's brows rose. "Where does it go?"

"Into the hypocaust," said Rhianne. "You'll see. I'm afraid it's not pleasant in there." She grabbed her bag and shoved it through the hole. Then she sat on the edge and slid in herself, landing lightly on her feet and wincing at the impact. Her head and shoulders stuck out of the hole.

Janto chuckled. "Not very deep, is it?"

"No. That's part of why it's not pleasant." She ducked into the dark, sweltering tunnel, turned around, and sat. "Come down."

Janto's legs and torso appeared through the hole, blocking the small rectangle of light that shone in. Then he crouched and turned about, searching for her in the darkness.

"Here," she called, igniting a ball of blue magelight.

His eyes met hers.

She crawled to him and pushed him lightly on the shoulder. "Move, please."

Janto dropped to hands and knees and backed up, twisting his head in alarm when his foot encountered a stone wall.

Rhianne reached up through the trapdoor, found the square of parquet floor, and lowered it back into place. The last slivers of illumination from her bedroom disappeared, leaving them in darkness except for the ghostly blue magelight.

A second ball of magelight flared in front of Janto's face. He eyed a massive heat-glow mounted on the floor. "How did you discover the trapdoor?"

She crawled past him on hands and knees. The wounds on her back flared with new pain at the movement, but she'd have to live with it for now. Once she was free of the palace, she'd find a Healer. "I didn't discover it. I had it made. Follow me—you don't want to get lost in here."

A scrape of fabric on stone told her he was trailing after her. "And Florian doesn't know about it?"

"No. I'll tell you the story. As children, Lucien and I had a tendency to get into trouble—"

"You mentioned that," said Janto.

"We'd done something, I forget what. Oh yes, we put fish in the baths as a prank on Lucien's older brothers. As punishment, Florian forbade us to attend the Consualian Games. We'd been looking forward to the Games all season, and I was a newly minted mind mage who'd recently completed soulcasting. I was drunk on the power, and I wanted to show off. So Lucien and I came up with a scheme. A carpenter came to repair a cracked seam, and

I used my magic to control him. I made him create that door. And then I made him forget he'd done it. It was wrong of me, illegal in fact, but I was a child and not terribly sensible or ethical. We had a fabulous time at the Games, sitting with the commoners and watching Florian up in his box, looking all stern and imperial."

"The trapdoor seems to have paid off for you."

Janto's voice sounded a little hollow and distant, so she paused and waited for him to catch up. "Lucien and I sneaked out so many times together. That was before he went away to war and lost his leg. I never anticipated I'd use it for something like this."

"Aren't these tunnels a security risk? Shouldn't the emperor be concerned about spies getting into them?"

She gave him a stern look over her shoulder. "Don't get excited. The floors of the Imperial Palace are spelled to muffle sound, as are the walls, so you won't hear anything through them. Aside from my trapdoor, there are no exits except the one used by the servants who change the glows. So the hypocaust is not the spy's delight you think it is."

She counted heat-glows, turned in the right places, and found the access tunnel. As the ceiling ascended, she stood, shaking her arms and legs to relieve cramped muscles. Behind her, Janto rose to his full height and brushed the dust from his clothes. He pointed to the door ahead. "That's the exit?"

"Yes."

"Where are the guards? Are they just on the other side?"

"No," she said. "There's a short hallway first. They're at the intersection of that hallway and the larger one."

"Good. Let's go." Janto headed for the door.

"Are you going to shroud us?"

"Already have. See the shimmer?" He eased the door open, peered out, and beckoned Rhianne through.

The two guards did not look in Rhianne's direction as she came out the door, but they were so broad in body they took up the entire hallway. "We can't get past them," she whispered to Janto, who slipped out beside her.

"Not to worry," he said, and gave the door a shove, angling it on its hinges to make it squeak.

The guards turned, suddenly alert. "Door's open," one of them said to the other.

The other rolled his eyes. "Well, shut it."

The first guard walked toward the door.

Janto placed a hand on Rhianne's shoulder and guided her first around the walking guard, then the stationary one. They left the palace through the slave entrance, and Rhianne took the lead, heading for the stables. She needed a horse for her journey, although she would not be able to keep Dice for long. All the horses in the stable were too imperial in appearance, too conspicuous. Also, she was secretly hoping she would need a second horse.

Janto had said nothing about going with her. He'd only said he would help her escape. She'd been afraid to ask if he would go with her, fearing she wouldn't like the answer, but there was no getting around it. She had to just say the words. When they were almost to the stables, she stopped him. "Will you come with me?"

He blinked. "You mean run away?"

"Yes."

His answer was a long time coming. "I can't."

"I know there's risk involved, but . . ." She blew out her breath, trying to settle her nerves. "I love you, Janto.

I want nothing more than a life with you. We can run so far away that Florian will never find us—even out of the country, to Sardos or Inya. You choose which." She took his hands and looked him in the eye. "I don't care if we're poor. I don't care if I'm not royalty. I just want to be with you."

"Rhianne . . ." He squeezed her hand, and he looked so sad that she knew his answer was not going to be the one she wanted. She felt the tears starting. He folded her trembling body into his arms. "What sort of man would I be if I ran off to enjoy a comfortable life in exile while my people suffer execution and enslavement? If I did that, I wouldn't be worthy of you. I have to save my country first. If I accomplish that, *then* you and I can be together."

"Mosar has fallen!" she said. "Your obligation is over."

"It will never be over," said Janto.

"Whatever plan you have, it is hopeless," said Rhianne. "You cannot retake Mosar. Even if you did, Kjallan forces would take it back from you. You will wind up enslaved or on a stake. My uncle has destroyed your country. Why let him destroy you as well? Let this be your small victory, your way of showing him he cannot win every battle. Come with me, and we'll build a life together. *Please.*"

"I can't do it." He stroked her hair. "However . . . you could come with me to Mosar."

She looked up. "And assist in your rebellion?"

He nodded.

She rested her head on his shoulder and sighed. "No. If you take back your country, I'll be cheering for you, but I'm Kjallan. I can't fight my own people."

"Then it seems we're at an impasse," said Janto.

Indeed they were; she could see no way around it. Rhianne closed her eyes and warmed herself in Janto's embrace until she could no longer bear the pain of their imminent separation. Why had she not brought a gift for him, something for him to remember her by? Perhaps she had never truly believed he would refuse her and stay behind. She would give him a well-wishing, since it was all she had to offer. "Soldier's blessing upon you," she whispered.

He smiled and drew three fingers down her forehead in the Mosari way. "Blessings of the Three: Soldier, Sage, and Vagabond."

She reached up and kissed him one last time. Then she headed for the stable, alone.

Back at the palace, Janto felt Rhianne's loss keenly, but he knew he'd done the right thing in helping her get away. Augustan was as bad an intended husband as he'd imagined—worse, in fact. He only worried that he had not helped her enough, that he should go with her to protect her and hide her from the guards who would inevitably be turned out to search for her. But he was king of Mosar, and his people needed him. Rhianne was smart and resourceful. He had to trust in her abilities. She had as good a chance of outrunning Florian's minions as anyone.

He'd been of half a mind to confess his true identity to Rhianne at their parting. What harm would it do now? But then, what purpose would it serve? Their paths were diverging. Let her memories of him remain untainted. She didn't need to grieve, as he did, about what might have been, had their countries never been enemies.

Donning his shroud, Janto collected paper, ink, and a

quill and returned to the hypocaust. In showing him this secret passageway, Rhianne had given him a magnificent parting gift. And until now, he hadn't even known of its existence! This underground heating system apparently lay beneath the entire palace, a thin layer filled with heat-glows that servants activated or deactivated as needed to keep the Imperial Palace at the desired temperature. Rhianne had claimed it was useless for spying, because it had only one entrance, and spells prevented sound from leaking through the walls and floors, but for all that he loved and trusted Rhianne, the uses of the hypocaust were easily something she might lie about. Or be ignorant about. She cared about him, but she was Kjallan, and, as she had just made so abundantly clear, she would not knowingly betray her people.

In a way, he was glad she'd refused to go to Mosar with him. It was a fool's errand; he would almost certainly be killed there. Better she should stay here on Kjall and begin a new life.

Gasping in the stifling heat, he summoned magelight and, with paper and ink, mapped the entrance corridor and everything he could see from the place he now sat, marking each individual heat-glow on the map.

Rhianne said that she and Lucien had sneaked out together through the hypocaust. She could have meant they both sneaked out through the trapdoor in her room. But wasn't it far more likely that Lucien had a trapdoor in his own room? If so, he needed to find that door. The rooms of the Imperial Heir could hold valuable intelligence about the attack, or feint, or whatever it was that was happening on Sardos. If Janto had to map every inch of the hypocaust to locate Lucien's trapdoor, he would do it.

Hours later, around dawn, guards began pouring into the once-empty hypocaust, and Janto knew Rhianne's disappearance had been discovered. They crawled up and down its sweltering passageways, searching perhaps for Rhianne herself, or else the exit she'd taken. No doubt they were bewildered, trying to work out how she could have slipped past the Legaciatti.

Their presence made any further mapping dangerous, so he left the tunnels. It was time for a new approach anyway. His all-night study of the hypocaust had impressed upon him the difficulty of mapping the entire system; the structure was enormous. Since his priority right now was finding a trapdoor into Lucien's room, why not find out where Lucien's room was located aboveground, and then, back in the hypocaust, map his way directly to that location? He headed into the north dome with that goal in mind.

23

Lucien Florian Nigellus, heir to the Kjallan throne, tugged an ear as he studied the Caturanga board. Should he make a bid for the Soldier? Or was it time to put his Traitor into play? He raised his eyes to the young man sitting across from him in case his opponent's facial expression might offer him any clues. Trenian was a student he'd discovered at the palaestra, where young officers-to-be were trained. At the end of the season, Trenian would earn his officer mark, and when that happened, he'd be transferred to a distant battalion, but Lucien intended to keep an eye on him from afar. He admired sharp minds, and this boy was one of the most promising Caturanga players he'd met. At the moment, Trenian looked absolutely guileless, which meant he had a trick or two up his sleeve.

Lucien moved the Traitor.

The door that led to his rooms groaned on its hinges.

"Gods curse it," he muttered, studying the altered board as he awaited Trenian's move. The boy was setting a trap for him, somewhere. But where? He called to his door guard, "Can it wait, Hiberus?" When there was no answer, he glanced up. Florian was striding into the room.

A bolt of fear shot through him. He seized his crutch, pushed back his chair, and stood. Trenian rose awkwardly, aware that he should not embarrass the higher-ranking Lucien by standing faster and more smoothly, but not wanting to appear disrespectful to the emperor.

It was clear from the length of Florian's stride and the tightness of his jaw that the emperor was angry about something. Lucien swallowed nervously. What had he done this time? He never *tried* to upset Florian. Indeed, he'd done his best to stay on the man's good side. "Father." He inclined his head as the emperor approached.

But Florian just kept coming. He strode to the small rosewood table upon which sat the Caturanga board, tucked his hands underneath it, and upended it, using his magically enhanced strength to fling table, board, and pieces across the room. "This. Useless. Game!" he shouted.

The board landed askew and broke. Pieces rolled along the wooden floor and under chairs and tables. Trenian stood frozen, horrified.

Lucien met the youngster's eyes. "You're dismissed," he said. "Go."

Trenian left the room as swiftly as he could without breaking into a run.

Florian advanced on Lucien.

Lucien took a step backward. "Is something wrong?"

Florian answered with a blow across Lucien's face that might have broken his jaw if his war magic had not signaled him to turn his head. Still the impact knocked him backward and off balance. He staggered.

"Oh, stand up," said Florian. "Sapskull."

Lucien set his peg leg and crutch firmly on the floor and recovered his balance. He worked his jaw, blinking rapidly. When Florian hit him, some childish part of him always wanted to cry. It was embarrassing and stupid, and he was never going to let that part of him have its way. Another part of him quivered with the furious desire to strike back, but that was an urge he absolutely had to suppress. No one attacked the emperor and survived.

"Rhianne is missing," said Florian.

Despite his still-rattling head, those words shocked him. "What do you mean?"

"Just what I've said. She's run away."

Lucien lifted his eyes to Florian's, perplexed. Hadn't he placed Legaciatti in front of the hypocaust exit just to prevent that from happening? "How did she get out?"

"It appears there was a trapdoor in her room leading to the hypocaust," said Florian. "But you already knew that. Didn't you?"

Lucien steeled himself for another blow. How was he to answer such a question?

"You must have known," continued Florian, carefully enunciating each word, "because you placed Legaciatti in front of the hypocaust exit."

"I was trying to *stop* her from getting out."

"You failed, because she got out anyway!" cried Florian.

"I'm sorry," said Lucien. "But I did my best to prevent that from happening."

"You didn't think to *tell* me about the trapdoor? I'd have sealed it up, put her in another room entirely—found some solution better than a couple of guards."

Lucien shook his head ruefully. "The trapdoor was something she used as a child. You were so angry with her already. I didn't want her to be in even more trouble. But how did she get past the Legaciatti?"

"We're going to find out," said Florian. "But right now I'm more concerned with you. How do you feel about facing a treason charge?"

Lucien gulped. "I tried to stop her from getting out!"

Florian frowned. "I don't care what you intended with your foolishness. You withheld information that led to her escape. However"—he held up a hand to forestall Lucien's protest—"I came here to grant you the opportunity to demonstrate your loyalty."

Lucien's neck prickled. He had a feeling he wasn't going to like this. "And how may I do that?"

"You will find your cousin," said Florian. "Some of your colleagues in the north, when you were in charge of White Eagle battalion, said you were a savvy tactician. Prove it. Use your best tactics and find Rhianne."

"Battlefield tactics and locating a runaway aren't the same thing." Lucien's mind raced. What if he tried his best and couldn't find her? She was smart, and Florian hadn't told him how much head start she had. Would he face a treason charge if he didn't succeed? He supposed deliberately failing at the task wasn't an option.

Florian's brows rose. "Are you making excuses?"

"No." He swallowed. "Have you considered that maybe you should just let her go? She's ungrateful and unreliable. Let her suffer on her own." He couldn't resist the opportunity to perhaps save his cousin from the fate the emperor intended for her.

Florian's brow arched upward. "Let her go?" He spoke the words as if they had a funny taste.

"Well . . . yes. For her to take a step this desperate, she must really hate the idea of this marriage. She'll never cooperate."

"I handpicked him for her," said Florian.

"She seems to disagree with your choice," Lucien murmured, discouraged.

Florian folded his arms, frowning. "Are you quite finished?"

Flinching from the contempt in his father's eyes, Lucien nodded.

"You speak as if I had a stable of imperial princesses to choose from and could simply swap another into Rhianne's place," said Florian. "I have only Rhianne and Celeste, and Celeste isn't of marriageable age. Rhianne *will* marry Augustan. And you *will* find her for me. Unless you'd prefer to face a treason charge for abetting her escape."

Lucien dropped his eyes to the floor. It appeared he had no choice but to drag his cousin back to this hated marriage, if he could possibly manage it. She'd never forgive him. "I'll find her."

Lucien stepped into the war room, followed by his father. He'd been here many times, but never in an advisory capacity. Always he'd been told to keep his head down and his mouth shut. For the first time, he would actually be dictating tactics. Too bad the circumstances were so unfortunate.

Officers and their lackeys crowded the room, some grouped together and speaking in low voices, others poring over a map spread on a marble table. There was something ironic about seeing all these men putting their heads together to work out a strategy not for winning a war but for capturing a runaway princess.

"Men," said Florian, "I want you to give Lucien your full attention. He knows Rhianne better than anyone, and I'm putting him in charge."

Some of the officers eyed Lucien sidelong as he limped

to the table. "What have you got so far?" he asked. "She escaped through the hypocaust. What else do we know?"

A tribune raised his wooden pointer and indicated a red flag that marked the town of Old Veshon, just north of Riat. "We know she was here around midnight. She visited a Healer for the wounds on her back. Then she sold her white mare and a substantial amount of imperial jewelry."

"After that?"

"The trail runs cold," said the tribune. "We're pretty sure she bought another horse. A stableman reports he sold someone a bay gelding during the night, but he can't remember details such as the exact time or whom he sold it to."

"Almost certainly that was her. She used a forgetting spell."

"We assumed as much." The tribune pointed to a semicircle of white flags marking the towns north and east of Old Veshon. "We figure she's in one of these places by now, most likely one of the northern ones."

"Why north?" asked Lucien.

"She rode north to begin with, and it's likely she began her journey in the direction of her ultimate destination," explained the tribune. "If she wanted to go east, why start by riding north to Old Veshon?"

"Because she was deliberately deceiving you. You're underestimating her. The radius of your search is too small—you've marked villages only twenty miles out. If she departed Old Veshon as early as midnight, and it's midmorning now, she could easily be a hundred miles from here."

Florian stepped into the crowd around the table. "Not likely. Rhianne is unaccustomed to travel."

"Doesn't matter," said Lucien. "She has a pile of money from Old Veshon—I assume she got good prices, with her mind magic?"

"She did," said the tribune.

"We must assume she rode hard all night, trading horses every ten miles at post stations or anywhere she could sell the old horse and buy a fresh one. Buying and selling are easy for a mind mage, even in the dead of night. She's skilled in the saddle, and she's desperate. We should assume she rode until she dropped—and she might still be riding."

Florian frowned, clearly unhappy with this characterization of his niece. "So what's your strategy for finding her?"

"I advise three strategies," said Lucien. "First, we track her through the horse. She bought a bay gelding in Old Veshon, and I'll bet she sold or abandoned it ten to fifteen miles from where she bought it. We pick up the fellow who sold it to her and take him to all the post stations within range; see if he can identify the animal. If we find that horse, we'll find the next one she bought, and so on. With luck, we can track her progress across the country." Lucien paused and looked around the room. He had everyone's attention now.

"Second, we use our signal network and notify the authorities of every town, village, and city within our search radius to be looking for her. Rhianne is clever, and her magic is powerful, but she has no skills for roughing it in the wilderness. She'll have to venture into civilized areas for food and other supplies, and as an attractive young woman, she's conspicuous. Forgetting spells are only worth so much. She may be seen from a distance by people she doesn't even notice, and of course mages are entirely immune to her magic. Have the towns mobilize search parties, and make sure every search party includes a mage. Offer rewards for information and for successful capture. And make it clear that there's a stake waiting for anyone who harms or despoils her."

"Third, mobilize any battalions stationed within the search radius and have them patrol the roads. A young woman traveling alone is a rare sight. If they see her, and they've got a mage in the party to ward off her defenses, they won't fail to recognize her."

Florian nodded his grudging approval. "Tribune Murrius, you're in charge of tracking the horses. Tribune Orosius, get on the signal network and organize the city authorities. Tribune Auspian, you'll organize the battalions. Move."

24

In the middle of the night, refreshed from a long midday sleep and a stolen supper, Janto reentered the hypocaust.

Rhianne had now been gone a full day. How was she faring? She hadn't been captured. He knew that much from the way the officers in the north dome were still dashing about the palace with gritted teeth and wrinkled brows. But she had to be frightened all by herself on the road. What sort of life would she find out in the Kjallan countryside, assuming she succeeded in her escape from Florian? Janto wanted her to be happy, but the thought of her eventually marrying some other man—even if it wasn't Augustan—bothered him, and the more he thought about it, the worse he felt.

Yet it was too late for regrets. He'd made his decision, and he would have to live with it.

He'd found Lucien's rooms aboveground. Now he just needed to locate the trapdoor, if it existed. He pulled out his hypocaust maps, which now sprawled over a dozen pages, and laid them on the floor, connecting them end to end. In his head, he projected the big structure of the palace onto the hypocaust and worked out which unmapped tunnel he needed to start working his way down. Two hours later, he'd mapped his way to the spot which, by his calculation, should be directly underneath Lucien's rooms.

He searched the ceiling with his magelight. There was nothing marked to suggest a trapdoor. He pressed upward, lightly, on each wooden square. All were quite firm—until he came to one that wobbled. Janto smiled. He pushed on the square again. It was loose, but there was resistance—probably a rug on top of it. He extended his shroud over the square to muffle any noise and pushed hard. The square rose enough that he could see that yes, he was lifting a rug. He slid the wooden square sideways, still beneath the rug, but away from the opening. Now only the rug blocked him. He reached up, probed for the nearest edge with his fingers, and folded it back. Through the gap, he felt a welcome draft of cool air. Sashi leapt through.

Clear? he asked his familiar.

All clear, replied Sashi after a moment. *The Imperial Heir sleeps.*

He dismissed his magelight and climbed up and out of the hole. He rested a moment atop the silk rug, letting his eyes and ears adjust to the new surroundings. Goose bumps pricked his arms. Sashi scouted silently, sniffing about the furniture.

Slow, rhythmic breathing emanated from a high four-poster bed. A crutch leaned against a bedside table.

Janto replaced the parquet square and opened the bedroom door, shrouding it to muffle noise. Through the door was the sitting room. He spotted Lucien's desk and hurried to it. He settled into the plush chair and opened the first drawer.

Inside were Lucien's personal letters. Skimming them, Janto discovered Lucien had several correspondents at the northern front with whom he discussed military strategy. The letters were detailed, going on about fine points such as supply lines and the locations of cannons.

They were useless to Janto, since they were a couple of years old and about Riorca. In each case he had only one side of the correspondence, but through careful reading he could piece together much of what Lucien had penned. What he saw confirmed his opinion of the Kjallan heir. The young man was a smarter strategist than his father—more rational, more detail oriented, and more innovative. Some of his ideas seemed to be controversial; at least, his correspondents reacted as if they were so.

Second drawer, more letters. One packet was from Rhianne, and when he saw her signature at the bottom—a signature he'd never before seen—something twisted inside him. He had nothing to remember her by. All they'd ever given each other were intangibles: conversation, love, and memories. He hadn't thought it important before, but now all of a sudden it mattered a great deal. He wished he had some sort of memento from her and that she had one from him.

She'd written the letters when Lucien was in Riorca. Their contents had no strategic value whatsoever, but Janto read out of curiosity, smiling at the flamboyant loops and whorls of Rhianne's handwriting. Then he stopped and set them aside, feeling as guilty as a kid caught listening behind his parents' door.

Third drawer, a treatise on military strategy that was interesting reading but entirely theoretical, with no specifics about Kjall. He set it aside. Below it, a three-day-old readiness report covering the entire Kjallan military. This, he realized as he paged through it, was gold. It named the location and destination of every ship and every battalion of soldiers, as well as status information such as the numbers of sick and wounded, stocks of provisions and ammunition, recent disciplinary problems, and the experience levels of the troops and their commanders. Janto put the other papers back in the desk.

He hadn't seen everything in the desk, but now that wasn't necessary. This was all he needed. He glanced at the bedroom door. How long could he risk staying here before Lucien woke? Maybe an hour or two. Or could he take the report with him?

No, it would be missed. He'd have to copy it.

The report confirmed that the Kjallans were sending a fleet to attack Sarpol. Twelve warships were involved, not just the three he'd already known about. The *Meritorious* was bound for Mosar—at least it had been three days ago, when the report was written—and Mosar itself had a garrison of three battalions and four warships. Janto winced. That was more than he would like to face in an uprising. Well, at least he knew.

Another six ships were bound for the port city of Rhaylet, which was odd.

Rhaylet was located on Dori, but Sardos controlled it. An attack on Rhaylet was an attack on Sardos and would certainly pull forth a defensive fleet. But a Sardossian fleet could not sail through the Kjallan-held Neruna Strait. It would have to go the long way around. Such a lengthy sail would leave it unable to render assistance in the defense of Sardos itself.

In terms of numbers, the feint seemed to give Kjall no material advantage. They could fight the Sardossian ships at Sarpol or they could fight them at Rhaylet; what did it matter? But in practical terms it mattered a great deal. Sarpol had ground-based defenses that gave them an advantage and rendered light ships useless. Anything Kjall could draw off was a win for them.

Janto shook his head in frustration. If only he could get word to the Sardossians! Then maybe they'd have a fighting chance at Sarpol. If the Sardossians could give Kjall a smashing defeat there, it would help Janto's cause on Mosar.

He read the document thoroughly and copied it onto his own paper, writing down even the small things, like the numbers of sick and wounded. Battles could turn on such details.

When he finished, he returned everything carefully to its place and went back to the bedroom. Lucien was still snoozing. Janto crawled back into the trapdoor. He pulled the rug over the wooden square and gently lowered both of them back into place.

About a mile outside the village of Hodboken, Rhianne's horse stumbled and went lame, nodding her head with each uneven stride. Rhianne pulled up and swung down from the saddle. The mare had thrown a shoe. Sort of. It was hanging on to her hoof by a couple of nails, clanking as the horse moved.

Rhianne clucked in sympathy—that had to be frightening and uncomfortable. She circled to the offending foot, the right fore, and picked it up. Lifting the hoof didn't tell her much that she didn't already know. The shoe had come loose and was hanging by two nails. It didn't seem possible to hammer the shoe back in without tools. Instead she pried it off, using the shoe as leverage against its own nails. Surely the mare would be happier with an absent shoe than with one that was half on, half off.

Tossing the useless shoe into the grass alongside the road, she led the mare forward experimentally, hoping the animal would be sound enough to ride. But the mare still walked unevenly, nodding her head.

"Well, old girl," Rhianne told the mare, "at least you didn't do this five miles back."

She led the mare up the road to the nearest farm. Some farms ran a cozy side business dealing in horses for travelers, and this one had a sizable-looking stable. She turned into the yard.

The farmer, when he came out to meet her, spotted the problem immediately. "Lost a shoe?"

"Back there on the road," said Rhianne. "I haven't been riding her since she threw it, and I don't think she's lame."

"There's a farrier in Hodboken could fix her up."

"Actually, I'd like to sell her and buy a new horse," said Rhianne.

He shook his head. "I've got animals for sale, but I can't evaluate the mare until she's reshod."

Rhianne reached out with her magic and embedded a suggestion in the farmer's mind: *I trust you. I want to help you.* She hated having to use her magic to win people's trust, but she had no time to earn it the proper way. "She'll be sound when she's shod. And she's a quality animal—nice paces, well mannered. So safe your children could ride her," she added, spotting a couple of youngsters peeping through the cottage window. "You could keep her for yourself or turn around and sell her for a quick profit after you get the shoe repaired."

The farmer chewed his lip. He checked the mare's teeth and felt each of her legs. After his examination, he grunted approval. "Perhaps we could work out a deal. You want to look at what I've got for sale?"

Half an hour later, Rhianne was cantering east, this time on a black gelding. While the travel was exhausting and she was sore all over from so much riding, she was, somewhat to her surprise, enjoying herself. She missed Janto, of course, and Morgan and Marcella and even Lucien, whom she supposed she'd eventually forgive for setting those guards at the hypocaust exit, but so far she didn't feel too lonely. She was meeting people every day, and they were so different from the people she'd known at the palace, so varied and wonderful. She was seeing tradespeople, innkeepers, farmers, housewives, and children.

She was more than two hundred miles from the Imperial Palace, and she saw now what Lucien had told her, that Kjall was not a wealthy nation. She understood how she'd been fooled. All her life, she'd been confined to the palace, where she'd been surrounded by the nobility in their fine clothes, with all their fine things. Even the nearby port city of Riat had been wealthy.

The rest of the country was different. While she encountered pockets of the well-to-do, mostly she traveled past shabby houses, lopsided barns, and grubby inns. Scraggly yards housed the family assets: more often than not, swaybacked horses and skinny pullets. And yet she loved the people she met. Even when she didn't use her mind magic, they greeted her kindly, gave her directions if she asked, sometimes offered her food or shelter. A few men leered at her, and still others thought of cheating or stealing from her, leading her to plant the suggestion in their heads, *I don't want to have contact with this woman.* But they were the exception, not the rule.

She found herself wondering what Janto would think if he were making this journey with her. As far as she knew, he'd seen only Kjall's royalty and nobility and their servants. Might he think better of her people if he spent time with the rest of the population, as she was doing now?

She was going through her hoard of cash faster than anticipated because she could not stop herself from pressing tetrals into the hands of children as she traveled. Twenty years she'd been alive, nearly all of them spent in a single building. How much of the world she'd been missing!

Lucien was crossing the bedroom floor with his crutch under his arm when he stopped short. Was that a white thread on the floor beneath his desk? He leaned down, touched a fingertip to his tongue, and touched the thread to lift it from the parquet square. It was nearly invisible. He had almost walked right by it.

He opened his desk drawer and pulled out the military's readiness report, careful not to tip it sideways. He opened it to page seven and chewed his lip. His suspicion was correct. The thread he'd inserted between the pages as an anti-tampering device was missing.

Who had been looking through his things?

He sat in his desk chair and went through the drawers, paging through each of his letters and documents. Nothing had been visibly moved, and nothing was missing. He wasn't dealing with a thief, but with a snoop or a spy. That was disturbing enough. How could a spy get into his rooms? They were warded day and night.

He frowned at the rug that covered his trapdoor into the hypocaust. Why had he not sealed that secret passageway years ago? He couldn't make effective use of it, not with his missing leg. But his father frightened him just enough that he liked the idea of having a way out in case of disaster. He could not easily crawl through those subterranean tunnels, but if sufficiently desperate . . .

What a fool he was. Someone had sneaked into his room, almost certainly through that trapdoor, and rifled his things. That person had looked through a document containing important and very secret military information. With Florian's idiotic attack on Sardos imminent, the stakes were unusually high.

There was a spy at large in the Imperial Palace, probably a Sardossian shroud mage. Now Lucien understood the bizarre incident in Florian's office. Augustan had tripped an enemy ward, yet his interrogation had come up clean. Important papers had gone missing that day. The event should have been followed up on, but then Rhianne had gone missing and all available resources had been allocated toward her recovery. An invisible spy must have entered the room at the same time as Augustan, triggering the ward so that the blame fell on the legatus. Then the spy had grabbed the papers. Clever bastard.

Lucien rose from his chair and shouldered his crutch. He limped into the sitting room. "Hiberus," he called to his door guard. "Send me a warder right away. And get me on Florian's schedule. I need to speak to him."

The spy ship was late. Three nights in a row, Janto had made the long trek out to the seaside cliff and signaled the ship, only to stare into the darkness and wait for a return signal that never came. He had, unknowingly, sent the ship on its relay mission just as the Kjallan fleet had been returning from Mosar. His ship might have sailed into that fleet and been destroyed. There was no way he could know its fate for certain at this point. But with the intelligence he possessed about the planned attack on Sardos, he could stand around and wait no longer. Somehow he had to get out of Kjall.

In the harbor, the *Meritorious*, bound for Mosar, rode at double anchor. One of its boats was at the dock, half loaded with casks labeled BEEF. Janto liked the look of that boat. He could more easily hide himself amidst cargo than among men, since cargo didn't notice when you bumped it.

Lots of guards, he commented to Sashi, who rode atop his shoulder.

Sashi's hackles rose. *Kill them?*

No. Too many. Janto felt the ferret's disappointment through the link and smiled.

Increased security at the docks was one of the side effects of Rhianne's disappearance. Some of the guards weren't in uniform and milled about in the crowd. With their erect, soldierlike posture, they were laughably easy to spot. The others were in uniform, and they stood before every boat tied to the docks, including the one Janto meant to sneak onto.

He needed a diversion to get past them. Something simple.

Shrouded, he trod along the wooden planking, dodging individual sailors and looking for a suitable group of three or more men. He would shove one of them while no one was looking, and masculine pride ought to take care of the rest. He spotted a likely-looking quartet on a spur just across from the *Meritorious*'s boat.

Just as he stepped forward to reach them, fireworks crackled in his ear, and he froze in terror. Fingers of orange and green lightning twined their way up from the ground, all around him. Gods! He'd tripped an invisibility ward.

He broke into a run. Men shouted and ran toward the ward, converging on his position. They couldn't see him, but they knew where he'd been a moment ago. He wanted to turn and make his path unpredictable, but the dock was straight with only a few spurs angling off it, none of which led anywhere but into the water.

He shivered in horror. He was pounding toward a dead end! He could go into the water, but he could not swim invisibly. His best chance was to turn around and go back the way he'd come—toward the guards.

He turned and ran back, ducking his shoulder as he dodged between the first pair of guards. His boots slipped on wooden planks he hadn't recalled being wet. Up ahead, a guard flung a bucket of seawater across the docks.

His stomach tightened with dread.

Something cold and wet struck him. He looked in the direction it had come from and saw an empty bucket in a guard's hands.

"There he is!" someone cried.

He extended his shroud, taking into it the water droplets that covered his body. But the ones that streamed off him could not be hidden. Another bucket of water hit him.

Someone collided with him from the side. He flew through the air and landed on the hard planks, wincing at a sharp pain in his knee. Sashi screamed as he was thrown clear. Janto tried to get up, but a heavy weight fell atop him, and another.

Run, Sashi, he commanded.

The ferret wriggled through a gap in the wooden planks and splashed into the water.

"We've got him! We've got him!" his captors were yelling.

Janto struggled, but the guards held him fast. His hold on the Rift and his shroud slackened, and he grasped at it mentally. *Sashi?*

If I go any farther I'll break the link, the ferret reported.

Through the link he sensed fear and exhaustion. *Are you still in the ocean?*

Yes.

Break the link, he ordered. *Get to dry land.*

Getting Sashi free was the best he could do—Janto was finished. He tucked his chin, scooping his necklace of glass beads into his mouth. He bit hard on one of the beads, cracking it open. Bitter liquid seeped onto his tongue. He gagged at the taste but forced himself to swallow.

He felt Sashi leave his range. He lost the link and the shroud and popped into visibility. The guards holding him down shouted in surprise.

"Hey!" A guard tore the beads off his neck and examined the one he'd bitten. "I think he took poison."

Another guard stood up and yelled. "We need a Healer here, right away!"

Janto's throat tightened. His vision narrowed around the edges and faded. Then he let go.

25

Janto woke disoriented. He swallowed with difficulty, finding his tongue thick and his throat swollen. He opened his eyes and for a moment wasn't sure he *had* opened them, since he saw only darkness, but as he shifted on his hard pallet, he located a broad rectangle of faint light halfway up the wall. Bars slashed across the rectangle. Prison bars? He tried to rise, but he was too weak. Also, something impeded his movement. Something heavy on his wrist.

A manacle.

Memories of the dock flashed through his head. His desperate run, the buckets of water they'd thrown at him, the poison he'd taken. How was it he still lived?

They'd called for a Healer.

He reached for the link to his familiar and, in a rush of relief, found it open and available. *Sashi?*

You're awake! the ferret crowed.

Where are you? How long have I been out?

Days, said Sashi. *I'm in the hypocaust.*

Janto could sense his ferret's position relative to him, now that more of his mind was awakening. *You're not below me. You're beside me.* Not in the same room, though. There was some distance.

You're in the prison, below ground, said Sashi. *The hy-*

pocaust doesn't go beneath the prison but runs alongside it. I'm as close to you as I can get.

I see. He was in the palace prison. This was extraordinarily bad news. They would have saved his life only in order to interrogate and torture him before staking him. He'd swallowed the poison to avoid such a fate.

They're going to kill me, he told Sashi. *You should get to a safe place—to the woods.* His death would not kill Sashi, but it would extinguish the fragment of his soul embedded within his familiar. Sashi would become an ordinary ferret.

You are mine and I am yours, su-kali, said Sashi. *I am with you until the end.*

The next day, Janto heard voices outside his cell door. He was strong enough now to sit up. The door to his cell was solid iron from the ground to about waist height. From there to the ceiling it was iron bars through which he had some visibility, but he was chained into a corner where he couldn't get much of a view. He stretched to the full length of his chains, trying to see out.

"Is that the one? The spy we caught at the docks?"

Gods curse it, he couldn't see who was speaking. That was a new voice, male, and it sounded vaguely familiar. In the short time he'd been conscious, Janto had learned most of the guards' voices.

"Yes, that's the one." That was Janto's guard, the one who'd brought him breakfast.

"When's he scheduled for interrogation?"

"A few hours," said the guard.

Janto shivered. Interrogation in a few hours. Lovely.

"I want to see him before you mess him up," said the new voice.

"As you please," said the guard.

The key rattled in the lock. Janto stopped contorting himself in an effort to see and retreated to a more natural position on his bench. The door opened. Lucien, the Imperial Heir, limped in on his crutch, looked at Janto, and did a double take. He turned back to the guard. "He's not Sardossian."

"No, he's Mosari," called the guard from outside the cell. "You didn't know?"

"I do now," said Lucien. "He's a shroud mage, isn't he? Where's his familiar?"

"Never found," said the guard. "It jumped into the ocean, and since he became visible while the guards were holding him, they think it drowned."

"You can't assume that. It might have gone out of range, or he may have made himself visible on purpose. He could have his magic right now, and if he does, he can make the familiar invisible. Send for a dog and search his cell. Search the entire prison. In the meantime, bring me a chair. I'll speak to him."

The guard gave a hoarse laugh. "Good luck getting anything out of him, Your Imperial Highness. He's silent as snowfall. You want him to talk, wait a few hours and we'll light him up for you."

Lucien's eyes bored into Janto's. "I can be persuasive."

Janto stared back impassively.

The guard brought a wooden chair into the cell. Lucien turned the chair backward and straddled it. After the guard had left, closing the door, Lucien said, "I know you."

Janto said nothing. He saw no reason to offer this man information for free.

"I wasn't expecting to find *you* here," said Lucien. "I

need to think about this." He rested his chin on the chair back. His eyes went distant. After about a minute, he lifted his head and spoke. "You're facing interrogation in a few hours. You can't be looking forward to that. They call it interrogation, but it's actually torture. You know that, right?"

No response.

"Here's what I'd like to know," continued Lucien. "Rhianne conspired with you on something relatively innocent—this plot to punish the slave overseer for his abuse of the slave women. But did she know she was working with a Mosari spy?"

Janto continued his silent stare. Why would he incriminate Rhianne?

"You think you're clever by not talking to me," said Lucien. "Here's why you should rethink that strategy. I'm a powerful man, and I can stop your interrogation from happening. You and I are enemies—we need not pretend otherwise. But in one matter, I believe our interests are aligned. We both care about Rhianne. Am I correct in that assertion?"

After a long pause, Janto said, "Yes."

"That was quite a trick you played on Augustan, with the enemy ward. I congratulate you."

A clumsy attempt at building rapport. Janto ignored it.

Lucien rolled his eyes. "I hate one-sided conversations. So, in the matter of Rhianne's welfare we are allies, and I will share with you something concerning her that you do not know. She is about to be captured. We've narrowed the search radius to a fifty-mile area in central eastern Kjall, and I believe she will be in the hands of the authorities within the next forty-eight hours. You may think fifty miles is a large area, but believe me, with our resources it is small. And Rhianne is making mistakes. She's giving away money to the village children, and we're tracking her through that."

"Rhianne has a big heart." It pained Janto that her generosity should be her undoing.

"I love her, but sometimes she lets her compassion override her good sense." Lucien rested his chin on the chair back. "If it were up to me, I'd let her go. I don't want this marriage for her any more than you do. But my power doesn't extend that far. All I can do is minimize the harm that will befall her when she is captured. Do you follow me?"

Janto nodded.

"If, in the course of your interrogation, it comes out that you and Rhianne conspired together, and that she knew you were a spy, that is going to be an enormous problem for her because that would be treason. I personally don't care if Rhianne committed treason, because I know that Rhianne is a woman of compassion and integrity. If she did such a thing, however ill-advised, it was because she believed it was right. The emperor . . . would be more concerned about it than I, but he'd still prefer to cover it up. He wants to marry Rhianne off to Augustan, not bring her up on treason charges. However, if the rest of the palace finds out — and they will, if you confess it in your interrogation — neither Florian nor I will be able to protect her from the scandal that will follow. If that's the situation we're dealing with, the only way I can protect Rhianne is to *prevent you from being interrogated*. So I think it's in everyone's best interest — mine, the emperor's, Rhianne's, and especially yours — if you start talking to me."

Janto swallowed. Did he trust this man? Perhaps he

should. Rhianne trusted him, and Lucien was making sense. "Rhianne knew I was a spy, though it was never her intent to commit treason. She threatened repeatedly to turn me in if I didn't leave the country."

"But she never followed through," said Lucien.

"No. She didn't want to see me tortured to death."

"Typical Rhianne. That's all I needed." Lucien rose from his chair and picked up his crutch. "Congratulations. Since your testimony would incriminate her, you just got out of your interrogation. But I can't save you from execution." He headed for the door, then stopped midstride, his eyes widening. "You know what? Maybe I can. Don't get excited—I don't know if it will work." Opening the door, he called for the guard. "Has his writ been sent up?"

"No," said the guard.

"Alter it," said Lucien. "Cancel the interrogation. This man is not to be questioned under any circumstances. Is that understood?"

"Perfectly, Your Imperial Highness."

"As for his execution, put it on hold. I've a potential use for him. Just keep him here for a while, and I'll be in touch."

Rhianne was resting her horse, letting him walk on a long rein, when she heard the rhythm of hoofbeats approaching from up ahead. Three horses came over the rise at a trot, each carrying a man in military dress. Their bridles and saddles were trimmed in white, and the soldiers wore the insignias from White Star battalion, but no blood marks. They were enlisted men, which meant they had no magic and were no threat.

She touched each man's mind in turn and dropped a

suggestion: *I am not interested in the traveler ahead.* Each man's gaze drifted away from her and back to the road.

Her tired chestnut gelding ambled along. Rhianne was hot and cold at the same time, sweating in the places where she was in contact with the horse while her ears and nose had gone numb from the morning's chill. She eyed the three riders as they passed alongside her.

Then the far rider broke ranks and cantered toward her. In a panic and uncertain of the soldier's intentions, she projected more suggestions at him. *I am not interested. I don't even see that woman. I'm in a hurry to get to my destination.*

Her suggestions weren't taking hold. He just kept coming! The other riders pulled up their horses, looking confused.

Rhianne snatched up her reins and kicked the gelding, hard. He surged into a startled gallop, but the other horse had momentum and caught up quickly. Her attacker seized her gelding's reins in one hand and her wrist in the other.

"Imperial Princess?" He smiled wryly. "There's quite a price on your head. Men!" he called to the other riders. "Get over here and help!"

"I'm not interested . . . ," one of them began uncertainly.

"Yes, you are! Get over here, and that's an order!" He turned to Rhianne. "Your tricks work on them. But they don't work on me."

"You're not wearing a blood mark," said Rhianne.

"It seems I forgot to wear mine this morning," said her captor as the other riders trotted their way.

*   *   *

The prison guards came with a dog, which sniffed around every corner of Janto's cell. After that, Janto's days bled one into the other, a shapeless mass of close confines, inactivity, prison rations, and a knot of dread he couldn't dislodge from his gut. He began to understand why prisoners scored the walls to mark the passage of time. He'd already become a little confused about whether it had been five days since Lucien's visit or six.

He had Sashi to keep him company, at least some of the time. The ferret stayed in the hypocaust during the day. At night, he left the sterile tunnels through one of many rat holes he'd found to hunt rodents in the palace's storerooms or gardens or sometimes all the way out in the woods. This involved putting enough distance between him and Janto that the connection between them was lost, temporarily disabling Janto's shroud magic. But with Janto locked up, there was no alternative. Sashi insisted he was stealthy enough to travel without the shroud, especially at night, and this appeared to be true since by morning he was always back in the hypocaust, regaling Janto with his tales of adventure. Then he would sleep most of the day.

Suddenly, the key rattled in the lock. Janto, still manacled to the wall, sat up on his hard bench. He didn't think it was dinnertime yet, but one could hardly tell in this place, and he was seldom hungry, though eating did at least give him something to do. The door opened, and he looked for his jailer.

Rhianne stood in the doorway.

Gods, she was beautiful. Disheveled and unhappy, her eyes all bloodshot, and it didn't matter. When he looked on her, the whole world fell away. His throat seized up — he didn't know what to say. She shouldn't be here. It meant she'd been captured and would be forced to marry Augustan.

Then he saw the man behind her, gripping her arm. Emperor Florian. *Forget him,* he decided. *They're going to kill me anyway.* "Rhianne, I'm sorry," he grated with a voice he hadn't used in days.

"Janto, I—" She yelped as the emperor did something to her arm and dragged her away.

Janto tried to rise from his bench to see where they were going, but his manacles didn't allow him to do so. He sat as quietly as he could, his heart thudding wildly in his chest. He cocked his head and tried to listen. He could hear them moving—more than two people. Perhaps some guards as well as Rhianne and the emperor. Were they leaving? No, they seemed to be entering a room down the hall from where he was. There was talk, but he couldn't make any of it out. Only the men were speaking, not Rhianne.

He heard what sounded like a blow and sat up very straight. Then came another blow, followed by a small cry from Rhianne.

She was getting another set of stripes.

He huddled against the wall, wincing as the blows came faster. Why had he not gone with her and protected her from discovery? Why had he not saved her from this?

26

Rhianne sat in Florian's office, leaning forward so her bandages didn't touch the chair. Her back was a searing wall of pain. Florian frowned at her from across his hardwood desk. Lucien was with them too, for what purpose she could not guess. He wasn't making eye contact with anybody, and he looked awfully uncomfortable. He sat on the same side of the desk as Rhianne but apart from her, his knees angled toward the door, as if he wished he could make a run for it.

"My patience is exhausted," said Florian. "You will sign the marriage contract, and you will sign it now."

Rhianne shook her head. "I'm not marrying Augustan." She needed to get this waste-of-time meeting over with so she could find out more about Janto. Why had Florian shown him to her? Had he been sentenced yet, and could she possibly get him out? He must have been captured recently—her people never held spies for long. Lucien would know.

"Foolish girl," said Florian. "Do you think I picked Augustan for you by accident? Do you think I don't know what you are? Do you think I don't know what *he* is?"

The hair rose on the back of Rhianne's neck. She lifted her eyes to meet her uncle's.

"You were a wild, rebellious girl who grew into a wild, rebellious woman. No surprise—I knew your mother well, and you're just like her. I knew you would need a stern, no-nonsense husband, one with a reputation for bringing to heel the laziest, most dissipated soldiers in the ranks—"

"Rhianne is neither lazy nor dissipated," protested Lucien.

"If he can tame the worst of my soldiers, he can tame Rhianne," said Florian. "So. You'll either sign, and we'll have a lovely imperial wedding with all the trimmings. Or I'll forge your signature and throw you on the boat with Augustan. We'll forgo the wedding, and he'll do what he must."

Rhianne sat speechless. How was she to choose between those two horrible options? And Soldier's hell, what was she going to do about Janto?

"Oh," said Florian, "Lucien has some alternative plan he wants to present to you."

She turned to her cousin with pleading eyes. Could he really help her?

Lucien swallowed. "Don't get your hopes up. It's not much of an alternative." He took a deep breath. "We've captured a Mosari man—he's down in the prison. I asked Florian to show him to you because I believe you're familiar with him."

Rhianne's heart beat faster. How much should she confess to? "He was a slave. He used to teach me the Mosari language in the Imperial Garden."

"Yes, well, as it happens—I know you weren't aware of this, but it turns out he was a Mosari spy named Janto." Lucien pulled some papers out of an interior pocket of his syrtos and handed them to her. "We caught him at the docks, trying to leave the country with these in his possession."

Rhianne studied the papers. They were written in Mosari, and hastily so. She couldn't make the writing out very well. There were a lot of numbers, and some place names. She picked out *Sarpol* and *Mosar*. "I'm not sure what I'm looking at."

"It's a rough copy of a military document. The point is he's a spy and he's been sentenced to death. I know you were fond of him at one time and might prefer he didn't die. Is that so?"

Rhianne nodded.

"Now it seems to me that you have something Florian wants, your signature on the marriage contract and willing participation in the imperial wedding. And he has something you want, the life of this man. I thought a trade might be brokered between the two of you."

Hope surged within Rhianne. Of course! She'd have thought of it herself if she hadn't been panicking and fogged with searing pain. She would trade her compliance for Janto's life.

"What?" said Florian. "I cannot spare the life of an enemy spy."

"Can you not?" said Lucien. "We could use a forgetting spell on him so he remembers nothing of what he learned here, and then exile him to Dori. He's Mosari. His country is already conquered and no threat to us. Why not show mercy in this one case?"

Rhianne looked Florian in the eye. "I'll sign the marriage contract in exchange for the Mosari man's life, but under no other condition." Exile to violent, unstable Dori, an island cursed by the gods, wasn't ideal, but she would do anything to save Janto's life.

Florian stared at the two of them, clearly stunned at the direction this conversation had taken. "You'll sign?" he asked Rhianne. "And you'll participate in the wedding without protest? In exchange for some worthless man's life?"

"You have my word," said Rhianne, "provided Lucien makes all the arrangements regarding the Mosari's exile."

"Done," said Florian. He held out his wrist, and Rhianne clasped it.

Another day crept by. Janto had been certain something would happen after Rhianne's capture. Either whatever Lucien had referred to would take place—something about finding a use for him—or he'd be executed. But instead he languished in his cell, wondering if Lucien had forgotten about him. And what was going on with Rhianne? Was she being forced to marry? He tried not to think about that.

Then two Legaciatti and a woman entered his cell.

"What's going on?" he asked in Kjallan.

The Legaciatti grabbed his arms and shoved him against the wall.

"I'm not to be interrogated. Orders from the Imperial Heir—"

"Quiet," said the woman.

One of the guards spat on the floor. "Personally, I think he should be flogged to death."

The woman placed a hand on his forehead. Janto twisted away, suspecting mind magic, which frightened him more than the prospect of being beaten. He touched the link to assure himself it was still there. Sashi was asleep but within range.

"Be still," said the woman through gritted teeth, grabbing a hank of Janto's hair to immobilize him.

I want to cooperate with these people. The thought ran through his head, confusing him because he *didn't* want to cooperate with these people, but the thought remained, persistent. Then his magic rose up within him and forcibly expelled the thought, leaving him clearheaded. A suggestion. She'd used a suggestion on him.

Not wanting her to realize that her magic hadn't worked, Janto relaxed in her grip.

"See?" said the woman to the guards. "No need for brutality. Quiet, now," she instructed Janto. "This is just a forgetting spell."

"What are you making me forget?" That was more disturbing than a suggestion.

"Your ill-gotten knowledge," said the mind mage.

"What does it matter what I know? I'm going to be executed!"

The mind mage sighed. "Actually, you're not. Someone has struck a deal for your life. You're being exiled to Dori."

Janto stared at them, unblinking. To Dori? Not his first choice of destinations, to be sure, but he wouldn't quibble. He had no doubt who had bargained for him, and it wasn't Lucien—not acting on his own, anyway. "What did Rhianne trade for my life?"

"I don't know what you're talking about, spy."

Probably she really didn't. Janto suspected the deal had been struck behind closed doors, and nobody knew the details outside the imperial family. He had a sick feeling it involved Rhianne's marriage. "Is the princess getting married?"

"Of course," said the mind mage.

Gods curse it. She'd traded *something*, and it couldn't possibly be good. She shouldn't have intervened. It was his failure, getting caught at the docks. He should be the one to suffer the consequences for it.

"Be still," ordered the mind mage. "This won't hurt. And once it's done, you'll be out of prison and off to Dori."

"Hope you like volcanoes," added a guard.

Sashi, called Janto.

Mm? answered the sleepy creature.

Wake up. They're shipping us off to Dori. But first—

He felt the unfriendly magic invade his mind, probing crudely against his defenses. It would be a simple matter for him to throw the spell off. But a forgetting spell was more invasive than a suggestion, and if he simply threw it aside, the mind mage might notice. Instead, he touched the repugnant magic tentatively with his own. The mage's spell was soft and pliable. In the domain of his own mind and body, his magic was stronger. Gently, he diverted the invading spell. He played with it, making it spin in harmless circles.

The magic vanished.

"It's done," said the mage. "He's forgotten everything that's happened in the last six months."

Janto feigned a look of blank incomprehension.

A Legaciattus chuckled. "Instant sapskull. I wish I could do that." He unshackled Janto's wrists. "On your feet, idiot."

Janto stood, his legs shaking with weakness at the unaccustomed effort. *Sashi, they're about to move me, I think to a ship at the docks. You've got to meet me there somehow.*

I have more distance to cover than you! cried a panicking Sashi.

Hurry. I'll try to delay them.

Going, said Sashi. The link died as he went out of range.

The mind mage left, and the Legaciatti led Janto up the stairs and out of the palace. Outside, a carriage awaited them.

He looked around desperately for his familiar. The link was still dead. He could orient on Sashi's direction—northwest of him—but he had no idea how much distance lay between them.

A Legaciattus opened the carriage door. "Get inside."

Janto yanked his arm out of the guard's grip and punched him in the face. A brief scuffle ensued. In moments, Janto was pinned in the grass with his arms wrenched behind him.

"What the fuck's wrong with you?" cried the Legaciattus he'd struck.

"He's confused," said the other Legaciattus. "He's forgotten everything, remember?"

Janto fought them as they hauled him up. He shoved a foot against the carriage wall as they tried to force him in.

"Let go!" cried a guard. Another kicked his leg aside, and they shoved him into the carriage.

His world lit up. The link came afire, and though he couldn't see Sashi yet, he threw a shroud over him. *In the carriage!*

The Legaciatti climbed in. One sat across from Janto while the others took places on either side of him, squeezing him in tightly. He craned his neck to see through the open door. A rust and white streak bounded over the grass, invisible to everyone but himself. Janto's heart leapt.

The carriage surged into motion. Nobody felt the impact, but Janto sensed it, when his ferret leapt onto the footman's seat in the back.

The ship they brought him to was the *Lynx*. It was a clipper, small and narrow bodied and fast. Unlike the big warships moored out in the harbor, the *Lynx* was shallow enough to be tied up right at the docks.

"You there!" called a Legaciattus to the man standing watch, high above them on the ship's deck. "We've got your passenger."

"Hurry up or we'll lose our tide," the sailor called down.

Sashi, get in now, advised Janto.

The shrouded ferret ran up one of the hawsers fastening the ship to the docks and disappeared through the cat hole.

The Legaciatti forced Janto to climb a rope ladder leading up the side of the clipper, one man ahead of him and one behind. Once on board, they showed him into the darkness of the ship's hold and chained him to the wall. Janto was prone to seasickness. On a ship's deck, his stomach was always a bit dodgy. Just the idea of being in the hold, belowdecks, made it clench, and his mouth began to water.

"Here are your orders concerning the prisoner," said a Legaciattus, holding out a packet of papers to the sailor. "Direct from the Imperial Heir, so don't improvise." Janto watched the papers change hands and hoped they didn't contain any surprises.

The Legaciattus tossed a sack at Janto. "By imperial

command, you are to have supplies when you reach Dori. There they are."

That had to be a good sign. If the Kjallans meant to kill him at sea, or when they reached land, why bother giving him supplies? Rhianne must have negotiated this deal carefully.

The men climbed hurriedly up the ladder to the upper decks. Janto sat very still, hoping to avoid seasickness, though he knew it would be unavoidable once the ship left port. When his nausea subsided, he opened the sack. Clothes, a blanket, a block of soap wrapped in linen, and food—hardtack and dried meat. All would be useful things when he landed.

He was not enthusiastic about his destination. Several decades ago, the gods had cursed Dori, destroying its coastal cities with a massive sea wave and its inland cities with a volcanic eruption. People still lived there—one could see lights when passing by the shores of Dori at night. But few dared to land there, except to drop off exiles. Mosar had twice sent expeditions to Dori to see if there was anything worth recovering from that broken nation, but neither expedition had returned.

Still, Janto had his magic. He might survive the gods-cursed island better than most.

His questing fingers discovered something hard inside the blanket. He searched through the folds, located the item, and drew it out.

It was an alligator, about half the length of his hand and heavy for its size. Cast in bronze and painted, the creature was openmouthed, revealing teeth carved of onyx. Janto ran his finger across them. They were sharp. Tiny gemstone eyes glittered at him in the darkness.

He stared at it for a while, his eyes swelling with tears. *I never gave her anything.*

His stomach began to gurgle ominously. He lay down against the ship's hull, pulled the blanket over him, and cradled the trinket against his heart.

27

Janto slept on and off for several days, weak and ill. His sleep was fitful and marred by discomfiting dreams. At first, the crew mocked him for his seasickness, but as he grew weaker, they became concerned. It seemed their orders required them to deliver him alive. They started bringing him a cup of broth several times a day.

A sailor named Bellus, delivering his morning broth, spotted the bronze alligator in Janto's fist. "What's that?" He snatched it up and ran his finger over the shiny onyx teeth. "Too nice a piece for a Mosari beast-worshipper." He moved to pocket it.

Janto launched himself at Bellus. His fist glanced off the sailor's jaw as the man scrambled out of range, leaving Janto to flail uselessly against his chains. "Give it back! Give it back, you jug-bitten, jack-scalded . . ." He couldn't think of anything sufficiently insulting. Sirali would have had the words on the tip of her tongue.

Bellus laughed and held the alligator just out of Janto's reach. He called to his mates who were rigging a pump nearby. "He's not so weak now, neh? Look at him!"

"Give it back!" Janto roared.

"Give it to him, Bellus," said one of the sailors at the pump.

"Why?"

"It's a talisman," said another of the men. "A good luck charm. You want to bring ill upon us near the gods-cursed island?"

Bellus pocketed the alligator. "If it's a good luck charm, might as well be my luck, not his, neh?" He winked at Janto and climbed up the ladder.

Janto sank back against the ship's hull.

He upset you, said Sashi, fierce and angry. *Kill.*

No, su-kali, said Janto. *It's a piece of bronze. Not worth killing over.*

But he already missed his alligator.

Janto awoke to screams in the night. He'd been dreaming of hunting rats. Kill! Kill! No. He shook his sleep-clogged head. That was Sashi's dream, spilling over the link.

"Help! Oh gods, there's blood everywhere!" came a yell from above.

What's going on? he asked Sashi.

Don't worry.

Don't worry about what? Janto sat up and looked for Sashi in the nest he'd made for him in a corner of the hold. The ferret was not there. *Where are you?*

On my way back, said the ferret cheerfully.

I told you it wasn't worth killing over!

I bit him in the neck. He won't die.

As the fog of sleep cleared from his mind, he could sense his familiar's movements. Sashi was scampering along the upper deck. Janto's eyes went to the far wall just in time to see his ferret drop through a hole to the bottom level. Sashi bounded across the ship's bottom, leaping over pools of bilge water. Chittering in triumph, he dropped the bronze alligator into Janto's palm.

It wasn't necessary, said Janto. *But thank you.*

The trapdoor to the lower hold flew open, and three men stormed down the ladder. Sashi, invisible, scampered for his nest.

One of the sailors pointed at Janto. "There he is!" They ran toward him.

One man picked up Janto's wrists, still manacled, and followed the chains back to the wall. "He's chained. He couldn't have done it."

"Look!" cried another sailor. "The alligator. It's in his hand!"

The men looked at it, gasped, and backed away.

"H-how'd you get that?" stammered one of them.

"I don't know," said Janto. "I woke up, and it was in my hand."

Their faces paled. "Fucking gods-cursed Dori," said one of the sailors. They retreated toward the ladder as if afraid to turn their backs on him, then climbed, casting frightened looks in his direction as they disappeared onto the upper deck.

That's not all I got for you during the night, said Sashi.

Janto turned toward him. *What else?*

Sashi bounded from his nest and looked up at Janto proudly. Clutched between his teeth was a ring of keys.

For the second night in a row, Janto awoke from a fitful sleep to screams. The ship was heeling frightfully. *What'd you do this time?* he asked Sashi.

Wasn't me. I think something hit the ship.

Oh gods, were they under attack? Janto scrambled into a sitting position. On the decks over his head, men shouted above the roar of wind-filled sails and the creaks of stressed wood, but he could not make out the words.

Through the cacophony came the whine of a cannonball. Janto clutched his knees and ducked his head, taking cover as best he could. The arc ended in a splash. Another cannonball whined, and he ducked his head again, waiting.

An explosion rocked the ship.

Janto slid to the full length of his chains, yelling as the floor tilted. Something struck him—a wooden crate. It ricocheted off him and slid to the other end of the ship. *Sashi, get over here!*

His bag of supplies, which he'd wedged against the side of the hull, began to slide. He grabbed it. The supplies weren't too important, but the keys Sashi had found for him were hidden in the bag. The floor was tilted too much for easy walking. To get some slack into his chains and reach the wall, where he'd have something to hang on to or at least brace himself against, he grabbed the chains and climbed up them.

Cold droplets spattered his face, and he looked up. Water gushed through a hole in the side of the ship. As he stared, the ship began to list to the other side. The crate that had smacked into him began to slide again, in the opposite direction.

Sashi was close. Clinging to his chains with one hand and pressing himself against the wall, Janto grabbed his familiar with the other hand and stuffed him into his shirt. *We're getting out of here.* He reached into the bag and searched for the ring of keys.

The hatch opened above him, and a crowd of sailors hurried down the ladder.

"Who's attacking us?" Janto called to them.

They ran past as if they hadn't heard, struggling through the bilge water toward the hole with hammers and canvas and a ship bung. Some of them began rigging the pump.

Janto wrapped the chains several times around his wrists so he wouldn't slide around, extracted the proper key, and snapped his manacles free. *Ready?* he called to Sashi.

The ferret trembled inside Janto's shirt. *Ready.*

He let go of the chains and staggered toward the ladder.

There was another terrible impact—a great lurch and the sound of splintering wood. The sailors shouted. Janto's feet slipped out from under him, and he splashed into the water. His hand found the base of the ladder, and he hauled himself up.

All right? he asked his familiar. Sashi was sodden and gasping against his chest, too stunned and terrified to answer. Weighed down by his dripping clothes, Janto struggled up the ladder to the upper deck and from there to the quarterdeck.

He emerged into the night air, which smelled of blood and gunpowder. Another splintering crash brought down the foremast, spilling ropes, sails, and men into the water. The deck beneath his feet was a horror, slippery with gore and seawater, littered with ropes and pulleys and shards of wood. An enormous warship loomed on their port side while another rode at their stern. Strangely, both seemed to be of Kjallan make. Beyond them were many more vessels, an entire fleet bearing Mosari and Sardossian flags.

"Why haven't we struck our colors?" cried Janto, searching for the captain or anyone with authority. His eyes went to the flag mast. The ship *had* struck. The Kjallan flag had been lowered and replaced with the Sage, but the enemies seemed not to be accepting their surrender.

An authoritative voice boomed nearby. "Clear away the after bowlines! Up helm!"

Janto turned and ran toward the man issuing the orders. "Why aren't they accepting our surrender?"

"Don't fucking know. Get to work." The captain shoved him away, looked into the tops, and cried out, "Clear away the head bowlines! No, not there, can't you see it's been shot through? Use the ratlines!"

"Sir, I'm your Mosari prisoner. I'm an important man among the Mosari. If we signal to those Mosari ships out there and tell them who I am, they may help us."

The captain turned and looked at Janto as if he hadn't really noticed him before. He called, "Signaler!"

A pale adolescent boy ran up. There was a splinter, thick as a man's thumb, embedded in the boy's arm. Janto gaped at it. "Yes, sir?" said the boy.

"Signal whatever this man tells you," said the captain. He turned back to his crew. "Lay the headyards square! Shift over the headsheets!"

The boy looked at Janto expectantly.

"Signal *Jan-Torres*," said Janto. "Spell it out. *J-A-N-T-O-R-R-E-S*. That should work in any language. If you have a signal for *valuable information*, add that."

The boy summoned an enormous magelight ball and began to signal letter by letter. When he reached the *N*, the nearest ship's cannons blazed orange. Janto and the others dropped belly-first into the wreckage on the deck. Debris rained down on them from above.

They staggered back to their feet. "Finish," commanded Janto. The signaler continued.

When the signal was complete, he and the boy watched, trembling in anticipation.

One of the Mosari warships threw up a signal. It was no

poor man's magelight signal, but a blast of colors and shapes of the sort that only a pyrotechnic could produce. The signal was repeated down the line from ship to ship, a rolling wave of fireworks that lit up the black sky. Answering signals rapidly followed. They rolled their way back through the fleet, finally reaching the two attacking ships.

The cannons stopped firing.

28

The small boat plunged down the crest of a wave, splashing everyone within. Janto wiped the spray from his face and looked up at the rapidly nearing Mosari ship he'd insisted the Kjallans deliver him to as a condition of their ship being spared.

"All right?" one of the rowers called to him.

"Quite all right," said Janto. Was it obvious he wasn't a sailor? His stomach, which had calmed considerably since the start of the voyage, was voicing its displeasure at the rolling waves. He hoped it didn't show. This was a bad time to display weakness.

Soon the *Sparrowhawk*, Janto's brother Kal-Torres's flagship, loomed above them. Sashi wriggled out of Janto's shirt and perched on his shoulder, virtually proclaiming Janto to be a shroud mage. Janto had finally allowed his ferret to become visible, and the rowers took turns gawking at the creature. Sashi eyed the ship as they approached it. The hackles rose along his neck and shoulders. *This task will fall to me,* he said.

What do you mean? asked Janto.

But his familiar was quiet, as if preoccupied.

The rowers turned the boat neatly until it thumped

against the hull. Kal's men dropped a rope ladder down the side, and Janto climbed up. Not wanting to make a poor first impression on these countrymen he hadn't seen in months, over whom he intended to rule, he mustered his strength to spring over the rails at the top.

Kal-Torres stood before him with his familiar, the seabird Gishi, perched on his shoulder. He'd matured astonishingly since Janto had last seen him, more than nine months ago when the war with Kjall had begun. He'd be twenty-two years old now, to Janto's twenty-five. The soft lines of his once-boyish face had hardened, becoming angular and masculine, while the sun had bronzed his skin to a deep copper and lightened his blond hair. *Still the lady-killer,* thought Janto, *but in a different way.* Faint lines on his brother's face suggested stress and worry.

Flanking Kal were his zo officers and their menagerie of familiars. Behind them stood the ordinary sailors, men who did not belong to the ruling zo caste and did not possess magic.

After a moment's awkward hesitation, Kal stepped forward and embraced him. "Brother. We feared you were lost to us forever."

Janto returned the hug, thumping him warmly on the back. "It's good to see you again, Kal."

They separated, and Kal studied him from arm's length. "You've seen rough treatment, *kali.* Sapo!"

A Healer stepped forward from the line of officers. "Yes, sire?"

Janto started at the title. Sire?

Of course. In Janto's absence, Kal-Torres had crowned himself king. He wasn't wearing the royal carcanet, but only because that symbol of kingship was back on Mosar, if it had survived the war at all. Would Kal renounce the title now that Janto had returned? Janto studied his brother. Kal's expression was friendly and his manner easy, but the set of his jaw and the intensity of his gaze suggested more complicated feelings. When they'd last parted, the war had been everyone's foremost concern, but Kal's jealousy still simmered beneath the surface, awaiting only an opportunity to boil over.

"See to his injuries," Kal ordered the Healer.

Janto held up a hand to stay the man. "He called you *sire*. But Mosar already has a king."

The crew fell silent, leaving no sound but the wash of the waves and the creak of the rigging.

"You were away," said Kal. "Unable to take on the responsibility. So of course—"

Janto nodded. "You held the title during my absence. Now that I've returned, I reclaim it."

There was a moment's uncomfortable silence. Kal placed an arm on Janto's shoulder as if to guide him belowdecks. "You are ill, Brother. Let Sapo tend to you. Get your strength back, and we'll discuss this when you are well."

Janto took a step back, plucking the hand off his shoulder. "There is nothing to discuss. I am Jan-Torres, your king. To treat me as anything else would be treason."

Kal's cheeks flushed with anger. "I *rescued* you from that ship. A *Kjallan* ship. You would have died, else. And these men." He indicated the officers at his flank and the enlisted men behind them. "Do you think they will follow a stranger over the leader they know?"

Janto's gaze darted over the crowd. The sailors

dropped their eyes. They knew he was the rightful king. Yet there was no doubt they would stand behind Kal if forced to choose.

Do not back down, said Sashi. *You are king. He is not.*

"You are not the king of Mosar, Kal-Torres," said Janto. "To pretend otherwise violates our country's tradition of peaceful succession. It insults the memory of our mother and father."

Kal straightened, emphasizing his slight advantage in height. "You're not fit to rule. At Silverside, your error in judgment cost us a dozen mages—"

"Ridiculous," Janto snapped. "You've always envied my crown. If our father wanted to replace me as his heir after that incident, he would have. But he didn't. Do you question *his* judgment? While you sat out the war, repairing your damaged ships after fleeing in the very first battle, I fought on the front lines in Mosar, and when the tide turned against us, I went into the heart of enemy territory, seeking intelligence that might help—"

"You left Mosar to get out of harm's way," snarled Kal. "You probably spent the whole time on Kjall cowering under your invisibility shroud—"

Kill! Sashi launched himself from Janto's shoulder with a chitter of rage and smacked into Kal's seabird. The familiars tumbled to the ship's deck in a ball of fur and feathers and flapping wings.

Kal's mouth fell open. "What the . . . Stop him, Janto!"

A chill ran up Janto's spine. He did not stop his familiar. He knew, at least from stories, the Mosari tradition of *quanrok.* Loosely translated from the old tongue, it meant "gods decide." More practically, it meant settling a dispute between two zo by allowing their familiars, the gifts and occasional mouthpieces of the gods, to fight for supremacy. Had Sashi invoked the old tradition? He took a step back, giving the creatures room.

Sashi had broken Gishi's wing with his initial leap, grounding the bird. The two of them grappled viciously on the ship deck, hissing and spitting and biting. Though injured, the bird was large and powerful. Neither animal had an obvious advantage.

Sailors and officers leapt out of the creatures' way as the familiars chased each other around the deck, the seabird thrusting powerfully with its beak and buffeting with its good wing. Sashi's lithe body flowed like water as he ducked in and out, skittering sideways to avoid blows and leaping in for a quick bite with needle teeth. The bird's blows were heavy, knocking Sashi across the deck when they connected, but the ferret shook himself off and reentered the fray as lively and fierce as before, while the bird grew slower. Gishi was weakening. The seabird reeled, unbalanced, and Sashi leapt like a striking snake, bowling him over and pinning him with a bite to the neck.

Make Kal-Torres yield, said Sashi, *or his familiar dies.*

"Get him off!" cried Kal. "Your ferret's killing Gishi!"

"Do you yield?" asked Janto.

"Do I *yield*?" Kal sputtered. "What are you talking about?"

"*Quanrok*. The gods have chosen. Do you acknowledge me as king of Mosar?"

Kal's eyes blazed fury. Slowly, as if it caused him physical pain, he folded his body and knelt on the deck. "Men, honor your king."

Sashi released the wounded seabird. All around Janto, the sailors lowered themselves to their knees.

*   *   *

An hour later, Janto watched a Sardossian boat row toward the *Sparrowhawk* as it rose and fell with the waves. He leaned on the rail to conserve his strength.

Kal, who'd been overseeing some detail of sail trim, walked up and leaned on the rail next to him. "Well, *sire*, perhaps you could tell me your plans for the fleet."

"Answer some questions for me." Janto pointed toward the distant lights that had to be land. "That's Rhaylet, is it not?"

"It is," said Kal.

"Here's what I think you've been up to. First, Kjall attacked Rhaylet and captured it with six light ships. Sardos sent a fleet to recapture the port, going the long way, south around Dori, since they cannot use the Neruna Strait. The Kjallan ships made no attempt to defend the port but fled the moment the Sardossians arrived."

Kal's eyebrows rose. "How did you know?"

"The time I spent on Kjall was not wasted. The Kjallan ships planned escape into the Neruna Strait, but then you arrived. You pinned the Kjallans between yourself and the Sardossians and destroyed their small fleet. Am I right?"

"Yes."

"It was an excellent maneuver, worthy of the Vagabond himself," said Janto. "You may have saved Mosar with it. But there's one thing I don't understand. Those two ships there." He pointed to the pair that had attacked the *Lynx*. "They are obviously of Kjallan make, so I take them to be prizes. But why do they fly a flag that is neither Mosari nor Sardossian?"

Kal grinned. "That's my favorite part. When we attacked the Kjallans, only four ships fought back in earnest. The other two fired sporadically, often at nothing at all. We gathered that their crews were in mutiny and left them alone. By the time we'd dealt with the other four, the two mutinous ships had raised the Sage in surrender. It turned out both ships had been manned with Riorcan slaves, who rose up against their Kjallan officers in the chaos of battle and tossed them overboard. They had to plead our assistance after the battle—they were under the influence of death spells that would kill them if a Healer did not take them off, and the Kjallan Healers were among those they'd flung over. So we removed those spells with our own Healers, who also tended to them, and they've joined the fleet for the time being. Those flags they're flying are makeshift Riorcan flags."

Janto looked out at the two ships with new respect. How long had it been since a ship had flown a Riorcan flag? Decades. History was being made.

"Just so you know, they're rather bloodthirsty," added Kal.

"I noticed. They wouldn't accept the *Lynx*'s surrender."

"Their hatred of Kjall runs deep," said Kal. "I think all they really want is to kill Kjallans, as many as possible. Because of that, they may be willing to help us retake Mosar."

"I'm not sure I want their help. They sound like savages who won't take orders. Do they have a command structure?"

Kal shrugged. "A rudimentary one. But they're all we've got. The Sardossians won't help. I've asked. They fear the attack on Rhaylet was a feint, and Sardos itself may be the next target. They're returning home immediately."

"What do you know of the Sardossian fleet commander? What's his name?"

"Admiral Llinos. He's a decent sort. Solid, reliable, and conservative."

"How can we motivate him?"

Kal shook his head. "No way to do it, Brother. He's Fifth Circle. Another promotion will move him to Fourth, which gains him a third wife. He talks often about that hypothetical wife—I think he's got someone specific in mind."

"Damned hive breeders," grumbled Janto.

"I don't care for them either, but the point is he's not going to disobey orders when he wants that promotion, and you can't blame him for putting his country's needs first. Count the Sardossians out. I figure with the help of the Riorcans and your shroud magic, we can take one of the Mosari harbors. I can have Gishi scout for the one that's least defended, now that the Healer has repaired his wing."

Janto shook his head. "No point. Even if we take the harbor, we'll lose the land battle. There are three battalions of ground troops on Mosar."

"So many. Are you sure?" Kal's brow wrinkled. "We can free slaves as we go and build up our forces before we engage them."

"An untrained, disorganized force of freed civilians will have no chance against a disciplined Kjallan battalion."

Kal snorted in exasperation. "What would you have us do, Jan? You walk in here and take command, and for what? To have us sail around aimlessly, doing nothing, while the Kjallans loot our country and exploit our people?"

"Be easy, Brother. We will take back what is ours. But we will not accomplish it by invading Mosar."

Kal spread his hands. "How can we recover Mosar without an invasion?"

"There will be an invasion. It just won't be on Mosar."

"If not on Mosar, where?"

Janto smiled grimly. "Kjall."

29

Janto stood with Kal-Torres in the middle of the deck, with the ship's officers fanning out on either side of them, to receive the Sardossian admiral as he came over the side. Admiral Llinos was a heavy man, big in all directions, with a tousled mop of dirty blond hair and bushy eyebrows. He bowed to Janto. "King Jan-Torres. I am sorry for your loss."

"I accept your condolences, Admiral. May I congratulate you on your victory?"

Llinos beamed. "You certainly may, though without your brother's assistance, we'd never have caught them." His smile faded. "Their quick retreat makes me think the attack was a feint."

"I know for a fact that it was," said Janto. "Shall we step over to the quarterdeck and I will explain?"

Kal had suggested holding the meeting belowdecks, in the captain's quarters, but Janto, knowing he was more likely to get sick belowdecks, insisted on clearing the quarterdeck instead. Gesturing at Kal and two of his brother's key officers, he led the way abaft the mainmast to the upper deck. Chairs and awnings had been installed there. He bade them sit.

Admiral Llinos spoke. "Your brother has already

asked for my assistance in retaking Mosar. While I'm sympathetic to your situation, I must decline. We think it likely the Kjallans are mounting an attack on Sarpol, and I'm under orders to return there upon securing Rhaylet. We are finishing critical repairs to our ships and will depart at daylight."

"The Kjallans *are* attacking Sarpol," said Janto. "Very likely the attack fleet has already sailed."

Llinos looked grim. "Then I haven't a moment to lose."

"You will not make it in time."

"If sailing conditions are good—"

"You will not make it," insisted Janto.

Llinos shrugged. "I am under orders, so I must try."

"Is there any situation in which your proper course of action would be not to follow orders?"

"Your Majesty, I am aware that your country is in desperate need, but I cannot offer help when my own country is threatened."

Janto scooted forward to the edge of his seat. "What if I said you could stop the attack on Sarpol completely? Avert *all* bloodshed and sidestep a costly invasion. Then would you consider not following orders?"

Llinos frowned. "Such a thing is not possible."

"I will tell you how it can be done. I was recently on Kjall gathering intelligence. I know the Kjallans' strengths and weaknesses. They are vulnerable right now, like a turtle rolled on its back. We'll stop the invasion at Sarpol, and you will be a hero to your people."

Admiral Llinos looked skeptical, but he cocked his head, ready to listen.

Janto unrolled one of Kal's nautical maps and began to explain.

* * *

"Legatus," Rhianne greeted her fiancé as he strode into the fitting room, draped with the silk syrtos he would wear at their wedding ceremony. It was unfinished, with pins marking the locations where alterations would be made and adornments attached.

"Princess." He looked her over briefly and turned away, allowing the tailors to converge on him.

Rhianne, by now, was also a veritable pincushion. The seamstresses had been at work on her gown for an hour already, and they weren't close to finished. One of them gently tapped her arm, and she raised it so the seamstress could pin something beneath it.

Since agreeing to the marriage, she'd seen astonishingly little of Augustan, which worried her. Lucien had warned her that through her rebellion she was offending the man, and now that she'd finally succumbed, she was facing a very difficult marriage indeed. She had never liked her fiancé, but at least when she'd first met him, there had been some pretense of friendliness between them. That was gone. But she was trying to make up ground. If the marriage was inevitable, she had to make the best of it.

"Are you looking forward to the ceremony?" she ventured.

He snorted. "Do not trouble me with your small talk. You have made *your* feelings about this wedding clear to everyone."

She swallowed. Perhaps she would have to make a more serious attempt. "Do you remember the Mosari cat you gave me?"

"A cat." His voice was scornful. "I vaguely remember."

"She turned out to be a brindlecat. Did you know?"

"A *brindlecat*?" He turned and stared at her. "It had no stripes."

"She has them now," said Rhianne.

"I had no idea. Thought it was a Mosari house cat."

A seamstress knelt at Rhianne's feet, pinning up the hem to her gown.

"Get out," Augustan snarled at the seamstress.

Startled, the seamstress dropped her pincushion. "Sir?"

He raised his voice. "All of you servants, get out. I want five minutes alone with my fiancée."

The servants froze in surprise, then filed out of the room.

"Close the door behind you," Augustan boomed. When it was closed and he and Rhianne were alone, he said more softly, "There are rumors about you."

Nervous at this unexpected tête-à-tête, Rhianne turned away. "In the Imperial Palace, rumors abound."

"Very specific rumors," said Augustan. "For a long time, you were dead set against this marriage. Now, suddenly, you are all compliance and friendliness. Why? Some say a deal was struck, and it had something to do with a Mosari man in the imperial prison."

Goose bumps pricked on Rhianne's arms. "Who says such a thing?"

"Though it may shock you, I do have friends here," said Augustan. "Did you dodge a treason charge, Princess?"

"What a ridiculous accusation!"

"I don't think so," said Augustan. "That Mosari man was flesh and blood—several sources have confirmed to me that they saw him. But if you check the records, he doesn't exist. No references to him whatsoever. There's been a cover-up, and I have a feeling you were at the center of it."

She could throw his own misdeeds back at him—the war crimes he'd committed, the people he'd enslaved, the lives he'd taken. What good was loyalty to emperor and country when loyalty led him to do such things? Could he really shame her, when all she'd done was save a man's life?

But she would say nothing. She was supposed to marry this man, and it was no good fighting with him.

"Don't think I don't know what *my* place is in all this," said Augustan bitterly. "I thought when Florian offered me his niece, he was presenting me with a reward for my faithful service in Mosar. How naïve! You are no prize. You're the bad seed, Rhianne. The family member he needs to send as far away from the palace as he can. And my job in the battalion, before I became a legatus, was to reform the troublemakers.

"Well, I'll do it," he said resolutely. "The emperor wants my service, and he'll have it. I'll reform his problem niece on the distant island of Mosar. And I don't expect you to appreciate it, though it's for your own good. But let's not bother with the small talk."

The *Sparrowhawk* slipped upwind toward Kjall in darkness. Janto climbed the ratlines to the masthead and settled in the crosstrees. Sashi leapt from his shoulder and scampered into the rigging, chirruping with pleasure; he was fond of heights. Janto shook the rainwater off his boat cloak, pulled out a spyglass, and studied the Kjallan harbor. Up in the tops, the natural motion of the ship was magnified, sending him around in great, nausea-inducing circles. Good thing he'd skipped dinner.

Kal came up, hooked an arm through the shrouds, and settled next to him. "You can go higher for a better view."

Janto glanced at the topmast above him and shuddered. Heights didn't bother him, but up there the motion would be even more exaggerated. "I can see well enough. Ugly night," he added.

Kal shrugged. "It's barely blowing. And the rain covers our wake."

Janto nodded. They'd left the rest of the fleet behind in order to scout the Kjallan harbor. He'd had to shroud the entire ship, something he'd never done before. It wasn't hard, but there was a dilemma—whether to shroud the part of the hull that lay below the waterline. If he did shroud it, he left a giant ship-shaped gap in the water. If he didn't shroud it, he left the bottom of the ship visible at the waterline. Either way, an enemy eye could spot the anomaly. Thus they'd chosen to scout at nighttime under cover of darkness. The rain was unplanned, but it helped. He raised the spyglass back to his eye.

"Well?" said Kal. "What's the word?"

"The attack fleet has left. There are only three ships in the harbor."

"Good," said Kal. "No waiting, then. May I?"

Janto handed him the spyglass.

Kal stared through it. "Those are seventy-five-gun ships. They outclass ours. If we double up on them, it'll be a fair fight, or it would be in open water. It's going to depend on your taking that battery." He pointed at the tower at the northwest entrance of the harbor.

"I'll take it," said Janto. "You can count on that."

"I'd like to have the Riorcans with us, for extra fire-power in case things go wrong."

Janto shook his head. "No Riorcans in the initial assault. I don't trust them to show restraint when fighting Kjallans."

"Under the circumstances, I'm not sure we can trust our own men to do that."

"If we cannot, Mosar is doomed."

Kal pursed his lips. "As you command. No Riorcans." He climbed down from the masthead. Moments later, signals flashed up in silent communication to the crew. Men raced to their positions, some scrambling past Janto toward the topsails. Sashi leapt back into Janto's shirt for safety, and the ship began ponderously to turn downwind.

Janto raised the spyglass to his eye and peered closely at the lettering on the stern of each Kjallan ship anchored in the harbor. The *Blue Rose*, the *Reliant*, and—gods help him, there it was—the *Meritorious*. He lowered the spyglass, his stomach tightening with worry. Rhianne had not yet left for Mosar. It was good news, in a way. Her wedding to Augustan might not yet have taken place. But she would be at the palace when his men landed. She would be in the direct path of his invading force, and in the chaos of battle, nobody could control the path of every bullet or the arc of every sword swing.

30

Rain sluiced across the black seawater and spattered into the bottom of the boat as it rowed away from the *Sparrowhawk*. Despite diligent bailing, water had reached the level of Janto's ankles and was seeping through his boots. Twenty-four men, handpicked for their skill at gunnery, pulled at the oars with muffled grunts of exertion, forgetting, as did most people inexperienced with shroud magic, that there was no need to be quiet. They pulled into the harbor, veered wide around the *Meritorious* and the *Blue Rose*, and headed for land.

Kill, Sashi muttered, his whiskers quivering with anticipation.

Janto's stomach clenched at the grim reminder. He'd never liked war.

The boat ground to a halt against the gravel shore. Janto jumped out, landing knee deep in seawater, and splashed toward dry land. He wobbled on his legs; the solid ground felt funny after so long at sea. The two brindlecats that partnered his war mages leapt gracefully from the bow. Several of the men grabbed the boat by its tow rope and dragged it ashore.

"Sire, shall we leave someone with the boat?" asked a young man with stubble on his chin.

Janto struggled to remember his name. "Palo, isn't it?"
The man's eyes lit. "Yes, sire."

"We'll not leave anyone behind, Palo. We're not going back. We're here to stay." Indeed, if they failed here, escape would be impossible.

The men divided themselves into two prearranged squads, each headed by a war mage. Janto gestured toward the steep, craggy shore. "Let's go."

There was no path. They had to scramble up the rocks, gear and weapons jangling on their backs and belts. The tower loomed above them, the gleaming barrels of its cannons peeking out from gaps in the walls. Lights glowed within.

Janto struggled up the final slope. As they reached the tower wall, one of the brindlecats growled a warning. Moments later, two men in the orange of Kjallan soldiers appeared around the corner.

Janto drew one of the three pistols he'd stuck in his belt and gestured to the war mage San-Kullen. "On three," he said, and counted. He and San-Kullen fired simultaneously, dropping both Kjallans. Sashi chittered in triumph. Janto extended his shroud over the dying men to muffle any sound.

It was possible the tower had been alerted, but not likely. The shroud muffled the sounds of the pistol shots, but not the initial cries of the men. It was a tricky business, knowing just when to extend his shroud to include the enemies. Too early, and the enemies would see him. Too late, and their cries would be heard. He examined the enemy soldiers to make sure they were dead, then shoved the spent pistol back in his belt and drew another. "Come on."

They jogged around the tower to the front gate. Two

more guards stood there. Janto's men shot them and entered the tower.

Inside was a large spiral staircase. Sashi leapt off Janto's shoulder and raced into the hallway beyond. *First door on the left, sleeping quarters,* he rattled off. *A dozen men in their beds. Second door, five men playing dice. First door on the right, kitchen, two occupants.*

They killed the sleeping men first. To avoid discovery, Janto extended his shroud over the enemies before his men slit their throats. Then they moved on to the men who weren't sleeping. The Kjallans stared in shock, uncomprehending, as their companions fell, blood gushing from the gunshot wounds in their chests, and then took bullets themselves. They turned to answer the cries of fellow soldiers, only to receive sword slashes to their throats. It was butchery, ugly and without honor. It had to be done.

Janto was in the kitchen, where a cooking fire burned and a haunch of venison hung from the ceiling, when the upper levels began to rouse. Heavy boots thumped on stone overhead.

"You and you," he said, selecting men, "go back and guard the front gate. Kill anyone who tries to escape."

Five coming down the stairs, warned Sashi.

Janto barked a warning, and the remaining soldiers closed around him, shielding him so he could maintain his shroud through the chaos of battle. When the Kjallan squad reached the door, the Mosari met them with a hail of bullets. Men screamed. Bodies dropped to the floor. Smoke filled the room, obscuring the doorway. Janto and his men held their pistols at the ready. Another gunshot rang out, and one of Janto's men screamed.

Janto found the faint outline of a man in the smoke

and fired. The man dodged the bullet—he seemed to have moved a moment before Janto pulled the trigger.

"War mage," Janto guessed. "San-Kullen! Tas-Droger!"

The two Mosari war mages launched themselves at the Kjallan in the doorway, swords drawn, their brindle-cats snarling and bounding ahead of them. The Kjallan ducked out of the room. San-Kullen and Tas-Droger followed. Steel clashed, accompanied by the terrifying growl of the brindlecats.

"To the stairway," Janto ordered the rest of his men. "We'll work our way up. You," he said, selecting a soldier at random, "help the injured man." He glanced back at Lago, one of Kal's time-honored veterans, who sat in a pool of blood, clutching his leg.

In the stairwell, one of the brindlecats stood possessively over a body. San-Kullen presented Janto with a topaz mounted on a chain, the riftstone of a war mage.

"Your victory, your token," said Janto. "Keep it."

They worked their way up to the second level of the tower, with Sashi scouting ahead and calling back to Janto with the numbers and positions of their enemies. The ferret's joy and bloodlust spilled over the link, but Janto resisted the vicarious thrill. He was no ferret who killed to survive; he was human, and these were fellow humans he was slaughtering. Rhianne's countrymen. No doubt they had families and friends who would miss them.

There were only a few Kjallans on the second level. His men dispatched them and headed back up the stairs, which ended at an open trapdoor. Rain had fallen through, leaving the stone wet and slick. Kjallan soldiers clustered around the opening, staring down and pointing their pistols at what must have looked to them like an empty stairway, though it was filled with Janto's invisible war band.

Janto scooped up Sashi and stuffed him in his shirt. No need for scouting. "Fire," he said softly.

Gunshots roared. The Kjallans returned fire, and the top of the stairs erupted into a chaos of screams and shooting and smoke. Someone slumped against Janto. Janto moved away, and the dead man, one of his own, rolled partway down the stairs. When the pistols were spent, Janto's men drew swords. They hoisted themselves up through the trapdoor. Janto followed, his hands slipping on rainwater and gore.

On top of the tower, his men butchered the last of the Kjallans. Tas's brindlecat ripped out a Kjallan's throat. Nearby, two of Janto's men flung a wounded enemy over the side of the tower. Janto wrapped an invisibility shroud around the man to silence his screams.

It was finished. His men stood quietly, panting with exertion. The air smelled of sweat, excrement, and blood. A few men were missing. Still, his band of two dozen had killed more than a hundred Kjallans.

Tas-Droger saluted him. "Tower's secure, sire."

Janto nodded. "Good work. Reload your weapons and catch your breath. Then we'll put these cannons to work."

After a short rest, they cleared the bodies away from the cannons. Janto set two lookouts, one on top of the tower and one at ground level, and sent men to fetch the wounded Lago.

Four of his men had been killed in the final action. That left him with seventeen to man the guns. The tower had ten thirty-two-pounder cannons, better than anything the ships in the harbor possessed. He had enough men to operate two of them.

"Double-shot them," he ordered, as they sponged the bores. The men loaded the guns with powder, shot, and wad, and ran them out, ready to fire. "Aim at the *Meritorious.* Her mainmast." He gave them a moment to aim, and extended his shroud over the cannons to muffle the noise. "Fire!"

The guns roared, plunging back against their harnesses. The smoky tang of gunfire filled the air.

"Reload," ordered Janto, rushing to the stone parapets to assess the damage. He could not tell where the balls had struck, but the mainmast still stood. Something had been noticed, however, because men began to swarm up on deck, milling about, confused.

The guns were ready. "Fire," he ordered. This time, the mainmast shuddered at the impact. Then, very slowly, it began to fall. "Next shot, below the waterline. We'll sink her if we can. Make Kal's job easier."

The *Blue Rose* and the *Reliant* were waking up. After sending several more shots into the *Meritorious,* Janto had his men aim at the *Reliant.* Sailors swarmed into the tops of all three ships, unfurling the sails. It seemed they had decided not to fire back at the tower. Their guns could do little damage against thick stone walls. They meant to sail out of the harbor to safety.

The *Blue Rose,* the least damaged of the three, got under way first. Janto smiled grimly. It would not get far.

His eyes went to Kal's fleet at the mouth of the harbor. The ships slipped silently over the water with all lights doused, nearly invisible to anyone who did not know where to look. The *Blue Rose* spotted the attacking fleet too late, wheeling to fire. Kal's lead ships got their broadsides off first. Another circled around to the *Blue Rose*'s stern. Two more moved to engage the *Reliant*.

"Concentrate fire on the *Meritorious*," Janto ordered. The ship was crippled, down at the stern and listing to port. Its sailors could not get the vessel moving.

In less than an hour, it was over. The *Meritorious* was sinking. Its surviving sailors clung to lifeboats or leapt off the ship and swam for shore. Kal's fire mages had set the *Blue Rose* and the *Reliant* ablaze. The ships were terrible pyres, the flames climbing up the masts to leap for the heavens. Black smoke spilled off them in great clouds.

Beyond a doubt, they know we're here. Janto's eyes went to the Imperial Palace at the top of the hill. Rhianne was there somewhere. Might she be looking down at the harbor even now?

A flash of color caught his eye. The tower beside the palace had sent up the fireworks of a signaling pyrotechnic. Soon he saw answering signals from the tower at the far end of the harbor, and from others more distant, on the horizon. It would not be long before they were relayed all the way across the continent.

Send word, thought Janto with satisfaction. *Bring reinforcements. A good first step is to recall your fleet from Sarpol.*

He turned his attention back to the harbor, where his boats loaded with ground troops pulled for shore. *Hold on, Rhianne. I'm coming for you.*

Janto shrouded two men and ordered them to retrieve the enemy. They did so, confiscating the man's musket. He was wounded but alive. The Mosari soldier he'd shot was in similar condition. Janto ordered his Healers to help them both. These Kjallan civilians posed no serious threat beyond the odd potshot, and they were Rhianne's people. She would not want them harmed.

Neither civilian resistance nor the enemy troops that awaited him concerned Janto; he had them outnumbered and expected a decisive victory. He had all of Kal's men plus a large Sardossian army, while Florian had only a few centuries of soldiers stationed near the palace, plus the contingent Augustan had brought with him from Mosar. Together, the Kjallan forces amounted to less than a battalion. The greatest danger to his operation was not the opposition, but temptation. There was not a Mosari man among them who hadn't lost something to the Kjallans—his parents, his family, his home. Now each soldier looked out at the Kjallan capital city, licking his lips and savoring the taste of vengeance. Each of these houses in Riat hid valuables they could steal, Kjallans they could rape or murder. Only discipline and Janto's authority could prevent them from doing so.

A few days ago, as they'd sailed toward Kjall, Janto had visited each ship in the fleet and spoken to the men. "This is not a mission of war," he'd said. "It is a mission of peace." Kjall was large and powerful, he warned them; it would rebound quickly from the damage they inflicted. If Mosar could not establish a lasting peace following this attack, Kjall's retaliation would destroy what was left of them. "Every Kjallan civilian you murder could bring about the murders of a hundred Mosari. Every Kjallan woman you rape could lead to the degradation of your wives, your sisters, and your daughters. Cruelty and brutality have no place here. Only restraint can win this war."

The men had avoided his eyes and shuffled their feet. Janto knew what they were thinking. How could peace be established with the Kjallans, who'd razed Mosar's cities, beheaded her leaders, and enslaved her children? How could such a nation understand any language *but* cruelty and brutality?

Janto knew it was possible. He'd met one Kjallan, so far, who spoke the language of peace, and he had hopes for her cousin as well. If he'd found two, there had to be more.

He looked over the column of troops, satisfied so far at how they were bearing up. He'd set a good example with his merciful treatment of the man who'd taken a potshot at them. He hoped his men had noticed it.

San-Kullen galloped up on a fine chestnut horse, entering the dome-shaped shroud Janto had placed over half his army. It was a rough shroud, poor in quality and with many defects, but at this distance it should serve. He didn't want Florian to realize how big the invading army was, lest he and Lucien perceive the danger, slip away from the palace, and escape.

San-Kullen leapt off the horse. "For you, sire," he said proudly. "The best we've found. My men are tacking up a couple more, but I thought I'd bring you this one directly."

Janto took the reins and hoisted himself into the saddle. "Thank you." The horse danced and tossed its head, rolling its eyes at San-Kullen's brindlecat. "He's not gun-shy, I hope. He? She?"

"It's a gelding, and no, we tested him. Fired in front of

his face, and he flung up his head, but that's all. He's levelheaded," said San-Kullen. "Most of the animals we can't use at all. They're afraid of the cats, or gunfire, or both."

"Find us some more," said Janto. "Twenty at least. Sensible animals, but they don't have to be perfect. We won't be using them for combat."

The war mage saluted and ran off.

San-Kullen and his squad returned later with thirty-seven horses.

As the army neared the palace, Janto dropped the shroud; its defects would now be obvious. The Kjallans would now see the full size of his invading force. He turned to his mounted war band, thirty enlisted men plus six zo and himself, and signaled them to follow. He rode to the head of the column where he found Captain Arvel, commander of the Sardossians, and Captain Kel-Charan, commander of the Mosari.

"We're going around now," he told the commanders. "I'll meet you inside."

"Yes, sire." Kel-Charan saluted, looking uneasy. They'd gone over their plan the night before. Kel-Charan had wanted Janto's shroud for the frontal assault, but Janto knew the fighting would go well enough for the Mosari and Sardossians without it. He had other important things to take care of.

"Remember: no looting, no rape. No unnecessary killing. Avoid harm to the emperor; his children, Lucien and Celeste; and his niece, Rhianne, at all costs."

"Yes, sire."

Janto wheeled the chestnut gelding and galloped with his band for the far side of the palace.

Kill? asked Sashi from within his shirt.

Soon, promised Janto.

The main assault would take place through the two south entrances and the servants' entrance. That left three unguarded entrances through which Kjallans might try to escape. The heavy oaken gate at the east entrance, when he reached it, was shut and barred, probably with defenders behind it.

He selected twelve men. "Keep watch on this gate and all the surrounding area, including windows," he ordered. "As long as the gate stays shut, leave it be. If it opens and someone slips out, or someone breaks a window and leaves that way, stop him. When possible, aim to wound, not to kill. And be careful; you won't be shrouded."

"Yes, sire."

"If a war band comes out the gate and they're more than you can handle, don't engage," he added. "Send up a signal and retreat. Reinforcements will be on the way."

He rode on to the northeast gate, where he left another dozen, and then to the northwest. It was closed like the others, which disappointed him. He'd hoped one of the gates would be open.

"I need to get inside," he told his remaining men.

One of the war mages stepped up—Janto couldn't recall his name—and said, "Yes, sire. Through the gate?"

"No. A window."

Leaving the others behind to watch the gate, Janto and the war mage rode around the palace wall until they found a suitable pane of glass, which they broke with the pommels of their swords. When no enemies appeared, Janto handed the reins of his horse to the war mage and climbed inside. "Go back to the others," he ordered as he dropped down onto the parquet floor.

He was back in the Imperial Palace. He had to get to Rhianne before his men did.

"Go. Just go!" Rhianne pushed Tamienne out of her sitting room, toward the doorway. Shouts and gunfire echoed in the distance.

Tamienne hesitated. She looked at the doorway, then back at Rhianne. "My duty is to protect you—"

"And you'll do it best by fighting with the others! It's ridiculous you should stick by my side at a time like this. If the invaders overrun the palace, how can you possibly protect me?"

Tamienne looked torn. "First I'll take you somewhere safe—"

"There *is* nowhere safe. Go," insisted Rhianne. "There's no time for this conversation." She waved the Legaciattus toward the door, and Tamienne went, breaking into a run. Lesser soldiers might have avoided the battle out of cowardice, but Tamienne held back only out of duty. Decades of training had prepared her for this, a short span of heart-pounding action after years of uneventfully escorting her charge around the palace. Rhianne knew she wanted to go.

She ran to her bedroom window and squinted into the darkness. All she could see were distant balls of magelight and the occasional flash of a pistol firing. It didn't look like much, not yet, but the enemies were out there.

She should not stay here alone, but to join the battle herself would be idiotic. She was not trained for combat. Her mind magic was defensive and required close contact. Someone would shoot her before she could get near enough to use it.

She would go to Lucien. He was crippled, but still a

war mage. Between the two of them, they could defend themselves if a party of soldiers broke through the defenders.

She ran for the door to her suite but stopped short when a shadow loomed within it.

"Going somewhere?" Augustan leaned into the doorway. Fingers of red and blue lightning crackled, running along the door frame.

He'd set off her enemy ward. *Why?* She took a step back.

Augustan shifted so his body blocked the entire doorway. "Aren't you happy to see your beloved fiancé?"

Her fear only increased his power over her, yet she couldn't still her trembling. She took a deep breath. "I knew there would be some soldiers too cowardly to fight at the front gates, but I didn't expect you to be one of them."

His expression darkened. Then he smiled and sauntered into the room, dragging the heavy door closed behind him. "Do you wish me dead, Princess? Have no fear. Your wish will be granted. I will fight and die with the rest of our forces, once I finish here."

Finish what? She backed away, taking one step for each he took toward her. "What do you mean, fight and die? Will our soldiers not prevail?"

Augustan laughed. "Prevail? When we're outnumbered two to one, both in regular troops and mages, and the palace is indefensible?"

"The invaders are going to take the palace?" Horror washed over her so thickly that she forgot her fear of Augustan. How could this happen? She'd always felt safe in the palace. Her uncle was the Kjallan emperor. He controlled the largest and best-disciplined army in the known world. Her enemies had always been political rivals; the people around her, other Kjallans. Never had she imagined that she and her family would fall into the hands of foreign enemies.

What would they do to her? To Lucien, to Florian, to little Celeste? To all the people she loved?

Augustan grabbed her arm, and she cried out in surprise. Reflexively, she flung a confusion spell at him, but it flittered away, useless. War mages were immune to her magic.

"Yes," he said. "They will take the palace."

"But we have reinforcements on the way! Didn't we send word from the signal towers?" She tugged at her arm. It was firmly held.

"The fleet's three days out. Ground troops are even farther."

"What can the invaders accomplish by holding the palace for only three days?"

"Bloodshed, looting, and murder. That's what you wanted, isn't it?" He dragged her, stumbling, into the bedroom.

"Of course not!" What did he mean, *what she wanted*? And why was he hauling her in here? Surely he wasn't after sex. No. More likely he meant to kill her. She could see it in his eyes.

"You engineered it, traitor."

"What?"

He shoved her against the bedroom window, pinioning her arms and mashing her nose into the glass. *"Look,"* he growled. "Look what you've wrought."

It was all blackness out the window. "I can't see a gods-cursed thing."

He yanked her away. "Jan-Torres the shroud mage is

at the head of that army. The Mosari king along with a horde of Sardossians."

"The Mosari king is a shroud mage? Aren't the Mosari kings usually war mages?"

"Usually," said Augustan. "This one's an anomaly. That's not the point."

Jan-Torres the shroud mage. Could it be? Surely not. "So the Mosari convinced the Sardossians to join with them in attacking us. What does that have to do with me?"

"We sent an attack fleet up the Neruna Strait to Sarpol just days ago. The Sardossian fleet could not possibly have known about the attack by now, unless your Mosari spy told them. The one you set free. *Traitor.*"

"No! That is not possible." She tried to pry his fingers off her arm, without success. "He could not have known! We used a forgetting spell on him and exiled him to Dori. There was no danger of—no, it could not have happened."

"It did happen. In all likelihood, your pet spy is in the midst of that army right now."

Rhianne looked out the window again. Was Janto somewhere in that blackness? Was it wrong of her if she hoped he was? Better that than dead or stranded on gods-cursed Dori. But she was not a traitor. Lucien had taken precautions.

"Perhaps he'll spare your life," Augustan sneered. "Perhaps he'll make you his mistress when all is said and done. Think he'll keep you to himself or share you with the rest of the army?"

She stared at him, shocked. He didn't know Janto at all.

"Fear not, Princess," said Augustan. "I won't let it happen." He hauled her to the bed and shoved her down onto it. She struggled furiously, but he climbed atop her, pinning her arms.

She looked up at him with a sinking feeling. "What are you doing?"

"Administering a little justice," he said grimly.

She gave her pinned arm a wrench and tried to twist away from him, but he was bigger and stronger. She couldn't break his grip.

"It must be done," said Augustan, running his eyes over her. "You're a traitor, and none of us are getting out of this alive—least of all you. Consider this the first and last of my husbandly duties." He brought a hand to her throat. "Wish I could make it last, pretty one, but I'm needed back at the front."

"Augus—!" His hand began to squeeze, and she could not finish the word. Or breathe.

Augustan's face became very intent.

Her chest heaved in short, unfinished gasps that brought little air. She writhed and struggled, clawing at him with her free hand. Before long, her lungs burned. As she weakened, Augustan moved his other hand from her arm to her throat, adding to the pressure. Her vision blackened around the edges.

It was only after the blackness was complete that she heard the pistol fire.

32

When Augustan's sword scraped from its sheath, Janto knew he'd missed. He dropped the spent pistol and drew his own blade, then glanced at Rhianne, who lay coughing and gasping on the bed.

Augustan pointed his sword at Janto and walked toward him through the tendrils of smoke. "Can't see you. But I know you're there."

He could escape Augustan if he wanted to. The man couldn't see through his shroud; he could only, through his war magic, sense impending danger. As long as Janto was a threat to him, Augustan would know his location. If Janto ceased to be a threat, Augustan would cease to know.

Then, of course, he would finish killing Rhianne.

Janto shook with rage. Augustan hadn't just put his hands on Rhianne; he'd been trying to *strangle* her. And he'd nearly succeeded. Somehow Janto had to keep Augustan engaged long enough to allow her to escape, and at the moment she looked too weak to stand.

He backed away slowly, holding his sword at the ready, and glanced behind him at the archway. In the sitting room, there would be more room to maneuver.

Augustan followed, leering. "Janto, is it? Our Mosari

spy, who returned with an army at his back? I'm glad you came. Now we can settle this in person."

Janto slipped through the archway into the sitting room. *Jump clear and hide,* he ordered Sashi. The ferret leapt from his shoulder and scampered beneath a settee. Looking around, Janto constructed a mental map of the place—where the furniture was, and anything else he might trip over—and made a tentative lunge at Augustan.

Augustan parried the blade with a laugh. "Slow. Terribly slow."

Janto circled around to the side and tried again.

Augustan, turning to orient on him, batted away the invisible blade as easily as swatting a gnat.

The opening sallies had told Janto enough. War mages nearly always outclassed him; he'd sparred with enough of them to know. Besides always knowing where the blows were coming from, they possessed preternatural strength and speed. Still, some war mages harnessed the magic better than others, and some were lazy in training. Janto could occasionally defeat a weak, inexperienced war mage, but never one at his peak. He had an idea now which category Augustan was in.

Augustan came at him so fast he was a blur. Janto whipped up his sword to intercept. Steel clashed inches from his neck, although Janto knew Augustan couldn't see how close he'd come to cutting him. He sucked in a breath of air, and Augustan's blade came at him again. He leapt back and parried, only to see steel lashing toward his chest. He swung his sword as fast as he could, beating off the attacks. He lost ground with every exchange. He unshrouded and shrouded himself, flashing in and out of visibility. It was the only technique he'd ever found that worked against a war mage, just because it was so disorienting to them.

Augustan hesitated, his timing thrown off by the flashing. Janto slipped in his blade and grazed Augustan's wrist, leaving behind a thin line of blood.

"Gods curse you," growled Augustan. He leapt forward.

The attacks came so fast Janto could barely see the flying blade; he backed away rapidly, stepping over a table, stumbling over the back of a settee, flashing visible and invisible. Augustan was adapting to the flashing. Janto knew beyond a doubt he could not win this fight. He lowered his weapon, removing the threat so Augustan could no longer sense him, and fled, invisible, to the other side of the room.

Augustan looked around, perplexed. "Have I beaten you so quickly? Did you run away? Or have I struck you down?" He turned to the still-closed suite doors. "You're still here, somewhere. You take a breather, then. I'll finish killing the traitor." He strode toward the bedroom.

No! Janto flung a shroud over Rhianne, who still lay gasping on her bed. But the shroud wouldn't stop Augustan—not for long. He would find her. And she was in no condition to run.

"Stop!" he cried, unshrouding himself. "I'll fight you."

Augustan turned back, grinning. He raised his sword and lunged at Janto.

Janto parried the furious attacks, again flashing in and out of visibility. His arm burned with fatigue. Augustan's sword strokes were not only fast but powerful. It took all of Janto's strength to block them, yet Augustan did not seem to be expending much effort.

Then Augustan's left arm drew back and flung something. A glass bowl struck Janto, shattering on impact. He drew in a sharp breath, choked, and coughed violently. The air was full of smoke. No—face powder.

"Now you can't hide!" Augustan's furious sword swings backed Janto into a corner. The war mage smiled. He knew he'd won. Janto glanced at the bedroom door. Maybe Rhianne was too far gone. Maybe she would not recover.

Kill!

Augustan shouted in pain and twisted away from Janto. Sashi clung to his leg, hanging on by his teeth.

Janto leapt out of his corner and lunged, powder flying off him in clouds. When it wore off, his shroud would be effective again. Augustan knocked his blade aside distractedly, then grabbed the invisible ferret, yanked its teeth out of his flesh, and flung the creature against the wall. Sashi screamed.

Janto checked the link. The ferret was injured but alive. Seeing a gap in Augustan's defenses, he swung his blade. Augustan blocked him and counterattacked furiously, stabbing at Janto's heart. Janto flung himself to one side.

The blade caught him in the shoulder. He cried out, nearly dropping his sword. Blood welled from the wound. Distracted by the pain, he lost his shroud, and Rhianne's.

Augustan advanced. "Shall I kill you slowly or quickly? Or perhaps I should finish Rhianne first." He began to smile. Then his eyes widened in alarm, and he flung himself to the side. A pistol cracked.

Rhianne stood in the bedroom doorway, holding the weapon in both hands. Janto recognized it as the one he'd dropped—she must have reloaded it. Smoke rose from the barrel.

Augustan chuckled as he rose to his feet, unharmed.

"Rhianne!" Janto cried. "Run! You can't save me. Just go!"

She hesitated.

Damn her. What was the sense in both of them dying? He tried another tack. "Go to the Mosari army—give them the name Jan-Torres, and they will not harm you. Have them send help!"

She glanced at the door but didn't move. He couldn't fool her; she knew any help would arrive too late.

"Go!" he cried in desperation.

Her eyes lit as if with a sudden realization, and she disappeared into the bedroom again.

Augustan swung his sword lazily, toying with Janto as he backed him into a corner. "That's the trouble with women," he drawled. "Too foolish to take orders, even when it's for their own good." He pointed his blade at Janto's heart.

Janto raised his own sword. His arm shook with fatigue. He didn't have the strength to resist the death blow. His eyes went to the bedroom door. Why wouldn't she run? She couldn't save him, but he could have saved her.

He heard the clank and grate of an iron door opening, and a furious snarling that made his hair stand on end.

Whiskers?

A brown and black streak flew out the bedroom door and tore across the room. Augustan hesitated, half turning to face the new threat. Janto used the last of his strength to fling a shroud over himself, leaving only Augustan visible. He thrust his blade at Augustan, forcing the man to engage his war magic and dodge the blow.

Whiskers slammed into Augustan, knocking him to

the floor. Augustan screamed, and the brindlecat tore out his throat.

Janto hurried through the hallways of the Imperial Palace, clutching Rhianne's hand, cocking his head to listen for shouts and gunshots. The battle was getting closer. He heard a voice he thought he recognized and turned into a side hallway.

The hallways were as deserted as the city streets had been before. Nearly all the doors were shut. Probably locked too, as those not equipped to fight hid themselves as best they could.

From within his shirt, Sashi made a sad mewling noise.

I'll get you help soon, Janto told him. The poor creature had a broken leg. He'd wrapped it as best he could, and Rhianne had wrapped his bleeding shoulder. They'd tried to coax Whiskers back into her cage, but she had ignored them utterly, consuming her kill. In the end, they'd had no choice but to leave her there; they certainly didn't want to become her next dinner. Janto wrote a note in multiple languages and pinned it to the door, explaining to his soldiers what was inside so they didn't burst in on a wild, battle-crazed brindlecat.

"You're bleeding through the bandage," panted Rhianne. Her voice was hoarse, and she was having trouble breathing. "Look at the floor."

Janto slowed to look, and grimaced. He was leaving a trail of blood.

She squeezed his hand. "You need a Healer."

"We'll find one." His eyes lingered on her. The red marks on her throat were going to develop into some truly spectacular bruises if they weren't dealt with soon.

She rubbed her neck, as if in response to his scrutiny.

"Janto, you've got to speak to your commander. This attack on Kjall is beyond foolish. It can accomplish nothing and will only bring about a brutal retaliation. What are your people after? It is just vengeance?"

"Not vengeance." He turned away, frowning. She didn't know he was in charge. Of course she didn't. He'd been so careful not to tell her who he was.

She laid a hand on his shoulder. "I know you. You don't want bloodshed any more than I do. You've got to convince your commander to call this off. Do you know how Florian responded to the fish riots in Riorca? And that was nothing compared to this!"

He grimaced. She believed he was a hapless participant in this attack. What would she say when she learned he was the man who'd orchestrated it? As he looked into her earnest, worried face, a confession half rose in his throat. But his courage failed him, and he swallowed the words. He'd tell her later. First he had to get her to safety.

Up ahead, a pair of Mosari soldiers stood guard at the end of a narrow corridor. *Thank the gods.* Still shrouded, he ran past them with Rhianne into a larger hallway that lay beyond. He saw a familiar face.

"San-Kullen," he called, releasing the shroud.

The war mage and the group of soldiers he'd been speaking to started, their gear and weapons jangling as they took in his unexpected presence. They looked equally surprised at seeing Rhianne.

San-Kullen dipped his head and came forward. "Jan-Torres. Sire."

Rhianne's hand tensed within his own. She knew a fair bit of the Mosari language and had not failed to note the significance of the title. Or perhaps it was the name.

Janto kept his eyes on San-Kullen, afraid of what he might see on Rhianne's face if he looked at her now.

"You're wounded," said San-Kullen, his curious eyes moving from Rhianne to Janto's blood-soaked shoulder. "You need a Healer."

"So does she," he said, indicating Rhianne, "and Sashi. How goes the battle?"

"The worst fighting was at the southern gate, where we ran into soldiers in orange uniforms with a sickle and sunburst on them—"

"The Legaciatti," said Janto.

"Fierce, fierce fighters," said San-Kullen, shaking his head. "We lost a lot of men, but we overcame them. There was some ugly fighting at the servants' entrance, but that's over now, and resistance is scattered. There's a team securing the north wing. We're waiting on reinforcements, and then we'll start on this one."

"Have you got the emperor?"

"We do," said San-Kullen cheerfully. "And unharmed. His guards didn't put up much of a fight. I don't think they're very fond of him. We're still looking for the son, the daughter, and the niece. Also, there's a group of Kjallans who've barricaded themselves behind a door upstairs."

Janto nodded. "This is the niece, so you can stop looking for her. I'll—"

Rhianne's hand slipped out of his own. He turned to see her flying from him, her syrtos billowing around her ankles, heading back in the direction they'd come.

"Rhianne!" he cried. Then to the guards, "Stop her!"

The guards shifted position to block her from the corridor. She did not slow but ran straight for them. They stumbled off to either side, allowing her through. Janto was perplexed and furious until he saw the guards' faces and recognized that dazed look he'd seen on Micah.

He ran after her himself, but after a few steps, he stumbled, too weak from his injury to catch up, and stared helplessly at her retreating figure. Images formed in his mind: Rhianne shot by one of his overzealous guards at the back gate; Rhianne caught by a band of troops, dragged into a room and raped.

A hand settled on his shoulder. "I've got her," said San-Kullen. A brown and black streak flew after her in pursuit.

"Don't let your cat hurt her."

"Don't worry," said San-Kullen. "Marci velvets her claws."

Janto clenched his fists.

The cat leapt past Rhianne, turned in midair, and landed facing her, hackles up, claws out, lips drawn back to reveal long, gleaming fangs.

Stop there, Rhianne, pleaded Janto.

Rhianne skidded to a stop and froze before the snarling feline.

San-Kullen's eyes were bright with affection for his familiar. "Nothing to it." He walked toward the pair, leisurely and unthreatening. He returned, gripping Rhianne's arm. The cat, now calm, padded along behind them.

As Rhianne entered the larger hallway, Janto ran to her. "Rhianne, I can ex—," he began.

"You gods-cursed liar!" she cried hoarsely, twisting in San-Kullen's grip. Grimacing, San-Kullen moved behind her and seized both her upper arms. But that didn't stop Rhianne from raging at Janto. "Augustan told me you were responsible for the attack. What a fool I was not to believe him. You made a traitor out of me!"

Horror trickled through him. Could he ever make her understand why he'd done this? "Rhianne, I—"

"I *sold* myself," she hissed. "For the price of your life, I would have gone to the marriage bed with Augustan. And you came here with an *army* at your back to murder and pillage everything that matters to me?"

He blinked, trying to formulate a satisfactory answer. He didn't have one.

"I'll kill you!" she shouted, wrenching one of her arms loose from San-Kullen's grip. "In the Soldier's name, I swear I'll kill you!" She lunged for him.

San-Kullen twisted Rhianne's other arm until she cried out in pain, and neatly recaptured the first. He twisted both until she gasped and stopped struggling.

Janto shook his head firmly. "San-Kullen, don't do that. She won't hurt me."

"The hell I won't!" Rhianne cried.

There was a hitch in her breathing that suggested she was hurting somewhere. Janto longed to go and comfort her, but he didn't dare.

"What shall we do with her?" asked San-Kullen.

Footsteps approached at a run. Tensing, Janto turned toward them, along with every other soldier in the room, but they were only fresh Mosari soldiers. "Looks like your reinforcements are here."

"Good," said San-Kullen. "And the prisoner?"

He looked sadly at Rhianne. *Prisoner.* He supposed she was. He could not explain himself to her now. The palace was not yet secure, and he was losing blood.

The new soldiers stared at Rhianne with predatory interest.

"You have rooms set aside for prisoners?"

San-Kullen nodded.

"Prepare one for her. I want a guard on her day and night—"

"I want to be *that* guard," someone muttered behind him.

Janto whirled, only to see carefully schooled expressions of innocence on all the soldiers' faces. "Two guards," he amended. "The most trustworthy men you have. This lady is the emperor's niece, a Kjallan imperial princess. It is essential to our plans that she not be harmed." He looked around the room, meeting the eyes of every soldier. "If any man harms this woman, despoils her in any way, or even threatens her, he shall be hanged. Is that clear?"

"Understood, sire," said San-Kullen. "Is she zo?" He glanced at the dazed guards, who were beginning to recover their wits.

"She's magical, yes. A mind mage."

"Then we have to take her riftstone. Unless you intend to guard her with zo."

Janto sighed. "We can't spare zo. We'll have to take the riftstone."

San-Kullen shifted his grip so he was holding both her arms in one hand. Then he reached for the chain around her neck. Rhianne arched away, avoiding him, and aimed a backward kick at his groin. San-Kullen blocked it with his knee and twisted her arms again until she winced and was still.

Janto couldn't stand it. "Release one of her arms," he ordered.

San-Kullen pursed his lips in disapproval but obeyed.

Janto stepped forward and spoke softly to Rhianne. "If you want to hit me, go ahead. I won't stop you, and I won't hit you back."

Rhianne glared at him, furious, but did not move. After a moment, she lowered her eyes.

He nodded, a little sad. He'd thought as much—she didn't really want to hurt him. "I need your riftstone. It's only for a little while. I promise you'll get it back."

Something seemed to break inside her. Her eyes closed, and her face crumpled. A fat teardrop rolled down her cheek.

"Please," he added.

She removed the chain from around her neck and handed it to him.

He cradled the precious object in his hand. "Thank you. I swear this is not a betrayal. I'll explain everything later."

Rhianne stared at the floor.

He turned to San-Kullen. "When the fighting is over, she is to have anything she asks for, within reason. Food, drink, books—whatever, as long as it's not something she can hurt herself with."

"Yes, sire."

"While we're waiting on the room, show us to the Healers," he said.

33

Rhianne found herself hurried along through the hallway, her arm gripped firmly by the Mosari war mage. His brindlecat loped on her other side, cutting off any possibility of escape. Her windpipe still burned from what Augustan had done to her, and as her breathing grew heavy from exertion, she gasped, unable to take in enough air.

"Stop!" cried Janto. "Look at her. She can't breathe."

The war mage stopped and had her sit, her back against the wall. She tried not to panic, and forced herself to breathe shallow and slow.

Janto approached, studying her, his eyes full of concern. "Can you bring the Healer here?" he asked the war mage.

"No need," said Rhianne. "I'm getting better." Her breathing was approaching normal, though every inhalation pained her.

"I could carry her," said the war mage.

"I can walk," Rhianne snapped, rising to her feet. The last thing she wanted was some strange Mosari soldier's hands all over her. "Just don't go so fast."

They continued at a slower pace, with Janto turning back frequently to check on her. *Not Janto. Jan-Torres*.

Augustan had been a nasty, evil man, and she did not

regret his death after what he'd tried to do to her, but he'd been right about one thing. She *was* a traitor. She'd freed this man, not knowing who he truly was, and he'd come back and invaded her homeland, killing who knew how many people she cared about. What was going to happen to Lucien, to Celeste, to Marcella, to the Legaciatti who protected her, the servants and slaves, the soldiers defending the palace? How many women in the palace were going to be raped tonight because of her foolish decision? And what about the citizens of the city of Riat? Janto's—*Jan-Torres's*—army had marched through there on its way to the palace.

Even Florian, whom she hated sometimes, she did not want to see executed. But Florian had ordered the death of Janto's parents. Gods, what a horror! Janto had seen his *own parents' heads* that day in the audience hall! It was understandable he should want to take his vengeance. But she would never forgive herself for the part she had played in allowing it to happen.

Gods, she was crying again. She swiped her free hand across her face.

Jan-Torres, staring back at her, looked as sad as she'd ever seen him. "Rhianne . . ."

"Say nothing." She blinked furiously.

"We'll have a long talk when this is over. I'll explain everything."

He'd talk to assuage his guilty conscience. Of course he would. But she understood already. He'd lied to her and betrayed her in order to save his country, or at least to take his vengeance on Florian and Augustan. He hadn't hurt her deliberately; she knew that. But she couldn't help feeling horrifyingly used. She'd *slept* with this man. She'd thought she loved him!

They'd arrived at a makeshift infirmary the Mosari and Sardossians had established in the Epolonius Room. The war mage directed her to an unused mattress on the floor while Jan-Torres disappeared into the crowd.

A short while later, he returned with another man at his side. "This is Mor-Nassen, one of our Healers. He's going to see to your neck injury."

The Healer studied Rhianne, shook his head, and turned back to Jan-Torres. "She's stable. Sire, you're still bleeding from that sword wound—"

"It's nothing," said Jan-Torres. "First Rhianne, then me, then Sashi." He settled onto the mattress next to hers.

Mor-Nassen frowned and returned to Rhianne's side. "Lie back and relax," he ordered.

She complied, closing her eyes.

The Healer's hands cradled her neck. She tensed, remembering the horror of Augustan's hands there. It seemed ages ago, but now that she thought about it, less than an hour had passed since the attempt on her life.

Mor-Nassen's touch was gentle, and she forced herself to think of other things. Quiet rides on Dice along tree-lined avenues. Swimming with Marcella in the imperial baths. The warmth of the Healer's magic flowed into her body, and by degrees her pain began to ease. She had not realized how exhausted she was. Was that an effect of being nearly strangled to death? Her limbs melted into the mattress, and her mind began to drift.

She was vaguely aware of Mor-Nassen patting her and telling her she was going to be fine and moving on to Jan-Torres. She lay where she was, sinking slowly into oblivion. She had some notion that there were other people in the room, other injured soldiers. They were men she didn't know—Mosari and Sardossians. She picked up disjointed fragments of their conversation, mundane and of little interest.

"Can you move your ankle in a full circle, like this?"

"They told me to leave the knife in. Said I'd lose less blood that way."

"Is the pain up here, by this rib?"

"You're going to him next, right?"

"No, it's a little higher. Up here."

Rhianne knew that last voice; she'd heard it many times. Was she dreaming, imagining things? No. It was *real*.

"Morgan?" she cried, opening her eyes and sitting up. She looked around, frantic. Where was he? There, about nine beds over. He looked pale and weak. "Morgan!" She leapt from her bed and made her way across the room, dodging mattresses.

"Rhianne!" shouted Janto.

The war mage and brindlecat intercepted her in an instant, the man seizing her arm and the animal snarling in her face. It was a grim reminder that despite the gentle treatment, she was still a prisoner.

"That's my friend over there. I want to see him!" she cried.

The war mage looked questioningly at Jan-Torres, who was lying on one of the mattresses, shirtless. Mor-Nassen sat beside him, closing the shoulder wound.

"Let her visit her friend," said Janto.

The war mage released her, and she hurried to Morgan's side. "What happened?"

"I must be dreaming. Is it really you? Got myself shot." He laughed, a weak sound. "Stewed to the gills, and I saw the invaders. Thought of you up in the palace, undefended with the attack fleet gone, and I turned my musket on them. Would never have done it if I hadn't poured my wits out with the wine."

She turned to a nearby Healer. "Why is he so weak? Has he not been healed?"

"He was shot in the streets of Riat," explained the Healer. "We stopped the bleeding to save his life, but the bullet's still in him. We'll have to remove it surgically, which means more blood loss, and he's lost a lot already. We're not sure he's strong enough, but we can't leave the bullet where it is much longer."

"Gods, Morgan." Rhianne flung her arms around him—gently, so as not to hurt him.

"San-Kullen."

Rhianne looked up to see Jan-Torres standing above her. His shirt hung loose about him, his arms were folded, and his expression was a dark thundercloud.

The war mage hurried to his side. "Yes, sire?"

"The princess's room should be ready by now. Take her there," said Jan-Torres. "We've lost enough time already, and we've got work to do."

Janto watched, uneasy, as San-Kullen and his brindlecat escorted Rhianne out of the infirmary. He wasn't sure why he'd reacted so strongly to seeing her hug another man. Normally he wasn't prone to jealousy, even back on Mosar when Kal-Torres, competitive beyond all normal limits, had deliberately seduced his girlfriends, sometimes with success. Janto had been philosophical about it then, theorizing that if a woman chose Kal over him, he was well quit of her.

Somehow it was different with Rhianne, perhaps because that hug was how he'd hoped and expected to be greeted himself. He'd rescued her from Augustan and delivered her from Florian's tyranny. But instead of welcoming him with open arms, Rhianne was livid about the invasion, and some other man he didn't even know was getting her tender affection. *Vagabond's breath, why?*

He'd have to figure it out later. One of his officers, the war mage Ruhr-Donnel, was striding toward him, clearly with something to say.

"Sire, we've got Lucien," said Ruhr-Donnel. "You were right—he tried to sneak out, but we had men at every palace entrance."

"I hope he didn't give you too much trouble."

"He and his escort gave us a lot of trouble. But we managed."

"I understand you have Emperor Florian as well?"

"Yes, sire."

"Bring him in. The emperor."

Ruhr-Donnel saluted and left.

Feeling better? Janto stroked his ferret, who lay cradled in his arms, uncharacteristically timid. The Healer had repaired his broken leg, but Sashi had never been seriously injured before and seemed to need a little reassurance that all was well.

The pain is gone, said Sashi.

Are you ready to get back on my shoulder?

After a moment, Sashi extracted himself from Janto's grip and scampered carefully up to his rightful place.

The thump of boots echoed from down the hallway, and six soldiers entered the infirmary, escorting a furious Emperor Florian. The emperor wore his imperial syrtos and loros, but his riftstone had been taken and his wrists were manacled behind his back.

Florian's eyes fixed on Janto. "You," he said coldly.

Janto smiled. "A pity we keep meeting in such unfortunate circumstances."

"You will die for this, spy—"

"Your Majesty," corrected Janto. "I am Jan-Torres, king of Mosar."

Florian paused a moment to process that. "Do you know why we don't keep a large garrison here, Jan-Torres?"

"Why?"

"Because no one is foolish enough to invade Kjall. When our reinforcements arrive, our retribution will be swift and merciless."

Janto sighed. "This conversation's just begun, and already I'm tired of it." He grasped the jeweled loros draped over Florian's shoulders, and lifted it over the man's head. "You are hereby removed from power, now and forever." He turned to the guards. "Confine him, alone, until we are prepared to render judgment."

By dawn, the Imperial Palace belonged to Mosar. The last of the palace doors had been broken open and the last of the Kjallan defenders killed or taken into custody.

Janto yielded to Mor-Nassen's admonishments and slept for a few hours. When he woke, he felt stronger. With a restored Sashi riding on his shoulder, he led a small, shrouded war band to capture the shore battery on the eastern side of the harbor. Resistance was light; many of the Kjallan defenders had deserted. He and his men took it easily. He then ordered his men to remove all the cannons, load the tower with explosives, and destroy it. By signal, he sent the same orders to the men at the western battery. He had a special plan for those cannons, and the demolished batteries should help him to execute it.

In the afternoon, he returned to the palace. His men had located a large, well-furnished meeting room and established it as command headquarters. He was weary and spent a few hours resting there, listening to the reports from his commanders, while Mor-Nassen tended his scrapes and bruises. Simultaneously with his attack on the battery, the Sardossians had launched an assault on the palaestra, but found it empty of soldiers. They'd returned with only a few terrified clerks.

Since he did not have the Mosari royal carcanet—it was either back on Mosar or lost forever—he'd asked one of the clerks to search the Kjallan jewelry boxes for a temporary substitute. The man returned with a golden three-tiered necklace. It was not as thick or heavy as the royal carcanet, but Janto donned it anyway. Any Mosari seeing it on him would know its intended meaning.

Kal-Torres arrived, trailing an escort of armed guards. "You're early," said Janto.

"I thought we might go over some details privately before we meet with the commanders."

"Very well." Janto rubbed his hands across his face. "I'm on my way to the slave house. You can walk with me."

"The slave house? Can't that wait?"

"I'm afraid not." Janto beckoned to San-Kullen and Mor-Nassen. "The slaves are under the influence of death spells, like the Riorcans on the Kjallan ships. Their abeyance spells will be wearing off this evening."

"But you don't need to attend to them personally."

"I want to," said Janto. "I worked with two of those slaves when I was acting here as a spy, and I want to bring both of them back to the palace. Also there's a man I need to arrest. San-Kullen, bring a few soldiers along."

They set out into the Imperial Palace hallways. "All of our ships sustained damage," began Kal. "The *Osprey* lost its mizenmast—we're trying to jury-rig one now. More worrisome is the *Tern*'s broken rudder. My men are working on it night and day. These are time-consuming repairs, and with the Kjallan fleet approaching, we've got to get those ships in fighting trim. Damage to the other four is minor. As for the direction of the reserve fleet's approach—"

"Sire!"

Janto turned in the direction of the voice. A Mosari man, not zo but apparently with some authority, hurried toward him. Behind him were four soldiers and two prisoners in wrist irons, all of them Mosari. "Yes?" Janto said warily. San-Kullen, who'd fallen into the role of his personal bodyguard, took a protective step closer to him.

The soldier bowed. "Sire, I'm the bosun's mate, *Osprey*." He nodded at Kal-Torres, whose chin lifted in acknowledgment. "Commander Kel-Charan said I should speak to you."

Janto glanced anxiously toward the palace gates and the slave house. "What about?"

"These two men, sire." He indicated the prisoners. "They were caught assaulting—uh, raping—one of the Kjallan prisoners. The commander wanted to know what he should do with them."

Janto sighed. This was just the sort of trouble he'd hoped to avoid. He studied the culprits, who avoided his eyes. "Is there any question of their guilt?"

"None, sire. They were caught in the act."

"Have we sent the victim a Healer?"

The bosun's mate bit his lip. "I'll find out, sire."

"Send one if we haven't. As for the men, execute them."

"Execute them, sire?" repeated the bosun's mate.

The prisoners stared at him in shock, then fell upon their knees. "But, sire!" cried the first. "Kjallans killed my wife!"

"Mercy, sire," cried the second. "We made a mistake. We will not do it again!"

Janto tried to tune out their pleas. He couldn't afford to relent.

"Jan—," began Kal-Torres in a tone of protest.

Janto rounded on his brother and snapped, "If I want your opinion, I'll ask for it." He turned to the prisoners. "I'm assuming the person you assaulted wasn't the Kjallan who killed your wife; therefore I fail to see how this is justice. You had strict, specific orders, and you disobeyed them. You knew in advance that the sentence for doing so would be death." He turned to the bosun's mate. "Tell Kel-Charan."

The bosun's mate nodded, ashen faced, while the condemned men wailed.

"Come on," snarled Janto to his entourage, and they swept off down the hallway.

For several minutes, nobody dared to speak. Then Kal put a hand on his shoulder. "Jan—"

Janto whirled on him. "Are you going to question my every decision?"

"You have no idea the kind of pressure these men are under—"

"I know *exactly* what kind of pressure they're under." He pointed in the direction of the chamber where Lucien was being held. "Over there sits a young man who has the power to destroy us. As we speak here in this hallway, he dreams of vengeance, and every crime we commit against his people brings that dream closer to his heart. Do you think I want to sacrifice everything we've achieved so that those two men can satisfy their lust? Should I give up the whole country for that?"

Kal-Torres blinked at him. "I just think that under the circumstances, a death sentence seems excessive—"

"I *know* it's excessive. I'm setting an example! The men will hear of this, and they'll know I mean what I say. Kal, if I'm lenient on this first incident, we'll have another dozen by tomorrow morning."

"Brother—" Kal glanced around at their escort. San-Kullen, Mor-Nassen, and the guards were staring at them, stunned. "May I speak with you privately?"

Janto growled assent. He signaled the escort to stay put and walked with Kal down the hallway.

Kal rounded on him. "Whose side are you on, ours or theirs? You're sounding like a Kjallan sympathizer."

Janto rolled his eyes. "Kal, we're going to have to negotiate with these people, and that means not only delivering them a few humiliating military losses to force them to take us seriously, but finding common ground with them and demonstrating that our intentions are to establish peace."

"Common ground? *They* attacked *us*."

"I know that. The Kjallans' thinking must change, and for that to happen, we must set the example. As to whose side I'm on, I'm on the side of peace and prosperity for Mosar. Are we done here?"

Kal looked away. "I suppose we must be."

Janto beckoned to San-Kullen and the escort.

As they approached, Kal gave him an odd look. "You've changed, Brother."

"War does that to a man."

They left the palace and set out on the long walk to the slave house that Janto knew so well. As they traveled, Kal enumerated the details of the fleet's status—damage to the ships, casualties, stores of gunpowder and spars and sailcloth. His report was thorough, but his tone was flat. He was clearly still angry.

When they arrived, the slave house was in chaos, but it seemed a happy chaos. The room was more crowded than ever, containing now both men and women. Apparently the two houses had mixed. Janto spied a few couples exchanging kisses in the back of the room, and one pair who'd gone considerably beyond that. The others were talking animatedly in mixed-gender groups. Many of the men were missing—the presence of the women had fooled him into thinking everyone was present. Perhaps some of the slaves had been in the palace when the fighting began. They might have surrendered to the Mosari troops and had their death spells removed. Others might have been killed.

Conversation ceased as he and his entourage marched in the door. The slaves took in his soldier's uniform and makeshift carcanet, as well as the uniforms of the men who surrounded him, and stared expectantly. Not one of them seemed to fully recognize him, though a few of the women cocked their heads as if trying to figure out where they'd seen him before.

"Attention," called San-Kullen. "Jan-Torres, king of Mosar, wishes to speak."

Janto stepped forward. "Where are Iolo and Sirali?"

"Here, sire." Iolo shuffled out from within a crowd of men. He seemed uncertain what to do with himself—approach, bow, or ask the questions that lay heavy on his mind. Sirali, across the room, stepped out from a group of people and just stared.

"Well, come up here, both of you!" cried Janto.

Iolo and Sirali walked to the front of the room, their eyes on San-Kullen's brindlecat. Iolo started to kneel, but Janto seized him about the shoulders and pulled him into a hug.

"I'm glad I found you." He released Iolo and embraced Sirali, who submitted somewhat stiffly to the attention. "Stand here by my side." He raised his voice to address the crowd. "As of this day, you are free men and women, Riorcans and Mosari and Kjallans alike."

A great cheer went up from the slaves.

"I have brought a Healer to remove your death spells." Janto indicated Mor-Nassen, who stepped up beside him. "Line up, please, behind Iolo and Sirali."

The slaves scrambled into a line.

"When your spells are removed, you may accompany us to the palace, where we have food and drink for you, and a safe place to berth. Now, there is more fighting to come, and we need every soldier we can get. Those of you who are able-bodied and willing shall be armed and assigned to a commander. If we succeed in the upcoming battle, ships will be available to return us all to our homelands."

The slaves cheered again.

Janto stepped aside to let Mor-Nassen do his work. Iolo and Sirali rejoined him after their death spells had been removed.

"Stay with me," he told them. "I want the two of you by my side, now and for always. When we return to Mosar, you'll be among my advisers in the palace, if that suits you."

San-Kullen edged toward him. "Where's the man you wanted me to arrest?"

"I haven't seen him yet." He turned to Iolo and Sirali. "Where's Micah?"

"No sign of him in a while," said Iolo.

"Right, and I know where he is," said Sirali. "I had nothing to do with it."

Janto and San-Kullen exchanged a look. "Nothing to do with what?" said Janto.

"Right, and you'll see." Sirali headed for the door. Janto followed her, accompanied by Kal-Torres, San-Kullen, and Iolo.

Sirali led them a short way into the forest, past the well. She paused at a clearing. "There."

Janto looked into the clearing. A shape lay on the ground. He advanced tentatively. Sashi wrinkled his nose. It was Micah's very dead, very mutilated body.

34

Janto stood outside Lucien's door, steeling himself for the encounter to come. The young heir was clever and would be more slippery to deal with than his father. Furthermore, this conversation actually mattered. Florian would never rule Kjall again, but Lucien might. Janto had some negotiating power now, and he would have still more if his forces managed to destroy the returning Kjallan fleet. He just had to convince Lucien that it was in Kjall's best interest to withdraw from Mosar.

"Shall I come in with you?" asked San-Kullen.

"No, wait outside," said Janto. "He's not going to attack me."

The guards opened the door and admitted him.

Lucien sat on a couch inside, his posture relaxed, his crutch leaning next to him. "Not a mere spy after all," he said, "but the king of Mosar. And poor Rhianne thoroughly taken in."

"It was never my intent to take advantage of her," said Janto. "Only to save my country by any means necessary."

Lucien narrowed his eyes. "If you think you've accomplished *that*, you are mistaken. How is it we missed your familiar?"

"He was hiding in the hypocaust."

"Ah."

Kjallans are fools, said Sashi from his shoulder.

Not exactly. "You underestimate them," he said to Lucien. "You Kjallans who've never known animal familiars. They're intelligent, like people."

"My father's mistress says that about her lapdog."

Janto felt his ferret's indignance through the link. He took a seat. "There is not the remotest similarity. Lucien Florian Nigellus, you are now the emperor of Kjall. Allow me to be the first to congratulate you." He held out the jeweled loros he'd taken from Florian.

Lucien's face went ashen. He accepted the garment with a trembling hand.

"I don't mean to shock you," Janto added. "Your father is alive. I am removing him from power until our council passes judgment on him."

"I see." Lucien gathered the loros into his lap, visibly relaxing. "Your arrogance, King Jan-Torres, can hardly be believed. The Kjallan fleet will be here in a matter of days, and our ground troops will arrive not long after. No matter what you do to me or Florian or anyone else in the meantime, my people will overwhelm you. Every last one of you will be staked. As punishment for this rebellion, Kjall will decimate the vassal state of Mosar. Do you know what that means?"

"It's not going to happen."

"One in every ten Mosari will be selected by lot and staked. That will be your legacy, Jan-Torres of Mosar. The suffering and death of thousands."

Janto swallowed, unnerved by the threat, which was marginally credible, but determined Lucien should not see weakness. "I do not fear the return of the fleet, Your Imperial Majesty."

Lucien leaned back, folding his arms. "We have thirty ships to your half dozen."

"An exaggeration. You have twenty-three ships. And I have the shore batteries." They were heaps of stone, completely destroyed, but he had them.

"With our numbers, it won't matter."

"I also think the return of the fleet will be cold comfort for you, young emperor, if you are dead before they arrive."

"Ah," said Lucien. "Here we come to the crux of it. You mean to kill me if I don't cooperate with your demands. What could those demands be?"

Janto smiled inwardly. Lucien was smart but inexperienced. His eagerness belied his attempt at nonchalance. Beneath that façade, he was afraid, and he wanted very much to strike a deal. "I imagine there are many Kjallan noblemen who'd be happy to rule this country in your stead."

Lucien snorted laughter. "They could not hold on to it! Every weak Kjallan emperor for the last three centuries has been deposed. That's what would happen to me if I gave in to your demands. What were they again? I only ask for the potential amusement value."

"Everything changes if your fleet loses the battle," said Janto. "Here are my demands. First, your troops must leave Mosar, now and forever. You will have no further claim on my nation. Second, we will establish trade agreements to foster peace between our countries. Third, if she consents, I would like to marry your cousin."

Lucien leaned forward, lowering his brows. "If you touch Rhianne, I will kill you."

"An empty threat if I ever heard one, prisoner. I don't need your consent. Only hers."

He sniffed and leaned back on the couch. "You are not marrying anybody. You will be dead within a week. Your demands are as ridiculous as I thought they'd be. Give up Mosar? Be serious. Here are my terms. You and your men will give up the palace and any other structures you occupy, return to your ships, and sail away. I cannot promise that there will be no punishment for Mosar for the crime of this invasion, but you will be treated as a vassal state and hence your people will have some value to us as slaves. Surely the lives of your countrymen mean something to you."

"I am not at all tempted by your offer."

Lucien's eyes narrowed. "When the fleet arrives, you will wish you had accepted it."

Janto shook his head. "No. I think we are done here." He rose to leave.

"King Jan-Torres," called Lucien. "The Sardossians loaned you ground troops. Did they loan you ships as well?"

"I cannot discuss such details with you." Turning his back, Janto headed for the door.

"Are you holding them in reserve? How *many* ships?"

As he opened the door, Janto turned and smiled at Lucien. He had as many ships as he was going to need if he and Kal-Torres pulled off the plan they'd worked out. "Good day, Your Imperial Majesty."

Rhianne had requested from the guard, and been granted, a list of known casualties of the invasion. The list was frighteningly long, but after reading through it, she'd realized it was long in part because it included the Mosari and Sardossians as well as the Kjallans. There were a lot of names she didn't recognize. But she recognized enough, and they shattered her. None of these people would be dead if not for her treachery.

She'd tried repeatedly to get an update on how Morgan was doing, but her guard didn't know who Morgan was and did not attempt to locate him for her.

When her door opened and King Jan-Torres strode in, her heart surged with both hope and trepidation. She was not at all eager to hear his self-serving justifications as to why he'd betrayed her to save his own people. But he *was* in charge around here, at least until the Kjallan reinforcements arrived. He had information, and what he didn't know off the top of his head, he could find out.

"Princess." Jan-Torres lowered his arm, letting his ferret scamper down to the floor. He moved about the room, taking in the furnishings and general surroundings, his eye lingering on the food tray that had been delivered an hour ago. Too grieved to eat, she'd barely touched it. The suite his guards had imprisoned her in, one of the palace guest rooms, was smaller than her own, with two rooms instead of three. Jan-Torres, who'd walked past her to peer into the bedroom, spoke again. "Have you been well treated?"

She twisted to glare at his back from her settee. "I am a prisoner."

"Are the guards kind and respectful? Have they brought you the things you need?"

"I have no complaints about the guards, save that they do not answer all my questions."

He turned and faced her. "I want to thank you again

for setting the brindlecat on Augustan. I'm sure you saved my life."

"You saved mine by showing up in the first place." Her hand strayed to her neck. "On that score, I call us even."

He strode back and took a seat across from her. He looked so little like the Janto she'd known in the Imperial Garden and at the bridge. He'd exchanged his bland, nondescript syrtos for a colorful Mosari tunic and a gaudy three-banded necklace of gold. But it was more than that—he stood prouder and straighter. Taller, even. He looked more commanding, more kingly.

She frowned. Some women would be impressed by that. Rhianne had seen any number of women fling themselves at powerful men like Florian and Lucien. Power was said to be an aphrodisiac, but Rhianne had spent nearly twenty years enslaved to Florian's tyranny. If the lure of power had ever been a temptation for her, Florian had long ago stamped out any such inclination. Let other women chase princes and kings and war leaders; the only aphrodisiac she wished for was kindness.

Jan-Torres settled himself on the couch. His ferret, which had been sniffing about the room, came running and leapt into his lap. Jan-Torres idly stroked the animal. "I want you to know that both Florian and Lucien are safe and unharmed. Your younger cousin as well, eight-year-old Celeste."

"For now. Do you intend to execute them?"

"I didn't come here to execute people. I came to save my country."

"If you want to save Mosar, invade Mosar. Why come to Kjall if not to spill blood in vengeance? You cannot hold the palace for more than a few days. Reinforcements are on the way."

"Please trust that I have thought this through better than that."

She shook her head. "Florian killed your parents, which was horrible and wrong. I understand your desire to strike back. But what purpose does it serve, answering violence with violence?"

"You're mistaken about why I came. I'm not going to explain why now, but the fact is that I couldn't save Mosar with a direct invasion. I needed the support of the Sardossians, and to get that I had to avert the attack on Sarpol."

Her finger brushed the casualty list that lay on the settee next to her. "Tamienne is dead. Did you know?"

"No. I'm sorry."

"Cerinthus is dead. You don't know Cerinthus—he was my friend Marcella's husband. Justis, Nipius, and Quintilla. All dead." She touched the paper again. "But perhaps they don't mean anything to you. They're just names."

"They mean no less to me, and no more, than the tens of thousands dead on Mosar."

She turned away, unable to bear his gaze. "I sent her."

"Sent who?"

"Tamienne. I sent her to fight at the front gates. That's why I was alone when Augustan came."

"I didn't know."

She shook her head in sorrow. "They're dead because of me, Jan-Torres. Because of you. If I hadn't bargained for your life—"

"Would you rather have sent me to my death?"

"I don't know." She stared at her fingers as if they were foreign things. "There was no right answer. There's supposed to be a right answer!" She shut her eyes, squeezing back tears. She'd always thought that if she just had the courage to make the right choices, even if they were hard choices, then at least she could live with herself, be proud of the person she was. If she had to make choices that made people angry, she could cope with that. But what did one do when there were no right choices?

Jan-Torres leaned toward her, his eyes soft. He tried to place his hand on her knee, the part of her closest to him, but she shifted and moved out of reach. He sat back in his chair, his mouth tightening. "Neither of us wanted this. It's Florian's war, not mine. Not yours."

Rhianne grabbed a pillow from the settee and hugged it to her chest. "I didn't love Tamienne. She was always reporting on me to Florian, tattling on me. But she was just doing her job. Florian employed her, not I. She was an orphan—all the Legaciatti are. She'd nearly finished her term. She was going to marry when it ended, start a family."

Jan-Torres was silent.

"And poor Marcella. What must she be going through?"

"When you requested that casualty list"—Jan-Torres pointed at the paper on the settee—"I granted your request, much as it pained me, because from now on, I mean there to be no more secrets between us. Every life lost is a tragedy, but that casualty list is short. We're counting the dead in the hundreds, and that's on *both* sides, my people as well as yours. Do you know how many of my people died on Mosar?"

"No," she said softly.

"Tens of thousands," said Jan-Torres. "All of your family members survived this invasion. Do you know how many of my family members survived your uncle's invasion of Mosar?"

She shook her head.

"One," he growled. "My brother, Kal-Torres. My parents are dead. My aunts and uncles, dead. My cousins, dead." His eyes grew hard and his tone more heated. "My anger is not directed at you. You didn't ask for it to happen, and you were not there. You did not see the horrors that were inflicted on my country, and this very minor invasion is your first taste of war. Of course you find it horrifying; you place a high value on every human life, a trait I admire in you. You have no basis for comparison; you've lived a sheltered life here in the palace, away from the realities of war. But I *do* have that basis for comparison, and I tell you that we have exercised remarkable restraint, and I will *not* be shamed for what I have done here."

Rhianne let her breath out carefully. She had never seen Janto angry before. He was an entirely different man now that he'd assumed his true identity, and he was a little bit frightening. "What are your intentions?"

"My intentions . . ." He frowned. "They depend on a few things that will happen over the next few days. But no matter what happens, I can assure you that no harm will come to you."

"Will you let me go?" It had occurred to her that Jan-Torres and his men might flee the palace before the reinforcements arrived, and if they did, they might take hostages. She would be a prime candidate.

He hesitated. "I can't answer that yet."

She looked away. This was a nightmare. She'd saved this man's life twice, once from Florian and again from Augustan. He'd saved her life too, but he had no right to lock her up and set guards over her. "What about Morgan, the man from the infirmary? Has he had his surgery?"

Jan-Torres's eyes narrowed. "Who is that man and how do you know him?"

"First tell me if he lives!" Rhianne protested.

"I'll send a runner to find out." Jan-Torres rose and went to the door. He conferred with someone and returned to his seat. "We'll have word shortly. How do you know him? He fired on my soldiers in the city of Riat—nearly killed someone."

"Please forgive him; he was drunk. Morgan is former Legaciatti, forced into early retirement when a Riorcan assassin wounded and disabled him. Florian denied him his pension for failing to kill the assassin. And those pensions are supposed to be guaranteed."

"Your uncle is a sapskull," said Jan-Torres, "if you'll pardon my saying so. If Morgan is disabled and without a pension, how does he support himself?"

"I supply the pension," said Rhianne. "Lucien and I have been privately pooling our funds, and I've been delivering them by sneaking out through the hypocaust."

Jan-Torres's gaze softened. "I should stop marveling at how many acts of kindness I stumble upon here that have your fingerprints on them."

Rhianne looked down at her lap. His words warmed her heart, but they did not change the fact that this man was now her jailer. She had loved the gentle language scholar she'd met in the Imperial Garden, and she'd continued to love him when she'd learned he was a spy collecting information to aid his people. But now he was the king of Mosar and the commander of an invading army. She had loved Janto. She was not sure she could love Jan-Torres.

The door opened, and Jan-Torres went to speak to his runner. "Good news," he called from the door. "Morgan survived the surgery. He's conscious but weak. It will take him some time to recover."

Rhianne leapt to her feet. "Can he be brought here, to my rooms? I could care for him while his strength returns. It would give me something to do, and I wouldn't be so lonely."

Jan-Torres's forehead wrinkled.

"Stop being jealous," she scolded. "You've no right to be. And you know better than anyone that Morgan has never been my lover."

He shifted uncomfortably. "I'll make the arrangements."

35

The much-awaited message from the sentries arrived two days later: the Kjallan fleet had been sighted in the Neruna Strait. Janto's stomach knotted. Here was the moment of truth. Now he would find out whether the plans he'd set in motion would save his country or destroy it.

Signals flew wildly between the palace, the cliffs, and Kal's fleet in the harbor, as the Mosari and Sardossians made their final preparations.

Janto had commandeered the suite of a high-ranking Kjallan official as his personal quarters. It was on the third floor, with a large marble balcony overlooking the city and the harbor. From the balcony, he watched the mastheads of the Kjallan vanguard as the ships glided closer. "Rosso," he called to his door guard. "Fetch Emperor Lucien."

He'd made arrangements for some of the high-ranking Kjallan prisoners to watch the fleet action from balconies and windows in the palace. Seeing it in person would have a bigger impact on them than hearing about it secondhand.

The young emperor arrived on his crutch and false leg, escorted by six guards. Janto beckoned him onto the balcony; the guards waited outside.

Lucien limped toward him. "Now we find out if you were bluffing about that reserve fleet."

"What reserve fleet?" Janto smiled and held out a bottle of Opimian Valley red. "Wine, Your Imperial Majesty?"

Lucien stared at the bottle. "You stole that from the imperial wine cellars."

Janto popped the cork. "I compliment you on its quality. My men have been enjoying it very much."

Lucien gave him a sour look.

Janto poured the dark vintage into twin crystal glasses and handed one to Lucien. "Your ships are forming up."

The first seven ships had maneuvered themselves into a line and were sailing into the harbor single file, skirting the western edge of the harbor, moving into a position that would allow them to engage Kal's fleet.

"Wait," said Lucien. "What happened to the shore batteries?"

Janto gazed at the sad heaps of crumbled stone. "We blew them up."

"But why? You control them—they give you an advantage!"

"They were complicating things."

Lucien's eyes narrowed. "You're up to something."

Janto smiled.

As the first line of ships rounded the edge of the harbor, more ships entered, but in a haphazard fashion. They had seen that the batteries were destroyed, so the only threat to them was Kal's fleet. The first seven ships would engage Kal's fleet while the rest sailed in behind them and landed troops.

Kal's fleet, waiting deep within the harbor, looked small and pathetic. *Gods, Kal, I hope I haven't signed your death writ.* But Kal had positioned his ships well. He'd stationed them as close to the docks as possible, so that no enemy ships could slip around and attack him from the other side. It negated the Kjallans' advantage of numbers. The Kjallans would have to fight Kal's six ships with a roughly equal number of their own; there was no room to bring in more.

Lucien sipped his wine, holding his glass with one hand. With the other, he gripped the balcony railing, his knuckles whitening as the first of the seven ships reached Kal's fleet.

The first broadsides went off almost simultaneously, producing great flashes of light followed by a terrible roar. Wood exploded. Sails shuddered, riddled with holes, and a Mosari mast came down. The Kjallan ships sailed along the line of Mosari ships, firing as they went, until they'd lined up one-on-one against Kal's ships. The extra seventh ship tried, without much success, to place itself so it could rake the last Mosari ship's stern.

"Hold them, Kal," Janto muttered. His own knuckles grew white on the railing.

Meanwhile, the rest of the Kjallan ships swarmed into the harbor and began dispatching boats full of ground troops. Janto had stationed his own troops, some mounted and some on foot, around the edge of the harbor to engage the enemy soldiers who landed. But most of them were former slaves, some of whom had only just learned how to fire a pistol. Their numbers were small, and the area they were covering immense. They could hold the Kjallans for a little while, but they could not stop a large-scale landing.

Kal's fleet was locked in a deadly melee with the Kjallans. Masts and spars tangled together; sails ripped and flew free. Cannons roared. From this distance, Janto could not tell who had the upper hand.

When does the battle start? asked Sashi from his shoulder. His whiskers quivered with excitement.

Janto's eyebrows rose. *It's going on right this moment.*

Oh. It's far away. The ferret retreated, disappointed, into Janto's shirt.

The first wave of boats hit the shore, where ground troops engaged them. Still more boats were on the way. His forces would soon be overwhelmed.

Lucien smiled. "Where is that reserve fleet of yours?"

Janto indicated the point of the harbor, where mountains blocked his view of the sea. The bows of two ships glided into view.

Lucien inhaled sharply, then blew out his breath in relief as it became apparent they were Kjallan ships flying Kjallan flags. He squinted at them. "Those aren't enemies. Are they?"

Janto was silent. More ships appeared in their wake—Sardossian ships this time, but also flying Kjallan flags. The new arrivals looked for all the world like the Kjallan fleet returning from Rhaylet, with Sardossian prizes in tow. The ruse would not hold under close scrutiny—there were too many Sardossian ships compared to the number of Kjallan ones. But in the chaos of battle, it would take time for the Kjallan commanders to work that out, and that time would make all the difference.

Lucien turned to him with a pained expression. "It looks like our fleet from Rhaylet. But it's not."

"No. More wine?" asked Janto.

Lucien wordlessly offered his glass.

By the time the Kjallans realized the new arrivals were not reinforcements but enemies, they were trapped in the harbor. They could not use their advantage of numbers and double up on the new ships in open water, but had to fight them one-on-one from the harbor, where they had no room to maneuver.

"We still have you outnumbered," said Lucien.

Janto clenched his fists. "Come on, Kel-Charan."

There it was: the signal. It flew over the palace in exultation, its purples and greens picked up and repeated from one side of the harbor to the other. Orange flashes lit up the eastern and western cliffs. The ships in the middle of the harbor tried chaotically to return fire.

"What did you do?" cried Lucien. "You took the cannons out of the shore batteries and lined them up along the cliffs?"

Janto nodded. "We had to lure your entire fleet into the harbor first. And the batteries were too-obvious a target."

Soon, the inevitable outcome of the battle became clear. Boxed in by Kal's fleet on the north, the Sardossians and Riorcans on the south, and the cliffside cannons on the east and west, the Kjallans had no room to maneuver. Many of them couldn't fire off a clean shot without harming their own ships. One Kjallan ship struck its colors, and then another. Kal's ships and the cliffside cannons aimed their deadly fire at the boats attempting to land ground troops, sinking many. Janto's ground forces finished off those that made it to shore.

The young emperor stared numbly at the ruins of his fleet.

Janto signaled for the guards and pressed the wine bottle into Lucien's hands. "Retire now, and think on these events. Tomorrow, you and I and the fleet commanders will discuss the terms of our peace agreement."

*   *   *

Rhianne's door opened, and a pair of guards entered. They carried a makeshift sling between them.

"Morgan!" Rhianne cried.

"Stand back, miss," said a guard as she approached.

She moved away obediently, seeing how they struggled with their burden. She didn't want her friend to be jostled or bumped. "Place him on the couch there, if you would."

The guards carried the sling to the couch and deposited Morgan on it. He looked up at her, ashen faced but alert.

"A Healer will come by later to check on him and instruct you in his care," one of guards told her. Then they left.

"Can I get you anything?" Rhianne asked anxiously. "Food, drink? Uh . . . chamber pot?"

"I'm fine," said Morgan. "I can walk short distances, so I won't be as much trouble as that. And if I'd known I'd be nursed back to health by an imperial princess, I'd take mad potshots at entire armies more often."

"Oh, hush." Rhianne pulled up a chair next to him. "What possessed you to do such a thing?"

"I'd say it was the wine."

"You need to lay off that stuff."

"I'll take it under consideration."

She folded her arms. "Are you patronizing me?"

"Are you mothering me, little girl who's half my age?"

"I'm not a girl, and I'm not half your age either." Rhianne picked up his hand. It was alarmingly cold. "You need another blanket." She went to the bedroom, fetched one, and tucked it around him. She picked up his hand again— it was enormous compared to her own—and rubbed it between both of hers, trying to warm it. "You really do drink too much. Are you unhappy, Morgan?"

He moved his shoulders in an approximation of a shrug. "A man's not made to sit around and listen to the gossip of his neighbors."

Rhianne frowned. Morgan wanted to work, but he was crippled and all his skills and training were physical. His right hand didn't work properly, and he had a hard time raising either of his arms above his head.

"I've been working up the courage to offer myself to that Mosari king," continued Morgan. "But I can't imagine he'd want me. I was useless before and more so now I've been shot."

"The Mosari king? You mean Jan-Torres?"

"Whatever his name is," said Morgan.

"You can't join his service," Rhianne protested. "You'd be a traitor!"

"Hardly," said Morgan, "when the emperor cast *me* out first."

"You don't know anything about Jan-Torres," she said. "He might treat you badly."

"Nah," said Morgan. "I've been in wars, spent time in hostile Riorca, and it's a miracle I didn't bleed my life away in the streets of Riat that night. Do you know how many military commanders will use their precious Healers to save the lives of enemy soldiers or civilians? None, that's how many. But the Mosari king did."

Rhianne considered this. "Aren't you furious about him marching in here and taking over?"

"I don't give a flying tomtit," said Morgan. "And anyway, he can't hold this place; not when the reinforcements arrive. I'm surprised he survived the arrival of the fleet—"

"The fleet's returned?"

"Yes, there was a monster of a battle in the harbor. Didn't you hear it? I suppose you're on the wrong side of the palace. Jan-Torres must have won, because his men are still here. But our ground forces are unstoppable. He's not here to hold Kjall, because that's impossible. He's not here for bloodshed, since I'd be dead if he was. So he's here to cut a deal. He's got Lucien by the cods—pardon my language—and you can't blame a man for wanting to save his country."

"No," said Rhianne. "I suppose you can't."

36

Janto met with Lucien again the next day.

The young emperor looked up as Janto entered the room. "Have the fleet commanders arrived?"

"Not yet, Your Imperial Majesty." Janto grabbed a chair from the far wall, casting a surreptitious glance at Lucien. The young man's eyes were hard and calculating. He'd recovered from the shock of losing his fleet, it seemed, and moved on to damage control.

Lucien shrugged. "Every day that passes brings my ground troops from northern and eastern Kjall closer to liberating the palace."

"We won't be waiting much longer for the fleet commanders. They've had casualties to attend to, and emergency repairs. Also, the harbor's a mess; it's impossible to maneuver in there. I don't envy the man tasked with cleaning it up." He smiled.

Lucien folded his arms and sniffed. "I hope you came here with a better offer than the one you brought before."

"Your fleet's been destroyed, and you think I've come with a *better* offer?" He set the chair in front of Lucien and straddled it. "You're lucky I'm not making it worse."

"I'm not giving up Mosar."

Janto shrugged. "For your sake, I'm sorry to hear that, since it will cost you the four warships and three battalions of troops you have stationed there. In a matter of days, the Sardossians, the Riorcans, and my own men will sail to liberate Mosar, and we are fully prepared to fight your outnumbered garrison."

Lucien was silent for a moment. "Perhaps an arrangement can be made."

"Give me your fleet's private signal and send with me new orders for your men, commanding them to return home in peace," said Janto. "Otherwise, I'll destroy them. My combined army outnumbers your three battalions on Mosar, and you know I've got more ships. I'm making this offer for one reason only: I'm tired of bloodshed. I want it to end."

Lucien's eyes narrowed in suspicion.

Janto sighed. "Let me also point out that without those four warships stationed at Mosar, you have no fleet."

"I have other ships."

Janto chuckled. "You're bluffing. Yes, you have more ships—the three that police the Riorcan harbors. Other than that, nothing. And don't give me any horseshit about putting guns on merchant ships; they're no match for real warships and you know it. We destroyed your Rhaylet fleet, your Sarpol fleet, and your harbor fleet. If you do not accept my offer—my *gift*, Lucien—you'll lose the four ships at Mosar and be left with only the three at Riorca. Which might leave you in some trouble, since Riorca now has ships of its own."

Lucien stiffened. "*Stolen* ships."

"That's a matter of opinion."

The emperor leaned forward, his eyes dark and angry.

"It is *nonsense* to speak of Riorcans possessing ships. Riorca is a province of Kjall and has been for decades. Those ships are in the hands of thieves and mutineers. Surrender them immediately."

Janto shook his head. "You're in no position to make demands. Even if you were, the ships are not mine to give. Take it up with the Riorcan fleet commander."

"There *is* no Riorcan fleet commander! The man who calls himself that is an escaped slave, nothing more!"

"By some accounts, *I* am an escaped slave."

Lucien scowled and folded his arms.

Janto rose. It was time to make his exit before Lucien could come up with any more ridiculous ideas. "I'll see you at the negotiating table, Emperor. In the meantime, think on my offer."

"Wait," said Lucien.

Janto paused.

"Return my stolen ships, and I will accept your offer. My forces will leave Mosar peacefully."

"The Riorcan ships are not mine to give. Even if they were, I would not betray an ally who fought at my side." Janto headed for the door.

"Jan-Torres, what do you want in exchange for those stolen ships?"

Janto waved a dismissive hand. "If you want ships, accept my original offer. It gives you four."

"I want the two Riorcan ships, and I'm willing to deal. What do you want? Money? Preferential trade agreements? Kjall would be a powerful ally for Mosar."

Janto hesitated with his hand on the door handle. Indeed, Kjall would. This was exactly the kind of agreement he wanted. But at the price of betraying the Riorcans?

There was no chance Riorca was going to come out of

this well. The destruction of the fleet would temporarily prevent the Kjallans from attacking Mosar or Sardos, but not Riorca, which shared their continent and was accessible by land. What difference would it make, in the long run, if he seized the Riorcan ships and returned them to Kjall?

No difference at all, probably. Lucien didn't need those ships; he was demanding them as a matter of principle. But there were lines Janto would not cross, not if he wanted to be worthy of his throne. And he didn't trust Lucien, not fully. It was in the young emperor's interest to break up the alliance between Mosar, Sardos, and Riorca. Janto had to make certain he did not succeed in doing so. "There is nothing you can offer me that will induce me to betray my allies," he said firmly.

"Perhaps we need only to hit upon the right lure. Did Rhianne accept your offer of marriage?"

Janto froze. "I have not yet made the offer."

"You were going to."

"I've been busy destroying your fleet."

"You haven't made it because you know she won't accept. She's hostile. Am I correct?"

"What do you care?" said Janto. "You said you'd kill me if I touched your cousin."

"Perhaps I've experienced a change of heart," said Lucien. "Rhianne once cared about you a great deal. Her happiness means much to me. So tell me: has she been receptive?"

Janto bit his lip. "She's angry about the lives lost in the assault and that I deceived her about my identity."

"You are making a mistake with her, and I think I know what it is," said Lucien.

"There's no mistake," said Janto. "She's angry about

the things I've done, and she'll either forgive me or she won't. If I had more time—"

"It's not about time," said Lucien. "I mean, yes, time would help. But it's unnecessary. Rhianne is rational; she's just not accustomed to war. If someone were to put your invasion into context for her, explain that you haven't been executing anyone, or torturing anyone, or even looting our treasury—"

"I did explain some of that."

"Yes, but she doesn't trust you right now. She trusts me."

"And you're offering to talk to her for me?"

"Yes, in exchange for the Riorcans," said Lucien. "Hand them over, and I'll return Mosar to you peacefully, negotiate trade agreements, and speak to Rhianne on your behalf, an act that might lead to an even stronger alliance between our nations."

The offer hit Janto like a punch to the gut. It was everything he wanted, absolutely everything. A peaceful recovery of Mosar, an alliance with Kjall, and, possibly, reconciliation with the woman he loved. There was only that small matter of betraying men who'd fought in good faith by his side. He forced his lips to form the words "No deal."

Lucien sighed. "I see you are intractable on this point. Come sit down, and I'll tell you something about Rhianne."

"In exchange for the Riorcans?"

"No. For free."

That sounded suspicious. "Why?"

"Because you're a terrible negotiator, but you seem loyal. This seems a point in your favor."

Wary, Janto returned to his chair and sat.

"You cannot put Rhianne in a cage," said Lucien. "It

is the worst mistake you can make with her. The story of the woodcutter's son and the horse of mist—do you know it? Is it told on Mosar?"

"I believe so. In our version, it's a potter's son."

"Makes no difference. The boy goes out late at night and finds a great black horse. He has no bridle or saddle, but he gets up on the animal anyway. The horse is so responsive he can guide it with his hands, and its gaits are so smooth he doesn't need a saddle, and he rides all over the countryside, and it's the fastest and finest of all horses. By morning, the horse has brought him home and gone off on its own, but every night it comes back, so every night he goes on this glorious ride. And he thinks, *I should capture this horse and make it my own.* So he gets a bridle, and that night he tries to put a bridle on the horse so he can keep it. And you know what happens?"

"The horse turns to mist and he never sees it again," said Janto.

"Exactly. Rhianne is the horse of mist," said Lucien. "My father thinks her confusing and impossible to understand. He could not be more wrong—Rhianne is the most straightforward of women. She's generous and openhearted, and most of the time she'll tell you exactly what she's thinking. There are only two rules you need follow with her, and they are absolute. First, don't mistreat her. And second, don't cage her. If you try to cage her, she will fight you with every bit of strength she has."

"I'm not *caging* her," said Janto. "I put her in custody to keep her safe."

Lucien rolled his eyes. "That's the mistake I was talking about."

*   *   *

While he awaited the return of the fleet commanders, Janto visited the wounded, settled disagreements, and attended funerals. As he went about these duties, he noticed a subtle but unmistakable change in his men. They saluted him more crisply; they stood straighter in his presence. They stared at him when they thought he wasn't looking. And high-ranking officers who had questioned his decisions in the past now deferred without a quibble.

He'd always craved the respect of his men, but now that he had it, he didn't enjoy it as much as he'd thought he would. He felt as if an invisible barrier, which nobody, not even his officers, dared to cross, had been erected around him. And with no one questioning his decisions, he had no sounding board for trying out ideas. What if he made a foolish decision and no one called him on it?

Folding his arms, he watched the military procession from his balcony. It wound its way up the switchbacks of the Imperial Road, bringing him Kal-Torres and the fleet commanders.

When they arrived, he met them at the front gates with as much pomp as he could muster. He had no musicians, nor could he spare even a single pyrotechnic from signaling duty. But he lined up his officers to receive the battle-weary men with salutes and shouts. Kal was first to enter, bronze and handsome as a living statue. He'd taken a bullet in the leg during battle, but the ship's Healer had done good work on him, and he wasn't limping. Gishi fluttered above him, keening in triumph. Admiral Llinos of the Sardossians followed, and then Admiral Durgan of the Riorcans. Durgan was a small, quiet man whom Janto studied curiously. As Lucien had mentioned, the man was a former slave. It remained to be seen whether he possessed the skills of a leader and a diplomat.

The kitchens had bustled with activity all morning. Freed slaves and soldiers too infirm to fight had busied themselves cooking a feast for the returning heroes. Janto led the fleet admirals and their officers to the grand ballroom and delivered the first of many toasts celebrating their victory.

Food and wine flowed copiously, though Janto drank lightly in order to retain his wits. When the party was beginning to wind down and an overstimulated Sashi had retreated into his shirt for a nap, Admiral Llinos pulled Janto aside. "Your Majesty, I want to confer with you on a matter of some delicacy before we begin the negotiations."

"What matter is this?"

"As you know, the Kjallan Empire has always been insular. They marry their imperial princesses to great Kjallan military leaders and the heads of powerful families, never to foreign heads of state. I believe this is part of the reason Kjall so willingly invades other nations. They have no ties to those nations. Now, the deposed Emperor Florian has two daughters—one daughter and one niece, actually—and the niece is of marriageable age. I understand she was previously betrothed, but her fiancé was killed during the invasion."

"That is correct."

"So she's available."

Janto nodded. "I plan to make an offer for her hand."

"Good, you and I are thinking along the same lines," said Llinos. "But an *offer*? Under the circumstances, an offer will be refused. You must make it part of the settlement."

Janto blinked. "Force it on her?"

"An imperial princess never has much of a choice in her marriage partner—nor does a king, as I understand it?" He raised his eyebrows.

"For the most part, no," Janto agreed.

"We must bring pressure to bear on the Kjallans to join the wider community and marry their women outside the empire."

"I'll think about it."

Admiral Llinos departed, swaying a little with drink.

Janto bit his lip, hardly able to sort out his feelings. He wanted Rhianne to marry him and return home with him as the queen of Mosar. But she was so hostile right now, and he had so little time. It was unlikely she would accept his proposal. Could he do as Llinos suggested and make it part of the peace settlement? Rhianne had nearly been forced into one marriage already. It didn't seem right to force her into another. And Lucien's advice lay heavy on his heart. He would never mistreat Rhianne, but under the circumstances, how could he avoid keeping her in protective custody? Lucien didn't understand the realities of his situation.

He sipped his wine. He was looking for San-Kullen when Admiral Durgan, the Riorcan, intercepted him and addressed him in fluent diplomatic Kjallan. "Your Majesty, may I speak to you in private?"

"Of course."

They moved to a quiet corner of the slowly emptying ballroom.

"What are your expectations for the upcoming negotiations?" asked Durgan.

"Well," said Janto, "Mosar will be liberated, either by

force or through peaceful agreement. I hope to set up trade settlements to promote better relations over the long term. Realistically, these agreements will work only if Kjall will truly benefit from them, since our influence over Emperor Lucien ends in a matter of days."

"And what of Riorca?"

"Admiral, I am willing to offer your ships and your people safe harbor at Mosar. My soldiers have scoured the city and freed more than a thousand Riorcan slaves—"

"This I already know," said Durgan.

"And I would be happy to welcome them to Mosar as free men and women. We have land available for them to settle."

Durgan's brows lowered. "King Jan-Torres, my people have no wish to be Mosari refugees. Our interest is in liberating Riorca. Am I to understand that these peace negotiations will offer no benefit whatsoever to Riorca?"

"What concessions do you desire in the negotiations?"

"No less than what you wish for Mosar. Freedom!"

"And how are we to negotiate for it?"

"We demand it in exchange for young Lucien's life."

Janto shook his head. "It won't work, Admiral. If we kill Lucien, someone else will rise to power in his place. If you can find a way to bring pressure to bear on Kjall such that they will give up Riorca, I would love to see it happen. But I don't see how. The only reason Lucien will withdraw from Mosar is that his fleet has been destroyed. He could not hold my country if he tried. But Riorca is accessible by land, and we haven't made a dent in Kjall's land forces."

"My people fought by your side, King Jan-Torres. Do you not now owe us the same favor in return? To liberate Riorca is not as difficult as you believe. My people would rise up. They have already! Even now, there are parts of Riorca Kjall does not control. If your fleet gave us support by sea—"

"Admiral, surely you are not proposing that my people begin another war."

"*Finish* a war, not begin one."

"Take it up with Admiral Llinos, not me. The Sardossians may be capable of fighting another war, but my people are not. We've lost nearly a fifth of our population. Some of our cities have been razed, while others are badly damaged, and we're heading into the storm season, during which we can neither build nor grow food. I fear the Kjallans have plundered our stores, and there's only so much food we can carry back with us. My people will have their hands full just keeping their children fed. A war is utterly beyond them."

"My people fought for you. We gave our lives for you. And you offer us *nothing*?"

Janto rubbed his temples. Negotiations hadn't even begun yet, and already his head hurt. "I offer your people land, safe harbor, and citizenship on Mosar."

Durgan glared at him. "I told you, my people have no wish to be refugees."

"Then I cannot help you, Admiral."

"I see," said Admiral Durgan coldly. He walked away, his back very straight.

San-Kullen, who'd been standing at a discreet distance, approached. "Sire? Are you feeling well? You don't look yourself."

Janto shook his head. "I'm just tired. Frustrated." He

made an exasperated gesture at Durgan's retreating form. "He wants things from me I can't give. Llinos wants things from me I can't give. So do Lucien and Rhianne. Why does everyone demand the impossible?"

San-Kullen smiled wryly. "Welcome to the Mosari throne, Your Majesty."

37

Rhianne's stomach fluttered when Jan-Torres entered her room. It was so irritating the way her body reacted to him. She knew intellectually that Janto and Jan-Torres were different people and one of them wasn't even real, but her body hadn't received the message. Her body remembered only that those were the hands that had stroked her, those were the lips that had kissed her, and that part of her, the *stupid* part, still wanted him.

"Rhianne," he greeted her. He turned to Morgan, who still rested on the couch. "Are you recovering well?"

"Getting stronger, Your Majesty," said Morgan.

"I'm glad to hear it." He turned back to Rhianne. "I'd like to speak with you in private."

Morgan struggled up from his prone position. "I'll move to the bedroom."

"No—stay where you are," Rhianne scolded. "Jan-Torres and I will go to the bedroom." When Morgan raised a worried eyebrow, she added, "We'll be fine. We're just going to talk." She had concerns about Jan-Torres, but that he would assault or molest her was not among them.

Jan-Torres escorted her to the bedroom, which was smaller and more intimate than the one in her imperial apartment. Because of the disruption in the palace, she had no servants or slaves looking after her and was glad she'd taken the trouble to pick up after herself and make the bed, not that she'd done a spectacular job. In a corner of the room, a few chairs nestled in a quiet reading nook. She claimed one of them, sitting up straight and rubbing her palms nervously on the fabric. Jan-Torres took the seat next to her.

"I have a few things to tell you," said Jan-Torres. "The first is that we will be negotiating the peace settlement this afternoon. You and Lucien will represent Kjall. My brother and I will represent the Mosari contingent of the invading forces, and we'll be joined also by Admiral Llinos and Admiral Durgan."

"Who are they?"

"The Sardossian and Riorcan commanders, respectively."

Sardossians. She kept forgetting about them and thinking the army belonged entirely to Jan-Torres. "What's this about a Riorcan commander?"

"A small contingent of Riorcans assisted us in the invasion, and Llinos and I have offered them a seat at the negotiating table. We need a tiebreaking vote if Mosar and Sardos disagree."

Soldier's hell, that was a terrible idea. "Riorcans are hostile to Kjallan interests. They're not going to negotiate in good faith for peace with Mosar and Sardos."

"I'm aware of the hostility," said Jan-Torres. "Because of it, Llinos and I will have extra motivation to present a united front. Don't worry about the negotiating part. It's Lucien's job, and he's well equipped for it. I just think you should be there."

Rhianne nodded. Anything to get her out of this gilded

prison and see Lucien again. She didn't like the idea of a Riorcan negotiator, but if the Riorcans had been part of the invasion, perhaps there was no avoiding it.

"I also came to . . . well, to clear the air between us." He shifted in his chair. "I'm sorry for any pain I caused when I concealed the fact that I was the Crown Prince of Mosar. Out of necessity, I dodged questions and withheld information about my family and upbringing. But there's no longer any need for secrecy. If you'd like, I can answer those questions now." He smiled hopefully.

Rhianne sighed. He wanted to reconcile with her, for what purpose she wasn't certain. To assuage a guilty conscience? Because he wanted something else from her, maybe at the negotiations? Or did he want to resume their love affair? "I'm not interested."

His smile faded. "The name *Janto* is real," he said, apparently determined to talk about himself anyway. "It's a common Mosari name, the one my mother gave me, and the one my friends and family use. At the age of fourteen, when I achieved soulcasting, I was granted the zo name Jan-Torres. It's formal—more a title than a name."

That was actually surprising, and something of a relief, since she'd thought the name *Janto* was a fake. But she kept her mouth shut. She didn't want to encourage him.

He soldiered on gamely. "Most of the things I told you in the garden were true. Obviously I've never been a scribe. But I *was* a language scholar, and I do speak five languages. It was part of my education as a prince, but I showed a natural aptitude, and beyond that, I was just really interested in languages. My brother, Kal-Torres, was the rough-and-tumble type, always wanting to wrestle or run a race or practice swordplay, and I always had my nose stuck in a book. I came here not because I was a trained spy—I wasn't—but because I was a shroud mage and my nation was desperate. I was in charge of Mosari Intelligence, but I'd had the post for only a short while and I had no field experience, so to avoid getting in trouble I stuck as much to the truth as I could. Most of what you know about me is genuine."

He paused. Rhianne eyed the ferret sitting in his lap. "Why are you a shroud mage rather than a war mage?"

Janto's eyes lit. "You're right to wonder. I was meant to be a war mage. It's traditional. The Mosari king's first son is always a war mage, and his second son a sea mage. If there's a third son, he's another war mage, and so on. In the zo crèche, they had an albino brindlecat waiting for me. Albinos are rare, and they save them for the royal family. I was visiting the crèche regularly, feeding my intended brindlecat and getting to know her, and then something happened. Are you familiar with the problems we have regarding ferrets and soulcasting?"

Rhianne shook her head.

He stroked Sashi absently. "Ferrets are ... difficult animals. They refuse the soulcasting bond nineteen times out of twenty. That success rate is just too low, after putting a candidate through all the training and bonding work, and then you end up having to start over with a different animal, and the candidate is set back a year or two. That's why we have so few shroud mages. Nowadays we don't even attempt to bond someone with a ferret unless the ferret shows a natural affinity for the candidate. We keep ferrets in the zo crèche and essentially wait for them to choose someone. Which a lot of them never do."

"Are you saying Sashi chose you?"

"He did," said Janto. "I walked past his cage several times a day, every day, to visit my brindlecat. And Sashi literally flung himself at the bars of his cage, trying to get at me. It created a dilemma, because the albino brindlecat had been set aside for me, and for me to become a shroud mage instead of a war mage violated tradition. But we have this concept in Mosar of *quanrok*. There's no Kjallan translation. It means, more or less, *gods decide*. We feel that sometimes the gods make decisions for us through familiars. My father and mother and some of the zo handlers and I came to an agreement that the gods had made a decision on my behalf. They wanted me to take Sashi as my familiar, not the brindlecat, and so I did. And I became a shroud mage."

His story raised half a dozen questions, about *quanrok* and this concept of an animal refusing the bond, but Rhianne kept them to herself.

"Any other questions?" asked Janto.

She shook her head.

Janto rose from his chair and took her hands, encouraging her to rise.

She stood, with some reluctance, since clearly he was up to something. He was being kind and, she had to admit, a little bit charming. But gods curse him, he was still her enemy. Her jailer.

"There's one last thing I want to talk to you about before the negotiations begin this afternoon," said Janto. "Before I head home to Mosar."

"What?" There went the butterflies in her stomach again.

"I know this is the worst possible time I could be doing this. But please understand, there *is* no other time. In a couple of days, I'll be gone, and once I go—"

"Doing what?" she demanded.

He swallowed. "Rhianne, since the moment I laid eyes on you in the Imperial Garden, I've been enraptured by your beauty. At the time, I was blinded by my prejudice toward Kjallans. But as I grew to know you better—"

"Janto, no!" Oh gods, he was proposing.

Twin lines of worry appeared in his forehead. "Let me finish before you make your decision. As I grew to know you better, I witnessed your bravery and your compassion for people from all walks of life. When I saw firsthand the steadfastness of your heart, my feelings grew from admiration to love. I would be honored if you would consent to marry me and rule by my side as the queen of Mosar."

She pulled her hands away. "I can't marry you!"

Janto, looking more sad than surprised, moved his hands awkwardly to his sides. "What is your objection?"

"You lied to me! You betrayed me!" Her hands shook. Her voice shook. What was wrong with her? This should be easy, telling him to go home to Mosar. "You took my riftstone and locked me up like a prisoner." Gods, the tears were starting. She brushed them away.

"I thought you knew why I had to do those things," said Janto. "You have the biggest heart of any woman I've ever known. Can you not find room in that heart to forgive, to understand my circumstances?"

Rhianne choked on sobs. "Just go."

"It would be good for our nations! Both yours *and* mine. It would promote peace between them. If you won't accept me for my own sake, would you accept me for the sake of Kjall and Mosar?"

Fury rose like bile in her throat. "Is that why you asked? Because it would be good for Mosar?"

He lowered his brows. "You know why I asked."

She shook her head.

Janto turned. "I'll see you at the negotiating table."

38

Janto arrived a little early for the council meeting, with Kal-Torres and a clerk in tow. He'd chosen a Kjallan council room for the negotiations, well-appointed but small, with an oval-shaped table in the center. Admiral Llinos and his adviser were already present.

Llinos clasped wrists with Janto and began to regale him with the tale of his battle in the harbor with the Kjallan ship *Relentless*. Janto sat down to listen, while Sashi climbed to the top of Janto's chair to nap and Gishi perched on the top of Kal's chair.

Admiral Durgan entered and took his seat. Janto nodded at Durgan and received a nod in return.

"We lost the foremast over the port bow—," Llinos was saying.

"Starboard," corrected his adviser.

"You were not on board, Eurig."

As Llinos's tale continued, Rhianne entered the room, escorted by a contingent of guards, and sat at the far end of the table. Janto stole glances at her, each one sending a shiver of yearning down his spine. Her expression was neutral, but a tremor in her hands betrayed her nervousness. He wanted to go and speak to her, but there was nothing left to say. She couldn't forgive him, and she didn't love him anymore.

"We knew it was unrecoverable, so we had to cut it free . . . ," said Llinos.

While Janto listened, increasingly impatient with the tale, Kal-Torres rose and crossed the room. He leaned casually against the table next to Rhianne, with his back to Janto, and apparently began speaking since Rhianne sat up alertly in response. Janto couldn't hear their voices from where he sat—Llinos was loud—but he watched out of the corner of his eye. Rhianne's back was very straight. She smiled, looking friendly but reserved. Kal picked up her hand and kissed it.

Janto tore his eyes away, fuming. Classic Kal. He'd figured out that Janto wanted this woman and was interested in her for more than political reasons, so now he was moving on her. He would steal her if he could, for no reason at all except to demonstrate that he could. Kal turned and smirked at Janto, confirming his intentions.

Llinos talked on, oblivious. "So then we had a loose cannon. You know what a disaster that is? If you don't rope it and catch it fast, it causes all kinds of damage. . . ."

Janto nodded distractedly.

A change in the body language at the far end of the table alerted him that something had happened. Rhianne snapped angrily at Kal, who recoiled from her.

Inside, Janto exulted. If he couldn't have her, at least Kal wouldn't either.

The guards arrived with Lucien, a welcome distraction for all parties. Kal came forward to greet Lucien.

"And then they struck their colors," finished Llinos. "Was it not a very fine action?"

"Very fine, indeed," said Janto.

The guards shut the door, sealing them in. Lucien limped to his chair, haughty and scornful. He took Rhianne's hand in a show of Kjallan solidarity. They leaned close and spoke in whispers.

Janto cleared his throat and began in diplomatic Kjallan. "Thank you all for coming. I'll begin with introductions—"

"King Jan-Torres," interrupted Lucien, "I object to the presence of that one." He pointed at the Riorcan. "He is a criminal, and he sullies these proceedings. Imperial Kjall will not negotiate with him."

"You gods-cursed tyrant," fumed Admiral Durgan. "*You* are the criminal!"

"Silence, both of you!" cried Janto. "Emperor Lucien, you are in no position to dictate who sits at this table. Admiral Durgan's men fought bravely and have earned their place here. If you cannot accept their presence, someone else will negotiate for Kjall."

Lucien subsided, grumbling, and Janto introduced the members of each delegation. "Our time is limited, so we'll get right to it. Our first order of business is to decide the fate of the former emperor Florian Nigellus Gavros. Bring him in, please." He gestured to the door guards.

Four men escorted a flint-eyed Florian into the room and took up positions around him. Lucien and Rhianne, who had not seen the former emperor since before the invasion, turned and stared.

"Florian Nigellus Gavros," Jantos began, "you have waged unprovoked war against Mosar, Riorca, and Sardos and committed numerous war crimes detailed in this list"—he held up an inked document—"including refusal to honor a Sage flag and the indiscriminate murder and enslavement of Mosari and Riorcan civilians." He repeated the words in Sardossian. "Do you have anything to say in your defense?"

Florian's eyes bored into Janto. "You will die for this."

Janto ignored that. "Admiral Llinos, has Sardos reached a decision?"

Llinos conferred with his adviser. "Yes, Your Majesty. We recommend the former emperor be exiled for life and kept under guard in Sardos or Mosar."

Janto nodded. "Admiral Durgan, Riorca's decision?"

"Death," said Durgan. "Former Emperor Florian is responsible for the murder and enslavement of tens of thousands of people. Exile is too lenient. If he is not executed, how can we be certain he will not someday return to power?"

That left Janto in the role of tiebreaker. He stole a glance at Rhianne, who watched Florian, wringing her hands in anguish.

He exchanged glances with Kal, who nodded. They'd discussed the matter at length already. "Exile. While Admiral Durgan speaks with honesty and passion about the severity of Florian's crimes, let this gesture of mercy demonstrate our willingness to forge a lasting peace. Since Mosar has been more injured than Sardos by Florian's actions, I propose we house him on Mosar, guarded by my own men."

"Sardos concurs," rumbled Llinos.

Admiral Durgan said nothing. His eyes smoldered.

Janto turned to Lucien. "He will be well looked after."

"Thank you," said Lucien. Rhianne stared down at her lap, her shoulders shaking. She seemed to be silently crying.

He nodded at Florian's guards. "Take him back to his room."

"You *will* die for this," said Florian over his shoulder, as the guards hauled him up and escorted him out. The door shut behind him.

"On that note," said Janto, eliciting a chuckle from his fellows, "let's discuss the removal of Kjallan troops from Mosar."

As Janto had expected, Lucien, denied any further opportunity to break up the alliance and turn his enemies against one another, agreed to peacefully withdraw his troops and ships from Mosar. He was going to lose the island anyway. This way he could keep his four desperately needed ships and spin it as a strategic withdrawal instead of suffering another humiliating defeat.

Janto and Llinos then began negotiating trade agreements with Lucien, who bargained with them in good faith while denying every request from Admiral Durgan.

To Janto's surprise, Rhianne, whom he'd expected to be a silent observer, spoke up often. Since Florian had never involved her in matters of state, her knowledge was limited. She was careful not to display her ignorance, but she intervened when discussions became too heated. She had a knack for smoothing ruffled egos and speaking sense in simple terms that couldn't be denied. It made Janto desire her all the more, not just as a lover, but as a diplomatic asset for Mosar. *Three gods, Florian, you've wasted this woman.*

However, Rhianne never spoke up for the Riorcans. Janto understood her reasons. Lucien would not survive as emperor if he appeared weak. To give the impression of strength after Kjall's crushing losses, Lucien had to take a hard line somewhere, and Riorca, the only country accessible to him by land, was his unlucky target. Admiral Durgan grew furious as the negotiations proceeded, and Janto felt bad for Riorca, but there wasn't much he could do.

By suppertime, they'd hashed out most of the important points. The delegations were growing tired and irritable, so he dismissed the group until morning.

The next day, when they reconvened, they worked out some sticky points regarding the use of the Kjallan-controlled Neruna Strait. After that, Janto proposed some changes in the treatment of Riorcan slaves, which Lucien firmly shot down. Admiral Durgan barely paid attention. He seemed to view the negotiations as a farce.

"Are we finished?" Janto turned to his clerk. "Cialo, when will you have a document ready for signing?"

Cialo lifted his head from the paper. "Very soon, sire. I'm copying the final passages."

"There is one more matter to discuss," said Admiral Llinos.

"Speak," said Janto.

Llinos turned to Lucien and Rhianne. "Kjall has long been an insular nation, rarely if ever marrying its women outside its own borders."

Rhianne's eyes narrowed. Lucien took her hand protectively and glared at Llinos.

"My delegation believes, as does the Mosari delegation, that this practice contributes to Kjall's culture of war, and that if the Imperial Princess Rhianne were to marry outside the empire, that gesture would further peace among our nations."

"Admiral Llinos, you are out of line," said Lucien. "It is not your business whom the princess marries."

"With respect, Emperor, you do not have a vote at

this council," said Llinos. "Now, the Sardossian First Heir has expressed a desire to wed the Kjallan Imperial Princess—"

"The First Heir has fourteen wives already," said Lucien. "It is an insult to suggest that the Kjallan Imperial Princess, the highest-ranking woman in Kjall, should be one of fifteen."

"By our laws, she would be his First Wife and thus of superior rank to any of them," said Llinos in a tone of practiced patience that suggested he'd explained this to ignorant foreigners before. "Rhianne's firstborn son would thus be First Heir to the First Heir."

Janto struggled to hide his annoyance. *If he survives to adulthood.* Ranking sons in Sardossian hive-families had a high mortality rate.

"However," added Llinos, "since Mosar has suffered the most in this recent war, I move that she instead be married to King Jan-Torres."

Everyone turned and looked expectantly at Janto. He opened his mouth as if to say something and closed it again. Rhianne folded her arms and glared at him.

"I second," announced Admiral Durgan. "Let the princess be married to the king of Mosar." He smiled. "That's a majority, Jan-Torres. We don't even need your vote!"

The delegates chuckled. Rhianne stared down at her lap, but he knew she was fuming. Lucien showed no emotion, not yet. He was waiting for Janto's response.

Which was going to be ... what?

He'd planned to vote against the arranged marriage, in accordance with Rhianne's wishes. But he hadn't expected to be outvoted before he even opened his mouth. Both Sardos and Riorca wanted the marriage to take place. Durgan was probably trying to cause mischief with the Kjallans, but Llinos's vote was sincere. Could Janto throw his hands in the air and say it wasn't his fault? He was outvoted.

No. Rhianne wasn't going to accept that explanation. She'd made a mistake when she'd turned him down. He was certain of it. She felt she didn't know him and couldn't trust him, but the man she'd fallen in love with, whom she'd trusted implicitly and offered her body to, was the real Janto. In time, given half a chance, he would prove that to her. A marriage would give him that time, that chance. Otherwise he would sail home to Mosar, and they might never see each other again. Should he not correct her mistake?

If he accepted the results of the vote, Rhianne would be his. Lucien would bluster, but he couldn't do anything about it. Kjall had no fleet. Mosar would be untouchable to him for years, and by the time Lucien had rebuilt, Janto would have won Rhianne over. She would no longer want to return home.

Rhianne trembled in her chair, avoiding his eyes. Could she not understand? Her experiences with Florian and Augustan had left their scars, but Janto was not like them. He would not abuse her. She would be happy on Mosar. Wouldn't she?

No. She'd run away from him, like she'd run from the others. Three gods, who was he kidding? If he forced her into this, she would never love him again.

"Respectfully, I must decline," said Janto. When Durgan opened his mouth to protest, he held up his hand. "I'm outvoted, I know, but this is my life we're talking about, and you two cannot vote me a wife, much as it may amuse you. While I greatly admire the Imperial Princess, I believe she does not desire this match."

Kal turned to Janto, his eyebrows raised expressively. Janto shrugged in response.

Lucien spoke. "King Jan-Torres, I am glad someone in this room possesses some sense."

Janto smiled wanly. He might have earned Lucien's respect, but inside he cursed himself for a fool. Now he and Rhianne would never have a chance to reconcile. It might be years before he paid a diplomatic visit to Kjall, if he ever did. By that time, who knew? She might be married to someone else.

He looked up to see Rhianne's eyes on him, warm and soft, and his breath caught in his throat. How long had it been since she'd looked at him like that? It wasn't love, though; it was gratitude. Gratitude for removing himself from her life. What was he supposed to say? *You're welcome*? Must she twist the knife? He turned away.

"Since the Mosari king refuses the match," said Llinos, "I move that Rhianne be married instead to Sardos's First Heir."

Durgan smiled. "Seconded."

Llinos's ruddy cheeks warmed. "Once again, Jan-Torres, we have no need of your vote."

Janto started to protest, but Lucien leapt up. "This is outrageous! My cousin the Imperial Princess will not be bartered about like spices or salt cod! Kjall will exact its vengeance on any nation that attempts to take her by force."

"With what fleet?" drawled Durgan.

"I must remind you, we will not always be without a fleet. And while our ground forces are far away, they remain strong. Furthermore," said Lucien, "Rhianne is in no condition to marry at this time. She was previously betrothed, and her fiancé was killed during the invasion. She is in mourning."

Llinos shrugged. "It is no object. We are prepared to wait the length of the traditional Kjallan mourning period before the marriage takes place."

"Admiral Llinos," said Janto, "may I speak with you privately?"

The admiral locked eyes with him. "Certainly."

Janto led him to a side room and closed the door. "You're making a mistake."

"No, I'm not," said Llinos. "Lucien's bluster is just that. Bluster. By the time he has a fleet capable of attacking Sardos, Rhianne will be fully invested in the Sardossian First Family, with children of her own. Kjall is not going to declare war on us. Marrying Rhianne into the First Family will make war *less* likely."

"Don't be so certain. I think Durgan is trying to stir up trouble."

"Of course he is," said Llinos. "Can you blame him?"

"It's more than just tweaking the Kjallans. Given that we've declined to help the Riorcans with their rebellion, what's the most useful thing he can do in these peace talks?"

Llinos shrugged. "Sabotage them. Stir up trouble between Kjall and Sardos, or Kjall and Mosar. Both, if possible. But consider this. It doesn't matter what Lucien signs or doesn't sign in these negotiations. Once his ground troops arrive, our influence over him ends, and he can throw these peace accords in the compost heap."

"Exactly!" said Janto. "We need his willing cooperation. We can't antagonize him."

"But if we take Rhianne, it gives us leverage. He doesn't have the power to forcibly remove her, not yet. And by the time he does, she won't want to leave. Everything we're negotiating today, he may reverse himself on, but not this. It's irreversible."

"You're assuming Rhianne will adapt to this marriage and come to enjoy her new life—that in the end, Lucien will not attempt to forcibly remove her because she's happy on Sardos. But that's not going to happen. Rhianne will fight you every step of the way. I know her."

Llinos looked skeptical. "Hm."

"She and her cousin have been confidants since childhood. I can easily see Lucien declaring war to recover her. It's a serious insult to Kjall, one around which he can unite and rally his people."

Llinos grumbled, his eyes going distant.

"Bringing back Rhianne as a wife for your First Heir may win you a promotion in the short term, but consider what may happen later on if that act leads to war with Kjall. You would be responsible for that war, Admiral."

Llinos frowned. "Perhaps this marriage idea is more trouble than it's worth."

Janto nodded. "It is."

They returned to the meeting room.

"I've changed my vote," announced Llinos. "I withdraw my marriage proposal, out of respect for the lady."

Rhianne looked at Janto with profound gratitude.

He managed a bitter half smile at her and turned to his clerk. "Is the paperwork ready for signing?"

"Yes, sire," said Cialo. He handed Janto four copies of the freshly inked accords, which Janto passed around the table. Janto, Lucien, and Llinos each put quill to paper.

Admiral Durgan refused to sign.

39

While Janto supervised from the palace, his ships in the harbor were loading, bringing on board soldiers and freed slaves, and filling their holds with provisions. His withdrawal from Kjall was, in effect, a controlled retreat. The final hours would be the most dangerous, with his occupying force at its smallest.

The amethyst riftstone was warm in Janto's hand as he approached Rhianne's door. He addressed the guards. "Brocah, Tassio, you're dismissed. Report on board the *Falcon*. We set sail tomorrow morning."

Grins split the guards' faces as they saluted and left.

Janto opened the door right into Rhianne, who'd been waiting just on the other side. Her hungry eyes sought the riftstone in his hand. No doubt she'd sensed its approach—indeed, her mind magic should already be restored by its proximity.

She looked up at him expectantly. "May I have it?"

He dropped the precious object into her hand. "I'm returning it to you." He bowed slightly. "You're free to go."

She clutched her riftstone to her chest and watched the retreating forms of Brocah and Tassio. "No more guards?"

Janto nodded. "No guards. Tomorrow my people sail for Mosar."

A line appeared in the middle of her forehead. "You too?"

"Yes, I'm going too." Was that regret he saw on her face? He waited to see if she would say something more. When the silence became uncomfortable, he cleared his throat. "I have a question for you."

She nodded, looking a little anxious.

"May we take Whiskers back to Mosar?"

"Whiskers?" Her eyebrows rose. Apparently it wasn't the question she'd been expecting.

"Yes, the brindlecat. I know you're fond of her, but she's dangerous if left loose, and it's unkind to keep her in a cage. We have better facilities for her on Mosar."

Rhianne lowered her eyes. "You're right. Please take her back to Mosar. May I say good-bye to her first?"

"Of course. I'll send word to my men." Once more, he waited for her to say something further, but again he was disappointed. "Do you remember this?" He pulled out the jeweled bronze alligator she'd sent with him when he'd been exiled to Dori.

"Oh!" She clasped her hands. "You still have it."

"He's been through a lot," said Janto. "An attempted theft, an attack at sea, the invasion here in Kjall. But I've held on to him. I wanted to give you the opportunity to take him back, if you feel that . . . Well, I know I lied about who I was, so if you feel the gift was given under false pretenses, here he is." He held out the alligator on the palm on his hand.

She looked hurt. "You don't want him?"

"I do. I just don't want you to resent having given him to me."

"Keep him," she said firmly.

He pocketed the trinket and smiled. "I only wish I had

something to give you. I hope to return several years hence for a diplomatic visit. I'll bring something then—I promise."

"You'll be away several years?" She sounded wistful.

He nodded. "The damage to my country is severe. We have much rebuilding ahead of us, and my earliest diplomatic visits will be to Inya, our ally and most important partner in trade."

"Oh." Her eyes were downcast.

One last time, Janto waited for her to say more, but she was silent. "I suppose there's one thing I can give you, before I go. Would you like a Mosari blessing?"

She nodded shyly.

He held up three fingers. "Blessings of the Three." He lifted his hand to her forehead, hovering so she could pull away if his touch repulsed her. But she leaned forward. He drew his fingers down her forehead. "Soldier, Sage, and Vagabond."

When she did not respond, he turned and swept out, retreating down the corridor. He felt her eyes on his back the entire way.

There wasn't enough space on the Mosari ships to load everything they wanted to take. Since he couldn't leave behind any of the human cargo, Janto had to choose between essential supplies like food and plundered Mosari treasures.

Jewelry and small pieces of artwork were no trouble, and he was also carrying back some rather grisly cargo: the heads of the former king and queen, for proper burial. But was it worth hauling back a marble statue when his people on Mosar might be starving for lack of provisions? Weren't his people's lives worth more than treasure?

While Sashi hunted rats, Janto walked among the collected Mosari artifacts on a cordoned-off area of the dock. A senior officer had already tagged the pieces, designating them either to be taken or left behind, depending on their quality, value, and size. Janto was looking over the rejected items in case he wanted to override any of those decisions. Those left behind would be stored for Mosar to retrieve later, but who knew for sure whether Lucien would ultimately return them?

Kal-Torres, returning by boat from a visit to the *Sparrowhawk*, walked over to join him. He ran a hand lovingly over the ears of a bronze brindlecat statue. "I used to climb this. Do you remember? Father used to swat me for it."

Janto smiled. "I got a few swats for that myself."

Kal examined its tag. "We're leaving it behind?"

Janto shrugged. "It's too big. We need the space for food. When we get home, we'll commission a new one."

"It won't be the same. How much food do we need?"

"I have no idea. If the stores on Mosar are truly depleted, we'll need far more than we could ever cram on board."

Kal frowned. "We shouldn't be taking the Riorcans."

"I promised they'd have a home with us." Admiral Durgan had relented and accepted his offer of asylum on Mosar. "Besides, they have their own ships and can carry their own food."

"They'll be trouble. Durgan tried to sabotage the negotiations."

"His interests weren't being taken seriously. People

make trouble when they're not treated fairly," said Janto. "I think we should see what happens when we treat them right. We've got entire villages that were wiped out and need repopulating, and these people need a place to live. If they can adapt to the Mosari heat and our storm season, this could work out well."

"The Riorcans don't like us. They don't know our ways, and they don't even want to be there," said Kal. "It's going to be another disaster—Silverside all over again. *And* you let that Kjallan princess go."

Janto balled his hands into fists. "Don't bring Rhianne into this."

"She's the best match you could possibly have made for Mosar. You couldn't bring yourself to face a few tears in the marriage bed, for the good of your country?"

"You're out of line, Fleet Commander," Janto snapped. "See to your ships."

When Janto arrived at his room in the Kjallan palace, he was tired and out of sorts. "No visitors," he growled to the door guard.

San-Kullen, his bodyguard, awaited orders.

Janto dismissed him with a wave. "Go to bed. Get some rest."

"Yes, sire. I was wondering—shall I send you up a woman? I think it would do you good."

Janto blinked. "San-Kullen, can you of all people have forgotten my orders regarding the Kjallan women?"

San-Kullen looked offended. "I mean someone willing. Since we freed the palace women, some of them have been, uh, friendly to the officers. I think we strike them as exotic. And they like our familiars. I won't have any trouble at all finding someone who wants to sleep with the king of Mosar."

San-Kullen was probably right; rank had its advantages. And it *would* do him good. On the other hand, a Kjallan woman would surely remind him of Rhianne — and that would cause him grief. And in the mood he was in, he wasn't fit for company. "Thank you, San-Kullen. Not tonight."

San-Kullen saluted. "I'll see you in the morning, sire."

The door shut, leaving Janto alone in his room. He rubbed the back of his neck, trying to relieve some tension. His supper tray sat on a nearby table. He passed by it without interest and stepped out onto the balcony.

An evening breeze ruffled his hair. The loading of the ships was still in progress. He could see it from here, trails of blue magelight on the water, some gliding toward him, others away. The ships' masts and rigging, outlined by glows and magelight, glittered like spiderwebs at dawn.

All three moons were out, which was unusual. The Vagabond would be full tomorrow. He'd have to produce enough spirits for everyone on board to deliver the customary toast. *Great one, pass us by.* He snorted. As if that ever worked.

You're in a mood, commented Sashi.

Sorry, he said. *This has been harder than I expected.*

Sashi's tail flicked over his neck in sympathy.

"Sire."

He jumped at the quiet voice. "I said no visitors!"

"I'm sorry, sire," mumbled the door guard. "But it's the Imperial Princess."

*   *   *

Rhianne fidgeted anxiously outside Janto's door. What if he wouldn't see her? The guard had refused her at first. She'd pulled rank and argued, saying she was the Imperial Princess and she absolutely had to speak with Jan-Torres tonight. After all, he was leaving tomorrow and wouldn't be back for years. The door guard held his ground for a little while, but when she'd persisted, he'd grudgingly agreed to see if Jan-Torres would make an exception for her.

Now the guard was returning, at an aggravatingly slow pace. His expression was bland; she couldn't tell from looking at him what his answer would be.

He trudged up to her. "King Jan-Torres will see you."

She let her breath out in a rush. "Thank you."

The guard stepped aside, and she hurried into the room. There was no sign of Janto. "Where is he?" she called over her shoulder.

"Balcony," the guard answered.

Odd that Janto had not come to meet her. Well, she was not at all certain how he felt about her. She hadn't treated him well for the past several days.

It appeared he'd installed himself in the rooms of one of Florian's advisers. She looked the place over, noting an untouched supper tray, and a pile of clothes and assorted items laid out on a chair. A light silk curtain, ivory in color, covered the entrance to the balcony, shimmering as the evening breeze tickled its edges. She pushed it aside and stepped out into the night air.

Janto leaned on the marble railing, watching the ships in the harbor. He turned, briefly, to acknowledge her presence. Then the harbor lights seemed to captivate him again—or perhaps he couldn't bear to look at her.

It stung that he didn't even smile in her direction, but

she couldn't blame him. He'd tried so hard to win her over, even proposing marriage, and she'd rebuffed him. She swallowed. "You're leaving tomorrow."

He nodded. "On the tide."

She stepped to the railing beside him and looked out into the harbor. "I couldn't let you go without saying good-bye."

The lump in his throat bobbed. "If that's what you're here for, you'd best leave. I've said good-bye already, and I can't bear to do it again."

Pox, she was fouling this up. Why had she even said that? It was so cowardly, and it didn't remotely hint at her real intentions. "That's not what I'm really here for." She didn't like the way he looked, tense and unhappy. His hair was a little mussed, and she wanted so badly to run her fingers through it. "I haven't seen you this quiet since the day we met. You don't look yourself at all."

"Bad day," he mumbled, staring at the harbor.

She slipped her hand into his. "How so?"

He stiffened, but then curled his fingers around hers and leaned closer, relaxing a little. "Do you remember the Riorcan fellow at the negotiations?"

"Admiral Durgan. Of course."

"I offered him and his people asylum in Mosar. Seemed a harmless thing to do, a bit of basic human decency, but now my brother's giving me a hard time about it, saying they're going to be trouble, and this is Silverside all over again." He exhaled forcefully. "I know it sounds trivial—nothing I should get out of sorts over—but it's always like this with Kal. I'm not good enough; my judgment is faulty; I should step aside and let *him* be king." He shook his head. "There was more, but I won't share it. Ugly stuff."

Rhianne slipped an arm around his waist. In response, he wrapped an arm around her shoulder. She leaned into him. It felt good to touch him again.

"I hesitate in telling you about the Riorcans," added Janto. "You're Kjallan. You see things differently where Riorca is concerned."

"The way we treat the Riorcans is wrong," Rhianne said softly. "I'm not blind to that. But Lucien has no choice. If he can't make a decisive show of strength following this humiliating invasion, he'll be challenged by a usurper, or several of them. We could have civil war."

"I know."

Dear Janto. Or was it Jan-Torres? Now that her anger had calmed and she was paying more attention to the way he'd handled the invasion and its aftermath, she realized it made no difference; he was the same man, and he was always trying to do the right thing, even when it cost him. Maybe she could help, in her small way. She slipped her hand under his shirt and found back muscles knotted tight with accumulated stress. "You're tense."

He nodded, groaning dully as her hands worked their way up to even tighter shoulders.

She removed her hand from his shirt and pointed at a wrought-iron chair, one of two that flanked a marble table on the balcony. Switching from diplomatic to the command form of the Kjallan language, she ordered, "Sit."

His eyes crinkled with amusement. "Yes, Your Imperial Highness." He sat in the chair.

She stood behind him, caressing his neck, but his collar was in the way. She tugged at his Mosari outer tunic. "May I take this off?"

He helped her remove it, and her hands went to work

on his shoulders, massaging and kneading. She was no professional, but it didn't seem to matter. His knotted muscles untangled anyway, melting to smoothness beneath her fingers. When she finished, he slumped groaning in the chair, his eyes half lidded—but he seemed in no danger of falling asleep. He eyed her over his shoulder. "Rhianne, are you seducing me?"

Her eyelids dropped, and her cheeks warmed. "Maybe."

He held his hand out to her.

After a moment's hesitation, she accepted it. He guided her to the front of the chair, pulled her into his lap, and hugged her. She wrapped her arms around his bare back and buried her head in his shoulder. Gods, she'd missed this. She'd been lonely without her Janto. "I'm so sorry. I assumed the worst of you, and I'm ashamed of the way I've been treating you."

"The blame's as much mine as it is yours." Janto pulled her closer. "Vagabond's breath, why did I think it necessary to lock up the woman I loved and trusted more than anyone in the world? No wonder you thought poorly of me—I was an absolute fool. Shall we forgive each other and never let it happen again?"

"Yes," she whispered.

"Good," said Janto. "That's settled, then. You met my brother, did you not? Kal-Torres."

"Your brother. I figured that was him. He looks so much like you, though not as handsome, of course."

"You don't think he's handsomer than me?"

"Gods, no. Also, he's too forward."

Janto chuckled. "That's his way. Usually it works for him."

Rhianne leaned back so she could see his face and

pushed away a lock of hair that had fallen over his eyes. "I know it's easy for me to say, but ignore your brother's empty words. You did the right thing in offering the Riorcans asylum, and you'll just have to be compassionate with Kal. Think how it must be for him, always in the great man's shadow."

He blinked. "Did you just call me a great man?"

"You're the greatest man I've ever known."

Janto's eyes glistened.

"I want you to know," she added, "that if Kal-Torres ever picks a fight with you again, I'm slapping him silly."

"Now I *want* him to fight with me, just so I can see that." He kissed her, slow and languorously, reacquainting himself with every inch of her mouth.

"Alligator," she breathed. "I missed you."

"You decided I'm the Janto you knew from the garden after all?"

"Janto and Jan-Torres were the same man all along. I just didn't believe it until you proved it to me."

He brushed the hair out of her face so he could look her in the eye. "And do you think you might love this Jan-Torres enough to marry him?"

"I don't think I could bear it if I *didn't*," said Rhianne. "I thought of you far away on Mosar, all by yourself, or maybe even courting some Inyan princess, and the thought horrified me! You're *my* alligator. I'm going with you to Mosar, and if you try to tell me otherwise, I shall be stowing away on your ship."

Janto broke into a grin. "We can't have stowaways, so we'd better make it official."

"I do have one condition," said Rhianne. "We take Morgan with us and bring him into our royal service. He's unhappy here and needs a new beginning."

Janto grunted his displeasure. "I don't like that Morgan fellow."

"Two conditions," said Rhianne. "You get over being jealous of Morgan."

"Do I get another kiss if I agree to these conditions?"

"Absolutely."

"It's a deal," said Janto.

Rhianne seized his mouth with her own, not giving a kiss but taking one. He was her delicious Mosari islander, and she'd been away from him for a long time, and they had until dawn. If Jan-Torres thought he was getting any sleep tonight, he was mistaken.

When they separated, he said, "What's Lucien going to say?"

"Since I'm going of my own accord, he won't interfere. I'll tell him."

"Not now, I hope." He nuzzled her neck.

"Tomorrow," she breathed.

"I have a confession to make," said Janto.

Her eyebrows rose. "What?"

"I'm a poor traveler. I get seasick."

"If you're going to get sick tomorrow, we'll have to get our fill of each other now." She sought his lips again.

Janto rose from the seat, lifting her with him, and laid her on the marble table. He leaned over her, framed her face in his hands, and kissed her deeply.

"Janto," she murmured into his mouth, "this table is marble."

"Mmm-hmm."

The kiss was lovely. The cold, hard surface beneath her, less so. She pinched him to get his attention. "Do you have any idea how hard marble is?"

"I know something harder," he growled. He straightened, lifted her off the table, and set her on her feet. "All right. Let's go inside and do this properly. *Now*, if you please."

"Yes, Your Majesty." Her laughter, born of pure happiness, floated up like bubbles in a champagne glass. She tripped toward the entryway with Janto at her heels.

Turn the page for a sneak peek at the next book in Amy Raby's Hearts and Thrones Series,

PRINCE'S FIRE

Available from Signet Eclipse in April 2014

Celeste smoothed the folds of her gown, wishing her tumultuous insides could be similarly reduced to a semblance of order. She was waiting in the anteroom on Lucien, who had trapped himself in a conversation with his adviser Trenian. Celeste drummed her fingers against her gown. When those two got going, they could prattle all night. It was unfortunate that the empress was out of town. Celeste would have taken some comfort from Vitala's presence.

At length, Lucien disengaged, stepped to her side, and took her arm. "Ready?"

She nodded. "As I'll ever be."

Lucien called over his shoulder, "Trenian, let's meet the Inyans." He nodded to the guards, who opened the doors, and they headed in to dinner.

State dinners were normally held in the Cerularius Hall, but Lucien had selected the west dining hall—a family room—for this meeting. While the significance of this gesture would be lost on the Inyans, Celeste understood it perfectly. It meant he was more interested in cultivating intimacy with his guests than in impressing them with opulence. The west dining hall lacked the Cerularius Hall's cavernous size and decadence. Still, it would hardly insult their guests. It was lavish on a smaller scale, with sculpted walls, silk tapestries, and a chandelier hung with a thousand colored light-glows.

The glows were dimmed, but Celeste had a clear view of the three Inyans as they milled about the room. They'd separated. One man stood alone and the other two stood next to each other, admiring the tapestries. Though they were the only people in the dining room, she'd have sorted them out easily even if they'd been strewn among a pack of Kjallans. Inyans stood out. Most were blond, and they all wore their hair long, the women in a variety of styles and the men in a braid that hung down the back. Celeste looked these men over, hoping to pick out her prince and fiancé.

The one standing alone she wrote off immediately. He was an older man and sallow faced. He couldn't be her twenty-two-year-old prince.

Next, the two who were together. Her eyes fixed on the leftmost figure. Tall and muscular, with his golden braid falling to his waist and a furred cloak slung about his shoulders, he put her in mind of a lion, maned and regal. His features were pleasant and honest, and he moved with an easy confidence. Though he did nothing to call attention to himself, she had the impression that everyone in the room was subconsciously aware of him and in his orbit.

Celeste's heart made a strange little jump. She clutched at Lucien's arm, feeling a little dizzy. *That one,* she pleaded. *Let the prince be that one.*

In the interest of fairness, she studied the third man. He was handsome too, but in a different way. Long and lean, a bit older, with well-defined features. She could learn to like him, but the man in the furred cloak—he was the one she wanted. It ought to be him. He was the only man who looked the proper age.

Lucien led her toward the two younger men. "Prince Rayn," he said, speaking diplomatic Kjallan.

The man in the furred cloak stepped forward and clasped wrists with the emperor. Celeste's heart leapt. The young lion *was* her future husband! But it remained to be seen how well he liked her. Or whether his character matched his good looks.

"Your Imperial Majesty," said the Inyan prince, answering in diplomatic Kjallan. "An honor."

She liked his voice: a pleasant, rumbly tenor. "Allow me to introduce the Imperial Princess, my sister, Celeste." Lucien held out Celeste's hand.

Rayn's eyes slid over her. He took her hand and bowed slightly. "Imperial Highness. Your beauty lights up the very room."

"Thank you," said Celeste, her heart doing little flip-flops. An empty compliment, obviously prepared in advance, but she appreciated his courtesy. Nervous, she pushed her hair back from her face. "I've heard much about you, Your Highness. The stories don't begin to do you justice."

His eyebrows inched upward, as did the corners of his mouth. "Let us hope you heard the right stories."

The onlookers chuckled.

Lucien waved Rayn and the others toward their seats. "Let's take our seats, and we can finish the introductions at the table. I don't want this to be overly formal. Are you comfortable speaking in Kjallan, or would you prefer we spoke Inyan?"

"Magister Lornis and I are fluent in Kjallan," said Rayn. "Councillor Burr knows enough to get by. I've always felt that when abroad, one should speak the host's language."

"Very well," said Lucien. "We'll translate if need be. Celeste and I speak passable Inyan."

Celeste took her seat directly across from her future husband. Lucien introduced his adviser Legatus Trenian, and Prince Rayn named the two men in his company. The man Rayn had been walking with when they'd entered the room was Magister Lornis, apparently a royal adviser or teacher or judge—she was not clear on the exact role. And the older man was a member of a Land Council on Inya that drafted laws and operated in some sort of power balance with the king.

The servants placed before each of them a white soup sprinkled with pistachios and pomegranate seeds. Celeste stirred and sipped at her soup, wanting to talk to the prince but feeling shy. Kjall needed this alliance, and she'd have gone through with the marriage even if the man had been a toad, but there was nothing amphibian about Rayn. He was so handsome, so charming, but she couldn't help noticing that he didn't look at her much.

"This soup is delicious," said Magister Lornis.

Lucien acknowledged the compliment and then turned to Prince Rayn. "For the benefit of we Kjallans who have never been to Inya, perhaps you could tell us a bit about it. Particularly the volcanoes."

Magister Lornis gestured with his spoon and grinned. "Now you've done it—you've said the magic word. He'll talk your ear off."

"I talk no one's ear off," said Rayn, yet he settled into his chair, making himself comfortable. He was clearly well practiced at speaking on this subject. "We've eight smokers at present, three on the mainland and five on the islands."

"Smokers?" said Lucien.

"Active volcanoes," said Rayn. "You're aware, I take it, that there are different types of volcanoes?"

"Not really," said Lucien. "We've not a single one in Kjall."

"That you know of," said Rayn. "A volcano can remain dormant for centuries before coming to life again. But you know about the ones on Dori. Those are a different type than ours. They *look* different. They're taller, more conical in shape. And when they erupt, they're more devastating, as you know by the recent catastrophe."

"The year with no summer," said Lucien. "Of course."

"Our volcanoes erupt frequently," said Rayn. "Some of them more than once a year. But they're rarely explosive. Occasionally they belch a little steam or ash, but mostly we have lava flows."

"Which it is Rayn's job to manage," said Magister Lornis.

Celeste, determined to be part of the conversation, jumped in. "How is that done? How can a person manage a lava flow from a volcanic eruption?"

Rayn opened his mouth to speak, but Councillor Burr cut him off, saying, "Rayn and the other fire mages use their magic to halt the lava flows before they make their way into the lowlands."

"That is *not* what we do," said Rayn.

"It ought to be," said Burr. "Fire mages of old used to stop the flows entirely rather than redirecting them. There are mentions in the old texts—"

Rayn snapped, "Hang the old texts! It depends on the volume of lava. Small eruptions, yes, those can be stopped. The major ones, no. It cannot be done."

The servants returned to the table and refilled the wineglasses. The silence stretched awkwardly.

Lucien leapt in. "I'm afraid we Kjallans don't understand. Please elaborate."

Magister Lornis said, "Prince Rayn is a fire mage, along with all of his extended family. For generations, their collective job has been to manage the volcanic eruptions. Whenever there is a lava flow, they stop it outright if they can, or if they cannot halt it, they redirect the flow into an unpopulated area where it can do no damage."

"That's wonderful!" said Celeste. "I love that the ruling family of Inya serves the people in such a direct and visible way."

Rayn set down his soup spoon. "Unfortunately, the Land Council upon which Councillor Burr sits authorized farmers to begin developing the formerly uninhabited Four Trees Valley, which leaves us no place at all to send lava flows from either Mount Fyor or Mount Drav, both of which are prone to serious eruptions."

Councillor Burr replied, "We cannot let that valley go to waste. Four Trees has the most fertile soil in all of Inya."

"As a hunting preserve, it was *not* going to waste. The soil is fertile because it lies in the shadow of two volcanoes." said Rayn. "Because we have sent so many lava flows there. Would you rather we sent them into Tiasa?"

"You must stop the flows," said the Councillor. "What

are our fire mages for if not to control the god in the mountain?"

"The god in the mountain cannot be controlled," said Rayn.

Lucien's eyes sparkled. "I see you care deeply about your people and the management of your country."

"I'm sure you would do no less for Kjall," said Rayn, tucking into his newly delivered second course, a steak of sturgeon with capers.

Celeste forced herself to eat, mechanically chewing each bite. Her insides were all twisted up. She liked Rayn. He wasn't just handsome but *passionate*, and about all the right things—protecting his people, making the right decisions for Inya. Whether Rayn or the Councillor had the right of the argument about stopping or diverting the lava flows, she couldn't say, but it was clear Rayn believed in the rightness of his arguments.

If only the tiniest bit of that passion could be directed toward her. He cared about his "smokers," but he had yet to address her, or even look at her, really. He answered her questions, but asked her none in return. He seemed to perceive this dinner as something to be borne as a courtesy, not as a valuable opportunity to get to know his future wife. Perhaps it was only nerves on his part. But he didn't seem like a nervous man.

There was only one answer that made sense: he didn't find her attractive. She hadn't expected that he would. Still, she'd hoped. She would marry him regardless; Kjall needed the match, and so did Inya. But it would have been nice if he wanted her.

Of the group, Magister Lornis struck her as the most diplomatically skilled. He was friendly and personable.

Councillor Burr, on the other hand, did not impress her. He reminded her of any number of corrupt government officials she'd met over the years—the ones Lucien was carefully weeding out of the Kjallan bureaucracy. Also, he'd drained his wineglass three times and was well on his way to being stewed.

"Princess Celeste." Magister Lornis nodded in her direction. "You're as lovely as the rumors foretold. The emperor and empress are known for their prowess at Caturanga. Do you play the game?"

"No," she said shyly.

"Celeste's interests lie elsewhere," said Lucien. "She's involved in the Mathematical Brotherhood of Riat. And, like all women from the imperial line, she's a mind mage."

"The Mathematical *Brotherhood*?" said Magister Lornis.

Celeste winced. This was embarrassing to explain. "They don't normally admit women. They made an exception for me."

"What sort of math do you do there?"

"A variety of things." Mostly cryptography and cryptanalysis, which she wasn't at liberty to talk about since she was working with Lucien to upgrade Kjall's ciphers to a higher level of security. She'd also broken Inya's ciphers as an exercise. It was probably best to abandon this subject. Her love of math wasn't likely to endear her to Prince Rayn, who already didn't seem to like her.

Magister Lornis smiled. "I think it's wonderful that we live in a world where there's something everyone can be passionate about. For the emperor it's Caturanga, and for you it's mathematics."

"And for the prince," slurred Councillor Burr, "it's volcanoes and blondes."

An uncomfortable silence fell over the table. Celeste was raven haired like her brother.

Magister Lornis steepled his hands on the table. "It's well known that Rayn dotes on his mother and sisters. And, Councillor, you've had more than enough to drink."

Can't get enough paranormal romance?

Looking for a place to get the latest information and connect with fellow fans?

"Like" Project Paranormal on Facebook!

- Participate in author chats

- Enter book giveaways

- Learn about the latest releases

- Get book recommendations and more!

facebook.com/ProjectParanormalBooks